B48 836 244 7

KV-233-065

Jane Elmor has lived most of her life in London, where her occupations have included playing in bands, dealing in vintage clothes and composing for short films and TV, among other things. She has three degrees, including an MA in Creative Writing.

Her first novel was *My Vintage Summer*.

# PICTURES OF YOU

Luna, a painter, is content living a bohemian life in London with sculptor Pierre. But when her estranged father dies, she yearns to discover what happened to her father and her family, and to start one of her own . . . Angie, a drama student, escapes her suffocating parents. Hitchhiking to the Isle of Wight Festival in 1970, she meets Dave and goes to live with him in his idyllic and free-living Welsh commune. However, Angie, as a mother with a baby daughter, makes a shocking discovery . . . Nat, a teenage mum on the run from the past, tries to build a good life for her kids in a new location. But can she escape the trouble that haunts her, and finally make her children safe?

*Books by Jane Elmor*
*Published by The House of Ulverscroft:*

MY VINTAGE SUMMER

JANE ELMOR

# PICTURES OF YOU

*Complete and Unabridged*

# CHARNWOOD
*Leicester*

First published in Great Britain in 2009 by
Pan Books
an imprint of Pan Macmillan Ltd.
London

First Charnwood Edition
published 2010
by arrangement with
Pan Macmillan Ltd.
London

British Library CIP Data

Elmor, Jane.
    Pictures of you.
    1. Mothers- -Fiction. 2. Family secrets- -Fiction.
    3. Large type books.
    I. Title
    823.9'2–dc22

    ISBN 978–1–44480–193–4

Published by
F. A. Thorpe (Publishing)
Anstey, Leicestershire

Set by Words & Graphics Ltd.
Anstey, Leicestershire
Printed and bound in Great Britain by
T. J. International Ltd., Padstow, Cornwall

This book is printed on acid-free paper

# Acknowledgements

Thank you to Pamela, Jabs, Gretch, Sarah, Kat, Simon, Joey, Jenny, Carey, Milly, Rebecca, Richard Brown, Ella Andrews, Jenny Geras, Clare Parkinson, Pan's people and Darley's angels.

# 2009

## Uffizi Gallery, Florence

I didn't see you so much as feel you. It was strange, but I just suddenly knew you were there. I was distracted and stroppy and the kids were playing up because they were bored, and I was still annoyed with my wife for the fact that they were here in the first place and not at her mum's, like I suggested. I mean, what little kids want to spend their holidays at art galleries in Florence anyway? I told her we should have a beach holiday with them later in the year, and just the two of us do Florence together. Get some time alone. I thought, you never know, we might even get to have sex for a change. But she wouldn't have it. 'We're a family now,' she said. 'That's what you wanted, wasn't it? Then we do things as a family. It'll be good for them, to learn about art from an early age.'

So there we were, finally, on the top floor of the Uffizi Gallery, having skipped loads of things I wanted to see as we'd already queued for ages. Bradley was whining, Zoe was crying and my wife was having a go at me for not booking tickets in advance. At last we were shuffling towards Botticelli's *Venus*, and I was trying to zone out all the white noise so that I could drink it in and appreciate it properly, and was thinking,

1

crap, I'm not feeling it — when I just knew. I'd lifted Bradley up so he could see over the heads of everyone in front and given him a sweet to keep him occupied, when this sensation went through me and made me look past his shoulder at the people in front of the *Venus*. I'm not given to believing in all that sixth-sense stuff and perhaps you were already in my thoughts anyway, because of the association between you and Botticelli I always make, which of course only you will know. All the same I froze, couldn't believe my own eyes, thinking it was the most ridiculous, mawkish cliché that the one time we should meet each other again was underneath the most famous Botticelli of all, the goddess of love. Of all the places and all the paintings in the world. You couldn't make it up. It would be too perfect, too impossible. I recognized you by the back of your neck, the way you tilt your head when you consider something, the wisps of soft neck hair that always escape their clasp. I studied your frame, forgetting all about the magnificent art I'd come to see. You were thinner. It suited you though, enhanced the grace of your long limbs. You had your hand in the back pocket of your jeans. That's very you. You still do that.

I was being inched forward towards you and I was holding my breath, waiting for you to turn round. My wife was out in the corridor with Zoe, trying to stop her crying. I became aware of Bradley's voice rising, 'Where's Mummy? I want Mummy!' as he struggled against me to get free. I let him slip down and push back through the crowd to find her. I was vaguely aware that I should be going after him but I couldn't lose my place. I couldn't lose you. I was mesmerized by the need to see your face, for your eyes to be looking into mine. I didn't know you could miss something as simple as that, miss it as much as the sun on your skin. The times you were looking at me I felt the best I'd ever felt, as though you verified my whole existence, exaggerated it so that I was big and powerful and everything I wanted to be.

I was closer now, with only a few people between us. I was close enough that if I said your name you would hear me. But I couldn't speak. My mouth was dry. And then you turned your head, not my way but to the other side and I could tell you were speaking. You were with someone. I felt my heart beating furiously. He turned towards you and smiled. He was young and dark, Italian possibly, with long, scruffy artist's hair which he shook out of his black eyes as he replied to you. I watched, transfixed, helplessly taking in more and more. The people between us moved and I saw you were arm in arm with him, intimate. You both turned back to the *Venus*, heads tilting up, standing in poses that mirrored each other, slouching on hips that were almost touching in matching, worn, paint-splattered jeans. You looked perfect and my heart ached. Of course you should be with someone like that. Not just each other's lover, but each other's muse. In a moment I saw your life as it must be now, filled only with art and love. I envied you so much it hurt physically, as though I had been punched. I often imagine

3

where you are and what you are doing, but, I confess, I held a secret hope that you no longer shone this way. That you grew older like the rest of us, gave up the romance, and the pursuit, settled for ordinary life and put it all behind you. But you didn't. I could see it in an instant. You were vibrant. I could feel the frequency of you, just standing there. It was this life in you that I loved, this way you have of being in every moment, knowing what it is to be alive. I was overwhelmed by the remembrance of what I'd had, and lost. I felt suddenly desperate, everything I'd built since you were mine collapsing. My insides were free-falling, my life shattering in an instant.

The tour group moved on, the room around us clearing, as though the crowd was just the chorus, moving into the wings. You were centre-stage, pointing at a detail of the *Venus*, and I could hear the hushed, excited tones of your voice amplified by the high ceiling, but not the words. I was rooted to the spot, not knowing whether to move those few steps forward and touch your shoulder and bask in your face when you turned it to me, or simply walk away. And then I heard Bradley running back to me shouting, 'Daddy, Daddy!', and then his mother's harassed voice telling him to quiet down and the sound of her hurried footsteps as she approached, Zoe still whimpering in her arms.

'Can you please keep control of Bradley?' she hissed at me as she came near. 'What were you thinking, letting go of him like that? It's a miracle he found me. I've got enough on my plate with Zoe.'

Bradley was already pawing at my jeans to be lifted up so I swung him onto my arm, whispering, 'Shush, shush,' I don't know whether to him or to my wife.

I glanced reflexively back in your direction and, your attention caught by our commotion, there you were, looking straight at me. All I could do was stare back into your eyes. I saw them take me in and recognize me, and then travel quickly over the rest of my entourage, my family. What did we look like to you? Me in a sweaty fluster, Bradley in his sugar mania, Zoe red-faced and swollen-eyed and squirming in the arms of my frowning wife. I saw you take us all in in one barely perceptible contraction, like a shutter clicking. It was not how I would have chosen you to see me. But then I think I saw a flinch of pain in your eyes for a split second, or was that just the pain I felt as I looked at you? Everything we went through, I lived it all again in a flash, the closest I have ever come to ecstasy, the depths of despair, madness even, and every emotion in between. You made me feel it all.

*I will fade away*, you said. *You will know a love that is stronger than anything you have ever felt, and I will pale in comparison, become nothing to you*. I have tried to believe you, tried to hate you, tried to forget you, and most of the time I convince myself I've succeeded and that you were right. But I knew in the moment our eyes locked again that you were wrong. I miss you like a part of myself. I love my wife. It is true

5

there is no love like the love you have for your children. I can't imagine my life without them, would die for them. But looking at you then, I realized I sometimes search for something in them that isn't there. I search for echoes of you.

We could have had it all, you and I. Not one part or another, this compromise for that, but everything. Instead all I have are the moments sometimes at the end of a day, when the busying about is done, when I have come home from work, when we have eaten, bathed, read bedtime stories, swapped the mundanities of the day and watched TV. When my wife has said goodnight and headed up to bed. When the night properly falls. I turn the TV off and pour another secret glass of wine, and remember you. Mostly I think of your eyes, your smile. Your body and the look on your face when we were making love. The laughter, the mischief, the abandon and the joy. The awe we felt for what we were creating. But always, by the bottom of the glass, I come back to the same thing. Were you true or false? Did you love me? Or not? All these years I've never been able to finally decide, one way or the other. But this moment, looking in your eyes, finally I felt I had my answer.

I wanted to hold you in my gaze forever, but then you began to move with a vague smile on your lips while the boy said something to you, connected and full of love. And then we were passing each other, close enough to almost touch, and then away into our own lives again, like the strangers we now were.

# ONE

*A painting. A woman at a window, looking out.*

# 2003

## Luna

Having sex in a cupboard under the stairs at her father's funeral was probably going too far, even for Luna. She was aware of it herself, as she undid the buttons of her silk shirt and placed Pierre's hand on her bra. It wasn't that she felt out of control so much as controlled by something else, something that dwelled deep inside her, a dormant beast she hadn't known was there until it began to stir.

She could smell the dry-cleaning fumes still lingering on the old granddad suit Pea dug out for such occasions, mingling with the mothballs in the pockets of the coats crowding around them. She fumbled with the fly of his black trousers, pressing her tongue into his mouth to shush his 'What's got into you?' And despite his protestations he soon responded, as she knew he would. This was a new side to their sex life that he couldn't resist.

They had always felt good together, in that way. But living together for six years had led to an inevitable decline of passion. The familiarity — the bathroom routine, the any-old T-shirts, the tiredness, the comfort of shared sleep — made it perhaps impossible to maintain. Until recently, when, for reasons she had not explored,

11

Luna had taken it upon herself to make spontaneous first moves. The first time, back from shopping in the mid afternoon after banking a cheque for a piece she'd sold and trying on new lingerie, she padded into his studio and positioned herself between him and his latest sculpture. Ignoring his initial bemusement and protests of 'I'm working, I'll be finished in a mo', she wrested him to the dusty studio floor. The splinters were worth it. His annoyance at being interrupted suddenly gave way to quick, hot sex of the kind they hadn't had since the early days. The next night she cooked in nothing but high heels and an apron. He laughed at first, the addition of sexual spice to their usual kitchen chores causing him some embarrassment. But he soon overcame it and joined in, playing his role by breaking crockery as he swept a space to lift her onto the worktop.

The following month she wore no underwear to a concert, making it known to Pierre in the van on the way. By the time they were travelling back home he was beside himself. Over the last few months they had had sex in the van, in the bushes in Victoria Park, in the toilets at a gallery opening in Shoreditch and in several comical positions around the flat.

This was the first funeral.

Luna knew it was probably disrespectful to her late father, but then — if it made it any less so — she hadn't known him, after all.

Pierre, in his sombre suit, was irresistible. It was rare to see him dressed up. Ninety-nine per cent of the time he was in his work boots and old jeans, with debris and dust in his mop of black hair. She loved him like that too, but the unfamiliarity of him in the suit, hanging so perfectly off his wiry boyish frame, and the seriousness of the occasion with all these strangers gathered afterwards at the uncle's pleasant semi-detached had somehow got the better of her. She was seized by an urgency, as though it had to be now, this minute, as though her life depended on it, as though a chance like this would never come round again. Pierre had begun to work on pieces for a forthcoming exhibition, a prestigious one at Flowers. He was working all hours in the studio trying to come up with his series and she had hardly seen him. Her own future over the next few months stretched ahead like space in a way she was unable to define.

That's what had got into her.

'I can't believe you just made me do that!' whispered Pierre afterwards. 'How the bloody fuck are we going to get out of here without being noticed?' He sounded panicked and Luna giggled, feeling suddenly far happier, as she pulled her skirt back down and groped in the dark for her missing shoe.

'Calm down, it'll be all right. Open the door a crack and wait till it's all clear,' she whispered. 'You go first and I'll wait for a while. Say I'm in the loo.'

'Christ,' Pierre muttered as he wrestled with the coats. She heard him scratching around for the door handle and then a filmy shaft of light penetrated the gloom. It seemed horribly quiet

13

out there. There was a lull in the conversation in the living room and she wondered how noisy they had been. When the talking began to burble up again and several shadows crossed the stream of light on their way in or out of the kitchen, Pierre made a bolt for it, as Luna shrank back into the depths of the cupboard to escape the flood of daylight. Her knees began to shake from the awkward position she had been in, and she knew she had to get out and stretch before she lost use of them altogether.

Just as she was closing the door behind her and straightening up, her mother appeared from the kitchen and eyed her suspiciously.

'I, er . . . thought I put my bag in here,' said Luna, pushing her fingers through her dishevelled hair.

'Why ever would you do that, darling?' Angie replied, in her loud, plummy voice. Luna cringed. 'Isn't that it?' She nodded at the banister to Luna's left, where her bag hung inches away, perfectly obvious to anyone who might be looking for it.

'Oh God. Stupid me,' said Luna, pulling a face. She took her bag and escaped up the stairs, trying to somehow act as though she needed it for a tampon or to redo her lipstick. Glancing at Angie through her wisps of fringe she saw that her mother did not believe her. The look on her face suggested she knew exactly what had gone on. However, she didn't appear displeased. In fact, quite the opposite.

Luna had, so far in her life, fully lived up to her mother's bohemian expectations.

'Life is for living,' she was fond of declaring. Sometimes it felt to Luna as though she was having to do the living for not only herself but her mother too.

'Go out and do Great Things,' she'd always said. 'Fuck settling down, darling. My generation of women paved the way for you. You have no idea of the fight we had to pass on to you young women what freedom you have today.'

And, 'God, what I would do if I were a young woman today! You have no idea how lucky you are!'

'I do, Mum, I do,' Luna always replied. It had been drilled into her from an early age and she was not likely to forget. For sure, her mum had been an inspiration, encouraging her artistic talent, equipping her with sex education and putting her on the Pill at the earliest opportunity to ensure she *didn't make the same mistake I made.*

On the other hand . . . It was almost beginning to feel like an inverted pressure, this always having to be creative and free and independent and living life to the full. She could somehow never relax for a minute on this trail her mother had so valiantly blazed for her.

Luna locked the bathroom door behind her and lay on the floor, taking deep breaths and trying to relax. When she got up she looked at herself hard in the mirror. Objectively she could see she wasn't doing badly for her thirties. If anything, she looked in the prime of life. She was lucky. Maybe it was genes from her father, of whom she had only a couple of hazy childhood

15

memories, which these days she thought she may have invented. Luna had never looked anything like Angie.

Her mother's looks had suffered from feminist idealism. No beauty regime, no moisturizers and too much early outdoor living had left Angie's face prematurely wrinkled. No quest for the body beautiful, no gym, no aerobics. Her bra-less youth had left her bosoms dangling so low that at first glance she appeared flat-chested. She still wouldn't wear a bra now, which left Luna in a state half admiring and half appalled. Especially at a gathering like this, with a bunch of nice, ordinary, Marks-and-Sparks-wearing stranger-relatives, where Angie stuck out like a sore thumb in her voluminous velveteen drapes. The scarves and beads hanging round her neck made her look as though she had been used to play hoopla. And every dangling piece of silver would have some meaning too, Luna knew; this Druid symbol for harmony or growth, that Celtic pattern for female empowerment, this pagan goddess of . . . etc., etc.

Usually Luna was proud of her mum. At her art shows in London a mother like this was an asset, with an unconventional quirkiness that showed Luna in the right authentic light. But here in a smart cul-de-sac on a new housing estate somewhere on the outskirts of Sheffield, Luna was frankly embarrassed.

She and Pierre, however, were doing well. They knew how to behave in situations — the sex in the cupboard aside. The fact that Dave's long-lost daughter was attractive and artfully dressed and apparently achieving some sort of success in a field they knew nothing about seemed to serve Luna well. And Pierre, well, Pea always charmed everybody, despite his unkempt hair. He seemed to appeal to the romantic in every woman, even prim, disapproving aunties and grandmothers. Men were unthreatened by his boyish affability and lack of macho posturing. He happily took their advice on routes avoiding congestion on the M1 interchange, and they could liken him, as a sculptor, to a tradesman, a stonemason perhaps, or a builder of garden ponds, as he politely answered questions about the tools he used and whether his van was diesel.

Luna stared into her own eyes in the mirror. She was told they were beautiful, an unusually dark brown for someone so fair, with a still depth that seemed capable of drawing people into her. These she knew were inherited from her father. Angie's eyes were pale blue, nothing like. It was one thing she knew about her mother's relationship with her father. It was his eyes that had got her.

★　★　★

She'd been shocked that Dave's relatives had got in touch with her and Angie when he died. It was so out of the blue. She didn't even know how they had tracked them down. Angie had cut all ties years ago and Luna had been given her mum's surname, of course — Morrigan, the name of a Celtic Goddess that Angie had changed her own to, as a feminist protest against patriarchy.

17

She had surprised herself even more by wanting to come to the funeral.

'Why on earth?' said her mother. 'You didn't know him.'

'Maybe that's why,' Luna had replied, which had stumped Angie for once.

'I understand if *you* don't want to go,' Luna continued. 'I don't mind going on my own.'

Which was probably the thing that made Angie insist on coming along for 'support'.

'God knows what this family'll be like,' Angie had said as she swooped into the passenger seat of Pierre's van while Luna clambered over the seat into the back, where she squatted on a pile of Pierre's sculpture-transporting blankets. 'I only met his mum once when you were a baby. She didn't approve.'

'Why not?' asked Luna. She hadn't asked questions about her father since she was a kid. She seemed to remember that she never got anywhere with them anyway. Angie had taught her that her father was irrelevant. It was just the two of them. Angie's own mother hadn't approved either. Growing up, Luna had accepted everything Angie told her as just the way it was. It was a new thing, this interest about her past.

'Well, there was nothing to approve of,' Angie smirked. 'Her son had dropped out of university to play rock music and live on a commune, of all things. We weren't married, we were hippies, I wouldn't have you in hospital, we didn't get you christened. We didn't give you their family name. We called you Luna Sprite — '

'Yeah, thanks for that,' Luna interrupted

grimly. 'Why again, exactly?'

'Oh don't be so boring. You should be proud to have an unusual name,' said Angie.

'Well, OK, Luna's not so bad, I suppose — apart from being nicknamed Loony by the school bullies — but Sprite, Mum? *Sprite?*'

'Oh . . . I don't know. I think I thought I saw one at your baby-naming ceremony.'

'You weren't stoned by any chance, were you?' Luna asked.

'Of course. We always were. That's another thing they didn't approve of.'

Luna sighed. Angie ignored her and carried on.

'And the time she came to visit I took off my top and breastfed in front of her and Dave's father. She was outraged. She thought we were depraved.'

'Didn't you ever get on? Later, when she got over the shock?'

'Oh she never had the chance to, darling,' Angie answered, not without pride. 'Your father disappeared soon enough into whatever life he found when he'd had all the free love he could handle.'

It didn't seem the time to be slagging him off, not on the day of his funeral. But Luna wanted to know.

'Why did he leave the commune, again?' she asked.

Angie shrugged Luna's question away. 'Oh I don't know, Lu. God, it was such a long time ago. We weren't a *couple*.' She said it as though it was a dirty word. 'I've told you, we really were living a completely new way of life. There's been nothing like it before or since. We didn't believe in possessive love, we weren't jealous, we all shared the kids. We were free.'

And some were freer than others, Luna thought, picturing her father deciding he'd changed his mind about the whole thing, walking off down the farm track in cheesecloth trousers and Jesus sandals, vaulting the rickety gate and hitching back to normality.

'So why did the commune come to an end?' she asked. 'If it was all so . . . idyllic?' She tried to keep the sarcasm out of the word but Pierre glanced at her in his rear-view mirror. Angie didn't seem to notice.

'Oh . . . well . . . ' She wafted her hand vaguely. 'I don't know exactly. Lots of reasons. None. How could it survive really, in a capitalist, patriarchal society?'

A typical Angie response. Down to politics again. Luna's first memories were of the commune and her mother's statements did tally up with the way she remembered it. It did seem idyllic, but whether nostalgia tinted the pictures she couldn't say. Sunny days running through long grasses that seemed as tall as she was. Starry nights in the open with women dancing freely as guys sat cross-legged on the ground playing guitars. Everything in glorious technicolour, everybody smiling. Always lots of people around. In later memories, when she was six or seven, there seemed to be only women. Or *wimmin*, as they spelled it, to avoid being adjuncts to men. Which came first, she

20

wondered, the split from the word, or the actual split, from the men themselves? Was it a false memory, that later on there were no men? Where did they go and why did they move out, leaving the women behind?

Her later memories involved a lot of rain and cold; huddling beside a wood-burning stove while drips plopped into buckets around them, being swamped in layers of heavy, itchy hand-knitted jumpers and still feeling damp and miserable. Surely it wasn't always sunny, and then always cold? But it was how she remembered the last era of the commune. Rain, cold and women with nowhere else to go.

She was seven and three-quarters when it ended — old enough to remember well what happened next for her mother and herself. There was a period with Angie's parents, in a nice middle-class house in Sussex, when she went to a proper school and was laughed at for the way she wrote *women* before she learned how to spell it correctly. A time her mother complained of afterwards as one of the worst times, a stifling phase of repression and unfulfilment, but when Luna had felt safe and happy and found out she was good at art. And then the time of Angie's absence, when she did a stint at Greenham Common and became a 'political lesbian' and then got a job in London working on a feminist magazine, returning at weekends in dungarees and a We Are All Prostitutes T-shirt that shocked her mother. Until she finally got into an all-female house-share in Wandsworth and announced during one visit that when she left

21

again on Sunday afternoon she would be taking Luna with her. While Angie had promised Luna would be coming back to visit loads, Luna and her grandmother had shared a stagily cheerful goodbye hug, keeping their broken hearts to themselves.

★　★　★

Luna was thrown as soon as they entered the service at the crematorium. Instead of hymns, whoever had put the service together had chosen some of 'Dave's favourite music'. As they walked in to the strains of Keith Jarrett's Köln concert and saw several people in bright colours instead of black she knew her mum's version of her father was not entirely accurate. Embarrassing tears sprang to her eyes as she recognized her own favourite piece of music, the beauty of the piano notes clustering in the reverent air above them like constellations. Pierre had introduced it to her when they'd met and it had become the piece she most often painted to, first on a cassette taped off Pierre's vinyl that had worn out, then on CD, and now on her iPod. She hadn't expected to be moved. Pierre squeezing her hand in acknowledgement of the poignancy of the music only made things worse. God, she couldn't cry over someone she'd never known, who'd effectively abandoned her before she ever had the chance.

'Although his life has passed he lives on in you.'

Luna was surprised and relieved to find that

the service director was a humanist, so they were spared the heaven-speak. He was referring to the people there who knew her father, not her. But as she glanced around at the sniffling friends and relatives it dawned on her that it was only she, Luna — she presumed his only child — who he really lived on through, genetically. It was a revelation to her, even though it was obvious. All the people who knew and remembered him would eventually die, and without her any actual traces of him would truly be gone forever.

Throughout the service she surreptitiously scanned faces for recognizable features. She didn't know anyone but some of them shared DNA with her. It felt peculiar, spooky. So did the fact that she learned more about her father from his death than she'd known in his fifty-odd years of life. The way Angie dismissed him she always imagined he'd sold out on their youthful ideals and gone on to settle back into society, get a proper job. She imagined him a salesman, or working for the council, or maybe an English teacher at a secondary school. Something dull that fitted with Angie's lack of respect, as though he never really meant it, never truly escaped the shackles of conformity the way she did. As though he was too weak. Or it was the other extreme and his weakness had made him a casualty, a sad druggie loser who lived in a bedsit. But it turned out he was neither. It turned out he was a photographer.

A long-term friend got up to speak first, a laid-back sort of guy with close-cropped grey hair, wearing chinos and a T-shirt under his jacket. He'd met Dave when they were both travelling back in the seventies. That figured. They'd hooked up and done India together, then Africa. The guy made the congregation laugh knowingly about Dave's long-haired, Buddhist era. He laughed himself. 'We were so *earnest*,' he smiled, and the group smiled with him. They obviously all knew about Dave's serious, socio-political days. 'But it was a different era back then. Less cynical. We thought if people knew about the poverty and the corruption they'd want things to change and be able to change them.'

As he went on Luna pieced together that he was a journalist. He and Dave had started working together as they travelled, a freelance team sending their words and pictures back to newspapers and magazines. She was stunned. She scoured the service leaflet for the guy's name. Matthew Brierley. Surely she recognized that name now? Had she seen it — correspondent Matt Brierley — at the top of articles in the *Guardian* and *Independent*? She certainly knew the type well, the sort that interviewed her when she had an exhibition for a piece in the *Standard* or the *Metro* or the Arts sections of the Sunday papers. The last thing she had expected was like-mindedness. Connection.

He finished his speech by talking about Dave's photographs. 'He had an original eye. Cuttingly perceptive and hauntingly tender. He caught things visually that I would never have noticed if he hadn't; he captured the soul of a place or a person. That was his gift, and is what he leaves

24

us, and I thank him for it.'

After Matthew Brierley was a piece of world music, nothing Luna had heard before. It sounded African, with a beautiful chorus of voices ringing out like glory across the bowed heads. She watched an old lady in the front row take a tissue from her bag and dab at her eyes.

The next person to stand at the front, a piece of paper trembling in his hands, was a slightly stout man, probably in his early fifties. He tried to look up and smile at the room, took a breath and looked down again at his paper.

'Dave was always my hero,' he began, in a broad Yorkshire accent. He cleared his throat and took a moment. 'Maybe big brothers are always heroes to their little brothers, I don't know,' he continued. 'But to me he was always bigger, braver, more adventurous than I would ever be. He never seemed afraid. I was quiet and bookish and when we were lads he was my protector. He was a tough act to follow — good at school and sport and art. He was always a trendsetter with lots of lasses after him, especially when he was in the sixth form and grew his hair long. He was the first in our family to go to university, but I suppose he was too much of a rebel to follow a conventional path. He dropped out, which was shocking at the time, but he were never afraid to shock. He had his own life to live and he lived it. He joined a commune — the most radical thing you could possibly do at the time — and then he went off round the world, way before it was a normal thing for young people to do. It was amazing to me, his kid brother. I never had his guts. I'd tell my friends the latest thing he was doing and they'd all sit round me in awe. I got a lot of mileage out of having him for a brother.' A murmur of fond amusement rippled across the room.

'I myself went into a much more normal, ordinary life, but I never stopped following Dave's. He never lost touch with me, wherever he was in the world. He always checked in to make sure I was OK. It was one of the best times of my life when I went out on holiday to Thailand, where he was living before his illness. I will never forget it.'

He broke down then. He took off his glasses and wiped his eyes with a tissue from his pocket. 'I'm sorry,' he said and blew his nose. He carried on, his voice cracking.

'He fought his illness bravely and without complaint and refused to be a burden on his family. We are all very proud of him, and everything he achieved. Not only that, he was a good, kind, true person, and we were all blessed to have had him in our lives. I thank him and I miss him.'

As he sat back down Luna felt a still tension in the air like a held breath, as though everyone wanted to applaud but couldn't in the sober circumstances. Instead a woman, probably his wife, put her arm round his shoulder and patted his sleeve.

That's my uncle, thought Luna. She wasn't expecting to like or feel for any of these people, and yet here she was, eyes brimming for him, and for herself, for the wish that good, kind, true Dave had checked in on her to make sure she was OK from time to time too. She looked along her uncle's row, at two men and a woman of her generation. Were they his children? If so, that would make them her cousins. She didn't have a good enough view to check them out. Did they know about Angie? Did they know about her?

As the service ended with 'No Woman No Cry', Luna tried to get a hold of herself, sneaking looks at the people filing out to see if there were any others like her. Perhaps he'd been married, had a family. She had assumed she was the only child, but now she felt ashamed of all her preconceptions.

As she approached the family outside the door of the crematorium, shiny-eyed and smiling as they shook hands and thanked everyone for coming, the old lady from the front row locked Luna into her gaze. She stepped unsteadily towards her and grasped Luna's hands in both of hers.

'You must be Luna,' she said.

'Call me Lu. Really,' said Luna.

'You look just like him,' she said, delight and anguish wrestling in her teary crumpled face. 'I'm so glad you came. I've been dying to meet you and get to know you properly. You are coming back to Robert's, aren't you?'

Luna swung round, looking to Angie behind her for confirmation.

Angie stiffened as she approached. 'Hello, Maureen,' she said flatly to the old lady, with none of her usual dramatic mwah mwah kissing,

27

and Luna knew for sure it was her grandmother, the woman who *disapproved*.

'Hello, Angela,' the old lady replied, sweetly. 'Thank you so much for coming. And for bringing this young lady too.' She still hadn't let go of Luna's hands.

'This is Pierre,' Luna said, to extract herself and lightly pull on Pierre's arm.

'Nice to meet you,' said Pierre, replacing Luna's hand with his in the old woman's clutch.

'And you. What a lovely couple you make!'

Luna looked at her mother in surprise. There were no traces of the sour old dragon of Angie's stories. Angie's face showed no emotion, an expression Luna knew belied what was really going on behind it. Angie glided past, and Luna and Pierre moved along the line to relieve the bottleneck that had started to form where they had stopped.

Luna had to run a few steps to catch up with Angie, who was locked in a determined forward motion to the van.

'Ange?' Luna called. Angie stopped abruptly and turned. 'Are we going back? For the wake?'

'I don't know about that. I'm sure it's family only. I doubt they want us there disrupting the status quo.'

Luna frowned, confused. 'She seemed genuine when she asked me,' she replied. 'And anyway, we are family.'

Angie hmphed. 'Well, it's the first I've heard of it. She's probably just trying to appease her guilt about rejecting you.'

'Mum!' Luna scolded.

'Well. There's nothing like a funeral for bringing out a load of insincere sentimental bullshit over *family*.' She said it the way she'd said *couple* earlier. It was another of Angie's distasteful words.

'For God's sake, Angie! Her son's just died. Give her a break!'

'Luie, leave it,' said Pierre, catching up to calm them down before one of their sudden heated rows blew up amid the mourners. Something in his look and the way he pressed her arm made Luna glance at her mother and she saw with some surprise that Angie was struggling to control her emotions. She would never admit to being upset at the best of times, and certainly not here. Still, Luna was upset herself and didn't feel inclined to spare any sympathy for Angie. She was angry with her, a horrible awareness dawning that her mother had denied her not only her father, but a whole web of family on her father's side. What if it wasn't all his fault, or his mother's fault? By all the accounts she'd just heard, he was a good guy. A great guy. What if, heaven forbid, Angie had had something to do with her father leaving them?

'Well, I think it'd be rude not to go,' said Luna. 'Now she's asked me directly to my face. I'll probably never see them again, so while we're here, what's the harm?' Angie didn't seem to have an argument. She shrugged lightly, as if it didn't matter one way or the other.

'Fine, darling, whatever you think. I can understand you being *curious*.'

Luna pulled an outraged face to Pierre as

29

Angie turned and walked to her side of the van. Why did it have to be as detached as curiosity? Why could she never allow her daughter something less hard-nosed and cold? What was so wrong with soft, tender feelings? Pierre winked to dissipate Luna's fury. Both mother and daughter knew how to push each other's buttons. To keep Luna from erupting he had to show he was on her side. Luckily he usually was, and certainly so this time. What he had seen in Angie's face as she saw Dave's mother greet Luna was a moment of terror at losing control. Bitterness and envy had crossed her face at the welcome Lu was given before she composed her features into blankness. He could understand it, if what Angie always said was true. In those days, having a child out of wedlock was a shameful thing and it must have been tough if all the relatives were against you, then you got left by the guy anyway.

★   ★   ★

Back at Robert's house, everybody circled the buffet set out on the dining table, loading vol-au-vents, coleslaw and potato salad onto paper plates. They stood eating and making conversation and trying to control the children, who had been looked after by a neighbour while the adults attended the funeral and had now been cooped up for far too long. Luna was introduced to a sea of faces, trying to take in who everyone was. Robert had two sons and a daughter, all with respective wives and husband

30

and kids. The eldest, David, proudly announced he was named after her father. It was peculiar for Luna, who had only heard him berated or dismissed. In this family, mention of him was accompanied by an air of admiration, and she too was welcomed as something special, just being, as her natural inheritance, a part of him. Reflexively she looked over at her mother, who had tried to stay in Pierre's van until she was reluctantly beckoned inside by Maureen, beaming as though this was the reunion she'd dreamed of for years, now introducing her to her 'other daughter-in-law'.

'Have you got kids?' Becky was asking Luna.

'No.' Her reply didn't seem enough and there was a slight pause, as though an explanation was expected. She didn't know how to fill it. She was used to being introduced as an artist, and people asked her about her painting, when her next exhibition was, her inspiration and what it all meant.

'Oh well,' said Becky. 'There's still plenty of time, isn't there?'

Luna smiled in what she hoped appeared agreement and took a bite out of a Scotch egg, eyes flitting to the pictures on the wall as a distraction. They were stark black and white photographs of foreign landscapes and street kids, at odds with the rest of the decor, which was creamy and floral with gold trimmings.

Becky followed her gaze and said, 'I suppose you recognize your father's photographs? My dad's whole house is like a gallery. Hey, Dad,' and she called Luna's father's brother over to show Luna around.

She followed Robert along the line of photographs that continued through the hall and into the sitting room as he talked about them. He was a keen amateur photographer himself, he said, wildlife mostly, but he could never catch an atmosphere the way Dave had done. He grew teary again as they stopped at the one he called his favourite, a photograph of an ancient man sitting in an old-fashioned armchair reading a newspaper. While Robert reached for a tissue and dabbed his eyes, Luna studied it.

At first look there was something ridiculously northern about it, almost to the point of caricature. It was a beautiful photograph, certainly, in its contrasts and composition and atmosphere. You could almost hear a grandfather clock ticking and smell the furniture polish. It was one of those oppressive, over-cluttered rooms of a bygone era, with a Victorian cabinet in the background, china ornaments on the mantelpiece and embroidered linen coverlets on the arms of the chair. There was even a pipe on the occasional table beside him, for God's sake. He was dressed in a Sunday best sort of outfit, suit and tie and waistcoat, with his thinning hair Silvikrined back. But as you looked, the thing that reeled you in was the expression in the old man's eyes as he looked up over his glasses towards the camera. Somehow the photograph had captured an entire lifetime in just that one snap, the moment of glancing up into the lens. You knew he had experienced every-thing: joy, sorrow, hard times and good, laughter, tragedy, boredom. The look into the camera conveyed it all and you, standing here receiving it on the other side, felt it. It made him seem like someone you really knew.

That's what made the photograph. That and the glaringly bright white eighties trainers on his feet. The more Luna looked the more subtle she realized the photograph was, and the more emotional she became.

'The trainers!' she said, and Robert's tears turned to laughter as he nodded furiously.

'I know! It took us ages to get Dad out of his boots and into those. He had murder with his fallen arches, but he wouldn't be told. 'Them's girls' shoes, for wearing to netball!' he said. It was only when we forced them on him he realized the support they gave. He'd only wear them round the house, mind.'

'So he's . . . my grandfather?' Luna asked, staring into the old man's eyes.

'Oh sorry, love. Of course. Have you not seen a photo of him before?'

Luna shook her head, not trusting herself to speak.

'Aah,' Robert replied, holding up a finger. 'I've got something for you.' He went over to the sofa and dragged a large battered suitcase from behind it.

'Dave didn't have much by way of possessions,' he said. 'He didn't believe in them, as I'm sure you know.'

Robert and Luna smiled together.

'But these are his photographs. There must be thousands that got lost along the way what with his Romany lifestyle, but I did my utmost to insist he kept his best ones. I went round to the last place he lived before he left for Thailand and salvaged what I could. He called me sentimental and said they weren't worth anything but he let me keep them anyway. I think he were glad of it later, when he came home . . . '

It sounded as though there was going to be more of the story but Robert trailed off.

'When was that, then?' Luna dared to ask.

'Only about nine month ago now. He tried to look after himself out there as long as he could but we insisted he come home when he got too frail. I wanted him to come and live with us but he wouldn't. He had a sheltered flat at first and then he went into a hospice. He never complained. He didn't suffer for too long, mercifully.'

He patted Luna's arm awkwardly, though it was he who needed the comforting.

'I'm sorry,' Luna said, at a loss for any other words.

'He wanted you to have these,' said Robert.

'Really? I mean — he said that?'

'He did, yes. He wished he had more to give you. Said he finally understood what possessions were for. Passing on and all that.'

'But . . . did he know about me? I mean, of course he knew about me, but . . . '

'It was him that asked me to get in touch with you. He seemed to know what you did and how to find you.'

'But . . . so . . . why didn't he get in touch . . . before he died?'

'I don't know, love. But by the time he came back to England he was very ill. My understanding was that he didn't want you to see him like that, after all these years. I think he thought it wouldn't be . . . very nice for you. Not the right thing. You know.'

Luna stared blankly at the suitcase. It was all so surreal. To suddenly be confronted with all this . . . *family*. Cousins, nieces and nephews, adoring grandmothers, a weeping uncle who was talking to her as though she'd always known him, a deceased father who'd secretly known all about her.

And now she felt a hand on her other arm, and turned to find herself looking into the old woman's eyes. Now that they were for the moment clear of tears, Luna saw with a shock that they were the same dark eyes as her own. Or rather, her own were exactly like her grandmother's. It was that way round, after all.

'He was very proud of you, dear,' she said. 'I want you to know that.'

The two women looked into each other's face a while longer in mutual recognition. This is what I'll look like when I'm old, Luna thought. She felt her mind warping as she was transported into her own old age. But it was only the face that was her future. She couldn't see herself in a house like this, filled with people. Who would be there with her? Angie would be long gone. Probably Pierre too — men always died before women. That's if their relationship lasted the distance. They'd never promised each other that they would always be together, in sickness and in health. It was, like most relationships were these days, for while it was good and what they both wanted. And everyone else — all the people she knew and took for granted in her full, sociable life — her dealer, fellow artists, buyers, friends . . . would she still know them then? Was the bond she had with them strong enough to take them into old age together? For the first time she felt the fragility of bonds that weren't glued with blood.

If she didn't start a family herself she wouldn't end her days surrounded by children and grandchildren. There would be no one coming after her, no one bound by love or duty to care about her. She would die alone. She suddenly felt like the person, last in line, who, in a record-breaking attempt to keep the ball in the air, dropped it and ended everything.

'Thank you,' Luna said.

'I hear you inherited his talent too,' said Maureen. 'Come and tell me all about yourself.'

She pulled Luna to the sofa to sit down, and Robert's wife brought them cups of tea. Luna perched awkwardly with her cup and saucer. Her mind had overloaded and gone totally blank. She was so used to talking about her life as it related to her work, but now that she was with a grandmother wanting to know the solid things, the bones of it, it all seemed weightless as air and she couldn't think of a thing to say.

'You live in London,' Maureen started for her.

Luna nodded.

'In a nice part?'

'No, not really,' Luna replied and tried to

laugh. So proud, normally, of her urban existence, living and working in a sky-high flat in a
tower block rising from the grim sprawl of East
London, it now seemed something to be ashamed
of.

'And you're an artist?'

Bless her for trying. But Luna had no idea
how to describe what she did. She had lived and
breathed making art since she could remember,
and it meant everything to her. And here it
seemed . . . like the sort of thing you should do
in your spare time, around the important things.

She nodded and smiled.

'Your Pierre seems lovely. How long have you
been married?'

Oh God. Maybe Angie was right and Maureen
was an old battleaxe after all. Every question she
was asking seemed to be chipping away at her,
making her feel more and more inadequate. Her
usual answer — that she didn't believe in marriage — failed her. Her arguments against seemed
inappropriate: the transference of ownership implied
in the change of surname, the giving away by the
father, the fact that in darker days women's lives
were dictated by who they married, that it was
rarely for love but survival . . .

'We're not married,' she answered instead,
finding herself adding a guilty, 'yet.'

'Oh,' said Maureen. Was there disapproval or
disappointment in her voice? Luna thought there
was something. 'Well, at least I haven't missed
the wedding,' she went on, more brightly. 'I love
a good wedding. You'll be sure to invite me,
won't you?'

'Of course,' Luna smiled, as though she really would have a wedding one day. What else could she say? I think it's legalized prostitution? It was already a bad enough day for a woman whose first-born son had died before her. Luna felt at odds here as it was, just being herself, her mother's daughter. She was shrinking, like Alice in Wonderland, until she was too tiny for all of this. It was strange that it was here, surrounded by family for the first time, that, also for the first time, she felt an outsider, afraid. It made her angry. Luna had never been scared of dying, or living. She had an urgent desire to get out. All these people were suffocating her suddenly. It was all too much. She was drowning in this quagmire of attachment.

She gulped down her tea quickly.

'Excuse me for a moment,' she smiled, making a gesture with her crockery to show she was returning it to the kitchen. The smile was fixed on her face as she wound her way through all the people, her eyes scanning them for Pierre. They had to make their excuses and go.

She saw him finally through the French windows, swinging a child round and round by his arms as his feet flew out. He was cackling maniacally, and another boy was jumping up and down excitedly shouting, 'Me, me, me! My turn, my turn!' Pierre was grinning patiently. Luna paused and watched for a moment. She knew already that he was *good with kids*, from his natural ease with the new children that had begun to pop up around them in friends' lives. Gradually couples were beginning to settle down and breed. Luna hadn't paid much attention. It wasn't something she and Pierre had planned to do, the way other people did, as soon as they got past the early romance and sex-at-every-opportunity stage. But it surprised her how well Pierre dealt with baby rages and tantruming toddlers whenever they were round at other people's houses. She presumed it came from being the eldest of five. As an only child, after the commune ended Luna had turned her back on childhood and forgotten how to relate to it. Children were boggling at best and generally rather irritating when you were trying to have a good conversation. They had a terrible sense of humour and no good anecdotes. Even so, she felt a stab of envy as Pierre stopped spinning and the children gathered round him clamouring for his attention. And a surprising pang of yearning for him.

She went into the garden.

'Sorry to spoil your fun,' she said. Pierre looked at her.

'Are you OK?' he asked.

'Uh-huh,' Luna replied, and tried to laugh at the boy pushing her away from Pierre's body so he could be whirled again.

'That's enough now,' Pierre said to him. 'I'm too dizzy. We'll be sick.'

The boy laughed and ran around making puking noises.

'I'm all charmed out,' Luna said quietly. 'Do you think it'd be all right to start saying our goodbyes now?'

'Sure,' said Pierre. It wasn't like her to be done

in so quickly. 'We've got the long-journey excuse. It'll be fine.'

'Thanks,' said Luna, relieved.

They made their way back through the conservatory. Everybody had gravitated towards the sitting room, but in the hallway Luna stopped and held Pierre back. It suddenly seemed daunting, to have to make an entrance and announce their departure. She didn't know how to do it. Was this the only time she'd ever see them? Or would they exchange contact details, arrange to meet up again? She felt teary again, and couldn't think of anything worse than actually crying as she said goodbye.

'Wait a sec,' she whispered. 'I'll be all right in a mo.'

They hung back, and Pierre put his arm round her. She put her face on his chest and steeled herself against the tears. He had a dip in his bony breast where she often lay her head, and it fitted, perfectly. She breathed in the scent of him. It was the only thing she could define as home. He smelled rich, the heat and whirling kids mingling with his fusty dry-cleaned suit and the aftershave he hardly ever wore. She was overwhelmed with need for him and reached up for a kiss. Thinking she only wanted the reassuring kind, she was surprised by an immediate sting of desire. From the way he was kissing her back she knew he was feeling it too. Luna glanced over Pierre's shoulder and seeing the cupboard under the stairs, gently pushed him towards it.

★ ★ ★

Luna had recovered her poise by the time she returned from the bathroom. Pierre had begun the lengthy process of goodbyes and was exchanging phone numbers and email addresses with Luna's cousins while Angie waited stiffly by the door. They gathered around Luna as she came in and she kissed everybody's cheek and gave Maureen's brittle bones a careful hug.

'Don't lose touch,' the old woman said, crying again. 'I want to see you again.' The way she said it made Luna think she meant *before I die*.

Luna managed to escape with her mascara intact, and the sentiment hardened into a stony silence once they were in the van with Angie once more. Even Angie seemed aware of Luna's fury with her, and had the sense to either snooze or pretend to for a large part of the journey home. They dropped her at her flat in Ally Pally, Pierre responding with a 'Not sure — we'll let you know' to her invitation to lunch at the weekend, filling the void as Luna ignored her.

'Lu,' he said quietly, squeezing her knee as she clambered over the seat once Angie's front door had banged shut behind her. Luna shook her head.

'Don't,' she said. 'How am I supposed to forgive a lifetime of lies?'

'Maybe it's not lies,' he tried, but Luna huffed and turned her head to face away from him.

Driving on down through East London was easy at this time of night. They slipped through a lucky run of green lights. It was raining now and

41

Luna watched the lights coming into focus and blurring again like watercolours as the windscreen wipers created their own two-second cityscapes. She loved London in the rain at night. Whenever they had been away, the drive back into town always excited and comforted her, a mixture of adventure and familiarity all at once. The city was her inspiration. Even the portraits she had been concentrating on in recent years were usually placed in a city backdrop. It often seemed part and parcel of the person somehow, inseparable from their psyche.

Tonight, for the first time, the landscape seemed bleak and filled her with such a sense of loneliness and alienation that she was amazed it hadn't ever done so before. It seemed obvious, somehow, that a city would do so, especially this poverty-stricken, bomb-blasted part of it. But until now the city had symbolized energy and life and connection to her, the best of human endeavour, that struggle to produce the finest of achievements that she herself had always been so desperate to contribute to.

They finally wound their way through their mottled patch, the warehouses, defiant single rows of Victorian terraces and wasteland scarred with roads and rail tracks, to their parking lot in the vast sixties estate. After the pleasant comfort of clean, leafy, sky-drenched suburbs, Beauvoir Heights loomed unwelcoming and sinister, and as they entered the lift the smell of urine was particularly pungent. At least it was working, however claustrophobic the rattly journey, and got them to the eleventh floor. They let themselves through the security door. This was a great improvement on how it had been when they moved in six years ago. Back then the lift opened straight on to grey corridors as grim as the building's exterior. Anyone could walk out of the lift and try their luck at any flat door, which was why they had been gated with wrought-iron bars and reinforced metal doors. The council had finally put in key-locking glass doors immediately the lift door opened, separate ones for the flats to the right or left, so that you shared a walkway with only six other neighbours. Because of this the corridor's paintwork remained graffiti-free and the smell was left behind when the door clicked shut.

Once up here it was a different world. Walking to their own door it was almost possible to believe they were somewhere swish. The concrete floor had been covered over with smooth beige marble-effect tiles and the flat doors had been replaced with ordinary, homely wooden ones.

As Pierre let them in and switched the soft lamps on, Luna felt a little cheered. They were home. Even at night — especially at night, maybe — the views across London were stunning. Living in the sky was better from the inside. They'd made the best of the flat interior, designed in that then futuristic, now retro-chic way. As you entered, the entire opposite wall was glass, which made Luna feel she could finally stop holding her breath. The sitting room was big; the kitchenette on one side had 'space age' serving hatches through the units that meant you could still see from end to end. The flat was unusual for a block in that it was a split level, the stairs turning round beside the front door to the bathroom and three bedrooms upstairs, two of which looked out the other side, across to the east.

Luna attempted to be upbeat as they uncorked a cheap Chilean wine and unburdened themselves of shoes and ties and hairpins. They lounged on their old velvet sofa and put the TV on for some mindless wind-down. But it was no use. The wine soon undid her efforts to hold herself together as though they were the laces of a bodice, and her maudlin mood was released like an exhalation. Pierre rubbed her arm as she lay against him.

'Heavy day, huh?' Pierre said. She began to cry.

'I'm sorry,' she said, getting up and moving to the kitchen where she blew her nose on a piece of kitchen towel with her back to Pierre. She wasn't a crier. From a young age she had prided herself on this, encouraged by her mum to be strong and brave. But these were tears that came from somewhere deep inside that couldn't be stemmed, that welled out of her as though she was sodden, flooded ground.

'It's OK,' said Pierre. 'Nothing to be sorry about. Of course you're going to be sad on the day of your dad's funeral.'

Luna nodded, still facing away. She wanted to leave it there, with Pierre thinking she was grieving a death, but she couldn't hold it in.

'It's not just that though,' she said. Her voice sounded small, not like her own, and she tried to compose herself. She didn't want to sound like a whining baby.

'I know,' said Pierre. 'It was kinda overwhelming today, huh? Meeting all these random people for the first time that are suddenly your family. It must've been, like, really weird.'

'Yeah, that too. It was.' She paused again. Pierre was putting words into her mouth. She didn't know if he was trying to help her out, or to make her answers the ones he wanted to hear. He fell silent as she turned, looking at her with an *I don't know if I want to hear this* expression. She baulked internally for a moment, then struggled on, groping for the words.

'The thing is, Pea . . . ' she finally blurted. ' . . . If nobody's born, all you're going to get your whole life is people dying.'

Luna watched Pierre's reaction as what she'd said sank in. Somewhere in her mind she was pleased with the way she had put it. It said it all, somehow, out of all the millions of thoughts and feelings tangled inside. It was a fact there was no denying, and he didn't try to.

'I mean . . . that's the reality of it, plain and simple. That old woman there, my grandmother. She's got her children and they've got children, and they've got their children, and when my cousins are Maureen's age they'll have their children and their children's children's children too. All spreading around them . . . and I'll just be — me. Sort of me. Only all shrivelled up and dying and then dead. It's not — it's not how life should be.'

'Are you saying . . . ? What are you saying, Lu?

45

I mean, I know that's what life *is* — being born, living, breeding, dying — I mean, sure. But . . . I don't know.' He stopped, cut to the chase. 'You're talking about us having kids, right?'

Luna felt embarrassed, as though the desire for children was something to be ashamed of. When they'd got together they had been high with the excitement of finding in each other the wish to follow an alternative path, chase different dreams, remain free from the inevitability of reproducing. And now she felt she was going back on a promise, letting him down.

'I don't know. I just . . . had a revelation, I guess. It's not like I've thought about it and changed my mind. It's more of a feeling.'

'Because you suddenly got scared of being alone when you're old? You always felt it was wrong that people had kids because of that. That it was selfish and we should be braver.'

'I know,' Luna replied. 'I still do. But it's not just that. It's like, I finally understand.'

'But haven't you always understood? We said we didn't necessarily have to do that just because it's, I dunno — a biological drive. We don't have to obey it, just because it's there.'

'I know, I know.' Luna felt defeated by the impossibility of trying to explain her feeling, so profound and wordless in the face of their usual logic and argument. 'I still think that. But . . . it's not that simple.' She rubbed her forehead and refilled her wine glass. Out of the corner of her eye she saw Pierre reach for his weed box and skin up. Her frustration rose as he sank back and took a long toke. Not that she was averse to a bit of blow herself, but weren't they getting too old for it to be cool?

'Look, we've had a knackering day. Perhaps this isn't the best time . . . ' Pierre's voice cracked as he held in a lungful of smoke.

'That's just it, Pea,' she said urgently, coming through from the kitchen and standing to face him, trying to get through to him before he disappeared beneath his glazed surface. 'I have this feeling that this *is* the best time. It's not that I've been planning or thinking anything. I just *know*. That now is the time.'

There it was. It seemed too bold a statement, so she softened it with, 'If we're going to.'

Pierre blew out, wafting his wild fringe away from his eyes.

'Christ, Luna. That's quite a thing to hit me with after today. Are you sure it's not just the funeral and everything? Maybe you need to chill out a bit, give it some time, see how your emotions settle down. I mean, you must be feeling all over the place.'

It annoyed Luna to have such an issue dismissed as her emotions. It was as bad as hormones, as though they rendered what she was saying invalid and unreasonable.

'I'm quite sure,' she said firmly. 'Today has only really brought to light what I've been feeling for a while.'

Her certainty wound Pierre up. He tensed defensively, took another toke.

'Well, you might be feeling that, but what about everything else? Have you thought practically, about our situation?' He gestured

47

expansively at the room around him, and, by extension, at their life.

Luna followed his sweeping hand and saw everything he meant. The flat was pretty cool for a couple, for artists with a studio each, but as soon as you put a cot and a buggy in the picture, an old carrier bag of dirty nappies at the door waiting to go out to the bins, it seemed . . . desperate. She'd always felt sorry for the kids living here, hanging around hunched in hoodies as grey as the scenery.

'We don't really live in ideal conditions for babies,' he pointed out, exhaling again. It would have been comical if it didn't make her feel so desolate, this scruffy guy dropping pot ash onto his Oxfam suit trousers. 'I thought we were against having kids, especially if we were in no situation to? We're barely supporting ourselves, let alone anyone else.' He struggled up, suddenly agitated, and began to pace around the room. 'And what about your art, anyway? How will you do that? You're on the brink of making it, Luna — we both are. Is it really the best time to put it all on hold like that to look after a baby? And there's my exhibition coming up . . . '

Luna sank under the weight of his words, her hopes buried by the implausibility of it all.

At her silence, Pierre turned to look at her. Her head hung dejectedly as though she'd been told off. He came to her and put his arms round her.

'Look, this really isn't the best time for us to be talking about this,' he said. 'We're both shattered. I'm not saying it'll never happen. Let's just think about it. There's plenty of time, Lu.'

For you, maybe, Luna thought. He could afford to concentrate on becoming a successful, famous artist. Or even sit around being a dreamy pothead for a couple of decades. If he didn't make it until he was sixty, he could still father a child. Not just physically. He'd still be able to attract young, fertile females, especially if he made it, had status and money. He'd certainly still be skinny and it looked as though he'd keep a full head of hair. He had the rest of his life, and then when a suitable girl came along he wouldn't even be disturbed from his work, because it would be her thing, to have the baby. To have it, look after it, bring it up. Yes, she thought, for you there is plenty of time.

But not for her. Somehow, though, she felt unable to argue the point. It wasn't just an argument with Pierre, but with herself and the life she had chosen. She felt split in two. She knew he was right, there was no way it was feasible. She still had to waitress most of the time, for God's sake, just to pay the rent. They were beginning to make names for themselves, but it was precarious. They could both go either way, still. If they were in the right place at the right time they could take off, or not. They had imagined they would be in this position five years ago. But it had taken longer to build their reputations, and they still hadn't got there, although they had both been happy to be immersed in their work, still trying.

But now, in her heart, there was a change, a drive for something else. She'd scorned the idea of a biological clock in itself, let alone the inability to overcome it, and here she was, being pressured along by its ticking hands. In her heart, suddenly, art didn't seem to be the thing that mattered. It was shocking to her. She certainly couldn't bring herself to say it to Pierre. It was too much of a betrayal, of everything they were to each other. Of everything she was to herself.

★  ★  ★

Unable to sleep, Pierre snoring next to her and taking up too much of the bed, Luna realized her eyes were open in the dark, settled on the shape of her father's suitcase standing by the bedroom door where Pierre had dropped it.

She slipped out of bed and took it into her studio, where she could put the light on and open it out on the large table along one side wall. She began to sift through the photographs, some packets of snapshots, a couple of boxes of negatives and slides, mostly larger black and white prints. Many were tatty or spotted with mildew. But still they had the same evocative beauty of the ones she had seen on Robert's walls. At first she tried to politely consider each one with the respect it deserved, checking her impulse to race through them to find others, ones that meant something to her. But the pictures were all of strangers in foreign places, and try as she might she felt nothing. She began flicking quickly, digging about to unearth some sort of link between her father and herself. It wasn't there. Eventually she lost her temper and chucked the entire contents into a chaotic pile on the table, wildly tearing through. She was on the brink of frustrated tears that she couldn't cry. He had been nothing in her life, and he'd left her with nothing now.

She took a deep breath and stopped. She would have to systematically place the photos back in the case one by one to ensure she hadn't missed anything. Finally, an A5 envelope revealed itself; she'd previously missed it in her furious hurry. There was nothing written on it to suggest what was inside, only his name and a Thailand address, a handwritten 'By Air' underlined in the corner.

She slid the thin wad of photographs out. The one on the top was in colour, making it spring to life against the pile of black and whites. Luna held it in both hands, staring. The camera was close to the ground, the lens peering through grass to a few feet beyond, where a man and woman sat cross-legged facing each other, kissing. The background was an unfocused impression of the colours and shapes of other people sitting and lying around, topped with postcard blue sky and sunlight beaming in from the edge of the shot. It was probably the photograph's only fault — the camera wasn't properly positioned in relation to the glare so the picture was a little bleached. But it was wrong to call it a fault. If anything, it enhanced the atmosphere of it, lending it a wistful, nostalgic quality. The man wore only frayed blue jeans and beads round his wrist. He was tanned,

51

long-limbed with a nice bare chest and wavy brown hair that hung in layers to his shoulders. The girl had a beautiful figure, wore only tiny cut-offs and a yellow macramé bikini top, and huge sunglasses perched on her head that held the waist-length pale gold hair away from her face. They held hands, resting them on their knees as they leaned in towards each other, their faces meeting at the lips, slightly smiling, eyes open. They were the picture of being in love. Luna flipped the photograph over. Inside a love heart drawn with biro were the words 'Me and Ange, Isle of Wight, 1970'.

On one level Luna had known it was her mother and father, but even so she hadn't recognized them. Not even Angie. She studied her in the picture, her smooth legs, slim brown arms, pert breasts, her face luminous with youth and desire. And her father, so lithe and — gorgeous, actually. Was it OK to think of your father that way? Luna didn't know. But he was. From his profile he seemed so handsome, a strong jaw highlighted with long sideburns, kind smiley creases around his eyes, a prominent straight nose nudging Angie's cute button.

The composition of the picture was astonishing, especially considering the position of the camera in the grass, which must have surely meant the shutter was set with a timer. The strip of sky at the top of the image mirrored the strip of grass at the bottom perfectly. The couple formed a triangle at the epicentre that drew the viewer's eyes in to rest on this still form they made together, a somehow sacred union. It felt like a special privilege to be witnessing this manifestation of love, set against the blurred motion of others, unnoticed beyond them. It reminded Luna of the device used in film, when the central characters were held still in a significant moment while everything else carried on, racing and whirling around them. But this was captured without any effect or trickery. It was beautiful.

The feelings all came at once — an indistinguishable surge of attraction, admiration, pride, joy, longing and loss. And then the rage, for everything she could have known, everything she had been denied.

# 1970

## Angie

Her mother would have had a blue fit if she'd known Angie was hitching to the festival. Or even going to the festival at all. But Angie was nearly out of her teens, had finished her first year at drama college, and it was her life. If they knew half the things she got up to they'd have heart attacks on the spot, but they were so square. Even getting them to agree to her going to drama school had been a huge battle. They seemed to think aspiring to become an actress was akin to deciding on a career as a prostitute. Her father aired his terrible disappointment that she wasn't going into teacher training before refusing to speak to her altogether until she changed her mind (which she didn't) and her mother tried to persuade her to at least go to secretarial college to 'have something to fall back on' when it all went wrong. Hoping, of course, that by the end of it she'd just get a nice job in an office and meet some boring man in accounts and get married. Had they really not seen that the world was changing? Men no longer had to be slaves to the nine to five, women didn't have to be stuck in the house having babies and cooking. They were so desperately out of touch. Her father even still refused to have a television in the house as he thought it a bad influence on the intellect. They sat round the radio in the evening, or read without speaking, or, if they were feeling particularly gregarious, played Scrabble. Honestly.

Angie had had such a sheltered upbringing that the Guildford School of Acting had been a bit of a shock, even though she'd been dying to experience something more like real living. Never mind what students got up to outside classes, the lessons themselves were astonishing. Angie had had no idea teachers her parents' age would read explicit scripts in class, encourage students to swear their heads off, or simulate orgasms in front of the entire group. It was way-out. It took a while for her to let go of her inhibitions, but once she had she felt released, and addicted. She had performed her end-of-year piece entirely naked. Mr Lennox ('call me Carl') had given her an A Plus.

She hadn't wanted to come home in the holidays, but the student accommodation was closed for the duration, and anyway, she'd run out of money. A few of the students with generous allowances from wealthy, supportive parents had asked her to go to Morocco with them and she was pig sick about having to say no. They said it cost next to nothing once you were there, and she had almost convinced her parents to at least lend her the money, which she would pay back by getting a part-time job, but she stupidly let slip that there were young men travelling in the party.

Being home had been a trial. She hadn't

realized quite how much she had changed over the year until she tried to revert back to the cooped-up person she'd been before she left, and couldn't. She found it amazing that her parents still insisted on knowing where she was going if she went out. (There was fuck-all to do — it was only ever the pub. Even that caused consternation — she had to pretend she was meeting people she knew, as young women shouldn't go in on their own.) They always stayed up until she got home. On tedious nights in, they expected her to go to bed at the same time as them. She found she craved pot as she knelt on her old bed, wide awake, smoking cigarettes out of the window. Her parents didn't even have any alcohol in the house, apart from the cooking sherry, which she had already drunk and replaced three times.

It was at the pub she'd heard about the festival. She ran into a guy she vaguely recognized from school days, who'd been a couple of years above her and dated Jill Jenkins, the prettiest girl in the fifth form. Turned out they'd had to get married when he got her pregnant, and whenever Angie went to the pub he was always in there with his mates. He flirted with her. She realized she had become interesting, glamorous, since she'd gone to college. He and his mates bought her drinks, but she wouldn't let them get anywhere with her. One of them wasn't bad-looking and worked in the music shop, but she wanted a better fate than the one Jill had ended up with. She was too good for this kind of boy now and wasn't going to waste herself on one.

When Jill insisted she'd leave Ray if he went to the festival without her — actually carrying out her threat by going back to her mum's when he tried to stand his ground — there was suddenly a ticket going spare. Angie claimed it immediately, without hesitation, without thinking how she would pay for it or get there. Ray was sweet. He said she could owe him for it, pay him back whenever. He did have a go at getting a sympathy shag off her by going on about how mean Jill was to him, and she knew if she put out she could have the ticket for nothing. But she decided she would pay him with money. She was determined to get a job when she got back, maybe one to last through the term time as well. She couldn't bear how limited she was with her grant gone and only the paltry allowance from her father, how beholden to her parents, how trapped.

She'd refused the offer of squeezing into Mike's Mini and travelling down with them, even though that would have made it a lot easier. She didn't want to end up feeling obligated to stick with them for the whole weekend. It was to be her adventure and she wanted to be free to experience it on her own, as the person she wanted to be. She regretted the decision at first, slipping out of the house at the crack of dawn before her mother rose at six-thirty, leaving a note to say she was going to stay with a girlfriend in Hastings for the weekend. She'd have a tricky interrogation when she got back home, but she decided she'd rather face it then than now, when they'd make a huge fuss asking for the address and telephone number in case of anything, and probably insisting on taking her to the station and seeing her off on the right train.

As she hurried out towards the main road her fear bubbled up into the crisp morning air like a hot spring and steamed into carefree exhilaration. Explaining herself and her disappearance to her parents could wait for another less promising day. The old Angie would have been worried standing at the side of the road on her own but the new one, budding for so long, was blooming at last and she dared to make eye contact with drivers, smile encouragingly. She had to wait only ten minutes before a van pulled over for her, as luck would have it, going all the way to the Portsmouth docks.

★　★　★

At the ferry port Angie was overwhelmed by the swell of groovy people trying to cram onto the boats to the Isle of Wight. In their midst she felt at first shy and suburban again. They seemed like the real deal, actually living it, their clothes worn and scruffy, proper dropouts. Although she felt an outsider, she was sure they were her people, the ones she belonged with. Her fresh cotton floral dress suddenly lost the hippy effect she'd intended, and she felt prudish and overdressed. Once on the boat, she went to the toilets and changed into fraying jeans and a thin cheesecloth top. She felt much better, squeezing out onto the deck with new confidence.

It was as she looked around her that she locked eyes with the most gorgeous man she'd ever seen. He was so handsome she caught her breath, like some silly bird in one of the cheap romances her mother read. Only he wasn't the usual romantic hero, clean-cut and wearing a surgeon's gown or a safari suit. He was looking at her with mesmeric deep brown eyes, leaning on the railing in the kind of close-fitting tie-dye T-shirt that girls usually wore, the wind blowing through his long dark hair. He held her gaze with an amused expression and she blushed at the thought that he might know she'd changed her clothes. At the same time, at least she had changed. She felt better now, and, despite her racing heart, secure enough to act cool, pushing her hand sexily through her mane of hair as she turned away, and swaying her bum as she climbed to the upper deck, knowing he might be checking it out in her tight jeans. When she put her shades on and dared a look back down to where he'd been standing she was disappointed to see he had gone. Still, his presence and attention lingered with her, adding to the thrill of anticipation she felt as the ferry headed for the island.

★　★　★

It was incredible, mystical even, that out of the thousands of people making up the throng, she kept seeing him.

'I guess we're meant to be, man,' was how he put it when he finally spoke, his voice soft in her ear. It was the fifth time as she'd wandered around the site trying not to be self-conscious that she'd looked up and seen him somewhere nearby, watching her. Evening had fallen, and she was standing at the edge of the crowd near the stage, listening to some folk singers she didn't know. The music spoke to her though, and she was lost in the beautiful harmonies. She turned and there he was again right next to her, smiling down with his beautiful eyes. He had an Indian blanket wrapped round him against the night chill, and he extended his arm to share it with her. Unable to do anything else, she laughed lightly and nestled in.

'Smoke?' he asked and she nodded, thankful for all the experimenting she had done at college, thankful she'd got past the stage when pot would make her sick. They sat down together while he rolled a joint, and finally lay back on the grass looking up at the stars, passing it between them, inhaling, holding, and blowing smoke into the sky. The warmth of his body against hers began to take her over until she was cocooned, not only in the blanket but also in him. She felt herself changed by him, his intensity, his silence. As she got high she lost sense of her edges, where her skin finished and his began. It seemed as though the blanket was the skin they both shared.

Some time later the music stopped and they lay as still as the ground beneath them, just watching all the people looming over as they passed. He rolled on his side to face her, began to stroke her hair.

'Where are your people?' he asked.

'I don't have any,' she replied. 'It's just me.'

'Just you,' he said. 'Someone like you shouldn't be just you. Someone like you should have someone like me.'

And with that he put his nose to hers, looked deep into her eyes and kissed her.

★   ★   ★

They made love where they were, in the middle of the field wrapped in the blanket. He was astonishingly good at touching her, as though he had always known her and had learned what turned her on. He was tender and slow yet with a building insistence that brought her to her first climax with another person. And her second. It wasn't anything like the fumblings she'd had so far with fellow drunk and inexperienced students, or the seduction she'd succumbed to by one of her married tutors — so promising in the lead-up, so disappointingly dry and soulless in the rendition. At those times she had been all too aware of the physicality of it, the mechanics. This time was like being taken completely out of her body to a better place, like being shown the cosmos by Superman. This was like love.

'You're so beautiful,' he said afterwards, still kissing her.

'So are you,' she said back, and he smiled above her, a smile that shone as brightly as the stars beyond.

Later, as their bodies chilled, he pulled her up from the cold ground.

'Where are you camped?' he asked.

'Nowhere,' she shrugged, nonchalantly. She picked up her haversack, which had a sleeping bag rolled and tied onto the straps. 'This is all I've got. I was just going to sleep wherever the night took me.'

He grinned right into her soul. 'Well, it seems to have brought you to me.'

He wrapped her in the blanket and put his arm tightly round her and led her towards the festival campsite.

'How will you find where you are?' Angie asked as they picked their way between the tents spread across it like a shanty town.

'I always know where I am, man,' he answered, as though her question was a deep philosophical one. She glanced up at him and saw the light from a fire catch a serene smile on his face, like he knew the secret of life. She had never felt so out of her depth and yet so right at the same time. So strange and so at home.

Far from her assumption that they'd finally stumble upon his dark one-person tent, he drew her to a collection of tepees with a crowd gathered in the middle of them round a fire, a guy playing guitar while others sang.

'Hey, where you been, man?' a guy asked him, putting his arm across his shoulder.

'Finding someone,' he replied. The other guy looked appreciatively at Angie, nodding.

Several of the others turned and welcomed them. A girl came to Angie and kissed her cheek, stroking her head.

'She's beautiful,' she whispered, her entranced

eyes following her fingers as they trailed through Angie's hair. Another girl came up to them, and together they drew her into the group by the fire, where Angie smoked the circling spliff until she conked out with her head in her man's lap. She still didn't know his name.

The following morning she opened her eyes to the sight of his face, as he rested on an elbow and smiled down on her. They were inside one of the tepees, the sound of a band starting up on the distant stage drifting across to them. She was sandwiched between him and one of the girls, all of them apparently naked inside conjoined sleeping bags. He began to kiss and touch her, and she felt the girl stir, press her body against Angie's back and begin to rub her foot with her own. Angie tried to be cool about it and hoped the other two didn't feel her body stiffen. As open and free as she wanted to be, she couldn't help an instinctive reaction against sharing her man with this other chick. But she needn't have worried.

'How about some breakfast, Rain?' he said to the chick, who smiled sweetly.

'Sure, Dave,' she said, slipping out of the bed and dropping a kaftan over her body. His name was so surprisingly boring and ordinary. Angie already thought of him as Jesus in her mind. She let his real name form on her lips.

'What do they call you?' he said in return.

'Angie,' she replied.

'Angie,' he whispered. 'Angela. My angel.'

They made love, Angie at first conscious of the open entrance to the tepee and the people right there outside, but she soon allowed herself to be carried away on waves of bliss.

Later he led her outside and introduced her properly to the group, as Angel. They all welcomed her with the same light of love shining from their eyes. There were about eight or so of them, she thought. The guys all had normal names — there was a Justin, a Roger, a Martin — but the women had all changed theirs to names of nature — as well as Rain there was Fern, Poppy, Star.

'Angel!' said Rain. 'You were meant to be with us!' Rain seemed so enthralled with the name it didn't seem the time to correct her and admit she was born plain old Angela. Angie felt another layer of her old skin shed as she slid forward into life.

They shared everything with her as though she was accepted and had always been one of them, a breakfast of some sort of porridgey gruel, something they called tea, which was water with bitter leaves in it, and tabs of LSD. Afterwards, Roger suggested heading down to the stage to check out Supertramp, a new band whose first album, he said, was kinda cool.

★  ★  ★

The long weekend passed by in a blur. She was aware of the smiling faces of new friends around her, the flames of fires becoming creatures to her eyes, the brilliance of blades of grass, the wonderful sensation of everything on her skin, being naked and running free . . . until security guards caught her and wrestled her to the ground. Laughter, then freaking out and being afraid, and all the kind faces and hands calming her, feeling safe again. And always this beautiful man and the sense of belonging. The music was like the soundtrack to her rebirth, always perfect for her every change of mood — folk when she was mellow, heavy rock when she wanted to break out. Bands she mostly didn't know the first couple of days, and then mind-blowingly big stars just suddenly there — Joni Mitchell at a time she felt raw and emotional, making Angie cry as she appealed to the people causing increasing disruption, wanting to get in for free. 'You're behaving like tourists,' Joni said, her voice cracking, and Angie wept.

'It's OK, baby,' Dave consoled her. 'It's not you — you're not a tourist.'

Angie felt right again. Yes, at last, she wasn't a tourist. She was right inside, in the centre of the innermost crowd, at the heart of everything.

Later The Doors, her favourite band, Jim Morrison the object of a painful crush for years. She was still wild with excitement when they took to the stage and Dave took her as close to the front as they could get. Jim Morrison was cool, but he was no longer a god to her. She had her own now, and Jim seemed to personify her past life of dreams and fantasy, her teenage life before it became real. Dave wanted to stay for The Who, and they shouted along to Young Man Blues' and danced together to the funk of Sly and the Family Stone, sexy, grinding dancing that Justin and Rain joined in with. The girls discarded their shirts as they sweated, Angie gyrating topless with Rain, the men's hands over their bodies. She felt powerful as a planet, liberated as the wind.

★　★　★

She was aware somewhere of the bad vibe around her, especially when Kris Kristofferson played on the last day while those on Desolation Row outside the fence were pounding on it to bring it down. There was an Us and Them atmosphere, a feeling there were establishment fat cats just out to make bread when music should be free, for everybody to groove to. The musicians were caught in between, bewildered and unsettled, somehow on the wrong side when they shouldn't be.

After Kristofferson's set, Dave sensed Angie fraying with the tension of it, and gave her a pill, this time to chill her out. They escaped to a far, quiet corner to soothe Angie's fragile senses. The sun shone on that last day, the strains of Free and Donovan reaching them while Dave set up his Pentax to immortalize their union, the festival the background to their love.

'That's right, that's right!' he whispered to her as they sat, nose to nose and smiling, waiting for the timer on the camera to release the shutter. Angie didn't know if they stayed like it for seconds or hours. But she felt their spirits flowing between them, like osmosis.

Finally, they made their way back to the stage to be ready for Hendrix when he played.

'Are you a photographer?' she heard her voice ask, the voice of that person she was before, light years ago.

'I take an image of things that matter. A record of perfect moments,' he answered. 'But I am who I am. I don't have a label.'

Angie felt suitably ashamed. So much of what she'd just accepted as the way it was was so wrong. The slightest thing, the most innocent of questions about what a guy did. She realized that for all her rebelling she hadn't really questioned anything, not properly. She felt herself adjusting to a new reality, living as it was really meant to be, underneath the man-made surfaces.

'I'm sorry — ' she began, but he shushed her with a finger to her lips and a kiss on her head.

'It doesn't matter, my Angel,' he said. 'We've just gotta let all that go.'

She nodded eagerly to show she was ready to.

'Like you,' he said. 'What do you do?'

'I . . . ' Any answer seemed like the wrong thing to say. But he smiled at her with such love that she laughed.

'Go on — you can tell me,' he encouraged, tucking her hair behind her ear.

'I'm a student. I go to drama college,' she admitted. He nodded seriously, as though he somehow understood everything about her.

'You needed to break out,' he said.

'Yes!' she said, amazed he got her so right.

'But now' — he shrugged and grinned as though the answer was plain and vibrant as a rainbow — 'you don't have to act any more. You've made it, Angel. You just are.'

He was so profound, what he was saying a revelation that shook her like an earthquake. He was right. There she'd been, trying to build her identity through artifice, when all she had to do was *be*. And with him, she just *was*. He brought out everything good in her, she felt her spirit shine out of her, and she knew by how people responded to her with love that it was true.

Hendrix was incandescent, blazing somewhere above all the shit that was going down. By his set, Angie was truly wrecked. She had lived through more emotion in those few days than the rest of her life put together. But she was up there with Jimi, flying high.

$$\star \quad \star \quad \star$$

On Monday it was raining and Angie woke to find she was coming down. People were streaming out of the fields, leaving behind a lake of mud and rubbish. It seemed to signal that summer was over. Angie felt reality setting in. Was she really going to head home now, shrink again when her mind had been so expanded? The group were already packing up their campsite and she stood shivering without any useful jacket, not knowing what to do.

'Don't be down, baby blue,' he said, coming over and stroking her cheek. 'Nothing lasts forever.'

She fought back tears and tried to be OK. Of course their thing was just a moment. Of course they didn't belong to each other. Who did? The image of her disapproving parents, their grim, pinched, 'worried sick' expressions as they sat grilling her at the dining table, flickered into her mind. They might even stop her going back to college, if 'this was what it was teaching her'. She didn't even know if she cared. Drama school seemed silly, the epitome of narrow-minded petit bourgeoisie, all those middle-class kids pretending to be something, anything else.

Still, Dave held her to him and carried her haversack as well as his tepee poles as they trudged towards the ferry. Rain and Poppy held hands and skipped, until Roger asked them to stop splattering his already bedraggled bell-bottoms with even more wet mud. They fell in then with the other tired lopers, arm in arm and heads resting together. They still seemed happy. It wasn't over for them, after all.

★ ★ ★

After the ferry ride back to Portsmouth, Angie tagged along to wherever they were going. She didn't know how to separate herself from them now she'd been part of them, like a drop of water on a window that had run into a rivulet and lost its own autonomy and direction. Dave showed no sign of letting her go anyway, clamping her to his side as if she were part of his load. They arrived finally at a car park somewhere, at a Ford Transit van, painted orange and purple with ordinary matt paint. Angie stood back awkwardly as they shoved their things behind the seats, hoping to say as private a goodbye as possible to Dave, wondering whether she would ever see him again. She looked around bleakly, trying to decide in which direction she should head for home. She already knew from sparse conversations on the ferry that they were going back to some place in Wales, the other direction. But as they all climbed in, Dave didn't even come over to her. He poked his head out of the side door, gave her a quizzical look as she stood back. Perhaps they assumed they would be giving her a lift somewhere better than this for hitching.

He smiled affectionately and said, as though she were a child, 'I know you don't want the party to be over, baby, but don't you wanna come home now?'

She stared at him until he got out of the van and came over to her.

'Come on, Angel. Come home.'

She looked around for her bag and realized he'd already packed it into the van with the others. It seemed to mean it was already decided, that there was no alternative. It seemed impossible to dig around and pull it out again, like a brick in the foundations.

'But . . . what about . . . ? I haven't got any of my stuff,' her old voice said.

'Is that all it is?' he laughed, reasoning with a child again, as though her stuff was as important as a balloon that had slipped out of her clutch and drifted away on the sea breeze. 'What do you need,' he said, 'other than what you have here?'

The huge swell of relief as she thought about it caused her to laugh with delight. There was nothing. She could do without all of it. He laughed with her and pulled her by the hand and she clambered into the van and headed home, surrounded by the smiling faces of the Children of Ceres.

# 1994

# Nat

By the time she got to the flat door, even before going in, Nat had already accepted it in her mind. It was miles from anywhere she had ever been before. The security seemed good: three different locks on the door to undo. She turned all the keys after she entered, locking herself in, but rather than feeling imprisoned she felt free. On the inside there was a bolt and chain to push across as well, which she instinctively did. It was safe.

There was more than one room, more space than she'd ever known. It was hard to believe it could all be for her. It was bare, with just a few remnants of the previous tenant — a foam sofa bed with a torn blue cover, a low table where a TV had been, a couple of odd dining chairs. In the kitchen there was an electric cooker, not just rings but an oven as well, a fridge with a small freezer. There was a bad smell, which she traced to the inside of it, where mould had begun to speckle since it had been switched off around bits of food stuck on the shelves. Nothing that a good clean wouldn't fix. In the big bedroom was a double divan with a base with crooked drawers, a built-in wardrobe with sliding doors. Far more shelves than she needed for her bag of clothes.

In the small bedroom was the frame of a kids' bunk bed but the mattresses were gone. A child's height chart with cartoon animals was Blu-tacked onto the wall, with marks made above it on the wall, where at least one child had grown beyond even the giraffe on the paper. There were still a few children's drawings taped up, some crayon and felt-tip scribbles over the paintwork. Perhaps she would paint over it, a bright cheery yellow. And some toys had been left behind, probably that the kids had grown out of — a plastic thing with buttons to press and wheels to turn, some tatty pop-up books, pots of glittery paints and felt pens, a soft sheep with floppy legs and stuffing coming out of a rip. It still baaed though, when she picked it up and turned it in her hands. She couldn't imagine any child growing out of this, however old. It was so cute. The mother probably said it had to be thrown away because of the stuffing. It was dangerous for children, maybe. She wondered if the kid missed it. It stayed hanging from her hand as she went to see the bathroom.

It smelled damp, a windowless box room with a bath and no shower. She tried to imagine washing in there, cleaning her teeth at the end of every day at the sink, looking at herself in the cabinet mirror, and couldn't quite. But she would.

She walked back to the living room and stared out of the window. Nothing she saw was familiar. She felt the grip of fear around her middle loosen a notch, as though she had released a belt she'd pulled too tightly on her jeans. It was the sort of place you could disappear. No one could find her if she didn't want them to.

Here she would be three removes away. It was like the game Linz had been showing her how to play, Chinese chequers. The refuge was the first move, the one that got her out of home. The B&B where she'd been while she was on the housing list was the second, a diagonal move in the right direction. This would be a massive leap across the board, as far away as she could imagine getting.

She looked around again, wondering how quickly she could move in, what she would need first. Paulette had said she could get help with stuff she needed for starting out, extra payments for things like a duvet of her own, a hairdryer maybe, things you needed in the kitchen for cooking. Maybe she'd be able to get a microwave. She felt excited as she wondered where the nearest Argos was, and whether it was in a shopping centre with other shops. There might be a New Look or something, and she could get some decent clothes, different stuff to go with her newly bleached, straightened hair. Someday soon she could stroll around the shops without always looking over her shoulder, in a place where no one knew her, or, even if they did, never recognized her. Even if they thought they did, she'd look blank, pretend she was someone else.

An alien phone ring went off in her jacket pocket and she jumped, the grip squeezing her again until she got the thing out and read the number. Even though it was Paulette's phone, on lend in case of anything, even though Nat didn't have a number that anyone could call her on, or any way of anyone contacting her, she still couldn't breathe. Not until she found out it wasn't that someone had turned up looking for her. It was the B&B payphone number so she picked up. It was only Paulette about Tyler. Linz had said she'd watch him, but he'd been screaming the whole time and she couldn't handle it any more.

'You better get back,' said Paulette. He was winding up the other kids.

'It's not his fault. It's his teeth,' said Nat. 'Tell her to give him his dummy. Or his bottle. There's some pop in the fridge. Tell her I'm on my way.' Her voice was echoey in the empty room.

'Is it any good?' said Paulette, before she rang off.

'Yeah,' said Nat. 'It's perfect.'

★ ★ ★

It wasn't until she'd let herself out and triple-locked the door again that she realized she still had the sheep hanging off her wrist by its elasticated loop. She didn't bother putting it back. It was hers now, she figured, if no one else wanted it.

# TWO

*A painting. A woman at a window, looking out.*

She sits on an old wooden chair, leaning forward with her arms on the sill, a loose dress draping over her form to her feet, which are bare. Her hair is swept up at the back to reveal the nape of her neck, stray locks falling around her shoulders. Her face is in profile, highlighted against the glass.

# 2003

## Luna

Luna had always expressed herself through painting. She had been precocious at school, sometimes shocking adults with her ability to capture psychological issues in her childlike drawings. There was the time (aged nine) she painted Miss Sparks 'inside out', with an exploding universe in her brain, before the teacher left suddenly, rumours flying about her nervous breakdown. Or when she depicted a group of girls who were teasing her for her strange handmade clothing as birds pulling at the threads of her jumper as though they were worms, unravelling it to leave her naked.

She had been sent to see a child psychologist because of the things she produced in art class. But she was found to be a surprisingly well-adjusted girl, and when they met the nice normal grandparents who were looking after her, the teachers encouraged her talent for seeing the things of the mind.

After moving in with the separatist feminists in Wandsworth she spent her teenage years in her bedroom making art from scraps of the political propaganda lying around the house and found urban objects. Already it was art that said something. She won a prize for the image she made of a bride and groom outside church. If you looked closely enough at the arch behind them, you saw the bricks were made up of words cut from newsletters about divorce, adultery, rape and domestic violence. Angie was thrilled with her. There was never any question of her doing anything but going to art school. She painted obsessively, and was given an unconditional offer at St Martin's. At art school at last she fitted in. She was no longer the odd freaky kid with the weird mum. Middle-class kids from normal backgrounds envied her way-out upbringing, actually, and her ability to use her experience to create work of far deeper maturity than they could yet muster. It would take years of living to catch up with her. But she found a circle of friends there, other misfits, whose outsider status gave them a certain advantage in the environment. They became the elite of their year, all managing to secure agents at their degree show and all still in each other's lives now.

Pierre was one of them. He and Luna shared a dedication to their work and had always been friends, but hadn't got together until they were in their late twenties, when it finally seemed ridiculous that they weren't. 'Meant to be' was what mutual friends called it. Neither had wanted or needed a relationship before — it would have only got in the way of their work. They had each had several lovers about whom they confided in each other in their studio rooms at an artists' workshop complex in Farringdon. It was only when the studio closed down to be refurbished as swanky offices for businesses that they found themselves the only two left, both yet to find somewhere to work. Their romance began then, when the crowd that had always been around them had dispersed and they looked up from their work and saw each other, finally. At the eleventh hour Pierre heard of the flat in Beauvoir Heights, then a squat, and, both beguiled by the light coming into the bedrooms directly from the sky, they had moved in together, sharing one bedroom, the smallest, to sleep in and turning the others into a studio apiece. Both had reservations about living and working together, but were so careful to maintain their own space in the arrangement that it worked perfectly. They were good together, understanding in each other the need to put work before anything else.

For six years now it had been ideal, giving them the solitariness they needed to fully immerse themselves creatively, without the real isolation that so often led to a loss of motivation and career rethinks, or early-onset alcoholism. They supported and encouraged each other, without invading each other's space. Fellow artists envied what they had. Pierre had the larger room for his sculpture and Luna the smaller, although it was the one that faced west, towards central London, rather than out to the east. Pierre didn't care about the view, just the light, and Luna didn't need as much space, although they both worked on a big scale, now restricted only by the size of door frames and the lift. They were becoming known for a rather old-school adherence to form, which luckily for them was seeing a renaissance in fashionable circles.

Luna painted large canvasses in oil. Her overriding theme was city life. At first she painted the environment around her: vibrant close-ups of urban decay, areas pre-and post-regeneration, the blurring, ever-moving neon energy of London at night. But increasingly she peopled her work, zooming out of the detail of place, refocusing on them, and zooming in again. She managed to capture not only people dwelling in the city, but also the way the city somehow dwelt in them. The way people inhabited their space, or lack of it. The way they managed to survive life crammed together. She had 'the eye of a psychological photographer', the critic had said, the first time she was given a decent space in the arts pages.

She was these days getting a name for her portraiture, often securing commissions from wealthy art lovers and even a couple of minor celebrities. Although having worked previously with bright, bold, even luminous colour, her latest work was muted in shade, using tones of beiges and greys. It had begun during a particularly harsh winter, when she had painted a series of market traders at Brick Lane and Columbia Road, when the East End had been drained of colour for months on end and veiled in a permanent mist, like a wash over everything. The pieces were well received, although she felt uneasy about their popularity, with a nagging concern that it was due to their ability to blend with the current fashions in interior design.

'I may as well flog them en masse to sodding IKEA,' she had moaned to her agent, Julian, in a moment of exasperation, when a request had come through for a complete 'East End' series to decorate the white-painted brick walls of a new restaurant that had opened up on Old Street in a converted fabric warehouse. Still, she had done the work and it had kept her out of waitressing for nearly a year and led to a drip-drip supply of commissions, so she couldn't really complain.

*   *   *

Luna woke late, to the sound of Pierre working in his studio and a feeling of loss. Her sleep had been so heavy she was unable to define what the feeling was for a few minutes as she came to, but finally remembered, sharply, her father's funeral. She'd been wrong to think she wouldn't feel any grief for this person she never knew. Now it was almost as if it was twice the loss, once for his passing and again for the time she had never had with him while he was still here.

Normally eager to get into the studio straight away, pulling on her painting clothes and only stopping to make coffee en route, today Luna lingered in bed. If anything, she had a sinking feeling when she thought about her current painting — a commissioned portrait of Amelia, the wife of a well-known businessman and nouveau collector, who had caught on to art as a cool way of investing. Commissioned portraits were, on the one hand, great, and on the other . . . difficult. What had been well regarded about

85

her portraits was the surreal internal landscaping she achieved, managing to place the person's character somehow outside them, in their surroundings — her work had been likened to Chagall, and 'a subtle Kahlo'. (The Kahlo quote had annoyed her — the comparison had only been made because she was female, she was sure.)

But now that people were paying her to paint their portrait she found she couldn't always depict what she felt from the person's 'aura', to use an Angie word. In this particular woman Luna could see only greed, vanity and smugness. There was no way she could paint the imagery that was coming to her. Instead she was having to paint her in her perfect Eden of a garden, where she had insisted on posing nude for several days in the summer. Luna had to flatter her, try to portray the image the woman wanted to show off — captured forever in eternal youth in her beautiful surroundings. It was making Luna feel like a prostitute. But, as all prostitutes would say, she needed the money.

Luna found her mind wandering to other ways she could spend her day. She had to waitress at Trey's later anyway. Maybe it was OK to take a day off painting after your father's funeral. Days off weren't something Luna ever usually needed from painting — waitressing, yes, but not painting. She wondered if there was anything she could do to help Pierre for his exhibition in the spring, but then remembered with a sinking feeling their conversation of the night before. She wished she hadn't brought up the subject of kids, but then again, if she hadn't she would still be waiting for the right time. Because it did need to be said. She still meant it. Her spirits lifted at the thought that maybe now Pierre was over the shock of it and the seed was planted in his head, it might take hold and grow. Maybe he would say, OK, if it's what you want. Let's start planning for it, at least. Or even, let's start trying.

She threw off the duvet and went downstairs to brew some fresh coffee, taking two cups up to Pierre's studio and smiling, 'Hi, Pea.'

But Pierre looked like shit. 'All right?' he answered gruffly, without looking at her. He took the cup she handed him and stood back scrutinizing his piece. 'Crap,' he said, frowning. 'I've really fucked that up. I knew I shouldn't have carried on when I was tired. Crap, crap, crap.'

'What's wrong with it?' Luna asked, trying to follow his gaze to see what had gone wrong. The theme for the show was technology. Although he was pleased with his idea, its execution was proving problematic. He was attempting to sculpt from the idea of pixelation, taking low-resolution photographic images and rebuilding them in 3D form — a kind of retake on Cubism. He and his agent were excited about the concept, but Pierre still hadn't found the ideal material for working the pieces. He had begun with his favoured material, chiselling at a block of stone, but the mathematics of it had beaten him. So he'd gone back to the drawing board, making 3D pixels in the form of cubes.

He'd bought a job lot of ready-made boxes, constructing pieces by gluing the cubes together. This worked better, but there was still the question of what to make the finished pieces from, whether the weight of the final pieces would withstand gravity. The difficulty meant Pierre was behind schedule and his work had taken on an underlying panic.

'It looks fine,' she said, but realized the words sounded like a weak effort at comfort. Pierre wasn't in the mood. When his art was going wrong he had an intensity that was impossible to penetrate.

After standing for a few seconds, Luna finally responded to the leave-me-alone vibes. They had an agreement that their working day was their working day, relationship or not, and, on the whole, they were good about not doing relationship stuff during it. Especially when either of them had a deadline or show. So why did it bother Luna suddenly, now? My dad has just died, for fuck's sake, she thought to herself as she padded back out to her own studio, but she knew that wasn't really it. She could deal with that on her own.

The awkwardness hung about in the flat, like someone who'd crashed on the sofa the night before and wouldn't take the hint that they were busy and leave. As she wandered into her own studio room she came face to face with the portrait of Amelia, leaning on the floor against the wall. Surrounding it, Blu-tacked to the walls, were the photographs of Amelia's two young children. Although she had posed alone for the painting, she had later decided she wanted her children in the portrait with her, 'Perhaps as darling little cherubs! Wouldn't that be rather fun!' She had wanted them, also nude, somehow draped across her body, swamped in her Earth Mother embrace.

Luna felt sickened. It wasn't so much that Amelia had everything, it was how pleased with herself she was for having everything. It didn't seem to matter to her that she hadn't earned it or didn't actually do anything meaningful herself. She had got herself a rich husband who had sorted it all out for her, like winning the lottery, and she didn't seem to feel anything but proud about it. She was the sort of woman, Luna felt, who'd never really grown into a fully fledged adult, never had to survive by her own means and look after herself. But suddenly she felt jealous. An alien thought crept into her head. What was so wrong with Amelia's approach? The only thing of worth she had done was give birth to children. And they were beautiful kids — Felicia and Oliver, of course — who had angelic curls and lucent skin, the seemingly natural inheritance of wealth. You could never imagine them snot-faced and screaming wretchedly. Their childhood would be an idyll of comfort and play, for them and for their mother. *Having it easy* was never a thing Luna had aspired to. But she saw for the first time why other women did. Rich husbands made it possible to enjoy womanhood as though it was a never-ending succession of treats, even motherhood. Luna hadn't seen child-bearing as

89

something you *had* to do as a woman. She had enjoyed rejecting it, exploring other ways of existing. Her art was her reason to be.

But now, just standing in front of this painting, this shrine she was making to the Madonna Amelia with her vulgar display of fecundity, felt like a slap in the face. Was what she was doing now as an artist any more important than what Amelia was doing in her life? Replicating the image, a flat, two-dimensional copy, of a living being who had breathed life into two new ones. Painting suddenly paled in comparison.

★ ★ ★

'Well, paint something you *do* wanna paint as well,' Pierre answered irritably, wolfing the fry-up she'd made to avoid getting down to work. 'Just see the commission as your bread and butter. It's better paid than waitressing.'

'I can't start something else — I've got to get it done. She keeps phoning, asking if it's finished yet. She's going to have a grand unveiling and she wants to get the invitations out early so that everyone can put her fucking party into their social diaries. I haven't got any time around my shifts for anything else.'

'Then cut your shifts down.' Pierre stood up and chucked his plate in the sink, hovering, ready to spring up the stairs back to his studio.

'Pea, we can't afford that. We're living on that money. Literally. Don't you know that?'

'Oh come on, we're all right. I should sell something at my show and we'll be laughing.'

90

'Well, that'd be nice, for a change,' said Luna.

'What's that supposed to fucking mean? In fact no, I haven't got time for this right now. I've got work to do. And so've you, as it goes. If you've got something to say we'll talk later.' He disappeared up the stairs, leaving Luna sitting at the kitchen table fighting an urge to throw her coffee cup at the back of his head. Instead she held it tightly with both hands and waited for the sudden rage to pass. Where had it come from anyway? It was probably PMT, although she would have killed Pierre if he'd suggested that. He would have been right, annoyingly. She should just get on with it instead of moping around letting her mood get the better of her, and go whoring at Amelia's party too, to get some more of the same from her circle of rich friends. It seemed there was nothing more appealing to acquire than a portrait of yourself, if you had more money than you knew what to do with once you'd filled your wardrobe floor with this season's designer shoes.

But dissatisfaction had lodged itself inside her. The life she had been so happy with felt flat and empty, as though it had suffered a puncture and deflated. Pierre, who had always been everything she needed in a partner, now appeared somehow lacking. It wasn't him, wasn't his fault, she told herself. Money was not something he was driven by. It was one of his good qualities. He wanted to succeed, but in terms of making great art. He was obsessed in an old-fashioned way; it was like a romantic notion, struggling against poverty and disease in his garret, transfixed and driven half mad by the need to replicate the incandescent beauty of form. It was one of the things Luna found most attractive in him. But not at this moment. Right now she couldn't believe how unthinking he was. He hadn't sold any work for a while and had maxed out on his credit card months ago. When he needed money he used the waitressing cash. Not that he needed it much, as Luna bought all the shopping, paid for spliff, got in the drinks when they went out. She was OK with that. It gave her a sense of pride to be able to support them both and she was sure he would do the same for her. Although, come to think of it, it had never been he who got the part-time job. But how could he stand there cheerfully saying, 'We're all right'? How could he not notice that Luna's job was keeping them? Not appreciate the sacrifice she was making, and had always made over the years?

The selfless pursuit of artistic achievement seemed, in this light, rather selfish. The romantic artist, suddenly, a loser.

★　★　★

At work she felt better. The cafe was busy with footsore art tourists visiting the White Cube, and the mundane but fast-paced routine was soothing and almost enjoyable, at least compared to the frustration and grinding effort of painting Amelia. Her mate Gina was on the same shift, which always helped. It was Gina who had got her the work. They had met at the Farringdon workshops where Gina had a studio stitching portraits of neurotic-looking women out of feminine materials — nylon tights, panty liners, make-up sponges. Luna had loved them on sight, and Gina was well known then. When the studios closed she had moved to the Cleever Street workshops round the corner from Luna's flat, but her work seemed to go out of fashion somewhere before the turn of the century and her sales diminished. It seemed her pieces had had their day as an artistic statement on the role of women, and depressed housewives made of household waste were no longer resonant in an age of domestic goddesses and yummy mummies. She had given up her studio space and was waitressing full-time, her art squeezed into the corner of her flat and life.

Gina was of Italian descent, petite with mad glorious hair, one of those people who were loud and expressive and made you feel uninhibited just being around them. Gina was the closest Luna had ever got to a girlfriend. She had never been one for the company of women particularly, didn't need women the way some women seemed to. Having been brought up around the *sisters* perhaps made her bored of it. The constant openness about every emotional and sexual detail, especially when expressed by her own mother, had left Luna repelled rather than attracted to the intimacy. She had been more intrigued by the reserved, less confessional nature of male company. But with Gina, Luna understood the attraction. When it wasn't with your mother, Luna found it was enjoyable to share and be girly.

Gina had, by her own admission, kissed a lot of frogs. She was always looking for the perfect man and no amount of feminist argument could dissuade her from the pursuit of finding Good Husband Material.

'What century is this?' Luna would exclaim in mock-and-actual horror at Gina's attempts to ensnare a meal ticket.

'But it's what I want and I'm going after it. I'm proactive. That makes me a feminist, innit?' Gina would reply, roaring with laughter.

After their afternoon shift they cleared up and made way for evening prep, settling into the corner table where they ate free leftovers before heading home.

'So, how's it going with — Adam, is it?' Luna asked as they kicked off their shoes under the table and tucked in.

A smirk teetered on the edge of Gina's wide mouth that she tried to straighten. She took a huge mouthful to avoid speaking.

'What?' Luna pressed. 'Tell me! You haven't moved on already, have you? Something's happened — what is it?' She couldn't help herself; Luna looked forward to the next instalment of the drama that was Gina's love life as though it was a good soap.

'No, really, it's nothing.' Gina played it down but her dark eyes glinted with the promise of *something*.

'Gina, come on, you've got to tell me. You can't pretend you've got nothing for me . . . '

Gina's grin spread and they both started laughing.

'See, I knew it! You can't hide it from me, *tell me!*'

'No, really. It's nothing. It might be nothing. I don't know yet, I can't say.' She was waving her hands as if to shoo Luna away.

'Come on, Gina, when have you ever held back before? Even when it might be nothing. It's not fair. Just say it.'

'You won't approve,' Gina said, daring a mischievous look into Luna's eyes. She looked deliriously overexcited. Luna's heart started to pump a little faster. It was something big. Had he proposed? He must have done, for Gina to say she wouldn't approve. She grabbed Gina's hand, looking for a ring.

'Come on — where's the rock?' she said. 'You've done it, haven't you? I told you this was gonna be the one. I knew it!'

Gina shook her woolly head vigorously and her smile faded for a moment.

'No, nothing like that. Not yet anyway.'

What, then? Perhaps Gina had started two-timing him for a better prospect. It was the way she often worked it, stringing two or even more along, hedging her bets.

'I shouldn't really say anything. It's too early,' Gina went on. She glanced up again at Luna's face. 'But as it's you . . . ' She looked a little nervous and glanced around at the other staff. 'Don't tell anyone.'

Luna leaned across the table.

'I'm late,' Gina whispered, as quietly as she was able. Her grin returned, triumphant.

'You mean you're . . . ?' Luna felt her throat

tighten around the word and she was unable to say it.

Gina giggled. 'I don't know yet for sure. But it's been two weeks. And I feel sort of different. My tits are like melons.'

Luna felt the smile fix on her face. A sinking heart wasn't the right response, judging by Gina's radiant beam.

'Oh my God, Gina,' she said, trying to match her conspiratorial excitement. 'What . . . how . . . are you happy about it . . . ? Silly question, you're obviously happy about it!' Gina laughed and shook her head with an isn't-it-crazy gesture. 'But, I mean, was it a mistake? Were you trying already?'

'Well, I was. I don't know about Adam,' Gina joked, expecting Luna to guffaw with her. But all Luna's attempts at joining in with the humour suddenly failed her.

'Gina, that's awful,' she couldn't help saying. 'You don't mean you really did that?'

Gina raised her eyebrows proudly as if to say *Why ever not?*

'But weren't you using anything? How did you manage that?'

'Oh come on, Luie, it's not so hard to persuade a guy it's fine in the heat of the moment. Stop playing so innocent!'

'I'm not playing anything,' said Luna, defensively. 'It's just so sudden and so . . . It's a shock. What are you going to do? How will Adam react?'

Gina shrugged. 'I've got no idea. It doesn't really matter. It's out of his hands really.'

'What do you mean?'

'Well, it is, isn't it? If I'm having his baby, that's that. He'll have to take responsibility for it.'

Luna sat back in her chair, astounded.

'But what about you? Your job? How will you cope?' As soon as she said it she knew it was stupid. Gina had sorted it so that she wouldn't have to cope. She only ever slept with guys with good prospects. She had shifted that responsibility to Adam.

'What if he's . . . what if he doesn't want a baby, Gina?'

'There's nothing he can do. If I'm pregnant I'm keeping it, end of story. He'll have to support his child.'

Luna saw that Gina didn't really mind if she and Adam failed. If she had his baby everything would be taken care of for her, whether she had him still or not.

'Look, I know it's a bit of a shocker. But I ain't getting any younger. We've all got to have our babies at some point, haven't we? I'll just have to give up my art for a little while, but then I can come back to it. I'll have more time for it when I'm a mother, probably, than I have now, having to waitress and support myself. And Adam will be a good father, I know it. First thing, though, I need to know for sure. Will you come with me and get a test?'

No way, was Luna's first thought.

'Please, Lu. I'm nervous. I don't want to find out on my own.'

Luna couldn't think of a good excuse. What

could she say, I don't *approve*? It would be ridiculous. After all, wasn't she pro-women, pro-choice? Why did she feel indignant on Adam's behalf? He was probably a complete arse, if Gina's other boyfriends were anything to go by, probably worked in the City and drove around in his BMW swearing at his secretary on his hands-free.

'OK,' she conceded, and found herself smiling as Gina crossed herself and simultaneously swore in Italian.

★ ★ ★

The man in the pharmacy on Hackney Road gave Gina a huge, gap-toothed grin as she purchased the pregnancy test.

'Your first?' he smiled, and clapped his hands in excitement when she said, 'I hope so.'

'I have four,' he said proudly. 'All growing up too fast. Time for another baby in the house.'

Luna smiled politely as she waited for the two new best friends to finish talking. Already Gina had been welcomed into the club with open arms.

'Aah, wasn't he so sweet?' Gina said as they made their way to Luna's flat. At first Luna had been reluctant to host this event in her home, with Pierre working in his studio along the landing. It seemed inappropriate. She had a flashback to her uncle's house, with its fitted carpets even in the bathroom, somewhere you could pad from room to room in your bare feet without getting splinters and drips of paint stuck to the bottom of them. That's the sort of home you should take a pregnancy test in. Somewhere you could lie on the couch in your dressing gown afterwards with daytime telly on and a diet hot chocolate and biscuits, flicking through a baby-name book and *Pregnancy Now*.

But Gina lived miles out in Stratford, and it wasn't the sort of thing you could do in a public toilet. Beauvoir Heights was just round the corner from the caff; it was the only place. And on the way there Luna felt a hope shimmer, like a late firework. It was a way of broaching the subject of kids with Pierre again, without actually having to broach it.

'Hi, Pea,' Luna called. 'Gina's here.' For a moment she thought he was out, but then a grunt sounded from his studio, followed by a lot of banging.

Gina had already opened the kit and was heading upstairs.

'Read the instructions!' Luna ordered. 'Make sure you do it right!'

'All I have to do is pee on a stick. How hard can it be?' Gina called back, clattering up the stairs. Luna followed her reading the pamphlet.

'It might not be that accurate at this time of day,' she called through the bathroom door over the noise of Gina's loud wee. 'And you should follow up with the second test to be sure.'

'OK.' Gina emerged holding the stick and straightening her tights with her other hand. 'How long do we have to wait?'

'Two minutes,' Luna said. 'Let's have a cuppa. D'you wanna coffee, hon?' she called to Pierre.

'Yeah, that'd be great,' he called back. 'I'll come down.'

Luna took Gina's hand and they went down to the kitchen. Gina stood with her fingers crossed for luck, watching the second hand going round on the clock. It was the first time Luna had witnessed fingers crossed for the positive outcome. Several times she and her friends had prayed for the negative. A couple of times, with a couple of people, the result had been positive but they had turned it into a negative anyway.

When two minutes had passed, Luna picked up the stick from where Gina had placed it on the draining board.

'Ready?' she asked.

Gina nodded. 'You look at it first and tell me,' she said, taking a deep breath.

'OK, here goes.' Luna looked in the window of the pen stick. She composed her face, turning to Gina with her best smile.

'Congratulations, Gina,' she said. 'It's positive.'

'Really? Oh my God! Let me see!' She snatched the tester and looked for herself. She screamed in delight and flung her arms round Luna. 'Oh my God, oh my God!' she exclaimed again, putting her hands over her mouth. 'Now it's real, it's so weird! Oh God, what am I going to do? Fuck, I've got to sit down.'

As she perched on the edge of the sofa holding her stomach and continuing her dramatic monologue, Luna turned her back and busied herself making cups of tea and coffee. She felt strangely left out, even though she was right there — the one Gina had chosen to share this moment with, even over the father. It was odd, to be having this baby's existence confirmed right here in her living room, in her life.

And it not be hers. That was it. It should have been hers.

Pierre bounced down the stairs.

'Hi, Gee,' he said cheerily.

'Hi, Pea,' Gina gasped, clutching the arm of the sofa.

'You all right?' he asked, concerned.

'Sort of!' she breathed.

Luna stepped through from the kitchen with the cups and her bright smile.

'Gina's just had a bit of news,' she said. Pierre looked at Gina.

'I'm pregnant,' she grinned.

'Hey, that's great!' said Pierre immediately, without even waiting to find out whether or not it was an accident. There was usually a subtle pause when this news was received, in case it was a bad thing. He gave her a hug.

'Congratulations. Does that mean your boyfriend'll be around long enough for me to meet him this time?'

'Pea!' Luna scolded, but Gina didn't seem to mind.

'That's the plan,' she laughed. This amused Pierre greatly.

'Oh I see. Nice one,' he chuckled, like a co-conspirator. Luna looked on, surprised. It wasn't the reaction she expected. How could a guy see the funny side of a woman tricking a man into making a baby he had to support for the rest of his life without him even knowing?

Pierre stayed downstairs for a change while he had his coffee, chatting with Gina. Luna tried to join in, but the feeling of being an outsider in her own home didn't go away. Pierre engaged completely with the whole thing, even advising Gina on how to tell Adam with the least adverse effect. He was being lovely, reacting just the way you'd want a guy to react to baby news. It was annoying. Or perhaps he'd had a change of heart. Luna looked forward to Gina leaving. She and Pierre could have another chat this evening. Maybe he'd even bring it up before she did.

★   ★   ★

She left it until they'd flopped back onto the sofa with their last glass of wine from the bottle. He hadn't mentioned anything about Gina or babies, only his work. He was in a much better mood though, excited even, as he'd finally found a way forward with his pixel constructions. It was as good a time as any.

'Hey, you were really sweet with Gina today, by the way,' she said, casually.

'How do you mean?'

'Well, you know — you were really positive about her having a baby, comforting. I think she was really reassured that it was a good thing.'

'Well, it is, isn't it?' he asked.

'Do you think so?'

'Well, yeah — I mean anyone could tell from her face she really wanted it.'

'But — does just really wanting it make it a

good thing?' Luna tried to make this sound like a light, just-out-of-interest kind of question, but of course it was no good.

'Oh I see,' said Pierre, grimly. 'I see where you're going with this. I'm talking about Gina. I have no vested interest. I'm not one of the parties concerned. I don't know Adam from . . . Adam. I'm not making moral judgements or saying what's right or wrong. She just seemed happy and I was happy for her. That's all. It doesn't matter to me how she chooses to live her life.'

'All right, I only asked a question. I think that's fair enough — I mean, it's just the opposite of what you usually say, that just really wanting it doesn't make it fine to go ahead and have it without thinking about anything else. Especially where kids are concerned. My God, you're usually the first to condemn anyone bringing a child into a world that isn't entirely fucking perfect.'

'No, I'm not — certainly no more than you. I don't care what other people decide to do, I just thought *we* had decided together that we wouldn't do it, especially if it meant sacrificing our art. We certainly weren't going to just because we felt like it.'

'Well, that's what Gina's done and it doesn't bother you at all. That's what everyone does, isn't it? Have one when they feel like it. When else would they?'

'Not everyone has chosen a life like we have, Luna. Most people have regular lives, with a steady income — a steady increasing income.

Having kids doesn't completely disrupt what they do.'

'I think you'll find it always disrupts what women do!' Luna retorted, outraged.

'Yes, of course it does, I didn't mean that — but they can manage because of their husbands or partners — '

'What about single mothers?' Luna interrupted.

'Single mothers scrape by on benefits and just about survive, never having a chance to do all the things they wanted to do with their lives . . . '

'Oh stop fucking stereotyping, that's ridiculous. Plenty of single mothers and artists and everything else have kids. If everyone waited until everything was perfect the human race would die out.'

They stared at each other, faces close. After a moment Pierre sighed and pushed his hand through his hair.

'But it won't die out if it's only us that don't have kids,' he said quietly, 'will it? That's what we always said, wasn't it?'

It was true, it had been what they said when they were first together, still filled with the ideology of a true artist's dedicated life.

'No it won't,' said Luna, finally. 'But I will. And I don't want to.'

'You will, whether you have kids or not,' he said softly, reaching out to tuck her hair behind her ear.

'Yes, but you know what I mean. And it's not just that, though. I feel totally differently about the whole thing. It seems . . . important now. Like the most important thing.'

Luna looked up into Pierre's eyes and he looked back at her, sadly.

'You don't see that?' she asked. He shook his head apologetically.

'I'm sorry, Luie. I still feel the same as I — as we — always did. It's you that's changed, not me.'

There was a pause, the heat gone from their row.

'Is that so bad, though?' Luna asked quietly. 'That I've changed my mind? I can't help how I feel.'

'I know, of course. But . . . '

'But you still don't want them.'

'I just don't know yet. Maybe I will, but you must see that we can't right now.'

'But that's what I'm saying. Other people cope somehow.'

'But we're not other people. And I'm not ready to make those compromises yet.'

Luna looked away. That's what it came down to. Gina would be able to jack in waitressing; Adam could afford it. If Luna did, Pierre would have to do something to support them instead. And he wasn't prepared to. Never mind that she had had to over the years. She suddenly felt really stupid. As though being responsible and supporting them made her a complete mug. Women who hooked themselves a rich man to look after them were the ones that ended up with the power, after all.

It was a shock that rooted her to the spot, unspeaking.

'I'm sorry,' said Pierre softly, touching her

arm. When she looked at him she saw he was full of concern and she felt a painful surge of love for him. 'What are you thinking?'

She shook her head. 'Nothing.' She gave a small smile. 'It doesn't matter.' She got up from the sofa and began to take the dishes to the sink.

'It doesn't mean I don't love you,' said Pierre. He came up behind her and put his arms round her waist, resting his head on the back of her neck. 'I do. Just give me some time. Let me get this show over, see where I am at the end of it. Let's think about it again then.'

It wasn't unreasonable. To give him six months to sort it out in his mind. Maybe this show would be the one that launched him into another league of artists, the league that didn't have to worry about where the next rent cheque would come from. Not that that was something that seemed to worry Pierre anyway, even if it should. But Luna had been here before, with Pierre's endless optimism that things would turn out and he would finally have the success he strove for. The next show was always the one that was going to turn things round. Luna had always believed it too, but what if . . . ? What if the next show didn't, or the one after that? What if there was never a show that turned things round? How long did she have to put her life on hold, waiting and hoping?

And who was to say it was Pierre who should get what he wanted anyway, while she made the compromise, again?

★　★　★

Autumn set in. Particularly misty, there was a damp sheen over the listless city, as though it was lying in a cold sweat like an ill person. Luna found herself staring out of the window more often than not as she struggled to paint Amelia's cherubs. The muted sprawl of grey beneath the colourless sky made the vivid, fertile colours of the summer portrait seem garish and vulgar, too showy. Her former feeling of omniscience — up here like a god looking down on everything — left, replaced by a trapped, removed sensation. Imprisoned in her glass turret, she felt like a mere onlooker, watching the rest of the world without actually being able to see it, as it hid its life away from her under roofs and the tops of buses. Without being able to feel it. It was as though her own life had left, without an explanation. I don't know what I've done wrong, she kept thinking, taking the blame, as the left ones always do. She could almost feel her confidence draining away like the rain off the streets.

A waitress at the cafe moved on — a young Australian girl, in love with *experiences*, who had met a New York artist and agreed on a whim to go and live with him in Brooklyn. Luna took on extra shifts.

'You don't want to do that, surely?' Pierre had said. 'We can manage till I sell something, we always do. And your commission's nearly done. We really don't need you to do this, Luna.'

But she insisted. 'Well, having the extra money'll be nice for a while. It's only temporary, until they get someone else. I've got nothing better to do at the moment. It'll give you some space to get on.'

'I have enough space,' Pierre argued.

But he couldn't talk her out of it and gave up trying.

'Well, if you really want to and it's only temporary . . . But don't complain about your lack of time and don't go all martyrish on me, 'cos you know you don't have to do it.' But he didn't get a rise out of her. She felt flat, emotionless, and simply shrugged.

'I know. It's my decision. I'm not having a dig at you or making a point. I just want to do it for now. It's not a big deal.'

'Fine.' Pierre watched her for a moment longer as she busied herself unloading the washing from the machine onto the lino and beginning to fold T-shirts and sort socks. He headed back up to his studio.

In spite of her words, Luna felt like a martyr as she took piles of laundry up to the bedroom and changed the duvet cover while Pierre worked away at his art. She knew it wasn't fair of her. She did hardly any more housework than Pea did, and he did his fair share of the cooking. 'God, I'm not *even* a housewife!' a panicky voice yelled up to her conscious mind from somewhere deep inside. What was her role exactly? *Being An Artist* didn't seem the all-important, all-encompassing job she'd made of it. In fact, it suddenly seemed like very little. She wasn't supporting herself through her work, it wasn't changing the world, or making any great splash. Not even just a little ripple. She didn't feel like an artist, she didn't have a career, she wasn't a mother. What was her life for? To make skinny lattes and clear tables in a caff? She saw into the future, when the Australian had been replaced by a new girl, but then Gina, big and round, had to give up, and Luna stepped in again, full-time, permanently. She would visit Gina and her baby in hospital and buy her flowers and a set of tiny Babygros. Pierre would have another show.

She was nothing.

★　★　★

Luna drove to her mother's house in a fury. She shoved the door open when the intercom buzzed her in and threw the photographs down on her mother's kitchen table. She stood trembling. Angie, unaware of her daughter's barely contained rage, was still talking as she flapped around in an orange kimono, making coffee. Turning, she came over to the table to see, and Luna watched the cheery animation fall from her face as the recognition hit. Angie recovered herself and after faltering for a split second, continued talking — something about the stupid art workshop her new friend was running. She turned to the stove to light the ring under the percolator. Luna folded her arms.

'Wherever did you find those?' Angie asked, keeping her voice light.

'They were in the suitcase Robert gave me. From Dad,' Luna replied. She was surprised how calm she sounded. Angie glanced at her face, seemed to overcome a reluctance and pushed herself to the table to look through them properly. She didn't pick them up but separated them where they were, on the table.

'We were so young,' she murmured. Luna waited for her to say something else.

'Is that it?' she asked finally. Angie looked startled.

'What do you mean?'

'Haven't you got anything more to say?'

'I don't know what — ' Angie began, but Luna's temper was beginning to gather itself and she spoke over her.

'Don't you think it's about time you gave me an explanation?'

'An explanation of what, darling?' Angie's insistent breezy innocence began to drive Luna crazy.

'An explanation of what happened when I was a kid that deprived me of my father.' Her voice was as low and menacing as a thundery sky. 'I have the right to know. I'm sick and tired of you wafting it all away as though it doesn't matter to me. All my life' — she began to come forward towards her mother — 'you've been telling me he didn't care about me. That he wasn't worth knowing, letting me believe he was a loser and I was better off without him anyway.' She snatched at the photographs, found the one of her mother and father kissing, in love. She shoved it in Angie's face. 'But now I know you lied.' She was shouting. 'You LIED. He had a family that wanted to know me. He cared about me enough to keep track of who I was, what I was doing. He did good things in life. He was talented and

— and beautiful.' She shook the photograph at Angie. 'And he left me his work. He wanted to pass something down to me. He wanted to KNOW me. And now it's too late. It's too fucking LATE.'

The shock in Angie's eyes turned to anger. 'For God's sake, Luna,' she snapped. 'Don't tell me you fell for all that insincere crap at the funeral. Everyone waxing lyrical about him because he's dead . . . '

'God, I don't BELIEVE you. That wasn't insincere. They LOVED him. He was lovable. Christ, even you saw that once.' She shook the photograph again. 'Before you got to be such a hard, cynical old bitch.' She slammed the photo on the table, turned away in disgust, gulping air to regain control of herself. Angie grabbed her shoulder to turn her round.

'Don't you dare bloody speak to me like that,' she yelled. 'You don't know what you're talking about. You have no idea how hard it was for me, raising you on my own.'

'Yes I DO,' Luna shouted back. 'It's all I've ever fucking heard. It was always you, you, you. I've just always had to tag along, fit in — and that's when you couldn't find anyone to dump me on. Believe me, you've always made it perfectly clear I was a weight around your neck. I ruined your life. I KNOW. I mean, God — LOOK at you!' She scrabbled at the photos, finding another one, holding it up as more evidence. 'I can see how fucking lovely your life was before I came along and spoiled the fucking party.'

Angie looked at the picture and looked away. 'It wasn't like that,' she said.

'Oh no?' A bark of a laugh escaped Luna's throat. She looked with mock incredulity from the photo back to Angie. 'Well, it certainly looks *like that,*' she said. 'How the fuck are you going to explain that away if it wasn't how it looks? But then I'm sure you'll find a way of justifying it to excuse yourself and expect me to believe it. Well, I'm not a stupid kid any more. I'm not *your* stupid kid any more. God!' She put her hand to her head and grabbed her hair in exasperation. Her temper had reached its peak, and she breathed out. 'You're so self-centred. You know, this is the perfect picture of you. You can tell just how much you love yourself. Of course there was never going to be any room for me. Or him.'

'Luna, that's just not true. It's not fair.'

'It's not fair,' Luna imitated in a whining voice. 'No, it's not fair. Nothing's fair. It's not fair when you have a mother who is incapable of love. Who denies you everything you could have had and could have been.'

'Now, come on, that's just absurd. For God's sake, look at you. You're bright, artistic, successful. You can insult me all you like, but you can't blame me for the way your life turned out as though it's some sort of mess. You have everything you ever wanted — you *are* everything you ever wanted to be.'

'NO!' Luna was shouting again. 'I have everything YOU ever wanted. I'm what YOU wanted me to be. I have the kind of life you wish you'd had, if you hadn't got saddled with me.

And I've only just seen it now — how utterly filled up I am with your crap. I've been completely controlled and manipulated. What about what I want? What about — ' She stopped abruptly.

After a pause Angie said, 'What about what? What do you want that you haven't got?'

Luna said nothing.

'What, Luna?' Her tone was softer now, with a real curiosity, rather than a defensive retort.

'Nothing,' Luna said quietly. 'You wouldn't understand.'

She began to gather together the photographs, now strewn across the table.

'Try me,' said Angie, reaching out to touch her arm. 'You know you can always talk to me about anything. I've always wanted us to be open with each other.'

'But that's just it, you see?' said Luna. 'You think we are, but we're not. You've been open with this — this construct of whoever it is you think you are. But that's not how you really are. I don't believe it. And I've never been open with you. Not about the real things.'

'But you can be, Luna,' answered her mother. 'I'm always here for you.'

Luna shook her head.

'Not until you can tell me what I want to know. About my father. You've never been open about that.' She waited, not looking at Angie, while she put the photos back in her bag. She heard her mother breathe.

Eventually Angie said, 'Luna, it's all in the past. How can it possibly matter now? Can't you just let it go?'

Luna waited a moment or two longer, giving her mother another chance to try again, before she walked out.

★   ★   ★

She Blu-tacked her father's photographs, the few in the envelope that were of his own life, in a short line on the wall. She spent a long time looking at them, trying to get the chronology right, swapping them around until they seemed in the right order. The one at the festival was first, definitely. All the others were on the commune, she was sure. The change in Angie, too, was evident. She was fresh in the first picture of her, just a girl. Then later . . . Luna pulled the second photo down to study it, the one she had used against Angie. She felt momentarily guilty for how harsh she had been, but it passed, flushed away with another wave of disgust. Why had her father taken this picture of her? How could he have just stood there, calmly photographing the woman he loved, sprawled naked, one man with his hands on her breasts, another with his face between her legs? And the expression on her face as she looked into the camera! The lascivious smile, straight at him, an arrogant awareness of her own sexuality and attractiveness, lapping up the male attention as though she deserved it. There were other nude bodies, out of focus in the background, a landscape of limbs. Again, Luna admired the composition, how the self-love on Angie's face was the central point, summing up the

114

narcissism of the scene — of the era, even. OK, it was the seventies. Luna knew what went on, and she wasn't a prude. But this was just pornographic. And her dad wasn't joining in, was he? Sidelined by these revolting lechers pleasuring her mother while she lay there soaking up the enjoyment, cuckolding her father with her stare, as though watching was all he was good for.

Luna wasn't surprised he'd left, gone on to do something serious with his talent, something other than taking pictures of seedy low-lifes. He went on to make a name for himself. Even though it had meant leaving his daughter too. Who could blame him? She wished he had taken her with him.

# 1970

# Angie

Home, as it turned out, was a crumbling old farmhouse in the middle of nowhere. All Angie knew was that it was in Pembrokeshire, South Wales. She wouldn't have had a clue how to get back to her old life if she'd wanted to. It had been inherited by Hugh, nearer her parents' generation than the rest of them but groovy for an old guy. Angie liked him the instant he welcomed her with his warm embrace as the festival-goers crowded round the fire in the farmhouse kitchen to warm up after their long, damp journey. His eyes crinkled sincerely as he then held her by her shoulders and looked deep into her eyes, searching her soul.

'You're one of us!' he smiled, finding whatever it was he was looking for. 'We have the connection — do you feel it?' he said. Angie felt that she did. He didn't ask any of the questions she would have expected in any other situation — where she was from and did her parents know where she was. It was an immense relief, she found, just to be accepted into a group of people without queries or assumptions or judgements. She was just here with them and that was good. It was like being given permission to be whoever you wanted, as though she was trusted, her own decisions respected, and whatever it was that had led her here was up to her.

Like the song Joni Mitchell had sung at the festival, Hugh had wanted to 'get back to the garden'. He was attempting to make the place a self-sufficient community, where its people could live off the gifts of its land, and love. The ethos was a mix of old-fashioned ideals of natural existence that didn't involve having to earn bread, and new morals that broke out of what he called the stifling hangups of convention. He had a wife and two kids, but she hadn't shared his vision and when he had inherited the farm she had stayed in their old house on a modern estate on the outskirts of Swansea. He was fine with it, he told Angie when she asked. People had to be truthful to themselves; not everyone could achieve the same spiritual level. In the place of his family he'd filled his house with about twelve adults so far, who had several kids between them. Angie couldn't work out who belonged to whom at first — something that pleased Hugh immensely when she asked whose gorgeous girl Willow was, a magical pre-pubescent child with an other-worldly elfin quality to her long white-blonde hair like silk and huge violet eyes. 'Children don't belong to anyone,' he answered, stroking Willow's head fondly. 'We are all mothers and fathers. And they are children of the universe.'

After eating soup from a huge earthenware pot on the Aga with chunks of home-made bread, Dave showed her around. The 'hang-out' was next to the kitchen, dark and incense-fumed, with a feeling of a cave or a womb perhaps, decorated with deep earthy reds and terracottas and lined with battered old cushions and beanbags. A threadbare Persian carpet and sheepskin rugs warmed the floor and the walls were hung with woven tapestries, what looked like children's artwork and instruments — guitars, a mandolin, lots of ethnic percussion such as bongos, wooden flutes, bells and chimes. There was an upright piano with worn, yellowing keys, its wood painted with psychedelic swirls and flowers. A curtained doorway led to another room behind it in which a slightly older woman with cropped hennaed hair was sitting at a loom weaving. She introduced herself as Hazel ('a lucky coincidence; I'm too old to change my name now'). She hugged Angie warmly and showed her the rest of the workroom: a spinning wheel and clouds of unspun sheep's wool, stacks of wicker, rag bags for patchwork and rag rugs, wool for knitting and darning, baskets of what looked like felt, with a half-made floppy hat someone had been trying to fashion. She showed Angie through the back door and out to a shed where they dyed the wool, using onion skins, dandelions and beetroot. They were experimenting with anything at the moment, which you could tell from the pungent farty smell of natural things reacting with other natural things, and rotting.

Dave took her round the farmyard then, showing her the barn, goats, cows, chickens, and the vegetable garden and the orchard beyond, where some guys were shaking apples out of a tree onto a tarpaulin. They stopped what they were doing to hug Angie in welcome. The teenage boy up in the tree — Crispin — leaped confidently down, his feet bare and hard from outdoor living, wild hair streaming behind him. He was extraordinary, more like an enchanted creature than a boy. All the children Angie had seen were like something out of a fairy tale. This whole place was. It was as though she had entered the pages of a storybook or gone through a magic wardrobe. She felt a little shy hugging the boy, but he wasn't. In fact he pulled her very close, his hand at the top of her buttocks, pulling her pelvis into his. They all hugged with proper unembarrassed contact with each other, human to human. After her initial self-consciousness, Angie decided it was a wonderful thing. On the rare occasions her parents had attempted to hug her, their hips would be halfway out through the doorway. She greeted Allun and Ken, then Dave led her back to the house.

'We all share the chores,' he said. 'Everyone contributes what they can. If someone's got a special skill, they'll do that mainly. Like Ken. He's a carpenter, so he does most of the fixing around the place, makes whatever furniture's needed, that sorta thing. But we're all learning all the skills we'll need to keep us going.'

'It's all so . . . like, wow,' said Angie.

Back in the kitchen, Dave took her knapsack and showed her upstairs. They passed the bathroom, where Poppy and Star were taking their clothes off and climbing into a bath together. He spilled her stuff onto one of the

119

mattresses on the floor in the bedroom. The walls had been knocked through to make a vast communal sleeping area, the mattresses arranged alongside each other to accommodate any number of people together. A few single ones at the end were strewn with home-made rag dolls and teddies, which she assumed were the children's. Dave began putting her things on shelves in an alcove. All clothes were heaped together, and he put her dress with the pile of dresses, her T-shirts with all the T-shirts, her underwear in a wicker basket with other pants. The bra she'd brought with her seemed to be the only one. He fingered the lace on it, saying, 'Haven't seen one of these for a while,' before dropping it in.

'We all wear, like, any clothes,' he said, reaching for her. 'Just help yourself to whatever you wanna wear in the morning. Possessions are, like, the root of all evil.'

She nodded.

He drew her to him and kissed her. 'Come with me,' he said, and pulled her to a wooden ladder leading up to the loft.

Up there were two rooms separated by a wooden-plank wall. Each had a mattress under the sloping eave and a curtain across the entrance.

'These are the privacy rooms,' he explained, 'for, like, when you need your own space? Some time out to chill. People come here when they're ill, say, and don't wanna pass it around, or the women when they're menstruating, you know? Sometimes they just wanna be left alone.

Crispin's been coming up here quite a lot lately. I guess he's started masturbating.' Angie nodded, cool, glad of her time at drama school when she had learned how to control her reactions, as well as discovering from the guys that that was a normal teenage stage.

Dave drew her to him. 'And it's where two people can come if they're just into each other at the moment, you know? When they don't dig anyone else 'cos they've just got this amazing vibe between them.' He started to pull her down onto the mattress. ''Cos that's OK too. It's a special, meaningful thing, you know, deep. While it lasts.'

The words *while it lasts* lingered with her for a moment, like a trail of bubbles left behind in the water, until he lifted her cheesecloth top and a new wave of desire swept them away.

★   ★   ★

Angie easily fell into the rhythm of the place, as though she was a natural fit, someone who had always danced to an ill-fitting three-time beat finally finding a waltz. There were no rules as such, only what was agreed by human instinct, for the good of all. Nobody had to do anything if they didn't want to, but everyone wanted to. They all shared the same purpose and this made it work. Hugh had become a Buddhist and he had a meditation session every morning at daybreak. No one had to go, but everyone did. Angie found herself waking every day with the light, which astounded her. She had never been a morning person, infuriating her parents with her lazy ways, and making the most of college by often not rising until the afternoon. But now she wanted to be awake, looked forward to the day ahead because she knew that whatever happened would be perfect.

After meditation they had breakfast together, knowing when it was their turn to make it, stepping in if the person whose natural turn it was was unwell or away or already working on the smallholding. While they ate they discussed the day and what needed doing, a kind of informal meeting really. Nobody took charge, although Hugh had the best knowledge, having grown up on the farm. It being his, the others tended to look to him as the authority — a position he strongly resisted. Then they agreed on who would do what. At first Angie was able to follow someone doing a different chore each day so that she knew how everything was done — how to spin and weave one day, how to milk the cows, feed the chickens, work the land. The children were home-tutored, the adults taking turns to teach to prevent them becoming indoctrinated with one person's knowledge and view of the world. Angie sat in with Fern in the little children's room behind the kitchen, putting her drama skills to good use for the imaginative play session. Learning was free-form, child-led, focused on creativity — they weren't made to do anything they didn't want to do but could write poems and stories, draw, dance, sing. It was fun. The children seemed so inspired, so self-assured and free.

Cooking was done on a rota, using food grown on the farm. Things they needed that they didn't produce themselves — flour, rice, honey — they went to the nearest market town for. Hugh was attempting to set up bartering systems with other local producers there, as well as the health-food shop where they could get things like halva, which they would never make here, however much they wanted to. Eventually they would use only what they could grow, but it would take time to get to that stage.

The evening meal felt like a dinner party every night, everyone crowded in the steamy kitchen together. After all the day's work was done they retired to the hang-out, where they smoked pot, played instruments and sang. It was here Angie felt in her element. Her singing voice was good, quite deep for a woman, slightly jazzy, and the lessons she'd had at college had taught her how to use it to its fullest. Everyone enjoyed her performances. She taught the group how to sing harmonies, some of the with-it songs from *Hair*, the end-of-year musical production they'd performed. A lot of the guys knew how to play Dylan and Cohen and Nick Drake songs, but were turning away from them now to learn old folk tunes and their own songs.

Dave wrote one called 'Angel'. He watched her as he played it to her, and afterwards everyone clapped and hugged her and she thought no one could ever be more loved.

★   ★   ★

At first Dave claimed one of the private rooms for the two of them and they spent the night — and several times during the day — in there. Eventually he said they should probably be thinking about joining the group sleeping area.

'We're a community, d'you know what I mean?' he said. 'We can all do what we wanna do, but we've also got to think about the whole group. We can't have, like, factions breaking off, couples forming and making their own little units. Else we're just back to the establishment, you know? And that's when feelings get hurt 'cos we start thinking we own someone, and other dudes feel left out 'cos it's got all exclusive, and then a hierarchy happens. Next thing you know, nothing's changed and we're back under oppression, living the lie. We gotta be open to everybody, to love.'

Overcoming a worry that he'd tired of her, she agreed. She *did* agree, reminding herself she'd run away from the uptight, repressed family she'd come from. The last thing she wanted was a marriage like her parents had, closed-up and frigid. She realized now just how claustrophobic and shackled it had been. She'd written them a letter the day after she arrived, hopefully before they called the police, letting them know she was safe and well and happy. She'd found the way of living for her and was leaving college, and them, forever. *I feel so right here*, she wrote, *it's where I should be*. She didn't give them her address. The South Wales postmark was the nearest she wanted them to know.

She was going to be the person she knew she

could be, with a big, open heart. She wanted to show Dave that she could. She couldn't bear to be a disappointment to him, and anyway, she wanted to be rid of these small, selfish feelings. She was brainwashed by her upbringing; it would take time to recover from that, readjust her mind, expand it. But she could do it. She was a Child of Ceres now. She was learning how everything in the universe worked, from the simplest of things like a seed growing. She had seen how much more beautiful women were without make-up and pinching shoes, how naturally happy men seemed working the land, how the more you shared, the more love came back to you. She had come to see the wonder of everything.

Dave lay with her on the first night in the communal room. The sex happened intuitively, without anyone having to initiate it, as though everyone just knew it was right and wanted it. Dave was kissing her and then someone else was on her other side, Justin, then she was kissing him. She felt Dave move away, became aware of shapes moving around in the room, heard whispers and moans. As the sound in the room grew louder she was bothered by the presence of the children in the room, and turned instinctively to check they hadn't woken. A ray of moonlight shone through a gap in the curtain on their perfect sleeping faces.

'It's OK,' Star whispered as she slid next to her. 'They never wake up. They're drifting in their dreams in a sea of love.' When someone lit a lamp hanging from the beam she saw that Star was so right — the moving bodies did look like a sea of love. She closed her eyes, to stop herself looking for Dave in the rise and fall of flesh. She felt Justin's hand reach over to Star's and place it on her. Soon she felt another man's tongue, another woman's breast. While others moved about the room, Angie remained pinned in place by the tide of new hands and mouths and thighs. Then someone was rearranging her, sitting her up to lie against a soft body, in between two breast pillows. A man kissed her mouth, someone else was touching her. Her knees were bent by strong hands. The tickle of a full beard on her thigh let her know it was Hugh. It was almost too much sensation, to have every part of her brought to response at once.

She opened her eyes to stop feeling overwhelmed, and there over someone's head was Dave, crouching, watching. He smiled at her, and she smiled back, relieved. She was still special to him then, and it calmed her, let her relax to the touches of the others. No one's hands were as good as his, but his being there with her helped. He came closer and she thought he would kiss her. But instead he held up his camera, adjusted the lens. Her alarm must have shown, because he lowered the camera again and leaned forward, rearranging her hair around her shoulders and whispering, 'Special moments.' She understood, then.

He moved back, brought the camera to his face and made a beckoning motion with his fingers. She knew it to mean she must give him everything she had, and secretly conscious of composing her face and body at the best angle for the camera, she projected all the love she had for him through the lens. Seeing how she was exciting Dave excited her, and she imagined it was his hands that were touching her. He saw the moment she surrendered to the feeling, because that was when the shutter clicked several times before he put the camera down and crawled towards her mouth.

# 1995

## Nat

'Fucking turn it down, Lee,' Nat shouted over the incessant shrieking siren on the hip-hop track. The bitch next door was banging on the wall again. Nat had already had one official complaint from the housing about noise and she couldn't afford to get another, or else they could evict her and she didn't have anywhere else to go.

Lee was huddled over the table with his back to her skinning up and either didn't hear her or ignored her. She went over and turned it down herself. TJ tried to turn it up again.

'Fuck's sake, it's worse than being at home,' he said, as she slapped his hand away.

'It's what happens when you become a mum,' Ashley smirked from the sofa. She was already out of it, but was still swigging from the bottle.

'Well, you're all worse than a bunch of fucking babies,' said Nat, swiping the bottle from her as she squeezed herself in between Ashley and Shawna. She pinched a fag off Paul and lit up. They all started making stupid noises at her. She was used to it by now. It had stopped bothering her when she realized they were jealous. They were the same age as her but she was far more mature. She had her own flat and her own

128

benefits, and however much they took the piss, they weren't going to stop coming round. What else were they going to do, hang out in one of their teenage bedrooms with their mums shouting at them? When she realized the advantage it gave her, nothing they ever said could make her feel bad. She had it a lot better than any of them and they knew it.

With the music down Nat could hear Tyler still yelling next door and remembered why they'd turned it up in the first place. She ignored him. It wasn't good to go running every time he called, she remembered that from the mother and baby group they'd sent her to at the refuge. But it was easier said than done, the ignoring thing. He'd learned how to shriek lately in such a piercing way it seemed to penetrate into the very core of her. He knew how to wind her up.

Lee started imitating him, 'Waaaah, waaaah,' coming close up to her on his knees, trying to get it right in her ear.

'Fuck off,' she yelled, hitting him. 'What are you, special needs?'

That made everyone laugh, turned it back on him. He kicked out at TJ and they began to fight, rolling around on the floor like a pair of wankers. 'Special, special,' the rest of them chanted. The vodka suddenly hit and Nat couldn't stop laughing. It was going to be a good night.

The next time the neighbour banged on the wall it was because of Tyler, who had managed to keep up his crying. They'd told her at the refuge that he would wear himself out if she didn't go to him, learn that it wasn't the way to get attention.

But did he, bollocks. She had to turn the music back up herself in the end. How long had he been at it now? An hour? Two? With the drinking and fucking about, Nat had lost track of time.

'Fucking fuck OFF!' she shouted at the neighbour, making the others laugh. She banged back on the wall, and the others joined in.

'Stop that fucking banging, will ya?' Lee shouted, in time with his pounding fist. 'We're trying to listen to some music in here.'

Nat was laughing so hard she thought she'd piss herself. Next thing, there was someone hammering on the front door.

'Fuck! That ain't fists, man,' said TJ. 'She's tooled up!' The thought of her neighbour being tooled up was hysterical but Nat tried to quiet everyone through snorts of laughter.

'You better fucking shut up in there right fucking now — I'm calling the police,' shouted a voice, a man's voice.

'Ooh, I'm really scared,' said Lee in a high whiney voice.

'Shut up!' said Nat, covering his mouth with her hand. He got her into a headlock while TJ turned the music up for a sudden deafening blast.

'Fucking stop it!' Nat yelled, trying to wriggle out of Lee's grasp. She was too helpless from laughing and had no strength. Shawna finally got to the CD player and turned it off. They listened for a bit for any more from the neighbours. It was totally quiet, even in Tyler's room. The silence seemed louder than the noise.

'Fuck, d'you think he did call the police?' asked Shawna.

'What if he did?' said Lee, skinning up again. 'What're they gonna do?'

'Only get me evicted, you stupid cunt,' said Nat.

'They can't do that, Nat,' said Ashley. 'You've got a kid. They can't turn you out onto the streets.' Her attempt at reassuring Nat only made Nat feel more afraid. What if they did turn her out onto the streets? The wild atmosphere turned sombre, then jittery. No one admitted they were nervous, listening out for real police sirens. Nat had kept thinking she could hear them, but they were just the echoes of the ones on the track.

'Fuck — you idiot,' Nat suddenly hissed at Lee. 'What the fuck are you doing, smoking weed when the cops are about to show up?'

'Oh shit, man!' said TJ. 'I've got Es on me and all.'

'Fuck, we've got to get out of here!' Everyone was half laughing, half seriously panicked, staggering up, getting their stuff together.

'Make sure you get all the drugs out of here,' said Nat. When they did hear the distant wail of a police car, Ashley let out a scream. They all bundled to the door.

'What about you?' Shawna asked Nat. 'We shouldn't leave you to get in trouble.'

'I won't answer the door,' said Nat, frightened now.

'You'll have to — they're the police. They'll break it down, else.'

Nat tried to think straight but she was too smashed. Somewhere she knew she'd be all right

131

if she just calmed down, waited for the knock, opened the door nicely and apologized for the noise earlier. She'd say she'd had a birthday party and that it was over now, she wouldn't do it again. But she suddenly couldn't stand to be left in the flat on her own. The siren was getting louder.

'Come on!' The rest had already run, but TJ came back for them.

'What about Tyler?' said Nat.

'He's asleep now,' said Shawna. 'He'll be all right for a bit. We'll come back soon.'

Nat ran to his door and peeked in. Tyler was flat out on his back, his hands up by his head still balled into little fists. Quickly and as quietly as she could, she pulled the door completely shut and turned the key in the lock. There was nothing dangerous in his room that he could hurt himself with. He'd be safe and he wouldn't even know.

She grabbed her keys and coat and ran after Shawna. Giggling, they stumbled along the corridor, trying to keep quiet, not clatter too much down the steps. They ran in the opposite direction of where the siren was coming from, following Lee's whistles. When they found the others everyone was up again, like the night was just beginning. TJ's brother Kel was DJing at a club, not far away.

'He might be able to get us in,' he suggested, grinning and waving his packet of pills. They huddled in a doorway taking them. Nat knew she should just hang out here for a bit then go back home. But being out with the cold night air sending thrills around her midriff felt too much like a freedom she had forgotten about. She felt light, as though she could fly down the street. She hadn't been clubbing since Tyler had been born. Since before. She'd only been a few times in fact, not nearly enough for a girl her age. The anticipation of a night just dancing was sweet. She was, after all, going to be seventeen tomorrow. She deserved to have fun on her birthday, right? You were only young once.

The police siren was disappearing again, not coming to the flat after all. Still, Nat found herself falling in with the others as they headed away.

# THREE

*A painting. A woman at a window,*
*looking out.*

She sits on an old wooden chair, leaning forward with her arms on the sill, a loose dress draping over her form to her feet, which are bare. Her hair is swept up at the back to reveal the nape of her neck, stray locks falling around her shoulders. Her face is in profile, highlighted against the glass.

The large window takes up most of the painting, placed at the very centre of it, looking out onto a dark sky. All that can be seen of the room surrounds the window at the edges of the painting: the bare white walls, the lack of curtains, the unpolished floorboards, a discarded stocking. The perspective of the lines of the floorboards leads the eye up to the woman's feet, taking in the figure tilting forward and following her gaze through the window, but we do not know what she can see outside.

# 2003

## Luna

Luna had tried to cancel. Since her row with her mum she'd felt like blowing it off, but couldn't quite bring herself to let Tomas down. It wasn't his fault, after all, even if he was a friend of Angie's. He was new to London from Poland, an artist Angie had met at a qigong day at her local holistic healing centre. It didn't bode well. But she had agreed to attend his weekend workshop on collage, of all things, to make up the numbers. It really wasn't her sort of thing, but then she'd thought, why not? A free weekend in the country at a nice B&B. And then after the row, when she'd called him with an excuse, she found herself unable to say it, especially after he'd been so grateful that she was coming. 'Thank you, thank you, Luna, from my heart's bottom, to be helping me! It will be so much fun, no? We can release our inner childs, be free of all this jobs and hard city life and thing. We shall see the sea!'

When he put it like that, how could she turn it down? He made it sound like playtime. She hadn't done any collage since God knows when, and the idea of sticking bits of stuff all over the place suddenly appealed. Art had been so bloody serious since she'd been making a living at it, perhaps it actually would be fun to go back to the basics. And how would she spend the weekend at home? Waitressing, struggling with her commission, forcing artificially natural conversation with Pierre, both acting as though there was nothing strained about their relationship.

And Tomas was OK, bearable in small doses. She and Pierre had met him at a private view. He was comical in his earnestness, dated, like an idea of an artist in a fifties film, with a shock of grey hair, a salt and pepper goatee and black turtle-neck jumper. He had zoomed in on Luna and Pierre, delighted to have met kindred spirits in a strange country. He had bowed and kissed Luna's hand and invaded their body space as he launched into a passionate tirade about art and politics.

'Is he for real?' Pierre had mouthed to Luna when Tomas had gone to get more drinks. But although they joked about him, they agreed afterwards they felt a real fondness for him.

'You just don't get people like that any more,' Pierre had said wistfully. 'I miss them.'

★  ★  ★

As soon as Luna clambered into Tomas's clapped-out old Fiat she wished she'd stuck to her guns about going on the train. But he had pleaded that he needed a navigator and she had given in. He had only just picked up his car and hardly knew London, never mind trying to negotiate his way out of it and into the countryside. As she threw her bag onto the back seat Tomas immediately grabbed her knee and squeezed, making direct eye contact in that insistent, un-English way, with his face too near hers to avoid.

'Beautiful Luna!' he declared, beaming. 'The Goddess of the Moon, are you not? It is so special that we share this wonderful journey!'

She didn't know if he meant the actual journey or the art workshop ahead — either way, her heart sank. She smiled and subtly shifted in her seat as she tugged at the seat belt, moving her knees to the door side of the car, out of his reach. Her hopes for some 'me time' faded as Tomas's need for companionship filled the stuffy air like his tobacco breath. She unwound her window a touch, as she adjusted her expectations and resigned herself to a long drive politely deflecting the bombardment of Tomas's person- ality. He lurched the Fiat back and forth out of the parking space and Luna turned her attention doggedly to the road map.

'We need to get to the North Circular,' she said. 'And then round to the A10.'

Disconcertingly, Tomas turned to face her fully when she spoke.

She glanced into his grinning face and couldn't help but laugh. 'Keep your eyes on the road, you mad fuck!'

He threw his head back and guffawed delightedly, swerving right onto the main road without stopping. Luna clutched the seat.

'Oh my God,' she groaned as a taxi horn blared.

★ ★ ★

After a thrill ride through the London roads and traffic, they found their way to the plenty-laned, relative safety of the M11 and Luna eased her grip on the car seat. It was a sunny day, with long, soft winter light and a white sky. Luna had never been to Norfolk, which for some reason pleased Tomas.

'Is first time for both of us!' he exclaimed. 'We are — how you say? — Norfolk virgins!'

In the outside lane, Tomas had at least calmed down, and although the car was rattling as he pushed it beyond its comfortable top speed, Luna began to feel good. There were worse ways to spend a Friday afternoon, like being stuck in her studio, painting a commission. She smiled internally with grim humour. It was the first time she'd pictured the scenario as anything other than her dream come true.

The motorway became a dual carriageway, then a single-file A road as they passed Norwich, and finally a series of winding, sand-edged B roads as they neared the Norfolk coastline. The land was foreignly flat, nothing like the lolloping, tree-frilly countryside of Wales and Sussex Luna knew from her childhood. It added to her sense of getting away, with the setting sun behind them throwing a glaze across the fields and the car's shadow always ahead of them, beckoning them on. Even Tomas sat back and allowed the quiet atmosphere to seep into him.

Luna read out directions to the farmhouse from Tomas's leaflet, but still they ended up on a track which seemed to be taking them past sand dunes and marshes straight out to sea.

'The sea! The sea!' Tomas was suddenly wild with excitement again. 'I've never seen the sea of this country!'

There it was, soaked in the sun's rays and spread before them like butter. The track seemed to be disappearing here and there, as it dipped under pools of seawater, but still Tomas drove forward.

'Er . . . shouldn't we stop now? The tide might be coming in,' said Luna, looking anxiously around for signs they may get stranded.

'OK, yes, you're right, we stop now.'

He jerked the car to an abrupt halt in the middle of the track and leaped out. He began to stalk towards the sea, stretching his arms out and breathing deeply. The wind whipped his hair, billowed his corduroy jacket and tugged at his trousers, defining the contours of his long thin legs and flapping the fabric behind him like windsocks. He turned to see where Luna had got to.

'Come on! What are you sitting there for? You must experience, Luna!'

In spite of herself and the cold, she found herself getting out of the warm car. The wind felt even stronger than it looked and was bitter, chilling her to her bones immediately. It scooped her hair up into the air and sucked the breath from her. Tomas roared with laughter as he came towards her with his hand extended.

'Let's run!' He grabbed her and began to lope forwards, stumbling up and down dunes until they petered out onto a wide flat beach. The sea seemed miles away, glinting like a mirage. Tomas pulled Luna on, leaping over pools of water or stamping through the ones he couldn't clear. It was a riot of sensation — the buffeting of the wind and attack of sand, the roaring in their ears, the dazzle of light on their eyes, the whirling hair, the mad galloping like children. When they finally reached the surf they were laughing, panting, half collapsed.

'Now what?' said Luna and they looked at each other, laughing helplessly.

'Now what? Now what! Ha ha ha!' Tomas repeated back at her. He kicked off his brogues, peeled away his socks, rolled up his trousers and jumped into the surf, yelping from the cold. 'Now what?' he yelled, splashing. 'Now what nothing! Isn't this enough?' He spread his arms emphatically and raised his face to the sky.

Luna was overcome by an insane urge to join him. Before sense could stop her, she stripped off her shoes, hiked up her jeans and ran into the water. The sharpness of the cold stung and made her scream. Tomas grabbed her and made her jump around with him in great splashy circles. Their clothes were getting soaked. But she felt wild with joy, utter joy. Just from flinging herself around in the elements. It was good to be alive. The euphoria was physical, the sort children get a hundred times a day, running, spinning round, skipping, standing on their heads. When did I last feel like this? she wondered. Fucking years ago. Sex was the closest they came to it as grown-ups, but even that . . .

Tomas began to pull her deeper into the waves, an even more evil glint sparking from his eyes. He gave her a playful shove, as if to throw her right in, the way boys always did. Luna didn't quite believe he would actually do it, but the next thing she knew she had lost her footing and plunged, totally immersed in the freezing water, and came up gasping with shock.

'Oh my God in heaven!' Tomas shouted, his hands to his face in horror. He pulled her to her feet. 'I didn't mean for that to happen, so help me God!' In spite of his profuse apologies, humour skipped around the edges of his wide eyes and mouth. Luna stared at him in disbelief, slicking her wet hair back from her face.

'You utter bastard!' she finally managed to exhale. Tomas started to laugh, he couldn't help himself, tried to hold the laughter in by clutching his mouth with his hands.

'But look at you! How beautiful you are!' He backed away through the surf as Luna lurched towards him. 'You are reborn! Like Venus emerging from the waves!'

He half fell onto the sand as he turned to run away. Luna gave chase as he zigzagged up and down the beach away from her. In spite of being in shock, frozen to the bone, every time he turned his hilarious idiotic face, she laughed harder than she could ever remember. He cut such a comical figure, and so must she, like one of the speeded-up chase scenes from the *Benny Hill Show*. She started singing the theme music — a joke Tomas got, which made him roar. When he eventually collapsed she grabbed him and

145

tried to soak him too, rubbing her hair on him as though he was a towel. They rolled in a tussle, getting plastered in sand. When exhaustion stopped them they flopped back looking up at the sky. She felt peculiarly new, as though she had actually been reborn, suddenly cleansed of her sin of despair. Her heart, pounding resoundingly against her ribcage, seemed to be shouting at her how very alive she was.

'We must seize every moment, yes?' said Tomas. 'Take all our chances. Live for everything that is good around us.'

Yes, Luna thought. Yes. As she lay there she made a promise to herself that that's what she would do. She began to shiver violently and Tomas, rather more gallantly this time, took off his jacket and wrapped it round her, tucking her under his wing and running her back to the car, where he gave her what looked like a paisley smoking jacket to wrap herself in and whacked up the car heater, although it seemed to make more noise than warmth.

\* \* \*

The B&B was an old farmhouse set in bleak fields a few miles from the beach, with a converted barn as the painting studio. The couple running it, Murray and Babs, were more conventional than Luna had imagined they'd be, ex-services perhaps. Babs glanced down at their wet sandy clothes as they stood at the door, causing Luna to stamp and shake the sand onto the doormat and make Tomas do the same

146

before they entered the house. Tomas wowed at the beautiful English antiques throughout as the couple showed them up the creaky stairs to their respective adjacent rooms. Murray and Babs left them and went to make a pot of tea, which would be waiting for them in the lounge once they'd freshened up.

Luna's room was fantastic. With double-aspect windows, it had views both over the farmland and outbuildings, and also over the fields and marsh land out to sea, which she thought she could just see, a glinting thread along the horizon. The room had low beams and was furnished simply with a dark wood chair and desk and a sumptuous bed. The carpet sank to the tread and was fitted through to the en suite, which was kitted out with thick towels and expensive-looking toiletries. The whole weekend suddenly felt like the treat Angie had claimed it would be, and not just a favour to be endured and made the best of.

Luna stripped off her cold soggy clothes and entered the shower — no dripping, no mildew, no leaping in and out to avoid freezing or burning. It was a wholly pleasurable experience, only marred, or enhanced maybe, by the muffled sound of Tomas singing the *Benny Hill* theme as he showered on the other side of the adjoining wall.

★ ★ ★

After setting out the studio for the following day, Tomas and Luna waited in the lounge for the other participants. First to arrive was an elderly lady, very sweet and chatty and utterly charmed by Tomas, who had changed into smart, tight black trousers (were they velvet, even?) and an open-neck, shiny black shirt, and done his best to sleek his hair back with pomade. He actually looked quite dashing and attractive, in a seventies ballroom dancer sort of way. Anyway, he was lovely with Millie, kissing her hand as he guided her to an armchair, pouring her tea and shushing her fears that she may be 'absolutely hopeless, I'm afraid'. She was followed by a young couple, Ian and Katie, teachers looking to refresh their art skills. Alex appeared next, a tomboyish woman a bit older than Luna, in her late thirties, or early forties perhaps. There was something open yet mischievous about her elfin face, framed by a cheeky black bob, and Luna smiled at her with the recognition of someone on the same wavelength. She headed straight for the chair next to Luna and began chatting. She too had driven from London, but from Acton, in the west. She had recently jacked in her career in publishing to retrain as an illustrator. Luna was amazed to find she had actually heard of Tomas and admired his work. Next was a young man, big enough to have to stoop to avoid banging his head on the beam in the doorway.

'All right?' he said in a loud, deep voice, with the same warm Yorkshire accent as Luna's new relatives. 'Jonathon Booker,' he announced, as he went round the room shaking hands. 'Call me Jon.'

Tomas asserted himself as the course tutor

and asked after his journey, nodding as though he understood Jon's explanation of his route from Leeds down the M1 and across on the A47.

'So. Where's the pub then?' said Jon, clapping his hands together, and when nobody knew he went in search of Murray or Babs to find out.

There was one just a few miles away in the nearby village, the Cock and Pheasant, and Jon took charge of organizing the two cars that would drive there according to who wouldn't mind having only one drink. Katie volunteered, and Ian, Millie and Tomas piled into her Citroën Saxo.

'You girls come with me then,' said Jon, pressing the remote to unlock the shiny doors of his silver Saab. Both Luna and Alex made to get in the back, but out of politeness Luna redirected herself to the front passenger seat. The interior was swish and immaculate with all the trimmings: a satnav, iPod player and holders for everything he could ever need holders for — coffee, mobile phone, change from his pockets.

'Very nice,' she said.

'Yeah, it's quality,' Jon replied, as he swung confidently around Katie's car, the fat tyres making the gravel crunch sweetly like cornflakes. He drove in a particularly *masterful* way that made Luna want to giggle, with very definite pushes and pulls on the gearstick, leaning back in the seat so that the arm on the wheel was at full stretch. In her peripheral vision she was aware of his large, muscly thighs pumping alternately at the foot pedals. It was the kind of car whose suspension made it swoop over the bumpy lanes rather than clunk or rattle, the kind which made Luna feel nauseous.

'So, what do you do, Jon, that affords such an impressive set of wheels?' Alex asked sweetly from the back.

'Advertising,' he replied.

'Aah! That explains it!' she said.

'Yeah. Creative Director.'

'So what's a proper grown-up like you doing on a course like this?' Luna asked.

Jon and collage seemed diametrically opposed. He slunk her a sideways look and seemed to sigh. Luna glanced at him. He had a big, sturdy sort of face. In profile you could see that his eyes were deep-set behind his black-framed designer glasses and his nose was surprisingly small and neat. He appeared to be searching for an answer, but then he spotted the pub.

'Here we go,' he said, and swung sharply into the car park.

★　★　★

The group was joined later by a shy, shuffling guy, Danny, a printmaker from Cambridge, who wanted to get some new inspiration for collographs. He admired Tomas's prints, which were apparently well known in printers' circles. Luna smiled at him from across the table. He was the sort of man she found attractive, slight and boyish, with an androgynous face. He had a goofy overbite and sandy, roughly chopped hair that he ruffled in a nervous gesture as he was

150

introduced. His soft green eyes really smiled when he said hello.

Tomas beamed round at the group and introduced the theme for the workshop.

'As you all know from the brochure, we are going to work in collage. As subject for the weekend we are going to concentrate on the portraits.'

Luna sighed. She was sick of sodding portraits. She'd been hoping for something lighter, less intense — to make attractive designs, a Norfolk view, say, or, even better, abstracts of nature.

'However,' Tomas went on, poised for dramatic effect with his hands raised, 'I want you to paint portraits with the perspective of a landscape.' He looked very pleased with himself. He paused, grinning round at the blank faces, waiting for his pupils to catch up with his genius. 'Our first task is a self-portrait. I don't want it to look like you on the outside. I don't need your painting of something I can see for myself. No.' He flourished his hand, like a diva. 'I want you to show me something of your inner being. You must go inside you and reveal something I don't know, none of us know. This is why, you see, we must all feel safe, like we can trust each other. Do you know?'

He looked directly at everybody in turn until they nodded their heads in uncomfortable acquiescence.

'So come now. We must toast each other as our contract and all drink to this agreement.' He made everybody raise their glasses. 'Look into the eyes! Look into the eyes!' Tomas exclaimed, insisting that they all took their turns clinking glasses one on one and staring at each other directly as they did so before taking a sip.

Jon stood back until Tomas dragged him towards Luna and made him do it in front of everyone else. Jon took off his glasses and gave an exaggerated stare, a piss-take that Tomas missed.

'Aah! Very good! Yes! Yes! Right into the windows of the soul!'

* * *

In spite of the luxurious bed, Luna had a disturbed night and started awake early from a nightmare — the childhood kind that really scared you and sent you running to your mother. She forgot what it was instantly, but even so she couldn't get back to sleep. So she rose and showered and made an effort with her hair, that, had Danny not been on the course, she might not have bothered with. She bothered with mascara too. She put on the man's shirt and loose chinos that she painted in (it was a bit of a pose, she knew — a homage, really, to female artists of earlier times — but she allowed it in herself. When she put them on she felt a certain gravitas — not for anyone else's benefit but her own) and headed down for breakfast. There was one long dining table for all the guests to sit around and it made Luna grin to see Jon sitting at one end and Alex at the exact opposite.

'Morning,' she said brightly, passing Jon to

slide in next to Alex, and then added more quietly, 'So, who came down first?'

'Me,' said Alex, smiling in amusement that Jon had been so unsociable. He made no effort to join in or appear interested in them as he tucked into his full English breakfast. Danny appeared, sleepy and ruffled, and, pleasingly, sat himself the other side of Luna. Ian and Katie were next, with Millie appearing last, breaking the rules about old people and early rising.

They were joined by somebody new, a woman who was local and not staying over at night. Suzie was already flushed and began to gush overexcitedly about her new-found identity acquired through driftwood sculpture. She started smiling at the sight of something through the French windows behind Luna, who turned to see Tomas in tight Lycra sportswear grinning in at them while jogging on the spot. He took some large intakes of breath and began to perform jumping jacks while greeting his group. Luna and Alex grinned widely.

'Hello, my wonderful people!' he exclaimed. 'It is a beautiful day for the spirit, yes?'

He gestured emphatically around him. The frost made everything magical, coating every surface like a shake of fine glitter. Realizing the final student had arrived, Tomas jogged round to enter the breakfast room and welcome her.

'Come now, people. I insist we experience the beauty of the special place in which we are so we can get in touch with the nature and ourselves and place us here today truly.'

Suzie was smitten. 'Wonderful!' she breathed,

clapping her hands together.

Tomas led the group out into the farmyard, heading towards the open fields rather than the barn.

'It's bloody freezing!' Luna complained.

'Not for long you won't be cold. Come on, we must warm up.' Tomas jogged back to her and ushered her forward with everyone else, like a sheepdog. 'Move! Come on! Fling yourselfs! I know you can, Luna, I've seen you!'

Alex looked at her, eyebrows raised.

'Don't ask,' said Luna.

They watched Tomas wheeling around as he advanced to the field. He opened the gate and began shepherding people through. Suzie was first, skipping loosely and wailing in a high pitch that sent a flock of black birds squawking up from the fields into the safe trees. The others trooped into the field, embarrassed and shivering, with their hands in their pockets or folded under their armpits.

'Nobody will be allowed into my art workshop without they do this first!' Tomas declared, flapping his arms and hopping round the huddle. 'It is an essential part of my course, believe me in its importance.'

Nobody moved. They glanced at each other awkwardly. Then Luna remembered her promise to herself that she would seize every moment. What did she have to lose? Apart from her dignity. She launched herself into the air before grabbing Alex's hands and whirling her around the way the hippies had done with the kids on the commune to get them dizzy at the fireside *happenings*. After all, Luna was no stranger to doing the kinds of things that excruciated most English people. She'd grown up in a place where not only the six-year-olds had run around naked, but most of the adults had too. *Movement* was practically a belief system. People expressing themselves freely and not caring how they looked was her heritage and at times like these it came in handy.

They progressed after Suzie across the field, running, skipping and leaping, making each other laugh with moves as stupid as they could think up. Luna looked back to see Tomas grabbing Katie and beginning to waltz her before passing her to Ian. More embarrassed to resist than continue, they blundered around the field. Danny, bless him, had offered Millie his arm and was falling in with her old-lady shimmy. Jon stood resolutely planted at the hedge, looking miserable. He couldn't do it on his own, or, worse, with Tomas. Luna ran back for him.

'We may as well get it over with,' she smiled at him, extending her hand. She began to do a piss-takey hippy dance that made him almost smile. He let her take his hand and strode firmly beside her as she skipped, making her feel like a child.

Tomas led everyone back in a big loop, until they were standing together again.

'Now we must make a circle all connected one to the other and breathe together and call for inspiration,' he declared, pulling people in to hold hands in a ring. Breathless and panting, they followed Tomas's lead in breathing in 'the

155

nature's creative spirits' and letting out the bad vibes.

Funnily enough it seemed to have worked, for most of them. When Luna opened her eyes again she did feel positive and connected, with energy pulsing through the hot hands of Jon and Millie, her waking feeling of being uninspired and anxious gone. Jon was the first to break the circuit, dropping her hand and turning to walk determinedly towards the barn.

★  ★  ★

The barn was L-shaped, with the glass-walled art studio taking up the long part, a kitchenette in the corner and a loungey dining area along the short side, carpeted with ethnic rugs. This is where Tomas led them first, making them remove their shoes before standing on the rugs. It wasn't over yet.

'Now is everybody warm? We are going to do some kind of yoga stretches to ground ourselfs in our creativity.'

He took them through a few light stretches and then they all lay on the floor and flopped out as he took them through a visualization to bring images to the surface of their minds. Finally they were allowed into the studio, where Tomas guided them around the boxes of collage materials he and Luna had laid out the day before.

'Today we have no pencils, no paint. No sketching, no drafts, nothing. Every shape, every definition must be made by the collage pieces. I

156

don't want to see your likeness on the page, I want to *feeeel* it . . . ' Tomas tapped his solar plexus with the flat of his palm, ' . . . *here.*'

Luna, Alex and Danny formed a triangle at the corner of a table and were having trouble controlling giggles.

'I've just remembered,' Luna whispered, 'I've got a really important commission to paint at home.'

'Yeah, me too,' said Alex.

'Don't leave me here.' Danny clutched Luna's wrist. 'Or should I say . . . *here.*' He imitated Tomas's gesture, hand on chest. Luna snorted. Uh-oh. He was funny too.

'OK, OK, it's good to laugh, yes?' Tomas tried a patient smile. 'But now I need for you all to get into the zone for the art.'

Luna's laughter subsided as she met Tomas's imploring eyes. He was genuine, if ludicrous, and working hard for their benefit; and anyway — however much they scorned them — his ideas for group bonding and mood setting had actually worked. As she had lain on the floor, in spite of herself, she'd felt something immovable shift, something cracking open. As it did so her dream emerged, like a chick pecking out of an egg, so clearly it was as though she was dreaming it all over again . . . She was climbing the winding steps of a high glass tower. When she got to the top all there was was a loo, so she sat on it and peed. When she looked out she saw with panic that the tower was alone, cut off in the middle of a vast lurching sea of blood. She was trapped in it. She tried to stop peeing and get off the toilet but she couldn't. When she looked beneath her she saw she was filling the bowl with sand. The sensations of vertigo and fear were so vivid she'd felt them physically and woken, jolting upright in bed. The imagery would certainly do for a *portrait with the perspective of a landscape.*

Luna had never worked in collage, and not even being allowed to make provisional sketches was like having her hands tied. Not being able to use paint flummoxed her completely. She'd wanted the shiny gloopy intensity of thick brush-stroked acrylic for the red sea. But then she spotted a flow of scarlet in a fabric box — a piece of silky dress lining. Too smooth, but a starting point at least.

The hours until dusk flew by. Nobody had finished, and all carried on straining their eyes in the weird half-natural, half-electric light. Eventually Tomas insisted they stop, physically taking their pieces from them.

'I don't care they are not finished. We as people are not finished, yes? So they make good the representation of you today.'

He shooed them all, complaining, into the lounge to take a break, making them stretch out their hunching shoulders and think about 'how to express your collage in words'. Luna felt nerves begin to rise. She didn't want to admit the symbolism of her dream to anyone, it was too exposing. She remembered why she disliked confessional work. If she wanted anyone to know things about herself she would tell them.

They took seats classroom-style, facing the end where Tomas stood with the art works. He placed Luna's piece on the easel first. She had decided to work on a rough piece of wood, and looking at it now it appeared makeshift and amateur. Her usual paintings were at least always aesthetically pleasing but this construction was just plain ugly. It looked like what it was, a collection of rubbish stuck on a board. However, there was nothing she could do now but sit out the embarrassing critique. She made a small circling movement with her finger to Tomas. He looked back to her piece to check it was the right way up. Luna pointed at the plastic drinks bottles at the centre, which he then prodded.

'Aah!' he said, as the bottle construction moved. Luna had filled one bottle with sand, cut off the top and inserted the other into it, gluing them fast together to make a double-ended capsule. She had drilled a hole in the wood and attached the conjoined bottles to it at their neck, making a brace with strong wire, so that the capsule could be rotated, like a propeller blade. As Tomas moved them round, he understood what would happen, and he turned the bottles so they would sit in their brace the other way up. As he did so the sand inside began to pour through to the other end, like an egg timer, beginning to reveal something on the inside of the upturned bottle, which everybody craned to see.

'Oh God! It's a face!' Suzie exclaimed.

Luna had fashioned it out of old tights from the material bin, stitched around a fuse-wire frame that she had managed to stuff inside the bottle. It was pinned, hovering in the middle of the bottle, with a spring pierced through the plastic on the back. She had wound golden threads for hair around the forehead and left a gaping hole for a mouth that the sand fell through. As the sand slipped further, two hand shapes that she had made in the same way appeared beneath the face, reaching out beseechingly towards the viewer. Luna breathed a sigh of relief as the sand slid past and the features wobbled but held. When the sand had fallen through, Tomas tipped the bottles again, and the sand began to fall back, this time gradually smothering the hands and face.

Luna had spent too long fiddling with the intricacies of the capsule to do much to the background. She had secured the capsule exactly on a horizon, the lower half of the board a red silk sea which she had glued down in waves and covered with blobs of red berries. Her sky was made of blue-white plastic, in the form of carrier bags, bubble wrap and cling film, stretched and pulled taut across the panel, with a huge half sun of gold chocolate wrapper sinking on the horizon, sending rays of gold netting across the sea.

'What do we think, people?' Tomas asked the group.

'It's a bit nightmarish?' said Danny, like a question. Luna gave him a slight nod. Yes, I'll say it's just a nightmare, she thought. 'It's like a sea of blood. And the plastic sky is so unnatural and . . . suffocating. Like the face in the sand. Trapped inside a plastic . . . tomb, or something.'

'Yes. It's quite disturbing,' said Millie. 'Like a

depiction of fear. The sea's so turbulent and stormy and the bottles look so precarious. Even if the figure could escape from the bottle, she would drown.'

The sand had fallen through again, so Tomas tipped the bottles. 'So, what do we make of this?' he said.

'This way round, the sand is falling out of the features,' said Alex. 'As if the person is losing something. But the other way round the body is being smothered by the same thing. And being stuck inside the bottle . . . that makes me think of an SOS — a message in a bottle. But the person *is* the message in a bottle. It's amazing. Really.' She gave Luna a wink.

'I think it's really powerful,' Ian said. 'I wouldn't want it on my wall though.' Luna laughed, relieved, hoping it was over. But Tomas didn't seem to have finished with her yet.

'So we've discussed the workings of it, and OK, so you know who it's by, but, as with all the pieces, we need to talk about what it says about the artist. What communication is she trying to make?' He paused and turned to Jon. 'You have been very quiet, Jon. Let's hear from you. What do you think this is saying?'

Jon leaned back in his chair, flicking a pen round and round between his fingers. Luna imagined he did that a lot in business meetings. He glanced away from the piece for a moment to Luna, and then back again.

'Does it say anything else to you?' Tomas prompted.

'Yeah, it does,' Jon replied. He shifted in his

seat. 'I don't know if it's what the artist is trying to convey or anything. I'm surprised no one else has said it, so maybe not. But, for me anyway, it hit me in the face. It's about fertility.'

Everybody turned back to study the work again.

'I mean, blood and sand — how much more symbolic can you get? There's the sea of blood, there're even fruit berries crushed into it — to me that indicates menstruation. The egg timer — the passing of time, is that a biological clock or what? The sun, even. It's not up high in the sky, is it? It's setting. The sand flowing out of the female, or, the other way up, the female being buried by it — sand, desert, symbol of barrenness. The sterility of the plastic in the bottle and the sky. And from back here, those dismembered features that aren't fully formed — they're kind of embryonic. Like a half-formed face and little baby hands in a test tube.'

A silence followed and Luna felt her face burning up. Nobody knew how to react, although Luna could tell that, yes, they could all see it now. It seemed so obvious now he'd said it.

'I'm not saying that's what I think the artist meant,' Jon added, seeing her flush. 'I'm saying that's what I got from it. I'm probably full of shite.'

There was a pause, which Luna knew she was meant to fill. She hardly trusted herself to speak, but she cleared her throat and said, as coolly as she could, 'Wow. That's interesting. It would definitely fit. I wish I'd been that clever. But it was just a nightmare I had — last night, actually.'

162

Her eyes flicked to Jon's. He was looking at her intently.

'Oh right,' he said. 'Just me being a pretentious twat then.'

Everyone laughed, dispelling the tension.

'I do think,' he continued, 'that as a piece of art it's fucking outstanding.' Luna stared at him. 'In spite of the constraints on time and materials and everything.' He shrugged and added, 'That's just my opinion,' leaning forward and folding his arms on the table.

'Thank you, Jon,' said Tomas. 'I think maybe your opinion is shared by some others.' He looked, fondly and rather proudly, at Luna. She willed him to move on, and he had either the psychic ability or the plain good grace to pick up the next piece.

★   ★   ★

Jon's work was last. It was nothing like the slick graphic design she'd anticipated, and was at first sight quite beautiful. The overall appearance had the dreamy quality of an illustration for a children's fairy tale. He had worked on a long, narrow portrait canvas, covering it in a pale blue chiffon. In the centre, a tree shot upwards, made from thin entangled mistletoe branches, ending at the top with most of the twiggy ends woven into a curving nest shape. Inside were a handful of the white mistletoe berries, which also exploded into the sky and began to fall around the tree, like a fountain. At a certain point on the way down, the berries were arranged in repeated patterns on the chiffon with adjoined mistletoe leaves, but nearer the bottom the patterns broke up, leaving a scattering of leaves and berries on the ground. As Luna looked closer she saw something else in the tangle of branches that formed the trunk of the tree. She left her seat and went close, joined by the others.

'It's a little man!' said Millie. A small figure in a dark suit, like a doll's house dad, was caught up inside, trying to clamber up the branches. Up close like this you could see that the tangled branches were cleverly intertwined, especially where they formed the nest at the top, as though Jon knew how to weave. There was something so unlikely about that, and it made Luna see him in a different light, realizing her first impression was wrong and she'd been stereotyping. She pulled back from the piece again. It was stylized and symmetrical and reminded her of art nouveau. In fact, mistletoe was often used in art nouveau designs, wasn't it?

Alex turned from the canvas and caught Luna's eye, grinning cheekily. Why was she doing that? Luna looked back to the canvas. Oh! That was why. Of course. How could she not have spotted it immediately? Now she looked, the trunk with a round nest at the top, the little hole filled with white stuff that was spraying into the air . . . Having just managed to cool down, she felt herself flush again. As she looked, it seemed as though the tip was angled towards her, and she took a further step backwards. She was completely used to analysing sexual imagery in art, but there was something a bit too personal

164

about Jon Booker's self-portrait coming in her face.

All the same, she found it hard to snigger with Alex. It was subtly done, the beautifully crafted woven tree, the berries looking more like beaded raindrops on the blue chiffon than semen. Further on their way down the canvas, the berries were attached to leaves. On each grouping, one pair of leaves pointed downwards, the other pair up, with a berry at the top.

'They look like . . . babies,' she said, turning to Jon. He rubbed his head, looking uncomfortable. At the bottom of the picture, the baby shapes were un-forming again, landing as separate limbs on the ground, like fallen fruit.

There was a hush among the students as they studied it. The piece was so at odds with Jon's gruff character, poetic and sensitive, with a fragility that was surprising in such a bear of a man.

'So, people,' said Tomas, 'come. Let's vocalize our thoughts here. What are we thinking?'

'Well, it's a penis,' Alex began. 'Spraying sperm into the air — with the potential to make babies dying by the time the sperm hits the ground.'

'Uh-huh, uh-huh,' Tomas agreed. 'Why mistletoe?'

'It's got to be a symbol of fertility, hasn't it?' Katie answered. 'What with all the kissing under it and so on. And it's evergreen. And the white berries — well, they speak for themselves.'

'What does Viscum Album mean?' asked Ian, peering at the words handwritten in the corner.

It was nice writing, another thing that didn't fit with the picture Luna had formed of Jon. She associated fluid lettering with middle-class southern girls.

'It's mistletoe's proper name,' said Jon, holding up a book on British plants he'd found on the book shelf. 'It literally means white fluid.'

'Aah!' There was a kind of group smile — the first one that included Jon.

'I like the little man struggling through the branches,' said Millie. 'It makes me think of Sleeping Beauty, when the Prince has to hack through all that overgrowth to wake Beauty up.'

Who's he trying to wake up? Luna found herself wondering.

'I *love* that it's such a *fabulous phallus*,' breathed Suzie, 'but that the tip filled with the spunky berries is also a nest. That's so . . . masculine. Not only is the piece bursting with sexual prowess but it indicates the tender, providing, sheltering side of a man. I think that's very *erotic*, for women.' Suzie's voice had grown more and more husky as she'd gone on. She finished by leaning sexily across the desk she was sitting on, squeezing her bosoms together and thrusting them towards Jon. His eyes widened in startled horror behind his glasses. As his eye flicked across and caught Luna's she was unable to stop herself smiling. There was a moment of connection between them that made them both look away.

'Luna? We haven't heard much from you. Do you have anything to add to that?'

She looked back to the piece. Suzie was right,

there was something deeply stirring about the imagery, although she wasn't going to admit it.

'It's beautiful,' she said instead.

'OK.' Tomas looked at his watch. 'We must finish for the day. I don't know about you guys but I'm starving and I need some nice glass of wine. We can continue our interesting discussions in the pub if so we like. I suggest an hour to freshen up ourselfs and then we meet downstairs in the lounge. Well done, everybody, for their efforts of today. Now we must relax so we can be refresh for tomorrow's new ideas.'

Everybody groaned, and then laughed as they filed out.

★   ★   ★

Luna and Alex had the kind of instant friendship that meant they immediately huddled together in the pub, talking in depth about anything, sometimes including others around them, sometimes not. Alex only broke off to use her mobile.

'I've just got to call Charlie,' she said. 'If I try now I might catch her before she goes out.'

'Flatmate?' asked Luna, already feeling the effects of the wine on an empty stomach and stuffing some bread from the basket into her mouth. Alex shook her head as she put the phone to her ear and leaned away from the chatter.

'Daughter,' she replied. Luna gaped. It hadn't occurred to her that Alex was a mum. She didn't seem the type. She was so youthful and spirited

167

and . . . unburdened.

'*Daughter?*' she exclaimed.

'Horrifying, isn't it?' Alex laughed. Her mobile connected and she stuck a finger in the other ear. 'Hello, darling. How're you doing?'

From the conversation about staying safe and not drinking too much or letting 'Ryan' stay over, Luna guessed Charlie was a teenager. Alex must have had her in her mid twenties at the latest. She'd made no mention of a husband or partner, so how had she managed? With her publishing job and art school and everything?

'I'm amazed,' she said to Alex when she came off the phone.

'So am I. It only seems like yesterday I was breastfeeding and now she's having sex with her boyfriend. It's crazy.'

'But . . . how?' Luna asked.

'Don't tell me I have to give you sex education too.'

'No, I mean . . . how on earth have you managed? Done everything you've done, when you had a kid so young? Your life, your career . . . '

'Oh I don't know. You muddle through, I guess. Christ, I wasn't going to be a stay-at-home mum at twenty-four. I'd've gone out of my mind.'

Luna must have looked bewildered so Alex continued, 'Life doesn't end when you have a child, Luna. It just kind of expands to include them.'

Over the meal, Luna pressed Alex for every detail. There had been a couple of years when she was 'tearing her hair out' in a flat with a baby, especially as the pregnancy had been an accident and the father hadn't wanted to be involved. But then there had been the salvation of playgroup, and a small publishing house where she'd previously done an internship needed extra readers. She progressed from there to editorial, and when Charlie started school she took a full-time job. She'd been a senior editor at a well-known house when she quit to retrain as an illustrator. The decision had nothing to do with finding it too hard to juggle a high-flying career with a kid. She just wanted to.

'Of course the childcare issue was difficult sometimes,' Alex said. 'But in some ways I think it helped me progress. A lot of my friends and colleagues were out there partying and having a life and didn't feel ready yet for the commitment of work. But for me the job was the thing I escaped to.' She laughed and added quickly, 'Not that it is all hard. It's fun too. Having Charlie never stopped me doing anything I really wanted to do. Sure, I couldn't go clubbing every night and no doubt she put off a few prospective boyfriends, but certainly not all of them. Not the good ones. I'm sure if you approach it with the right attitude it doesn't take over your life. Kids can be a nightmare at times, but they are a joy as well, you know.'

A joy. Luna felt the word take hold inside her and knew it would spring up again, like a daisy.

'In many ways I think it's harder for you thirty-somethings,' Alex said. 'I had an accident and had to deal with it whether it was a good time or not, before I'd really started my career. It's different for you. How do you decide when's a good time to interrupt everything you've been working towards? But there's never a perfect time, Luna. Now's as good a time as any.' She paused. 'Do you want kids?'

'Yes,' said Luna, simply. The admission felt strange on her tongue, like a lie. But it wasn't. It was a relief, more like unburdening a secret.

'Don't wait for the right time, it won't happen,' Alex said. 'Go for it.'

Luna pulled a face. 'I . . . I want to, but . . . It's not so simple. Pierre isn't so sure yet. He's got this big exhibition coming up and he says we're in no position . . . I mean, he's right really.'

'But you'll manage. And it's worth it, I promise. I mean, I hadn't had long enough to think about kids or anything, so I had to get used to it pretty quick. But it's amazing how you adapt. And it's not your whole life that comes to an end. Only a few months or years. And they shoot by, believe me. And, not being rude, but you're getting on. It's not really fair of your boyfriend to put it off. Especially if you want more than one. You haven't got forever.'

Hearing Alex's words was like an affirmation of Luna's own inner voice. It suddenly seemed outrageous that it should be Pierre who dictated when she could or should experience mother-hood.

The next morning, Luna emerged from her sleep as somebody different, like waking in a foreign country with a new experience ahead.

She had lived in Florence for a few months the summer after leaving college, studying an art course on the Renaissance. She had woken up in her apartment with the Tuscan sun streaming in through the open shutters onto her face and felt new. It was exciting. She was just starting out and her life was spread before her like the view. She was embarking on her life as an artist. This feeling was like that. She was entering a new phase of her life, one that would give her a new identity, not as an artist this time but as a mother.

★   ★   ★

'Today you can sketch, you can use paints, any mark-making at all is OK, you can do anything,' Tomas declaimed in the studio after breakfast and Yogic breathing. 'Although, of course, the one rule is that you must incorporate an element of collage too.'

Just as everybody relaxed and began chatting he recalled their attention.

'Wait! Wait! You don't know yet what the exercise is for today. Today you are going to paint portraits of each other.'

The group began instinctively to gravitate towards the partners they wanted.

'No, no, NO!' said Tomas, holding up his palm in a stop sign. 'I'm afraid it is not allowed to choose yourselfs. I have chosen who I want to capture whom.' He looked at his notebook and then back at the students, nodding. 'Yes. I think this is right. Alex and Ian. Millie and Danny.

171

Katie and Suzie. Luna and Jon.' He looked up, beaming. 'This is good, I think.'

Luna's heart sank. She didn't know if she wanted to be studied by the guy who'd exposed her subconscious fears so deftly.

'This time your work may be more figurative,' Tomas continued. 'But also there must be some things that you feel you see in your model that maybe they don't see, some kind of psychological thing, or emotion or quality that speaks to you. It's *your* interpretation of this person, not a straight portrait for a gallery or some such thing.'

The partners set up positions facing each other around easels and tables.

'OK, everybody, get in the zone,' said Tomas. 'Now we will have ten minutes' utter silence while we study our subject and become ourselfs filled with their presence.'

The task itself was well within Luna's comfort zone — to eke out a person's deep character and represent it through visual imagery. However, staring at and being stared at by Jon Booker was not. She closed her eyes to compose herself for a moment, get herself grounded. He still had a huge presence, even with her eyes shut. She could feel his heat radiating towards her, as though she was sitting in front of a hot stove. She realized she didn't know anybody else like him. Most people she knew were flitty and light and quick, but Jon had a weighty, rooted quality about him. When she opened her eyes she became aware of a softness in him she hadn't seen before. She tried to locate it in his big frame but couldn't. He didn't look like he worked out but he had one of those physiques that was heavyset and masculine, naturally strong, like a bull almost. She thought she saw the fold of a slight paunch above his waistband. Some softness there. And in his round cheeks, more noticeable without his angular specs. He had big soft lips too, very red, with a surprisingly pronounced Cupid's bow nestled in his stubble. But these things were only hints at softness, not the softness itself.

He had started to make provisional sketches of her with bold, confident marks of charcoal. His eyes wandered over her with an expertise that was unnerving. He was good at sizing things up, a bit too good. She attempted to focus on her own work but it wasn't easy under his scrutiny. She wasn't used to being the observed. She too began to make marks on the page, just to sketch his outline. She couldn't think how to portray his personality but she knew she should trust her method well enough that it would come to her as she worked. The secret was in beginning, allowing it to form and take shape. As he sat there in front of her, however, he remained impenetrable. He was someone who held his cards very close to his chest. The collage element, too, remained elusive. She had no idea how she would incorporate anything other than thick acrylic on her canvas. She could envisage him dressed in a black suit, despite his weekend attire of dark jeans and T-shirt. But if she put him in a suit would that be a cliche born of her interpretation of his job in advertising? Could she fashion his clothing in textiles — give him a jacket that opened to reveal . . . what? No, such a childish idea. She felt herself frown and tried to clear her forehead, aware again of Jon's watchful eye.

Before lunch she got up to stretch, rummaging in the collage boxes for an idea. She finally found something, following the others through to grab some lunch and mull over her idea. It was hardly attention grabbing, but in lieu of anything else she decided she would have to make it work. She rose quickly from lunch to get started on the collage pieces. She wished she had time to make up some papier mâché, but instead had to make do with pieces of card, placing and sticking them on the canvas in a way that forced them up into relief. She then cut her material, placing it carefully over her sketched shadows.

The atmosphere of the afternoon built into a mixture of panic and amusement, as they all watched each other with maddened curiosity, applying their collage pieces to their portraits, trying hard to keep focusing on their own work. Jon had cut some textiles into tiny pieces, and was attaching a length of string — and was that a small doll's face he was trying to conceal in his palm? Luna wished she'd spotted one of those the day before — it would have saved her hours of trying to fashion a face out of bloody wire and stockings. She craned to see but Tomas was invigilating as though they were in exam conditions to ensure nobody looked at anyone else's picture.

'It is *aperitif* that no one's creativity gets muddled up by someone else's!' he boomed. A few chuckled at his misuse of the word. 'Focus, people! Focus!' But his words only added to the air of hilarity in which the afternoon was ending as everyone raced to get their pieces to some kind of finished state before they were shown. They were all comforted by the fact that everyone was in a similar frenzy, more like contestants on the *Generation Game* than any serious art class, and eventually there was no point in even trying any more. Alex and Ian gave up before anyone else.

'Well, there's no saving that,' Alex admitted cheerfully, sitting back and laughing at her own efforts. 'Apologies in advance, Ian.'

Luna was grateful for their attitude of abandon. She finished her piece with a great blob of acrylic that would take days to dry. Tomas took a last prowl around the tables, assessing each work with an actorly studiousness, deciding which pieces to display first. He stopped for a long while at Jon's, glancing up and catching Luna's eye as she shared jovial remarks with Millie.

'I dread to think what's on that canvas,' she laughed. She even smiled at Jon, who pushed his glasses back up to the bridge of his nose and looked away.

'Well, let's not keep you suspended,' Tomas decided. He took the canvas from the easel and staggered with it to the front of the room.

It was a busy piece with a lot to take in and a slightly awkward silence fell as people attempted to interpret it. The first thing to stand out was that the figure at the centre was literally a blank canvas — an outline of Luna, accurately depicted, the charcoal marks still showing where they drifted inside the figure. But there was nothing within the figure itself, making her look unfinished. Behind her was strung a washing line, on which hung the doll's face, with the same thread that Luna had used in her own self-portrait as the blonde hair, attached to a miniature replica of Luna's painting outfit — shirt and chinos roughly cut from fabric, her shoes tiny leather scraps stapled to the trouser cuffs. A doll's hands were attached to the cuffs of the shirt, holding a matchstick like a paintbrush. The figure sat on a chair as she had, looking into a mirror. The mirror image was a ghostly figure, rendered in fractured pieces of something flesh-toned beneath a layer of semi-transparent shiny paper to imitate glass. But it wasn't exactly a mirror image. It had a definite curve to the stomach, an actual bump in fact, raised from the canvas, rounded like the tip of an egg. The mirror image was pregnant.

As she took the portrait in, Luna felt as stripped as she was in the picture. He had undressed her and hung not only her clothes but her body parts on the line. What was he saying exactly? And she had her back to them, looking instead at herself as she wanted to be, a mother. It was too true, too close to the bone, but still she felt insulted. She was glad of Alex diverting attention away from her by talking rapidly about the technical cleverness of the washing line of clothes, while Luna composed herself.

'So, what do you think, Luna, of this

interpretation of you?' asked Tomas, after several people had commented while skilfully avoiding mention of what the painting was saying.

'Well,' she said. 'It seems to be saying my artist persona is an outfit I wear. That stripped of it I'm nothing. As for why my reflection is pregnant, I can only assume that the artist imagines that motherhood is the only thing a woman could possibly aspire to.'

There was a nervous pause, until Jon said, 'Hold up a minute — that's not what I meant at all.' He was suddenly very red and had broken out in a hot sweat.

'OK, OK,' said Tomas hurriedly. 'Perhaps you could tell us what you meant?'

Jon struggled to find something to say.

'I didn't mean anything by it. I just — it was — to be honest I don't know what I was doing. The pregnancy thing was just a facet of womanhood I bunged on in a panic. I actually couldn't think of a thing to do to represent Luna, and I ran out of time. The body parts on the washing line — I just nicked that idea, actually. I couldn't think what the fuck else to do.'

Luna looked at him. His reaction was unexpected. She was sure he'd known exactly what he was doing, so why the backtracking, the false confession of failure? Was he trying to spare her feelings, now he'd seen her distress? Luckily they were running out of time and Tomas decided to move on quickly to another piece. Luna struggled to contribute as they progressed through the other portraits, but she couldn't help

177

feeling as lacking as she was inside her outline in Jon's painting.

It wasn't until hers was placed on the easel that she finally felt her sense of self return. She hadn't realized quite how successfully she had caught Jon's likeness. His shape and especially the slope of his shoulders she had managed to get right with the curves of the card. Aesthetically, too, the painting pleased her. It had the atmosphere of American art, a Grant Wood perhaps, the solid figure in black against a bright blue background. She'd painted Jon in a room with a window. The background was reversed so that the wallpaper (and she had cut and attached strips of paper up to a balsa-wood picture rail so that it really looked like wallpaper) had a design of summer sky and printed repetitions of white cloud. Outside the window was an office — tiny grey filing cabinets and little beige desks in rows like crops. It worked far better than she had thought it would. Seen from this distance the perspective was perfectly imperfect, lending a surreal quality. The composition was spot on, the colour and lines bold, confident. Luna felt excitement flooding her like a sunrise. She would have been proud of it if she'd had weeks to work on it.

'That's amazing,' said Alex, leaning over to squeeze Luna's arm. 'Really incredible.'

Danny agreed, followed by the others. Millie pointed her hands towards Luna and applauded. Luna felt suddenly emotional again and fought back tears. She hated people getting gushy at their own triumphs, like actresses winning awards. But it did feel like a triumph. It was a really good painting. Tomas had been pacing — looking at the painting from all angles, near and far.

'So, the general feeling is we like this work?' he asked the group.

There was a resounding 'Yes'.

'So then we need to know why. Why do we like this painting? What does it achieve, how, and cetera.'

Quickly, the group chimed in with everything Luna had wanted to convey: not only Jon's physical presence, but the suggestion of softness. It was Suzie who got it, from the clothing, which was mainly heavy-duty grey-black sandpaper but with all the creases and folds and shadows formed with black velvet. The materials worked far better than paint would have done, the depth of the black in the velvet compared to the lightly shimmering sandpaper, the pile of it giving the effect of bursting through the flat sandpaper.

'It's as though the tough exterior can't quite hold the softness in . . . it's like the folds of material are cracks that his inner self seeps out of although he tries to keep it contained! Oh I love it! *Pleease* say that's what you meant!' Suzie gasped, making everyone laugh. Luna broke into a grin, hoping she didn't look too self-satisfied. She felt it though.

'Jon?' asked Tomas. 'What would you like to say about this piece?'

'What can I say?' Jon replied, sitting very still, like his image on the canvas. 'It's so like me it almost freaks me out.'

When he made no further comment, Millie

asked, 'I love the sky wallpaper and the interior placed outside. Why did you do that?'

Luna shrugged. 'I don't really know. The idea just came to me and I liked it. I wasn't saying anything about Jon, particularly.'

'Weren't you?' asked Jon, not aggressively but with a sort of sad acceptance.

'Why, what does it make you feel about yourself?' asked Tomas.

'Like I'm missing the point,' he answered.

'Oh what do you mean?' asked Millie.

'Well, it's a kind of *what's wrong with this picture* thing, isn't it? I'm focusing out of the window at an office interior, when the sky's inside. But it isn't really the sky, it's wallpaper. I don't know what it means, I can't work it out. It makes me feel unsure. I guess that's the point. It's very clever, that.'

'Is that what you meant, Luna?' asked Tomas. 'To make Jon — us — feel unsure?'

'I'm not sure,' Luna smiled. 'I just got the feeling Jon was . . . unhappy about something. I knew he had a stressful job. It made me want to put him in an office, but it seemed trite or obvious to have him staring longingly out at the sky. So I just turned it around. I didn't think about it much. I didn't have time.' Everyone moaned in agreement at the problem of time. It seemed to wrap up the proceedings.

'Right,' said Tomas, clapping his hands. 'Well done, everybodies. You have all worked so hard and I'm so very proud of all you have achieved here this weekend. I hope you all will take away somethings that you can use in your future artistic endeavours. Now may I suggest we all go to the pub and get — how you say — blattered?'

Alex stood and thanked Tomas and they gave him a round of applause, at which he almost cried. As they packed up their stuff and helped tidy the mess of materials into Tomas's containers, an end-of-exams party atmosphere took over. Ian and Katie would come for a bite to eat and a quick drink but had to head back for work on Monday morning. Luna was staying anyway, stuck with her lift back with Tomas. Alex, Danny and Millie decided to stay at the B&B for another night too, so they could really make a night of it, and Suzie showed no signs of going home. Only Jon seemed apart from it, gathering his things together as though he would set off there and then. Luna felt sorry suddenly that she'd denied the truth of his painting, and also grateful that he'd let her.

'How about you, Jon?' she asked. 'Can you stay over — bunk off work tomorrow morning?'

He looked up in surprise and grinned like a kid.

'Are you sure?' he said, as if it were up to her.

'Of course,' said Luna.

'Maybe I will,' he said. 'I'll phone it in tomorrow, literally.'

He was less OK than he seemed about being on the outside of a crowd.

★   ★   ★

The evening was a raucous affair. Luna got to sit next to Danny, which, as she'd had little chance

181

to chat with him all day, was a boon. He seemed more shy of her than before, and, as the drinks flowed, she got the feeling it was a fancying sort of shy. She hoped so, anyway. She felt fanciable again, now that she had impressed with her painting, confident and back on form. The nagging worry that Jon's depiction of her was right — that she needed her artist's clothing to feel like somebody — she gulped down with a glass of house red. Who didn't need an idea of themselves anyway? Wasn't Jon's identity centred on his job title and his flash car? His whole look was typical for someone in his industry, with all that black attire, angular specs, cropped hair and sideburns. She poured herself another glass from the bottle on the table.

They were an unapologetically loud party. Tomas's voice alone startled the pub from its usual Sunday night quiet, as he moved around the group, squeezing in next to each member to congratulate them earnestly on their work and discuss ways to improve and move forward. He really had studied everyone's work and wasn't just making a show of doing so as he'd stalked around the class stroking his goatee. Everyone felt enthused about using collage in their future work. Even Luna was inspired to use it, and told him so when he pulled up a stool — annoyingly between her and Danny. Tomas put his arm round her and hugged her to his chest, kissing her head.

'My Luna!' he exclaimed. She gave Danny a look from beneath her fringe. 'How well you did today, no? Your beautiful portrait of Jon — my feeling is you excelled yourself, am I right?'

Unfortunately, she and Danny were the last two Tomas had come to, and so there he stayed until last orders, in between them both. It was probably just as well, thought Luna drunkenly. But as the group finally got up to go, chivvied by the bar staff, she felt Tomas's hand on her back, and then — did he just reach round beneath her arm and deliberately touch her breast? Or was that an accident? She wasn't sure but somehow his hand had been there. She looked at him and he smiled at her as though he'd done nothing. In the car park, she clutched at Alex and they swerved towards Millie's car.

'Do you girls need saving?' Millie asked sweetly, smiling at them in her rear-view mirror as she sat up to see over their heads to back and turn.

They arrived at the B&B to find Tomas waiting outside the studio, clinking together the wine bottles that he'd had the foresight to buy earlier. The new acknowledgement between the three women that Tomas was on the prowl made them giggly. Millie headed for the middle of the sofa in the barn lounge, and Luna and Alex dived next to her, leaving no room for Tomas.

'Suzie, would you like to sit with us?' Alex asked, squeezing up as Suzie entered the room, but Suzie shook her head and followed Tomas to help hunt down some wine glasses in the kitchen area. They returned triumphantly, and Tomas sat on his haunches on the rug, displaying his crotch to the three on the sofa, and uncorking the wine with his penknife. Suzie hovered around him, holding out glasses to be filled. He did so with the flourish of a tourists' waiter, showing off. When Suzie had passed the glasses round she knelt next to Tomas, attempting a graceful slide into a provocative lying position on her side. She puffed out her chest and let her top slip to show her cleavage. Something about sitting on the couch in a row watching this display, like birds mating, was hilarious. Luna knew Alex and Millie were finding it as funny as she was, the sofa shaking as they attempted to stifle their laughter.

After several of Danny's lethal spliffs the night grew more mellow. Despite their body wall of defence, Tomas managed to end up squeezed onto the sofa between Millie and Luna, and persisted, quite unashamedly, to come on to Luna. A friend of my mother's is trying to get off with me, she thought, trying to keep the facts straight in her warping mind. It was unbelievable. Through the haze she noticed that at some point Millie left for bed, Jon was trying to appear interested in an animated monologue from Suzie and Danny had drawn his armchair towards Alex, where they were, for some reason, examining each other's fingers in great detail. With Millie's absence, the feeling of coupledom with Tomas was increased. The wine and spliff had taken away control of her limbs, which felt as though they were melting into the sofa. She couldn't tell where her skin ended and the cushions began, they were one and the same. As for her mind — she couldn't form a sentence to tell him it wasn't OK. She became aware of

184

Tomas stroking her hair, his other hand on her thigh. His intensity was too much, his face too close. It reminded her of getting off with boys at foundation — the smell of tobacco and alcohol as they leaned in somehow attractive, the sweet anticipation that soon they would be moving in for a tentative first kiss. The awful thing was, she realized, she wanted to be kissed. Though not by Tomas.

With a great effort, she lurched up suddenly, her arms flaying forward to propel her off the couch.

'I need some air,' she mumbled, and picked her way to the barn door. Trying to walk, she realized how out of it she was. Nausea rose and the gravel drive tilted as she tried to focus. She drew in lungfuls of air as she leaned against the barn. Just as she began to feel herself steady up she heard the crunch of footsteps coming after her. She dared to look up, hoping it was Alex. But it was Tomas, as she knew it would be. He placed one arm above her on the barn wall and pulled her towards him with the other.

'Luna, you know I'm crazy about you,' he whispered into her ear, pushing his pelvis into her stomach.

Oh dear God. Of course he thought she was leading him on — 'I need some air,' she'd said. The absolute clichéd come-on when you were really saying, *Let's go outside*. She couldn't believe what she'd done. Tomas tried to kiss her and she attempted to push him away. But her arms were feeble as excuses.

'No, Tomas, that's not what I meant,' she tried.

'I know, I know,' he replied, inexplicably, as he pulled her hips into him and rubbed.

'Stop it!' she attempted to shout but it came out husky, like another come-on.

'We can't stop now, you know it,' he said, feverishly.

'I mean it!' Luna finally found her voice. 'Don't!'

'We must!' Tomas replied and pushed her back against the wall. Somehow he got his tongue in her mouth. Luna pushed against him with all her might, and he suddenly jolted backwards.

'Listen, pal, she said no.' It was Jon. He shoved Tomas as he spoke, overbalancing him so that he staggered comically in slow motion to the ground. Jon stood with his fist raised, ready for a fight. Tomas was in shock. He raised his hands in surrender as reality hit that he'd gone too far. He got to his feet looking dazed.

'What am I doing?' he said, melodramatically. He put his hand to his forehead. 'Luna,' he came towards her but she took a step back and Jon put out his arm to defend her. 'No, no, no,' Tomas said, arms outstretched. 'I'm not going to hurt her. I would never hurt my moon goddess! Oh Lord God, what must you think of me? I am some kind of monster tonight!'

'Oh Tomas, for God's sake, shut up,' she said, smoothing her shirt down as he clutched at his hair in despair. 'We're all just too fucking stoned.'

'But you must hate me for being like this,' he cried, 'having no respect for your person. I am despicable.'

'Just calm down, mate,' said Jon, sternly.

'OK, OK. I'm sorry, I'm sorry. Please accept my apology . . . '

'Look. Just go back inside. Leave her alone, all right?' Jon's tone was threatening and he moved towards Tomas.

Christ, he was going to hit him. Luna instinctively stepped forward too, thinking she should break it up. But, surprisingly, Tomas meekly followed Jon's orders. It was bizarre, so Neanderthal, to be pounced on by one male, who was then chased off by another. What the hell was going on? Luna would have laughed out loud if she wasn't so embarrassed, and suddenly sober. She and Jon stood awkwardly.

'You all right?' Jon asked.

'Yes. I'm fine,' Luna replied. 'It was my fault. I'm stupid.'

'You're not stupid,' said Jon. 'It was obvious you weren't interested. He's stupid for not realizing.' Luna felt a girlish gratitude towards him, which she tried not to show. 'Blinded by love, I suppose,' he added.

'He's not in love with me!' Luna said.

'I wouldn't bet on that,' said Jon. 'Surely you can see it? Or maybe you are stupid.'

Luna laughed. 'Stupid enough that he's the person I came here with. Fuck knows how I'm going to get home.'

'Shit. Do you want a lift?'

'You're not heading to London, are you?'

'No. But I will do if you're stranded.'

'Really? God. Thanks. But actually Alex'll be heading to London. In fact, I must catch her before she goes to bed in case she slopes off early in the morning.'

She started towards the door but Jon put his hand on her arm, walking before her like her protector. He poked his head into the lounge area, Luna peering round his shoulder. Danny and Alex had disappeared. Tomas was sitting on the floor leaning on Suzie's legs with his eyes closed, while she massaged his temples. Jon and Luna flinched back to remain unseen and grinned at each other. Luna shook her head. 'Unbelievable!' she mouthed. She coughed loudly.

'Goodnight, you two,' she smiled sweetly as she looked in again. Tomas jumped up guiltily and came towards Luna with a tortured, beseeching gesture, but she just raised her eyebrows and turned away.

'Yes, goodnight, Suzie,' Tomas called flamboyantly, as though he too was leaving. However, he didn't follow Luna and Jon. He was absurd.

On the B&B landing, the embarrassing sounds of moaning and a rhythmically squeaking bed were emanating from Alex's room, too loud to pretend not to hear. Luna winced as she caught Jon's eye.

'Breakfast is going to be interesting,' he remarked as they parted ways.

So, thought Luna as she thankfully closed her bedroom door behind her, turning the key in the lock. Danny and Alex. She felt a mild disappointment that there hadn't been anything special between herself and Danny after all, but it passed. She wasn't too stoned to realize that the flirtation hadn't really been about *him*, but some other thing that was going on with her. Something that perhaps Tomas had picked up on.

★ ★ ★

Luna lay awake, listening for sounds of Alex stirring. She didn't want to miss her lift. At five, when all was still, she hastily scribbled a note to that effect and tiptoed to Alex's room to slip it under the door. She showered, dressed and packed early so she was ready for immediate departure. As soon as she heard Babs in the kitchen she slipped downstairs and got the studio key off her, to tidy up and sort the work, ready for quick collection.

Back in her room she heard everybody rise and head downstairs for breakfast before Alex and Danny. Typical, that they would be having a lovers' morning together, when she needed to make a hasty exit. In the end she knocked at their door. Alex eventually opened it a crack, wrapped only in a sheet and an afterglow, looking at Luna with one gleaming eye.

'Not a good time,' she whispered huskily.

'Alex, I know, I'm sorry, but did you get my note? I've *got* to get a lift back to London with you. Please, I can't go with Tomas.'

Alex's eye widened. 'Well, I'm not going till later. Danny and I are spending the day together.' She grinned lasciviously. 'But, sure, if you're OK to hang around until this evening.'

Luna's heart sank. She wanted to be out of there.

'OK. See you later,' she said as she went back to her room, already making other plans. She couldn't stand to wait all day. She heard voices outside and car doors banging and then Millie trilling goodbye as she left. A knock at her door made her jump.

'Who is it?' she finally called out when there was another knock.

'Jon.'

She let him in and shut the door behind him.

'Tomas is skulking in the studio,' he said. 'I thought I'd take the opportunity to come and check you're all right before I go. For a lift and that.'

'Thanks,' said Luna. 'I can get a lift but Alex isn't going till later. I'm going to have to kick about somehow until then.'

'Offer of a lift's still there,' said Jon.

'No, really. It's too much to ask. Although . . . where's the nearest train station, do you know?' Luna suddenly brightened up at the thought. 'If you could get me to a station that'd be brilliant.'

'Sure — good idea. I'd be far happier not leaving you here with that . . . predator.' They planned to meet at his car in ten minutes, like escapees. Jon would smuggle her art out of the studio as well as his own. She got there as he was hefting her pieces into the back.

'They're pretty heavy,' he said. 'Are you sure you can manage them on the train?'

'I'll be fine,' said Luna automatically. 'I can get someone to pick me up at the other end.'

As they were about to leave Tomas rounded

the corner from the studio and saw them.

'I'm going home by train,' she said, looking at him evenly. 'I've got my work already.'

'Luna,' he said softly, so contritely she almost felt sorry for him. 'Please, let me give you a lift home. I know I did wrong and I am sorry. We must make up before we get back to our normal lifes.'

'It's OK, Tomas,' she replied. 'Let's just forget about it.'

'But . . . ' He was about to come forward but glanced at Jon, hovering watchfully behind Luna. 'What will I tell Angie why you're not with me coming home?'

'Tell her what you like,' Luna said. 'Not my problem.'

She felt a pang of guilt as she swung into the passenger seat of Jon's car, Tomas standing forlornly watching them go. Apart from the leching, he'd been great. It was a shame it had spoiled things. Jon passed her the road map to find the nearest train station as he skidded out of the drive.

'Well handled,' he said as they headed for the main road.

'Not really,' she replied. 'I could've gone back with him. He wouldn't have tried anything on. I've been overdramatic.'

'No you haven't,' said Jon. 'Not from what I saw last night. I wouldn't've been happy about you getting into a car with him.'

Luna glanced at him. Why he had taken on the role of protector with her she didn't know. Maybe he was the sort of guy who did that sort of thing for ladies. It made her smile. It seemed quaint and old-fashioned. But as she sat there next to him in his big safe car she had to admit it felt nice.

'What are you smiling about?' he asked.

'Oh nothing,' she said. 'I'm not usually such a damsel in distress.'

He laughed. 'No, I'm sure. You can look after yourself, I bet.' He said it in an admiring way, she thought. She busied herself with trying to find the nearest station.

'There's one at Wroxham,' she said. 'It looks tiny, but I'm sure I'll be able to get a connection. All trains lead to London eventually.'

'You don't want to be carting those heavy things around all over the place,' said Jon. He gestured to a road sign. 'Look — I've got to take the A47 past Norwich. Why don't I nip into Norwich station and drop you there? It'll save all the arsing about.'

'No, I'll be all right, honestly. It's too much out of your way.'

'No it's not. It'll probably be easier than trying to find some little station in the middle of nowhere. And then you might not get home till Wednesday.'

He drove on. It seemed to have been decided, without her agreeing to it. She wondered if she minded but found she didn't. It was just good to be chauffeured out of there. She put down the map and sat back, watching the roads gradually widen as they left the sandy tracks of the coast and glided towards the dual carriageway.

At the station Jon insisted on carrying her bag

as well as her paintings onto the platform, and waited with her for the twenty minutes until the train to Liverpool Street.

'I'll be fine — you don't have to wait,' she protested.

'I'll help you on with your paintings. I'm in no hurry,' he replied.

There was no arguing with him. He was decisive, seemed used to having the final say.

'Why don't you call someone now to come and get you?' he suggested, but Luna didn't feel quite like speaking to Pierre yet, in front of him.

'It's OK, I'll call from the train,' she said. 'I don't live far from Liverpool Street.'

After an awkward pause he added, 'Look, I really didn't mean to insult you in my painting. If it helps make it up to you, I'm in awe of your work.' Luna reddened.

'Thank you,' she said. 'Actually, the feeling's mutual.' He wrinkled his nose in dissatisfaction with his own work.

'Don't humour me,' he said.

'I'm not,' she said. 'I do really like your pieces. The first one was just beautiful — really strong composition and such a delicate . . . theme. And my portrait — I know I got offended, but . . . It was clever, you know. I'd have been pleased with it if I'd done it as a self-portrait.'

'Would you?' he said, doubtfully, but with a hint of hope that she might mean it. 'How much would you sell your portrait of me for?' he hurriedly added. Luna was taken aback. 'If I wanted to buy it. How much would you sell it for?'

Luna searched his face to see if he meant it but couldn't read him.

'I want to buy it,' he clarified. 'How much?'

'It's not for sale,' Luna finally said. 'How about swapping it for yours of me?'

'Oh no,' he said emphatically.

'Why not?' she asked, laughing.

'Mine's just not . . . it wouldn't be a fair swap. I wouldn't like you to have mine of you. It doesn't catch you right at all.'

The announcement for Luna's train interrupted them and they both turned to watch it entering the station.

'I'd like to paint you again,' Jon blurted as they gathered her stuff to get on the train. 'Properly this time.'

Luna didn't answer. She was too flustered, preoccupied with lifting her things into the carriage to think about what he was asking. There was suddenly not enough time. As he closed the door behind her Jon motioned for her to open the window. He passed her a business card through it.

'Email me,' he said. 'Please. I really want to paint you again.'

'All right,' said Luna. They stood, not knowing how to say goodbye through the window. The moment seemed to have become heavy with significance, but that was silly. They were just unlikely people who had met on a weekend, strangers. 'Thanks,' she added. 'For the lift and everything.'

'No biggie,' he replied. The train began to move and he raised his hand in a wave, watching her as it pulled her away.

★  ★  ★

There was a message from Angie when she got home asking how the weekend went, but Luna still wasn't speaking to her.

'She's trying to make up with you,' Pierre said gently. 'Can't you let it go?'

'How can I?' Luna said. 'She didn't want me. I was a weight around her neck, but she just carried on trying to live her life as though I wasn't there. And now that I've realized she feels guilty and wants me to make her feel better. Why should I?'

'You don't know all that,' Pierre tried.

'I do,' said Luna. 'I've felt it all my life, without really understanding what the feeling was. But I can see it for myself in the photographs. As soon as I saw them I knew it was true.'

'Perhaps you're reading too much into the pictures. They're just snapshots, Luna. Of moments. They don't necessarily tell the whole story.'

'Well, they tell me a damned sight more than my mother ever has,' Luna snapped. 'They're all I've got to go on. I trust them a lot more than anything she says.'

She stormed up to her studio. She felt changed by the weekend, expanded beyond the constraints of her life before it, and now it seemed impossible that she could somehow fit back in, like a Pac-a-mac. She tried to feel more empathy towards her mother, tried to believe that what Pierre said was true. But as she looked at her minimal gallery of photographs, if anything she felt more aggrieved than ever. The photograph she had placed third in the row was of Angie pregnant with her. Now that the only thing that mattered to Luna was having a child, her own mother looking so downright miserable with her added insult to injury. Not only that, she was smoking a fucking joint. Surely by 1971 they knew you shouldn't smoke when you were pregnant? Even if they didn't, it had to be blindingly obvious that getting stoned wasn't the best idea.

Angie was slumped carelessly in a beanbag, using her bump to lean her elbows on, the joint dangling from her fingertips looking as if she might drop it at any minute, without the slightest care for herself or her unborn baby. There was a neglected air about her, as though she had given up caring for herself at all now that her body had been invaded by this other being. She was draped in baggy things and blankets like an old bag, and her hair was lank and dark, unwashed.

She appeared to have just that second looked up, realized through her stoned haze that she was being photographed. She hadn't had time to rearrange her face, and the camera had caught an expression that chilled Luna, darting resentment and hostility towards the lens, and through it, on the other side, her father. Everything about her, her look, her demeanour, said, *You bastard, look what you've done to me. Now fuck off.* The picture said it all, as far as Luna was concerned. She felt the strongest connection with her father then, like he was trying to communicate with her through time, from that past into this future, when Luna would see the picture and realize the truth of how it was for him, why he never had the chance to be close to his daughter.

# 1971

# Angie

Every few months, a group of the women drove together into town to attend the Family Planning Clinic for their contraceptive pills. They attracted a great deal of unpleasant attention when they did. In the street, people always stared at their long wild hair and strange, brightly coloured clothes, and in the clinic itself other women tutted and commented under their breath and moved away. The doctors themselves were only just civil, sometimes not even that, as their disapproval filled the room like a bad smell. Sometimes they gave them lectures about the health risks of promiscuity and gave them details of the Special Clinic to get check-ups, as though they were prostitutes, as though the love they expressed together was some sordid business exchange.

It never bothered Angie, in fact she quite enjoyed it. She felt sorry for everyone else, if anything. They had no idea of the glorious bliss that came with true liberation — sexual, social, emotional. They seemed so constrained, these people, so uptight and unhappy with their crushing ideas of right and wrong. Their morals were like cages. They were jealous of the love the Children of Ceres exuded as they held hands openly, chatted and laughed together, refusing to sit quietly like the others, who looked down guiltily and twisted their wedding bands. Because of the Pill, women were able to enjoy their sexuality in a way they had never been able to do before for fear of unwanted pregnancy, and this was a cause for celebration, not shame.

Angie was unlucky though. As the months wore on she found her body didn't react well to the Pill. She often felt nauseous and was afflicted with headaches, and she put on weight. At first she was pleased with her fuller breasts, but they became sore to the touch, heavy and uncomfortable without a bra, her nipples scratched by cheesecloth and wool. She tried her best to accept her new flesh as part of her womanhood, adhering to the group's ethos of loving yourself as you were, regardless of society's ideals. But the flesh around her hips and stomach didn't feel like her. The real her was buried underneath it somewhere. It made her feel bloated and inhibited, especially when Dave seized a handful and wobbled it. Some of the men enjoyed it more, but not him. He'd liked her as she was. She noticed that in the lovemaking he was drawn towards Poppy and Star, the skinny girls. Angie tried to overcome her jealousy. People were allowed their sexual preferences. It didn't mean he loved her less.

They saw dieting as a form of oppression, but even so Angie secretly ate less and less, skipping meals when she could get away with it, always opting for the most physical jobs on the farm. She was glad when autumn rolled round again and she could more easily hide her body with thick baggy clothes.

Along with provisions, Allun brought a vile sickness bug back with him after trading in town, which of course went round everyone at the farm like wildfire, adults and children alike. Probably because of overexertion and undernourishment, Angie was particularly badly stricken. She was given one of the private rooms for far longer than anyone else and had to stay in bed for days, too weak to help out and unable to keep anything down. Although she felt awful, it was at least pleasing to feel her stomach flatten under her palms. When Dave climbed up to join her one night during her recovery — tired of the countless sleep interruptions from coughs and phlegmy snores and children's wailing in the main bedroom — she felt proud of herself again under his touch.

Despite the physical ecstasy she experienced in the group lovemaking, it felt profound and intense to express feelings one to one with Dave again. She did love everybody, of course, but in her heart of hearts there was only him, he was the only one who could make her feel so special. They made slow, silent love for hours into the night, and when he finally slept she lay in his embrace, feeling their breaths rising and falling in time.

As early as the following morning, she felt the change in her. It manifested itself a few weeks later, when she became violently sick again. It was Hazel who first recognized the signs as something other than the bug. She took advantage of a quiet morning, when most people had left for the fields or the market, and asked if she was pregnant. Angie knew she was, even though she shouldn't be.

'I don't know how,' she said. 'I've been taking the Pill.' 'It's not always effective if you're sick,' said Hazel. 'But you didn't make love then, did you? Weren't you up in the loft?'

Angie looked at her. 'Yes I was,' she replied. 'But not always alone.'

★  ★  ★

Hugh was especially happy about it.

'It's about time we had a new Child of Ceres,' he beamed. 'The other children are growing up so fast. It'll be the first one actually born in our community!' He organized an impromptu celebration for that evening, despite Angie's request to tell Dave privately, keep it between themselves for a while longer first.

'There are no secrets here,' Hugh said. 'You are special as the child's life-givers. But never forget it does not belong to you.'

Angie was then so swept up in the preparations she was unable to give it another thought. As it was the first conception, they had to quickly invent a Creation of Life Ceremony. All their big celebrations — the solstices, the harvest, the first buds of spring — were held outside under the night sky around a big bonfire. Hugh set Fern and the children the task of finding apt songs and poems to read, a piece about the goddess Ceres, a Khalil Gibran quote.

He organized the other women to prepare a feast for the occasion and dress and adorn the mother, while he hid himself away for an hour or two to write a dedication to the new life.

'What's going on?' Dave asked Fern on his return at dusk.

'I can't say,' said Fern excitedly. 'Hugh's going to announce it at the celebration.'

'Celebration of what?' asked Dave, but she just smiled as she rushed past him with her clutch of straw to the hangout, from where he heard conspiratorial giggles as she made sure she closed the curtain behind her.

Autumn made it difficult at first to think what symbols for new life they could use.

'It would have been a lot easier if you could have timed this for spring,' Hazel moaned to Angie.

'But you know what's far out?' said Fern, coming in breathlessly. 'It's a full moon tonight! Doesn't that symbolize the child-bearing woman? How, like, perfect is that?' The other women wowed in appreciation.

'That's so amazing!' breathed Star.

They used silver to represent the moon, hanging Angie with as much silver jewellery as they could find, as well as daubing her and themselves with silver make-up. Fern and Hazel made corn dolls as good-luck charms for the baby's growth over the winter and summer arrival. In the kitchen, they made up a stew with every bean and vegetable they had, to imbibe the nourishment of the fruits of the earth, with whole bulbs of garlic for protection and baby-shaped dumplings. They decided apples were the perfect symbol of life and set about baking enormous apple pies, which would be served with copious amounts of cream — an obvious sexual reference that delighted the women into much throaty laughter.

★  ★  ★

The ceremony was beautiful. It was a perfect, cloudless night, the full moon sending an ethereal glow over the scene, the stars like holes poked through from heaven. Hugh made the announcement as they gathered round the fire and gave the blessing he'd written to the new Child of Ceres. They ate before the readings and singing, cracking open the turnip wine a couple of the guys had attempted to make — which was disgusting, but lethal.

It was the best night of Angie's life. She was not only part of the universe, she was at its very heart. Everyone was celebrating her, the power she had to create life. She realized the miracle of it all and was so happy to be bringing this child into their utopia, surrounded by nature's gifts and love. They were truly blessed, she and her baby.

She didn't have a chance to connect with Dave alone all evening, as he whirled about documenting the event with his camera. He had kissed her stomach to welcome the new being, but then so had everyone else, in a circle moving around her. She battled through her fatigue to the end of the night to catch her moment with him. She sat on the ground next to him as he gently strummed a guitar by the dying embers.

'I'm sorry I couldn't tell you myself, alone,' she said quietly.

'Why?' he said. 'Don't be.'

'I just wanted to. I thought it was right that you knew before everyone else. But Hugh said no.'

Dave looked up at her, uncomprehending. 'Why should I know first?'

'Well, you know — being the father,' Angie smiled. Dave looked at her for a moment, then back down to the guitar.

'Oh right. Yeah, well.' He gave a small shrug as he carried on playing. 'Maybe I am. Who could know, though, for sure?'

Angie was taken aback. 'Well — I know. Of course I know.'

'You can't possibly know,' he replied. His voice was calm and low — offhand even.

'I do,' Angie insisted. 'It must have happened that night, that last time we were together alone.'

'Why then? Why not the time before with someone else? Or one of the times after?'

'Because I haven't . . . ' Angie thought about it. It hadn't occurred to her that one of the other men could be the father. But she was absolutely sure. 'I haven't been with anyone else since. And it couldn't have been before, because I was on the Pill — '

'Yes, what about that?' Dave interrupted, smoothly. He stopped playing abruptly, his hands on the strings to still the sound. He lowered his voice in the silence. 'That's what I

204

thought. You were on the Pill. So how did it happen, exactly?' There was enough light to catch a glint of accusation in his eyes.

'Well, that's the thing. Hazel told me it's not always effective when you're sick. But I didn't know.'

'Right,' he said. 'Might be the sorta thing you should know, don't you think?'

Angie thought she could make out a small smile on his face, and gave a little laugh. 'Yeah.'

There was an awkward pause. His smile, if it had been there, had gone.

'Hugh's really happy about it,' Angie added, as though that would somehow make Dave happy too.

'Great,' he said. He sounded like he meant it, but was it sarcasm? She couldn't read his voice at all. 'Maybe it's his?' he added, pleasantly.

'It isn't!' Angie said. 'It can only be yours.'

'His, mine . . . ' Dave said, swinging the guitar upright and leaning on it as he uncrossed his legs and stood, stretching. She looked up at his dark frame, looming over her like a shadow of doubt. He smoothed her hair and lifted her chin. 'Roger's, Allun's, Martin's . . . doesn't matter! That's just it, babe. What we're trying to get away from here. Nobody owns it. It's a beautiful child of the world, man. We'll all love it equally, right?'

Angie said nothing.

'Right?' he said again. She nodded.

'Sure,' she said. 'Of course. I just thought . . . '

But he was already bending and kissing her forehead to say goodnight.

'Hush, my beautiful Angel,' he said as he swung the guitar over his shoulder and headed inside.

★ ★ ★

With the first pregnancy, new issues arose that the group discussed in their morning meeting. There was some debate about what was cool and what wasn't with regards to the lovemaking. Angie being pregnant seemed to throw people. Hazel, for example, had a problem with Angie fucking a lot of guys when she was with child. She was shouted down by some of the guys as being repressed by convention; there was no physical reason why Angie shouldn't — in fact it was probably healthy for the baby that she should. Hugh was particularly adamant that the baby — and Angie, of course — should feel the love from all of them, and their most visceral, joyous way of expressing that was through sex. Why should she be left out? She wasn't ill. That seemed like rejection. It was peculiar for Angie to feel that her body belonged to the community as much as it did to her.

It was Fern who finally said, 'Isn't it kinda up to Angel? What feels right for her?'

★ ★ ★

As it turned out, it was the baby who decided, at least in the first trimester. Angie was the sickest she had ever been, too fragile to even think about sex.

'Poor you, you're unlucky to get it so bad,' Hazel comforted her as she threw up for the umpteenth time. Her morning sickness wasn't only confined to the mornings, it was throughout the day and night. Angie could hardly bear to be touched, she was so nauseous and sore. Her skin reacted badly, becoming oily and breaking out in rashes and spots. Her luscious hair became lank and straight and greasy, and when she washed it great handfuls came away. She also bled sometimes, and Hazel insisted she was excused from all duties. She spent these times just lying on the beanbags, like an ill cat. She had cravings for meat and salt, both of which were absent from the commune. Hazel, a former nurse, was so concerned for her nutrition that she ordered that vegetarian house rules were broken, and sent someone on a mission to the butcher's.

The baby took over her body like an alien invader. Angie felt all her energy being sucked into her centre, as though all that remained of herself was a husk. Yet despite it all, she was happy. She didn't mind being used by this miraculous creature inside her. She would lie stroking it through her belly, telling it stories and singing. Along with all her energy, she felt a breathtakingly fierce force of love surge towards the being, like radiation. And she in turn was replenished by the love of the community around her. As her body cradled this new person, so the family cradled her. She couldn't imagine how women coped in the normal world, with just their husband out all day at work, expecting dinner when he got home, and only their mother, or, worse still, their mother-in-law, for support. It was better this way. Dave was as kind to her as everybody else. But no more. Up in her private loft, when she heard the sounds of love begin in the room below, she tried not to think about who he was with, as the waves of nausea lurched up and she groped for the bucket by the bed.

★　★　★

Hugh was big on creativity and self-expression. Art, writing, photography — not only for its own sake, but so that there was a good account of life on the commune, for history. He himself wrote a detailed journal, and encouraged others to do so too. He was very into the idea of keeping an extensive photographic record. Although the camera, like everything, theoretically belonged to everyone, it had been Dave who had brought it in with him. Although it wasn't his possession, nobody else really knew how to use it and he had become the chief chronicler. He'd persuaded Hugh to spend out on a dark room in the cellar, so that they themselves could print those photographs that would probably have alerted police attention if they'd sent them off to the Kodak lab. He got more and more serious in his dedication to the art form, and hardly ever did anything without the camera around his neck. He would often enter a room with it already raised in front of his face, to capture people in a natural state, before they became self-conscious in front of it.

Angie began to resent it. It was as though he wore it like a mask, so that he could remain an unreachable observer behind it, there yet not there. It was like the embodiment of the intangible barrier he placed between them, a one-way barrier, like a peep show, where the woman was on view, exposed, but with no idea of who the voyeur was.

He was obsessed with capturing the 'reality' of things, which for him seemed to mean snapping people unawares in vulnerable moments, a child crying, someone naked pulling on a sock in an unflattering position — even Angie when she was bent over the toilet bowl throwing up. She found it invasive, and tried to say so in a morning meeting. But Hugh urged her to allow it, for the common good.

'We must have records of what we're doing here, people,' he said. 'It's revolutionary. We're making history, man. One of the first groups to be changing society. They'll look back on this in the future and see where it all began, that we were the first. It's really important.'

Dave was hurt that she'd brought it up in front of everyone.

'You could have just asked me, man,' he said coolly afterwards. 'I thought you'd have wanted pictures of you with your baby, but hey.'

'I do,' said Angie. 'Just not always the bad side of it, when I'm at my worst.'

'We gotta keep it real,' said Dave. 'But, yeah, let me know when you think you're at your best and I'll try and get there in time.'

His comment was ambiguous at best, but

when Angie looked at him he smiled warmly.

'Or if you wanna be left alone, that's totally cool with me.' His offhand shrug. He did that often these days, so much so that it was almost a tic.

After that he mostly ignored her. She found that being watched at her worst was better than not being seen at all. He would still take the odd perfunctory shot, for Hugh's all-important records. Angie tried to tell herself she was being paranoid — it was her hormones — but still she was sure he only pointed his camera to her when she was looking bad. She found herself searching out the lens on days she was feeling good, with newly washed hair, or a pretty dress. But he would only smile at her then, as though he knew what she wanted, the camera resting firmly against his chest until he looked around, always somehow finding something more interesting to his photographer's eye. It seemed to become a game to him, one that he would always win, with the camera as his weapon, as unbeatable as a gun.

The last time she was ill before her second trimester, before she began to grow strong and blossom at last, she sat alone in the hang-out with a streaming cold and a thumping headache. She had come to lie down in the quiet, away from the others in the noisy, too-bright kitchen, hoping a couple of secret puffs of blow would dull the pain. She had given up smoking, tobacco and weed, as soon as she'd fallen pregnant. She was too ill and also too happy to miss it. But her recent insomnia was exhausting her, and she yearned for just one decent night's sleep. When she heard footsteps in the corridor, she just knew it would be Dave. He'd joked at the table about how terrible she looked, had noticed when she slipped away. She was in no mood for the game.

'Don't photograph me now,' she ordered, as she heard his steps approach. The curtain at the door flicked and at the same time the camera lens poked through, Dave's fingers turning the focus round.

'I said, DON'T!' Angie shouted, furious, staring at the lens defiantly. She was too weak and fat and in pain to move.

The shutter clicked.

'Why do you do that?' Angie shouted. She tried to struggle out of the beanbag, but it held her prisoner as she wriggled. Dave laughed, whether at her flailing like a woodlouse on its back or because he thought he was cute and funny, she didn't know.

'Hey, cool it,' he said. 'You don't wanna harm your baby.'

Your baby. He always called it that.

# 1997

## Nat

'Fuck off, you little bastard.'

Tyler had climbed onto the bed and was trying to prise Lee's eyes open to wake him up. There was a thump as Tyler accidentally tipped off the bed and hit the floor. He started wailing. Nat sat up groggily.

'Fuck's sake, Nat, get him out of here,' said Lee, rolling over and putting his head under the pillow.

'What the fuck did you do to him?' said Nat. 'It's OK, Ty. I'm coming.'

She got out of bed and tried to scoop Tyler up to take him out of the room, but Tyler fought her as usual.

'No, no, NO!' he shouted, punching out with his fists, catching Nat in the stomach. He gave his piercing scream.

'Shut the fuck UP!' Lee yelled, kicking out from under the duvet in their direction.

Nat caught hold of one of Tyler's wrists, secured it with both hands and began to drag him across the floor to the door. He tried to twist round on his bottom so that he could stop her with his feet, kicking at her legs and stomping the tops of her feet with his heels.

'OW! Stop it,' Nat ordered.

He bit the back of her hand to make her let go. It worked, but she managed to hold on still with the other one. She cuffed him round the head with her free, stinging hand.

'I said, STOP IT,' she shouted. She pulled harder. Tyler screamed louder. He wedged his feet against the door frame so that Nat couldn't pull him through.

'FUCK'S SAKE!' Lee shouted, slamming out of bed. He grabbed Tyler's legs at the ankles and took them off the door frame, and the force of Nat pulling his arm slid him along the floor on his back. Lee slammed the bedroom door and went back to bed.

Another wail started up from the kids' room.

'Now look what you've fucking done, you idiot,' said Nat, dropping Tyler's wrist and leaving him to have his tantrum on the hall floor. She went into the kids' room and picked up the baby, jiggling it up and down mechanically as she went through to the kitchen. She picked up the long roach on the ashtray, lit it and took a toke to calm her nerves, trying to block out the cries, one kid in each ear, like stereo. She put milk into Jade's bottle and warmed it in the microwave, placing her in the baby chair. She was a good baby, so quiet she hadn't even tried to talk yet, much easier than Tyler. When she cried Nat could always shut her up with her bottle or a pacifier. She'd never been able to do that with Tyler. He'd always fought her over everything, never stopped making a noise. Even before he'd been able to get around by himself she'd had a nightmare just getting a nappy on

213

him while he squirmed and kicked angrily. Now he was impossible to control, a whirr of limbs, into everything. She looked at her watch on the table. They were late again.

She gave Jade the bottle and went to dress Tyler.

'Come on, it's time for school,' she said, taking her advantage while he lay flat out with his face on the floor, grabbing him from behind. He tried to make himself stiff and heavy to resist her, but she got his hips between her legs and managed to slide him forward on his knees.

'I'm hungry,' he shouted.

'You can't have anything till you got your clothes on,' said Nat, dropping his weight on the bedroom floor.

He was almost too big for her to handle now. She couldn't always win. Her body was permanently sore, bruised and scarred from their battles. She thought she'd got away from all that. She picked up his jeans and top from the floor and chucked them at him. Rooting around on his bed for his pants, she felt that he'd wet it again.

'Tyler!' She swung round, grabbed him by the shoulders and shook him. 'How many times do I have to tell you? That's NAUGHTY!'

Tyler's face twisted as though he was about to cry, then twisted again. He screwed his eyes up hatefully. Nat flinched automatically, expecting a kick or a thump. Instead Tyler spat, laughed as his drool hit Nat's face.

'You little SHIT!' She gave him another shake, harder than she meant to, and let him go so that he fell backwards, banging his head on the floor. He let out an angry shout and kicked at her, but she had already sidestepped him. She got to the door, swinging it shut behind her before he could get his hands and feet in the way to prise it open. 'You're not coming out till you're dressed,' she said, locking the door. 'Then you can have something to eat.'

She went to the bathroom, finally had the piss she was desperate for, put on her trackies and stood in front of the mirror scraping her hair back into a ponytail. The shadows under her eyes were darker than ever but she didn't have time to put on make-up. Even if she did, she couldn't be bothered. Hopefully she could go back to bed and crash once she'd dropped Tyler off.

When she opened Tyler's door again he still wasn't dressed so she wrestled his clothes onto him, cajoling him now with offers of biscuits, which made his limbs more compliant as she thrust them into sleeves and legs. In the kitchen, she gave him the rest of the packet to keep him still while she put on his reins to stop him running into the road. Jade had finished her bottle and dropped it and was trying to wriggle out of her chair. Nat found a pacifier in the sink, rinsed it off and plugged it into her mouth.

'I'm taking Tyler to school,' she called. The baby would be all right for five minutes.

★　★　★

Nat let Tyler go from his straps, corralling him into running in the right direction down the

215

corridor. She turned and left quickly, before Tyler could decide he didn't want to be there and came screaming back after her, before the teacher saw her and came out to say something about the time. Once out of sight of the school, Nat felt the calmness come down over her nerves. She dawdled along the street, not wanting it to end too soon, savouring the lightness. What would she do today if she could? Jump on a bus, literally jump on, without having to hold everyone up as she folded down the pushchair and tried to heave it on with one arm while carrying a child with the other. Just her. She'd go to a shopping centre maybe, somewhere massive like Brent Cross, spend the whole day trying stuff on, without the ordeal of buggies and feeding and nappy changing and tantrums. Every day she tried to think of somewhere different she would go — the seaside, a funfair, the pictures. Sometimes it was a job. An office, where she'd wear a smart suit and high heels, or a shop where she could be more funky. Probably a shop. When Jade was older and going to school with Ty, she'd be able to get a part-time job. It would all get easier when they were older. Tyler would calm down, and Jade wouldn't be any trouble. And Nat would still be young enough to start her life.

She walked an extra time around the block for the few minutes more of freedom. As she got close to home, she felt the tightness return, gripping her insides and squeezing with the strength of a man's hands.

She heard the baby screaming before she even

got to the door. In the kitchen, the high chair was on its side. Jade, with one leg still trapped by it, was lying on the kitchen floor with blood on her forehead where it had hit the cupboard as she tipped. Lee hadn't even woken up.

# FOUR

*A painting. A woman at a window, looking out.*

She sits on an old wooden chair, leaning forward with her arms on the sill, a loose dress draping over her form to her feet, which are bare. Her hair is swept up at the back to reveal the nape of her neck, stray locks falling around her shoulders. Her face is in profile, highlighted against the glass.

The large window takes up most of the painting, placed at the very centre of it, looking out onto a dark sky. All that can be seen of the room surrounds the window at the edges of the painting: the bare white walls, the lack of curtains, the unpolished floorboards, a discarded stocking. The perspective of the lines of the floorboards leads the eye up to the woman's feet, taking in the figure tilting forward and following her gaze through the window, but we do not know what she can see outside.

It is lighter inside than it is out. Because of this all that can be seen through the window is the artist's reflection suspended in mid-air in one of the panes. He half-sits against a tall stool, painting at an easel. The way he is painted contrasts with the detail of the woman — each contour, each lock of hair, each toenail, each fold of her dress, painstakingly captured. His figure, a barely-there impression.

# 2003

# Luna

Impatience tugged at Luna like little hands. That first night back home, she stood in the bathroom and popped the first pill of her next packet after the seven-day break. Instead of taking it she turned on the cold tap and watched the water gather the tablet in its stride and slip it down the plughole. What did the Pill do to you anyway? She couldn't remember how it stopped you getting pregnant. She had known once, she was sure. She had begun to take it as soon as she was old enough, under Angie's advice. She knew she had armed herself with all the facts about what the Pill did then, but whatever they were, it hadn't bothered her. Did it make your body think it was in a constant state of pregnancy already? She had that in her mind, somehow. If it did, she was suddenly repulsed. All these years, she had been playing this awful trick on her body. It seemed really wrong, some sort of abuse. She remembered the sand she was bleeding in her dream, while the blood all around her was outside the glass dome she was trapped in. The imagery was stark, unsubtle. It felt as much of an omen as a big black crow crashing through the window.

The next night she did the same, feeling a sense of control returning. Why shouldn't she be the one to steer her life? And then, the night after that, there was no going back.

★ ★ ★

She remembered to email Jon, to thank him again for the lift to the station. *And,* she added, *for intervening so masterfully when Tomas got out of hand.* It made her grin, and imagined it would do the same to him — that blink-and-you-miss-it amused twitch at the side of his mouth. She also wrote about the train journey home — how the plastic bottle with the dismembered head had been jiggled off on the train and rolled away, causing great consternation to an elderly lady who picked it up for her. It had led to a good conversation though, when she'd explained what it was, about the lives of women then and now. They'd swapped phone numbers by the end of the journey. She'd had to get a cab home as nobody was around to pick her up.

He wrote back the same day.

> No problem. I'm glad I got the chance to apologize for my shite portrait of you. It wasn't a true likeness. I was just trying to be clever. I meant it when I said I really like your art. And seriously, would you consider selling your portrait of me? I know how much your work goes for, so don't be shy about the price. Jon

She sat in her studio, considering the portrait and wondering how he had known about her

224

prices. She felt foolishly pleased at the thought he'd Googled her when he'd got home. She couldn't decide on a price, and knew she should really go through her agent, but . . . Even though he would price it higher than she would, he would still take his half, making her no better off. If she sold it to Jon herself she could get more for it than a percentage, and it would do Jon a favour too. But still, she couldn't come up with a figure. Partly it was because it felt unfair to charge him for a piece that she'd done as a student on a course and which had taken only a day to complete. And partly because she was strangely attached to it and wasn't sure she wanted to let it go. Why, she couldn't say. She was proud of it, certainly, and it perhaps marked a moment that she considered a breakthrough. So much so that she couldn't think why on earth she hadn't thought outside paint in her work until now. Somehow the use of collage, however naive it had been, had loosened her, broken her free.

She had returned easily to her painting when she'd got back from Tomas's weekend, even pulling a sickie at Trey's to get on with Amelia. She worked into the night and survived on little sleep, the way she could when she was inspired. The solution to finishing the portrait seemed so obvious on her return it was practically crying out to her. The second she looked at it, it seemed peculiarly dull and flat, despite the colour in it, like an old painting whose gilt had worn off with time. It needed shiny gold. With a nod to the religious paintings of the madonna and child of past centuries, she finished Amelia as a kind of graven image under a sacrilegious gilt halo, her children as a pair of cherubic gilt Jesuses placed on her lap in each arm. Luna spent hours perfecting the way she dangled them from each of Amelia's ears, as though they were jewellery. It gave Luna the secret satisfaction of saying something in her work, and doing it in such a way that Amelia would only be pleased with it. It gave her a buzz, as she painstakingly finished every golden curl of the children's heads, to half-disguise the hoops attached to Amelia's earlobes. It didn't matter if nobody else saw them, as long as she herself knew they were there.

It made all the difference, somehow. She worked every moment she had over the days after the course, completely focused and adrift from the rest of life, the way it was when art was going well, the way it should be. Art meant something when it took you over like this, and it was an enormous relief to reconnect with the person she had always been, the person she thought she had lost. She hardly noticed Pierre. Or was it that she didn't care that he hardly noticed her? While she was away he had found the way of working the pieces for his show, making the cubes in transparent plastic and melding them together. He was utterly absorbed, and while they both worked this way their relationship seemed back on track. Luna could push aside the thought that they weren't a proper couple but two individuals who only slotted in together because they both had the same uncompromising attitude, and could put up with it in each other. When one of them flagged — when *she* had flagged, at any rate — it had suddenly seemed that there was nothing between them but a shared space and a mutual self-absorption. It was a relief to feel the passion again, if only for the fact that it balanced out Pierre's. During the previous weeks everything had been aslant, like being too light on a see-saw, wriggling helplessly in the air.

But it didn't matter now. She was happy again to race up there when she came home from Trey's, happy not to bother with mealtimes, or any kind of interaction with Pea.

There were still details to finish on Amelia, and she wanted to frame it too, in a heavy, gold, old-fashioned gallery-style frame, to enhance the nod to classic works. Something in the style of it had reminded her of Botticelli's *Venus* — she thought probably the turquoise colour of the sky against the gold hair, the pinks of the flowers — and she'd pored over books of his work to further enhance the reference, defining the detail in the curls of the hair and the leaves of the garden trees, adding flowers floating in the air. It was a nice touch that the art aficionados among Amelia's friends would appreciate. She'd got the light in the garden right, the honeyed soft afternoon glow that lit up the faces, which Amelia would find flattering. It gave her a saintly quality as she looked benevolently on her dangling offspring. Luna was sure Amelia would be unaware of the cynical undertones that Luna had added, creeping through the garden around her — symbols that she hoped were discreet and obscure enough to get past her *patron*. It pleased her immensely. She felt she'd discovered the cunning of creating the perfect commission, producing a work that satisfied both the client and the painter, not necessarily for the same reasons.

She needed another opinion before she showed it to Julian — another expert opinion, from someone who wouldn't mince his words — and for this it was Pierre to whom she usually turned.

'It's not finished yet,' she said, as she ushered him into her room, feeling the need to apologize. He did his best to focus on it, although his mind was obviously still on his own work. He stared at it, moving up close, touching the gilt, then standing back.

'Yep,' he nodded, finally. 'I think Amelia'll love it.'

'Right,' said Luna. 'OK. That sounds good. I think. Is that good?' She gave a half laugh.

'Of course it's good,' he said, hanging at the door in an I'm-not-stopping pose. 'You gotta give the client what they want.'

Luna looked at him.

'Er . . . but what do you think of it? That's what I'm asking, really.'

'It's good, Luie,' he said impatiently. 'You know I think your work's good.'

'But that's a generalization,' she said. 'Not everything I do is 'good'. And anyway, it's nothing like my usual style, and I'm not sure that I am giving the client what they want in this piece. Can you see anything . . . she might not like about it?'

'No,' he said, casting his eye quickly over the painting again. 'What wouldn't she like?'

'*Look*,' Luna said. 'Look properly.'

She felt him control a sigh as he forced himself to regard the portrait again.

'Luna, I really can't see anything she wouldn't like. Although that tree there doesn't seem the right perspective compared to the roses. Aren't they nearer the foreground?'

'Yeah,' said Luna. 'That's the bit I haven't finished yet.'

'All right then,' said Pierre, already turning to head down the corridor to his own studio.

'Pea,' Luna said exasperatedly to his leaving back. 'What do you think of it?'

She saw his shoulders tense as he turned around to face her and reply.

'Lu.' He came and placed his hands on the tops of her arms. 'You don't need me to validate your work. You should be able to see for yourself that you've executed a very fine commission for a difficult client. I think you've done brilliantly. But what I think is neither here nor there.'

'So you don't like it?'

'For fuck's sake, Lu! When did you become the sort of woman who fishes for praise? I've always liked it in you that you've known when a piece is good enough or not — to your own standards and judgement.'

'I'm only asking what you think of it. I'm allowed to do that, aren't I? You've never had a problem giving your opinion before.'

229

'I think it's really good. That's my opinion. OK?'

Luna didn't respond.

'OK?' he said again.

'OK,' she said, and let him go. But she was left feeling unsure of herself. She looked at the painting again. Was it crass? She really couldn't tell. Pierre was right though — she had never *needed* other people's opinions before. But then, Pea had always happily given them, without her having to dig for them in such a needy way. Still she felt she wanted a proper opinion before Julian saw it, let alone Amelia. She was pretty sure Amelia wouldn't decipher her hidden meanings, especially as Pea hadn't. But then, Pea hadn't gazed at it at any length, the way she was sure Amelia would, for days and months and years. If things hadn't got so ballsed up with Tomas she could have asked him. Whatever he was like as a man, she valued his artistic opinion. But still — there was the matter of what he was like as a man, all the same.

She wondered about asking Alex. She hadn't yet met up with her, although they had been in email contact, catching up with each other on how the weekend had panned out for both of them. Alex had had a blissfully romantic Monday with Danny, having lots more sex in the morning, going for a stroll on the beach, booking another night in the B&B and having lots more sex again. Luna wrote a suitably contrasting droll account of her time with Tomas and Jon Booker and her ensuing struggle home with her canvasses, which amused Alex greatly, but left

Luna feeling uncharacteristically jealous.

She wasn't enjoying her new friend as much as she hoped she would, finding it strangely painful to hear about Alex's new romance. They were trying to find time to hook up, but Danny was coming to London for the weekend, and although Luna could easily have met for a drink one evening in the week she'd found herself emailing that she was too busy with her commission. She knew as she wrote this that it was partly a bit of one-upmanship to be pointing out that, whereas Alex had a new romance, Luna was a proper artist with work to do. She found herself mentioning Pea a lot too, how he was working away simultaneously in his studio for his show at Flowers. Written down like that it portrayed her life as an artistic idyll. She'd never felt the need to compete before, yet here she was, overstating what she had, as much for her own benefit as Alex's. It was as though Alex was ahead of her in some kind of race, although she wasn't, professionally. Alex was starting out. She might not even make it, a thought which Luna found shockingly comforting. The thought of her having had a child, a money-making career, this new relationship with a younger guy, and still having the possibility of becoming a successful illustrator Luna found hard to take. She'd always thought that to be an artist you had to put it first, sacrificing the rest of life. Alex could prove her whole belief system wrong.

No, she couldn't bring herself to ask Alex. Petty but true. The same went for her other artist friends. Gina . . . well, Gina was otherwise occupied. Luna felt another surge of envy about that too, like a seventh wave.

The only person she could think of was Jon Booker. She tried to dismiss him, considering it was just because he'd flattered her and she wanted more compliments. But out of everyone she knew — even those closest to her — she got the feeling that he was the one who would actually put his mind to the task, completely. Not be distracted with whatever was going on in their own head, whether that was their own art, or their new boyfriend, or their baby. She reached for her digital camera, and began to take snaps of Amelia to load into her laptop to email.

Jon replied within the hour. A really long email.

I'm just going to write thoughts as they come to me. First off, I have to say, it's breathtakingly beautiful. But in an edgy, sinister way that I can't place. There's the nod to religion, with the halo, the cherubs and madonna-esque pose in some kind of Eden. The sitter's lovely, as are the children. But something gives it an eeriness. Something in the woman? She's flatteringly painted, but I'm starting to feel I don't like her. She's too perfect, maybe? Her surroundings, the garden and even the children, are opulent. It's like there's a knowledge in her face that she has so much, but she's proud of it — in fact, her expression's pretty immodest for a Virgin. It works well juxtaposed against the saintly halo. The

232

way she's holding her children slightly forward, presenting them like they're for show,
her accessories . . .

There's something else though. The
garden. Is that a magpie in the tree?
Symbol of covetousness and greed for all
that glitters . . . ? Am I on the right lines?
The green of the garden is so unnaturally
vivid it almost shimmers — does that
mean something? (Green — the colour of
envy . . . ?) Now I'm looking closely I'm
seeing loads of insects and weeds and
brambles. The flowers seem overblown, like
they're at the very end of their bloom. And
the thorns on the rose stems — is it my
imagination, or are they more pronounced
than they really are, larger and darker? And
the gilt — it's on the edges of the flowers,
the apples on the tree . . . things that have
value in themselves and don't need gilding.
In fact, apples that are made of gold can't
be eaten. It speaks of unnecessary, flaunted
riches, like King Midas and his wish that
everything he touched turned to gold. Hey
— and I've just spotted the drips of gold
coming off the woman!

I must be right! Am I right? Is this a
commission of someone you don't like, by
any chance? Please tell me I'm right! And
if you're worried, I'm sure the woman is
too vain and smug to see the vanity and
smugness in herself!

I love it. I absolutely love it. Not only is
it an exquisite piece of work, ravishing to

look at, but you've managed to say something about your sitter in such an
underhand way that Amelia will never
notice in a million years. You're a genius.
And just in case I haven't been enough of
an arselicker already, it reminded me of
Botticelli. Seriously. Jon x

Luna laughed out loud and actually clapped
her hands together in glee. Jon had spotted every
single oblique reference in the work apart from
the fact that the children were earrings, but
— God! Close enough. Full marks to him! And
at the same time he'd been utterly sure that it
was covert enough for Amelia not to notice.
Even if some arty friend of hers did (and would
they really point it out to her?) it was subtle
enough that Luna could deny it, or at least
excuse it by playing innocent and saying any
symbolic features were for the sake of referenc-
ing classic art, and not intended in any way,
Amelia, to say anything derogatory, yada yada
yada. She felt a rush of happiness. Jon had
confirmed her hope that she would get away with
it. He'd also called her a genius, of course, which
somewhat added to her feeling of elation. She
called Julian and told him she would have the
painting finished by the end of the week and was
very specific that it had to be framed in heavy
gold, so could he lay out for the cost as she was
skint? And did he think that would be OK with
the client?
  'Only if it's real gold, darling, knowing
Amelia,' he replied. 'I'll put in a call to her now

— you never know with her, she might have a very strong opinion about it going with the decor of whichever of her *salons* it's going in.'

They shared a laugh. Julian was *one of them*, really, operating in their circles, which was how Luna had obtained the commission in the first place. She could hardly hold him in disdain about it, although she teased him as though she did. It was how the art world worked, and without Julian as an agent she would be nowhere, she knew that. With Julian and his marketing, she was acceptable to that world. They thought of her as the real thing, authentic, living in Hackney, a proper edgy artist — it was exciting for the wealthy classes to own a piece of her work. Without Julian to sell her this way she disappeared from their view, becoming one of the faceless poverty-stricken struggling masses, to be swept past in a cab on the way to any private view that had the misfortune of lying east of Bond Street.

And anyway, Julian had a self-deprecating awareness of their ilk, added to a sharp sense of humour that made him more than bearable. Lovable, in fact. He enjoyed Luna's cutting remarks about the pretensions and pomposity of those in the business of art, and for his benefit she played up to his idea of her as cool and streetwise. Most of all, though, in spite of his oft-used Andy Warhol quote that he was 'deeply superficial', there was actually a depth to Julian that was often curiously absent in his acquaintances, considering how well educated, well travelled, well brought-up, well 'everything'd' they were.

'You sound marvellous, Lu,' he said to her now. 'You've got over your hatred of the piece and forgiven me, then?'

'Yeah,' she laughed. 'Sorry about that. I took it out on you, didn't I?'

'Not at all, darling. You only shouted, 'Thanks a fucking bunch for making me fucking worship at the fucking shrine to that fucking bitch from hell all fucking day long when I could be doing some proper fucking art,' when I dared to ask how it was going.' They laughed uproariously.

'Oh my fucking God, I'm so fucking sorry,' said Luna.

'That's quite all fucking right,' he replied. 'I usually pay good fucking money to get that kind of abuse.'

When their laughter had died down Luna said, 'Well, I think I've managed to turn it into a proper piece of art after all. No thanks to you, of course, you absolute bastard.'

'Ooh — tell me again how bad I've been,' Julian groaned.

'I'm going now, sick fuck,' said Luna, 'before I have to start charging you. Check your email in a mo.'

Jon's confirmation of the work had totally banished her doubts. After sending Julian *Amelia I* she checked the time. Half four. Jon must have picked up her email and written to her at work. She should thank him before he left the office.

Heh heh! Ever thought of becoming an art critic? Or a detective, maybe. You're spot

236

on. As always. Though that doesn't necessarily put me in the most flattering light,
when I think of your portrait of me. It's
you that's the genius. At least, I hope so. If
you're a halfwit and you still worked out
my hidden 'theme' of the painting, I'll
never work in this town again.

She grinned at the word halfwit. She could
imagine Jon chuckling at it in his deep cough of a
laugh, which was somehow in a northern accent
even though there were no words to it. She
paused and wondered how to thank him properly, without being too gushy, but still conveying
how touched she was that he'd bothered.

Anyhow, you've given me the impetus to
finish the fucking thing and deliver it. It's a
weight off, really. I've had such trouble
with it (for the reasons you so intelligently
deduced, smartypants, i.e. loathing the
subject). Actually, it's the portrait I did of
you on the course that seems to have
renewed my inspiration. So I seem to be in
the position of being indebted to you.
Again! Luie x

She closed her iBook and went back up to her
studio, where she studied the painting, attempting to keep hold of her critical eye. But pride
bloomed in her chest like one of the overblown
flowers. It wasn't just her own vanity that had
seen a resemblance to Botticelli. Jon had seen it
too. She hummed as she took her brush to the

last tree forming the edge of the scene, the only thing Pierre had found worth mentioning.

Hmm . . . so I have you in my debt, do I? I'm ashamed to admit I like that thought. I'll try my hardest not to abuse my position, although I must confess it's sorely tempting.

Was he being suggestive with her? Luna gave a bemused laugh. Where had that come from? Before Danny and Tomas at the weekend she couldn't remember the last time someone had flirted with her, and anyway, Danny didn't count because she'd been wrong. There had been the guy that kept coming to the caff, pretending it was his local until he let slip he actually had to catch a bus to get there. He'd given up eventually, after Luna's repetitive drip-drip of the words 'my boyfriend' into their conversation. But that had been — God, it was over a year ago. Luna now felt the loss of it. It seemed the feeling of being young, fertile, desired, had fuelled her self-confidence without her realizing it. It had been an intrinsic part of who she was, as much as her own character, her own talents, her mind, her very self. Young women had so much power and they didn't even know it.

Luna left her laptop abruptly, hoping to share a nightcap with Pea, with a spliff perhaps. But the light was off in his studio and she poked her head round the bedroom door to see he was already in bed, crashed out after having worked through the night yesterday. Her heartbeat quickened. It was another chance she was missing, at the perfect time of the month for trying, because their body clocks were out of sync again.

She closed the bedroom door and went back down to look out through the glass at the city, still pulsating way beneath their perch. She was a long way from being able to sleep. She could feel life beating through her, waiting to spread itself. Too much life to be contained in this stillness, in sleep, in this poky flat, cut off from everything. I could go out, she thought, slip into the stream of life out there, like a corpuscle. But she knew she couldn't. Not round here, at this time of night. It was asking for trouble. She was trapped, like a woman in a tower in a fairy tale. Or a nightmare.

She poured the last of the red wine, skinned up and took the spliff back to her computer. She would have to conk herself out with substance abuse. She tapped the computer out of sleep mode and saw Jon's email still there. She reread it and smiled. What was wrong with a little harmless flirtation? She took a mouthful of wine and hit reply.

Don't get too excited. I don't like owing anyone — it makes me feel dirty. And not in a good way.

She laughed, looking at the screen. Was it too much? Yes, definitely. But all the same, it was funny. Her finger hovered over the send button. She shouldn't really. She deleted it and spent a while trying to think of something else instead. But the thought of it making him laugh and

239

blush as he opened it at work was irresistible. She typed it again and pressed send.

When she checked her emails the next morning, he had already written back.

In that case, I won't keep you in suspense for too long. Just give me this afternoon to spend a few delicious hours thinking of ways you can repay me.

She found herself peculiarly touched by his response. There was something sweet about such a big, solid, earth-bound Yorkshire-born-and-bred type flirting with her. He was so in control of himself that it made it interesting to imagine him spending delicious hours dreaming of ways she could pay him back. It made her feel powerful, to be able to move him in that way. Danny types — soft and romantic — were easy to affect. Tomas would go after anything, as he had proved, and anyway, he was old. But someone like Jon wasn't easily stirred.

Of course, she could be running away with herself. It could mean nothing — the way it did with Julian. Some men couldn't operate on a level with a woman that wasn't flirtatious. But she hadn't seen that in Jon. He was a serious sort of guy and she couldn't imagine him coming on to women for the sake of it. Though what did she know? He could be the kind of person that completely belies their appearance, like funny life-of-the-party guys who were manic-depressive when you lived with them, weeds that turned out to be violent little bastards.

It occurred to her as she left work for the short cycle home (it didn't need to be cycled, for it was a short journey, but through the unlit back streets and archways it was potentially dangerous) that he could actually be a stalker or a pervert, or, at least, a bit of a creep. Worse than Tomas, even. It should have bothered her, probably, and maybe would have done if he had lived in London. She would perhaps have been aware of the possibility of him suddenly appearing out of the shadows a few nights or weeks from now. But the distance between them made her feel safe. That and her memory of him, his voice and accent so like that of her new-found relatives on her father's side, warm, homely, safe. And the fact he had rescued her so valiantly. There was something old-school about him, in the way he had stepped in when Tomas had got out of order. He was probably quite young, now she thought about it, but he had an old head on his shoulders. She thought again of her uncle, her granddad, the way they flattened their vowels when they spoke, lengthening their words. There was a fatherly comfort in the tone, a kind of 'there, there, pet', but she didn't know whether it was real or imagined. Did she carry in her subconscious the sound of her own father's voice, or did she just hope that it was there?

★   ★   ★

Pierre had nearly completed a piece. He was wired with a manic energy. The piece worked. A life-size figure standing, holding his head, made

241

up of plastic cubes about three inches square. The figure was leaning forward, looking close to toppling and collapsing, as though he would if you pushed in the right place with your finger.

'Try it!' he urged her, his eyes huge. She did, but the piece was firmly planted and wouldn't budge. Pierre was like a mad professor who had made a belief-altering scientific discovery.

'He's wonderful,' Luna said, her eyes taking in the figure. It was incredible how much pathos there was in the piece, how your heart went out to this figure made up of transparent plastic. He appeared on the verge, as if he'd just that second stopped being able to cope with modern life, trying to hold his head together, and failing.

'I'm thinking of calling it 'Balancing',' said Pea. 'I don't know if he should be part of a series or if all the pieces should just have their own thing. Whichever, anyway — I'm up and running!' He gave Luna a squeeze and went back to his work. She watched him, two things entering her mind simultaneously: a sudden reconnection with how deeply she loved and admired him and his beautiful work, and a rather alarming thought that he could be bipolar. It was the sort of condition that sometimes didn't show itself until later in life, when the madness of youth died down and let you see what you were made of underneath. He would be up for days now, working feverishly and ranting away, completely immersed, exhilarated. He would never once have his mind interrupted with the tiresome notion that he should eat something or buy a pint of milk or pay a phone bill before they were cut off. It just wouldn't occur to him.

Another month would go by.

Luna asked if he'd like a cuppa, knowing he wouldn't reply. She made him a tea — he would have overdosed on coffee already — and took it back to his studio with some leftover frittata in a polystyrene container from Trey's.

'Eat!' she ordered as she left, but she knew that if he did it wouldn't be until the early hours when it had long gone cold. As she closed his studio door she felt filled with a love and longing she didn't know what to do with. The lack of sleep over the past few nights, working at Trey's but also up late finishing her commission, had begun to catch up with her, and she felt frazzled. But still, she did not want to go to bed alone. She made herself a strong coffee, deciding to try to channel the last of her energy and emotion into her final touches on Amelia. It was one of her more recent discoveries — that she could sometimes produce her best work when she was driven not by the desire to paint itself, but by the mournful want for something else, something unreachable that painting could only fill the absence of.

⋆　⋆　⋆

She wrote an email before she finally went to bed, the dizziness of relief at finishing her painting showing itself in typos and the running on of sentences without punctuation, which she didn't bother checking before she pressed send.

Well it's 4 thrity am and I know your
probly fast asleep in ur bed but i had to
write 2 you NOW as i've finally finished
Amelila, every last blade of grass every hair
on her hateful head evrything, and its
THANKS TO YOU that i got herein the
end — i just had to share this very special
momen twith you even tho your not here,
atlthough it kind of feels like you are here
— i swear your portrait keeps smiling at
me behinfd my back but evry time I tun
round youve got yor poface on again!!! just
the trace of it on your lips, im sure that
wasn't there bfore . . . ???
   Anywy — cheers 2 you! (last glulg of
wine)
   Lol LU xx
   ps I#d cash in my IOU now if I were
you while I'm feeling particularly gratful!

Jon replied at 7.43 the following morning.

Let me paint you. Properly this time. My
attempt to capture you before was a dismal
embarrassing failure, which showed me up
to be the con man my job has made of
me. It said more about me than it did
about you. I want to do you justice.

Luna remembered he had asked this before,
in rushed last words at the station as she boarded
her train home. It had taken her aback, but
then there was no time to answer anyway, in the
awkward scramble to get her things together

onto the train. She realized now she hadn't really forgotten, just pushed it to the back of her mind while she got on with life. But once again, she found the idea alluring, flattering. She remembered the strangeness of having another artist's eyes looking over her, being the observed rather than the observer. She'd felt so vulnerable — especially when Jon had exposed things about her that she wanted kept hidden. She'd felt undone.

The fact he was persisting still in saying that his portrayal of her had been wrong meant a lot. Although she had tried hard to not care what someone like Jon saw in her, that his opinion wasn't the truth, she hadn't succeeded. It had shaken her, that someone had seen her identity was built on being an artist, and not a woman. It had hurt and she had railed against it — she was a person and an artist, what did femaleness have to do with anything? But the fact was, she had come to a point in her life when it had everything to do with everything — for her. He wanted to do her justice, he'd said. Something about that awoke a curiosity in her she couldn't shush back to sleep. She had spent too long being hard on herself for being a woman after all, for having female instincts that had let herself down as well as Pierre, and that ultimately got in the way of their lives.

She wondered what a version of her that did her justice, saw good things in her, would look like. The thought gave her a glimmer of something that felt like hope.

She wrote suggesting she could send him

photographs to work from and set about finding pictures of herself she liked.

He wrote back immediately.

I can't work from pictures. I hate it. I need you to sit for me.

PS I'm not expecting you to do it for nothing. I'll pay you for your time, of course.

PPS I could come to you, if that helps.

Luna tried hard to dismiss the idea. It was ridiculous that she would have to pose in person for him. But she couldn't quite get it out of her mind. It was the word 'need'.

He *needed* her to sit for him. There was an urgency that should send her running. Most people — normal people — would put 'I'd prefer' or 'I'd rather', or 'ideally' or 'is there any chance that'. Wouldn't they? But it was peculiarly enticing, somebody *needing* her to sit in front of him while he captured everything about her.

He couldn't come to her, of course. Luna had cycled to Frameworks now she had the go-ahead from Amelia for the gold frame ('I trust Luna completely of course, but can you just say that I don't want it to be too shiny — the darker the better, cost no object'). She'd chosen the frame gleefully — the most expensive she'd ever gone for — and was now in no mood to go straight home. It was a crisp, sparkling winter morning and she decided to cycle meanderingly to Victoria Park to make the most of it. She could stop off at the Approach, where she'd had a show the previous year, say hi, remind them of her — and treat herself to brunch somewhere she wasn't a waitress, now she knew she had a good wad of money coming in. Maybe she'd text Pea to join her, maybe not. She'd see how she felt.

As she cycled her mind wandered over the reality of Jon painting her in person. She suddenly wished she wasn't so broke, that she had enough money to rent a proper, separate space for herself, somewhere someone like Jon could come that would live up to his idea of a successful London artist. She had another pang of yearning for the security of a salary. Jon earned a good wage, she was sure, good enough that he would have absolutely no idea of the kind of poverty she and Pierre often lived in. They were sometimes pretty flush, yes, but it was always balanced out with the times when there were months after months of not selling, when she relied on waitressing tips to keep her above the minimum wage. It was nearly time for her to do their books again. She had a quiet dread of finding out in black and white figures exactly the amount of money she and Pierre were living on. Usually, being artists somehow saved them from the harsh statistics, allowed them to feel they weren't branded by the poverty-line grouping that their earnings dictated. But, recently, with the earnings, the dour estate underneath the gloss of 'artist territory', the thought of bringing up children in these harsh streets . . . in spite of her alternative upbringing and bohemian status, she was beginning to feel she was — as her tax returns revealed to the taxman — poor.

She had always been so good at ignoring status anxiety, the pressure that others seemed to be increasingly under — what was that measure people used? That your salary should be the same figure as your age? She was sure that her and Pierre's combined salary wouldn't equal either of their ages this year. An underlying panic was seeping into her framework, like floodwater creeping under doors and lapping at the stairs. It made her feel as though she had been shockingly innocent before, like a child. She really, truly, had thought that art was everything. How naive, it suddenly seemed! To have ever thought money didn't mean anything! Were times different before? Had things changed since she was young, growing up among anarchists in communes and squats, or had money always mattered and she just hadn't clicked on? Her mum had taught her that art was the important thing, creativity. Yes, she'd wanted Luna to be successful, always, in a feminist way — competing work-wise for status with any man — but success was never about careers and money; it was based on independence, freedom, not living as a man's partner but a woman in her own right. Luna still had the book to prove it.

Was Angie wrong after all? To think it was all right to scrabble about to support yourself as long as you had independence from men and freedom of expression? All at once the idea seemed hopelessly out of date to Luna, her mum like a figure from history! Nowadays it was the norm to have a great career and salary and kids and a husband, and, and, and. Luna felt outmoded and left behind, to be sacrificing one or the other to be the thing she wanted to be. She only had one facet of the things that made up a successful woman in this day and age. You could — should — have it all now, as if it was no big deal.

The only other people in the park were mothers chatting to mothers, wheeling babies and patiently waiting for kids under school age to wear themselves out kicking around in the leaves. Luna had always thought it appeared painfully frustrating and tiring, putting your life on hold like that and talking kiddy talk when there were so many other things you could be getting on with. But today, having what felt like a day off after completing her commission, it looked companionable and fun. The women were laughing at their children's antics and the things they were shrieking. They probably only knew each other through these daily walks in the park. Luna felt excluded. She couldn't go up and join in with their conversation, not without a child in tow. She would seem more like a weirdo than another woman with experiences the others could relate to.

Further along an old woman was feeding mouldy bread from a plastic bag to the pigeons and babbling to herself. Luna felt more able to strike up a conversation with her than the mothers. We have more in common, she thought. The old woman might have children somewhere, of course, but something about her derelict appearance made Luna think not. A mum who had children somewhere in the world, even if they never visited, wouldn't be left to wear the same dirty coat each winter and talk to pigeons, surely? Luna cycled on quickly, feeling guilty. She didn't want to feel horrified by a person, but she was.

She stopped off at the Approach, having a quick look around the gallery upstairs. She didn't recognize the work, by a young female Danish artist new on the scene. She didn't recognize the bloke in the office either, which gave her the excuse not to self-promote, at least this time. She had lunch in the pub downstairs, waiting to see someone she knew. She tried to browse the papers, but couldn't concentrate. She felt self-conscious, an outsider, even here. She was usually pretty high after finishing a commission that she was pleased with. It's just a mood, she told herself; but she left, unconvinced that it was a passing phase. She cycled home along Bethnal Green High Street, where the market was full of stalls selling Christmas glitz and toys. Everywhere she looked there were mums loading up with presents for their kids, to be hidden when they got home and before the children got in from school.

Christmas had never meant much. Luna and Pierre usually celebrated it with her mother, although of course for Angie it was a pagan celebration of the solstice and a welcoming in of the new year. It was always a civilized, adult affair with Angie's great collection of interesting misfits, followed by partying with friends over New Year. But over the last couple of years, the number of friends that could go out clubbing had diminished. Babysitters were too expensive, or spending the time with their kids was preferable. Who would come out this year? It had always worked perfectly well, but when she thought about it now, without going to Angie's, she saw a void followed by a flagging routine, and she wanted a change. She tried to block out thoughts of a Christmas with children running around excitedly, filled with the magic of it all. She wondered if she and Pea could do something altogether different this year — get a cheap flight to somewhere else — Prague, or maybe even somewhere warm. Somewhere she wouldn't see families with children everywhere she looked.

When she got home she stood at the west-facing window in the lounge, where she could just make out the Christmas lights along Oxford Street trying to ward off the misty dusk as it fell, wrapping up the day. It felt significant, as though a scene of her life was ending in a slow fade to black.

She heard Pea coming out of his studio and heading down the stairs.

'Oh hi, babe,' he said, surprised to see her there. 'I didn't hear you come in. Cuppa tea?'

He was cheerful, sweet.

'Thanks, that'd be great,' she said.

He put the kettle on, came up behind her and hugged her. 'D'you get your frame all right?'

'Yeah, that's sorted, finally. All done. Thank God.'

'Yeah, really,' he replied. 'D'you wanna

celebrate? Fancy lunch?'

'It's half four! And I've eaten already,' she said. 'Sorry — I grabbed something while I was out. I wasn't sure if you'd want to tear yourself away.'

'That's OK. I should probably keep at it. On a bit of a roll,' he said. 'Maybe later? Let's go out.'

'Yeah, maybe. See how we feel,' Luna said.

'What are you up to now?' Pea called over his shoulder as he headed back upstairs.

'Oh . . . this and that,' she answered unconvincingly, but he wasn't waiting for a response. His question was left, looming in the room for her to deal with alone.

She felt she was on pause, waiting for the next scene. She had to turn her mind to what to focus on next. She should get on to Julian about getting her another commission — hopefully the portrait would spark some interest from Amelia's competitive friends. Start thinking about pieces for next year's shows. The thought tired her. The only task she could think of that she could face doing right now was answering Jon. She had to put him off the idea of coming to paint her here. It just wouldn't work. But she felt disappointed. The thought of being paid to sit while someone else painted her was appealing. It would take the weight off for a while, letting someone else worry about making art while she earned money not waitressing. But she couldn't picture it here in her studio, with Pea banging around in his room along the corridor. She couldn't imagine what Pea's reaction would be. He would find it odd, she was sure. He would probably say it was a waste of her time when she herself should be painting. He wouldn't like Jon. He wouldn't like anybody coming into their space, but especially not Jon. He would be suspicious about it. Maybe it was suspicious, some guy they didn't really know *needing* to paint Luna so badly that he would travel across the country to do so.

But, somehow, it didn't put Luna off. It didn't make her write a polite email declining with a sweet apology. Instead she wrote that her own studio wasn't suitable, with a casual mention of her boyfriend working noisily on sculptures in the next studio along. She worded it in such a way that Jon wouldn't know the truth, that it was because she felt her own life might not measure up to his expectations of her.

> I'm in between projects, so actually I could do it. In fact, I'd like to. It'd give me a bit of thinking time, about what I'm going to do next. And I admit, I am just the tiniest bit curious as to what you'll make of me this time. It's really just a question of how and where, etc.

Each time Luna opened her email she expected a response from Jon. Days went by with no reply from him. She pretended to herself that she wasn't really waiting, but still she reread her own email several times to make sure she hadn't put him off by mistake. It must have been the mention of her boyfriend. She felt foolish for having wanted to be painted and wished it had been her that had said, thanks, but no thanks. She had lost some self-respect somehow. It made her feel exposed again, that she had shown Jon her silly eagerness to sit for him again.

Between waitressing shifts she forced herself into the studio, but even her new inspiration seemed to have deserted her. She tried not to think that it was something about Jon that had inspired her, but now, without his communication, it was hard not to make the connection. She made herself work. If she didn't then she really would be just a waitress, a thought far more difficult to overcome than the block about what to paint next. But all she could do was make up collage sample boards with thread, fabric, plastic, old packaging. She would keep at it until she broke through this barrier, find a material, a method, that took the practice beyond what felt like Art GCSE. She panicked that she was wallowing, directionless. The way she was working before was perfectly all right, wasn't it? Why now start mucking around with bits of junk when she had established a form and style that was being appreciated? But she couldn't think of a straight painting to do either. There were still several weeks before Amelia's grand unveiling — perhaps there would be something after that. She told Julian that's what she wanted to do at the moment, but her heart wasn't in it really. He recommended some exhibitions coming up the following year that she should work on pieces for. There were themes of regeneration, waste, mental health — quite interesting, she should be able to produce some good stuff for those. But nothing excited her.

*It's something else I want to create.* The

thought kept rising from her subconscious, flapping like a disturbed bird. She tried to hold still so that it would settle again, quiet and ignored.

★　★　★

It was five days before she heard from Jon, long enough for her to think that he had become one of those randomly met people who almost make it into your life, but who fade away before they really appear. It happened a lot in these days of emailing — you gave out your address to loads of people, and it was far easier to send a quick line than to phone, so you did. More often than not, after an initial dash of correspondence, one or other of you didn't get round to writing back, and that was that. It was an easy yet somehow false way of communicating. Some email friendships never found their way out of it into real talking, real meeting, real connection.

She felt nervous when she saw his name. She was sure it would just say, sorry I've been busy — shame we couldn't make it work, never mind. Instead she sat, stunned, rereading his message.

Can you get to Leicester? Actually I know you can — it's just over an hour from London (St Pancras). Of course, I'll pay your fares on top of your fee. A mate of mine has a studio there, and asked me if I knew anyone who wanted it for a few months. It seems ideal — halfway between us both! Whaddya say?

255

The tone of his email seemed excited, and she felt a rush of adrenaline herself. She shouldn't do it really but she couldn't help thinking, why not? It was a job, quite a nice 'meantime' kind of job, something different, related to what she did, without her having to do it herself. She should think about it first; but she found herself emailing yes before she got up from her desk. She could always back out if something made her realize it was a bad idea — Pea's reaction, or a sudden commission. But she thought of Jon's character and imagined him sorting it all out immediately — committing himself to his friend's studio, paying a deposit there and then, looking into possible dates for a first sitting, which would be sooner rather than later. He would make a decision and act on it. There was something strong about that, even if the decision was a bad one. It had felt good to do the same, email a definitive answer immediately, without prevaricating, without running it by Pea, without sorting out other commitments first. God, what have I got myself into? she thought, clasping her hand over her mouth, in horror, before the laughter broke through.

★　★　★

Two weeks later, on a Tuesday, Luna set off at ten-thirty for a lunchtime shift at Trey's. A lunchtime shift she had already swapped out of. Although Jon hadn't said anything, she had an instinctive idea that there would probably not be much in the way of sittings at weekends. It wasn't logical really — it would be reasonable to imagine that, working full-time, he would only be able to paint for himself at the weekend — but with those first suggested dates (Tuesday lunchtime or Friday morning) she guessed that weekends were out of bounds. He hadn't mentioned a wife, but Luna had seen a band on his wedding-ring finger when she had sat beside him in his car on the way to Norwich station. It had struck her as it caught the sun and glinted in reflections off the glass, more chunky than most, making more of a statement, and it had surprised her. He had seemed young to be married, and she had wondered if he was just wearing a ring on that finger. But then he wasn't the sort to wear jewellery for no reason. He was, though, the sort to be married young, settled down. It fitted. Probably a childhood sweetheart.

Weekends didn't mean much to her and Pierre. They had days off when they wanted to, and it had always been a pleasure they had shared — they had their own rules, the privilege of picnicking on Hampstead Heath when most of the world was stuck in the office. He wouldn't notice a change to her routine when they didn't have one. All the same, she set off for work on Tuesday, omitting to mention she had swapped her shift to Saturday, leaving him still in bed after a late night working. He had slipped into a pattern that was getting later and later, so that the neighbours below had begun to bang on their ceiling at the noise when he didn't realize the hours were sliding into night. He was trying to get up earlier and fit into a more usual working week, but so far, luckily for Luna on this day, he hadn't achieved it. Had he seen her as she set off he might have wondered why she was so dolled up for waitressing. She usually didn't bother but today she defined her eyes with mascara and dark eyeshadow, put her hair up, even dabbed herself with scent. She wore a gold shirt with big cuffs and puffed sleeves — one of Angie's seventies affairs — with a black A-line skirt and suede, heeled boots under her shaggy-haired coat. As she descended in the lift surrounded in her own fug of perfume, she felt ridiculous. She'd really overdone it, but she couldn't go back in case she'd woken Pierre up banging the door closed, or woke him up now going back in. How would she explain herself? She couldn't.

As she walked to Old Street tube she tried to get into the frame of mind in which she wore clothes like this every day — after all, a lot of women did, and there were plenty she was overtaking tripping along in far higher heels. It's all about confidence, she told herself, and catching her reflection in a window she felt a little more at ease. Her idea of 'overdone' was really quite understated. She wasn't even smart enough to work in an office dressed like that. She looked suitably boho — her clothes obviously vintage. She had a feel of Julie Christie *circa* 1974, which pleased her. She felt peculiarly womanly. Why that should feel peculiar, she wasn't sure.

As she crossed Kingsland Road and passed the cafe, walking on in the opposite direction, she panicked. What if Pea decided to pop in to see her at work for something? He hadn't done it for a while, but it wasn't uncommon, if he needed cash or breakfast or had locked himself out. Thoughts of what she would say when she picked up her mobile to him, or when she got home later, rushed through her mind. *Oh I forgot — I swapped my shift.* She practised the casual breeziness internally as she carried on striding away. *As I was already up and about I went into town to do some Christmas shopping . . .* Would it matter that she didn't have any shopping with her? Or she could say she had gone across town to meet up with someone. Whatever she said would be an easy, safe lie. In a vast city it was so easy to be swallowed up with some business or other for a whole day, without anyone spotting you or being able to prove different.

She could tell the truth and say someone had asked her to sit for them. If she left out the part about going all the way to Leicester to do so it seemed a lot less weird. She could say it was Alex who wanted to paint her, and she was going over to west London. It took pretty much as long on the tube as getting to the Midlands anyway. Though that was a lie that could get sticky. She imagined that Alex would become a part of her real life at some point; she'd meet Pierre one way or another, maybe even just bumping into them at some show, and of course Pea would ask how the portrait was going. Luna would save that lie for the future, to use if she had to explain herself when her other excuses for her absences were wearing thin. She could say she'd been embarrassed to tell him because she knew he would think she was wasting time she should be spending on her own work.

By the time the Leicester train pulled out of the station, pulling her forward into this other life, she had constructed an internal database of potential lies she could tell Pierre, if and when he noticed anything unusual. It was so unlike her, to be this closed off and shifty with him. Until the baby thing, they had been completely open with each other, without it taking any effort whatsoever. It was only now, when so much of herself was becoming hidden from him, that she realized quite how good their relationship had been. They'd been so in tune with each other, their thoughts and desires and attitudes, and as she felt herself dragged at speed away from him and home, she was aware of just how acutely she had been missing him. It was so bad she got up at the first station stop to get off, turn round and get the next train back. But just then her mobile bleeped a text, and she stopped at the door to check it, hands trembling. It was from Jon. *Did u make the train? Stuck in traffic but shd b in time 2 meet u! J.* Other people were trying to get on, so she turned and sat down in her seat to get out of the way. And then the train was pulling out of the station and she was texting back: *Yes — c u there!*

★   ★   ★

'Hi,' she said, nervously, and leaned forward to kiss him on his cheek. At the same time he put his hand out to shake hers, before changing his mind and retracting it, embarrassed. They laughed as they touched hands clumsily, and slightly missed each other's face as they tried to kiss. Luna looked around for the way out as they stood feeling foolish.

'Oh. It's this way,' said Jon, and they began to walk to the exit. 'You made it then,' he said.

'Yes. And you.' They glanced at each other as they fell into step and laughed again.

'I'm sorry. I don't know what to say,' Jon said after another awkward silence. 'This is surreal.'

'I know. It really is,' Luna agreed. Outside the station she said, 'So. Hello, Leicester.'

'Have you ever been here before?' he asked.

'No, I don't believe I have.'

'I don't suppose you've had reason to,' he said. Another embarrassed laugh from both of them.

'How about you? Do you come here often?' she asked, playfully. He laughed, relaxed a touch.

'I've been once or twice for business. But not to invite strange girls up to my studio, no,' he replied. It was odd how natural the innuendo between them seemed when it was so improper and out of place.

'I'm not that strange,' she replied, laughing.

'Here's my car,' he said, as they approached it.

'So it is,' she smiled.

He unlocked the doors with his remote, but still opened the door for her, and shut it once she'd folded herself lightly in. She watched him walking self-consciously round to the driver's side, wondering if anyone had ever opened a door for her before.

They sat in silence as he pulled out of the car park, the windows beginning to steam up. He seemed embarrassed by it, and turned the air conditioning on high for a blast.

'It's not far,' he said. 'It's walkable. I just didn't have time to go round first. I hope it's not too cold in there. I haven't had the chance to get the heater on. It shouldn't take too long to warm up though.'

'Well, I won't strip off right away then,' she said.

He braked suddenly when he realized the traffic light was red, and swung his head to look at her, in shock.

Luna grinned at him.

'Oh. You're joking,' he said. He turned to look straight in front and shook his head at himself, ruefully.

They both began to laugh, contagiously. She threw her head back on the headrest to really chortle.

'Very funny,' he said dryly, and drove on, both of them laughing again.

He tried to open her car door for her when they stopped at the studio, but she had already swung herself out, thrusting her hands into her coat pockets and looking up at the building, a converted Victorian school. He got his things out of the boot and they climbed the stairs to his studio on the second floor, probably former offices or storage rooms. It was surprisingly homely and comfortable, a rug and a sofa with a crocheted throw in a kind of chill-out area by the sink and kettle. He had a table along one wall with his art supplies on it, and an easel set up by the window. It was very clean, for a painting studio. He got the convector heater going and filled the kettle while she stood hugging her coat tightly round her.

'Do you want a cuppa?' he asked.

'Tea would be lovely. Milk and two sugars,' she replied.

'That's my girl,' he said.

'What's so good about that?' she laughed.

'I don't know.' He shrugged. 'Most girls are on a diet all the time. They're like, I can't have this and I can't have that. Some of the secretaries in my office will have, like, half a biscuit. *Half* a biscuit! And that's only after hours of going 'I shouldn't really, I'm soooo fat.'' Luna smiled at his impression of a girl's voice.

'I love biscuits,' said Luna. 'Have I passed your test?'

'Yes, I suppose you have. Congratulations.' He looked up from the tea bags and met her eyes for a second. They grinned. 'Plus, I had you down for a fruit-tea type,' he added after a pause.

'A fruit-tea type?' she spat out, in mock disgust. 'How dare you, sir!' She put on a posh southern voice as she said it. She saw a look flit across his face that let her know he'd liked it.

'It's what you southern jesses drink, in't it?' he added, overdoing his accent for effect.

'Don't be silly, darling,' she replied, overdoing hers. 'We only ever drink overpriced bottled water or champagne.'

'Even in Hackney?'

'Especially in Hackney, darling.'

He gave her her tea and she stood warming both hands round the mug, blowing on it so she could take sips. She took a step sideways, to allow him to get some of the benefit of the hot air blowing out from the heater.

'Cheers, love,' he said, and they stood together, too close for normal body space, but allowable in the circumstance of the narrow stream of warm air.

'So, you haven't got any of your other paintings here?' She was looking around at the bare walls and table top.

'Er — no. No. As you know, I've only just taken this over off a mate. I didn't think it was worth bringing old stuff.'

'Where do you work usually?' He looked embarrassed and didn't answer. 'At home?' she suggested.

'Well, yeah. If I ever get the chance. I don't, to be honest. Not these days. Other things are just — more pressing.' She nodded. 'I suppose that's why I want to do this. Before I actually forget how to paint, how to make the kind of art I like. Look, I really appreciate you agreeing to sit for me.' His usual air of professional confidence seemed to leave him. 'I don't even know if it's going to come out any good. I hope you don't end up feeling it's been a right waste of time.'

'I won't,' she smiled. 'To be honest, I can't paint myself at the moment. I don't know why. I'm more than happy to let someone else do it for a change.'

He looked as though he was going to ask more but stopped himself. There was something touching about Jon being nervous. Luna couldn't imagine him being in situations that caused him to be nervous very often. They began the awkward process of starting what they had come here to do. She knew by the way he rubbed his head while suggesting where he thought she could pose, the way he shuffled his already perfectly positioned easel several times by minute amounts, that he was uncomfortable. She got the feeling he didn't paint models often. He was hesitant about beginning, shy almost. He asked to take several snapshots of her first, and he relaxed again while he did so, back in his comfort zone. He was probably used to advertising shoots, she thought, as he clicked quickly and proficiently around her with an expensive camera.

It was warm enough now for Luna to take her coat off, and she discarded it over the back of the sofa. It slipped onto the floor, but she didn't bother to pick it up. She felt her self-consciousness return at revealing the gold shirt. She knew she looked good in it, but however tatty and faded it was, it was still too glamorous for the occasion.

'Is that what you want to be painted in?' Jon asked. In truth, she hadn't really thought about it. She felt herself colour slightly as she realized she had chosen her outfit with seeing Jon in mind, rather than what she would be painted in.

'Um . . . ' She looked down at herself. 'Oh I don't know. Is it all wrong? For your, you know — 'vision'?' She drew rabbit-ear quotation marks in the air, feeling silly.

'Oh — no, no. Not at all.' She liked the way he lengthened the a in 'all'. Something about the drawing out of it stressed it and made him sound sincere. 'I only ever picture you in your painting shirt.' He looked embarrassed suddenly and added, 'I mean, when I've tried to envisage my painting, that's what you've got on.'

'Of course,' said Luna. 'I should have thought to ask if there was anything particular you wanted me to wear.' Oh God. It made her sound like a call girl with a client. Neither of them seemed able to stop making remarks that sounded suggestive. 'I mean — for the painting,' she added. They caught each other's eye and quickly looked away.

'No, it's me that should've thought of it. It doesn't matter today, any road. I doubt I'll get further than a few preliminary sketches and that. But I'll have a think how I want it to look and let you know for next time.'

'OK.' Reflexively she rubbed her upper arms, although she was no longer cold.

'Not that you don't look good in that,' Jon blurted. 'You really do. I mean . . . '

'It's all right!' Luna laughed. 'I won't take it personally. I do understand that you'll want a certain look for your piece.'

'Of course you do,' said Jon. 'I just didn't want you to think, you know, you look awful or anything.' Again the long 'a' in 'awful'.

'Thanks,' Luna said. 'That's good to know.' It was good to know. She unzipped her boots and kicked them off, curling her stockinged feet under her on the sofa and rubbing her toes. 'You

266

don't mind do you? My feet are killing me.'

'No, go ahead. Make yourself at home.' He stopped to look. 'Actually, that's nice.' He snapped a few more shots. 'Can I sketch you like that a minute?'

'Er — sure,' Luna replied. She rested her head on the arm that was leaning on the back of the sofa and settled. She stared out of the window at the bleak midwinter sky, able to see only a few black birds sometimes careening across the grey-white expanse. Watching them, waiting for the next ones to glide into shot, helped to lull her into a stillness that she could hold while Jon's hand swished across the paper. He sat wide-legged on a stool between the easel and table, drawing quickly. She was aware of him starting several pages before finally staying with one. Again she felt his presence, and the strange yet strangely familiar feeling of his eyes moving over her. It made her, in turn, aware of herself, her body, as though his gaze somehow centred her. She became acutely aware of the feeling of something missing deep inside.

'What are you thinking about?' Jon said, bringing her back into the room. He looked concerned suddenly. Was he reading her mind?

'Nothing. Why?'

'It's just that your face changed. As though bad thoughts were crossing it like clouds.'

She smiled. It was odd to be so . . . noticed. It was so peculiarly comfortable between them, the way that if something disturbed her calm he could read it in her face, the way he was watching her without (she hoped) picking her apart the way his portrait had done before. Perhaps this time he would put her back together again. Perhaps that was why she had agreed to do this. He was the one with the power to do that, having been the one to fracture her, and analyse the parts so accurately in his last portrayal.

The afternoon wore on, Luna sitting and Jon watching, drawing her, and each moment filled Luna with a renewed sense of herself, as though she was slowly returning to form.

★  ★  ★

The composition of his final drawing was perfect. Included, huge in the foreground, were her discarded boots, one lying on its side and the other standing but with its length flopped over crookedly. The exaggerated perspective of them led the eye in to the curled figure on the couch, the dropped coat at her side. He had concentrated on the detail in the shagginess of the coat hair, the pattern, now wonky, on her twisted tights, a small hole in the toe. The folds of material in the shirt around her breasts, and the gape between two buttons that revealed a snippet of lace on her bra. The messy drape of hair, the crease in her face from where she was leaning on her hand.

'God, I bet that's still going to be there by the time I get home,' she said, peering into the mirror over the table and rubbing at it. But still, she felt pleased. She could see that he had captured something of her, even if it was mainly her outer garments that he had focused on. In the same way as she had worn the clothes that day because she felt right in them, he had drawn attention to them as significantly *her*. The woman in the drawing had her kind of relaxed style; she sat like her. She seemed to be thinking like her. She nodded.

'I recognize her,' she said. 'Or should I say me?'

'Well, it's a start,' said Jon. 'I've cheated a bit, concentrating on anything but your face. I chickened out of trying too much in case it came out all wrong.'

'Still — what you've done of it seems right. The eyebrows are good, and the set of the jaw.'

'Yeah, but I wanted to get . . . '

' . . . the thought clouds scudding across it?'

He nudged her with his elbow. 'Don't take the piss.'

'I wasn't, honestly,' Luna said. 'I'm looking forward to you capturing my thought clouds. You can keep them too.'

'Thank you very much. I'd be happy to.'

It was such a sweet idea, to bear the burden of her thoughts — old-fashioned and gentlemanly, like walking on the outside of the pavement as protector from the world's splashes.

'Are you hungry?' Jon said, looking at his watch.

'Starving!' said Luna.

'What time do you have to be back? Have you got time for a bite before you go?'

'That'd be great. I don't have to be back for anything in particular. My trains are on the hour and half past.'

He nodded yet looked at her quizzically. A

look that suggested he wanted to know why she didn't have to be back in time to make somebody's tea. She thought he seemed to like it about her that she didn't. In fact, she felt particularly independent as she straightened her tights and zipped up her boots and strode in her heels towards the door, swinging her coat around her shoulders. She felt carefree and breezy, interesting. There was nothing like being studied for making you feel — worth studying. The Julie Christie feeling came back as she clattered down the staircase swinging her bag. All at once, she felt incredibly groovy, and the word made her want to laugh aloud. She could feel Jon watching her still, as he followed her down the stairs. She turned to look at him suddenly, just to catch him doing so. She wasn't disappointed. He pushed his specs up the bridge of his nose again, a gesture he used often, almost to conceal something he didn't want to give away.

He took her to a cafe on the way to the station — funnily enough, insisting on walking on the road-side edge of the pavement. She was above average height for a woman and of a broad build, but walking beside this bear-ish man made her feel petite and slinky, and in heels and a skirt as well, she felt uber-feminine. In the cafe, Luna swung her feet happily as they sat on high stools at a bar and shared a panini. They had a jokey, easy conversation that Luna couldn't quite remember the details of afterwards, only the feeling it left her with that kept a smile playing at the corners of her mouth as she sat on the train home.

* ★ ★

Luna stared at the photograph of her own birth. It filled her with horrified fascination, now more than ever. All the pictures surrounding the time of her creation stirred an emotional response, but this one could make her cry. It was a brutal shot, sparing the viewer nothing, taken between Angie's knees, so her face was a blur in the background, turned away, Luna noticed, as though she couldn't bear to see what was happening. Angie had never told Luna anything about her birth, even when Luna asked as a curious child, had never told her she was worth the pain, that seeing her for the first time, holding her, was the best moment in her life. But her father had been there, more present than her mother, capturing for her the violent glory of it. Between the bloodied legs was Luna's head, forcing itself through, her mucky, scrunched face upturned towards the camera. It was at once dreadful and miraculous, base and sublime, earthly and ethereal. It left Luna with no doubt that birth was what life was about, that without experiencing it herself, she would die incomplete, bereft of true meaning. She stood at the picture now, her heart beating with excitement and sheer terror at the knowledge that she too would go through this. She was going to make it happen, would fight now for the line of life in her to continue. It was hers to give and she would, for the sake of that little baby blasting its tiny way into existence and surviving.

271

# 1972

## Angie

The last six months of Angie's pregnancy had been perfect. She was in tune with the seasons, as she and the baby unfurled from the harshness of winter, blossomed through spring, and ripened into lush fruit in the summer, ready to drop. She became huge, grew to love the feeling of being a big nest for her baby. The sense of excitement grew with the heat of the sun as the birth date drew near towards the height of summer. Angie couldn't wait to meet this new being she already loved more intensely than she'd known was possible. She was nervous about the birth, but she had Hazel and the experience of the other mothers to help her. As the date approached they decorated the main bedroom in readiness for the labour and the welcoming party. A private room had been suggested, but Angie wanted it to happen in the communal room. The loft reminded her of misery and sickness, and she didn't want that atmosphere for the baby. She wanted it to be born in the room of love, the heart of the community, where anybody could be present for the miraculous event if they wanted, the children as well.

'But what if the labour goes on for ages?' Roger said. 'What if people need to crash, man?'

'Then couldn't they be the ones to go to the

private rooms, or the hang-out?' Angie replied. 'If they really don't want to be part of this amazing thing.'

The others agreed. The children were set the task of making pictures for the walls and toys for the baby, soft rag dolls and sparkling mobiles to hang from the ceiling. Ken had made a beautiful wicker crib. Angie's birthing bed was created, hung with muslin that could be draped around to keep the flies and mosquitoes off. Fans were woven with straw or strips of material, so that people could help waft Angie some air as she laboured in the stifling heat.

Her contractions began late one morning. Angie went out into the fields to be at one with the nature bursting all around them, and helped the kids pick wild flowers for the birth room. She wondered aloud whether she should give birth outdoors, but Fern smiled and said the baby would probably come in the middle of the night. Later in the day, as the contractions intensified, she was glad to go and lie down on a bed inside, and found the others had anyway brought nature inside, bowls of summer fruits to hand and a trellis of daisies and buttercups on the muslin around the bed. It was the perfect way to bring someone new into the world.

She didn't give birth that night though. She spent most of it pacing around the house, in agony and with increasing anxiety, trying not to disturb the people who were crashed all over the place. Panic rising, she asked if she should go to hospital, but Hazel reassured her that it was fine, completely normal. In the morning they sang to her, ran her a bath, massaged her, but nothing seemed to bring the baby on. She didn't want to freak out but the thought of anything going wrong made her lose it. They gave her a joint to calm her down but it made her sick. She wished there were doctors who would give her proper drugs for the pain, who had the means to get the baby out, who would be able to do something if it all went wrong. Hugh kept trying to get her to meditate with him, kept wafting over her the smoke of some foul-smelling herb bundle that he'd lit. She had to bite her tongue to stop herself from shouting at him to fuck off. Everything began to rip her nerves to shreds. The children, picking up on the fraught intensity, were running around, crazy and feral. People were trying to be helpful, she knew, but they were making her feel worse, milling around her bed arguing over what she should do, getting her to chant or scream or squat or bend. Angie wasn't surprised the baby wanted to stay put. Hugh was even suggesting nipple stimulation, for fuck's sake.

If that wasn't helping enough, with the group's collective wisdom, many of them decided it was a good time to drop LSD. Some time later, Roger brought in his bongos and started beating out what he called tribal rhythms, thinking they would encourage the baby. Poppy started up what she called summoning the spirit of Mother Earth, which involved shaking maracas as she danced naked, emitting an incessant high-pitched wail. Angie gripped Hazel's hand and focused on her face, trying to push, as the grotesque figures behind her loomed in and out of her vision. This is chaos, she thought, before she passed out.

\* \* \*

She came to with somebody pushing her up and forward, someone else squeezing a sponge of cold water on her face, excruciating pain in her belly.

'Come on, Angel. We've got to get this baby out now.' Hazel was being calm and firm but Angie picked up her sense of urgency. Dave was hovering excitedly with the camera.

'It's stuck,' she gasped. 'It won't come. We're going to die.'

'No you won't. But come on. You're nearly there. You've got to help it.' Hazel looked to see if the baby had crowned. Angie heard her say something hurried and low to Fern about face first, needing forceps.

'What's wrong?' cried Angie.

'It's gonna be OK,' Hazel said. 'Stay calm. You have to keep going.'

Angie collapsed back in agony, pushing with all her might. She felt a searing pain as she ripped, and the warm gush as her bloody insides spilled. She heard the shouts of joy as the baby tumbled out, Hazel yelling, 'She's here! She's a girl, Angel!' Angie raised her head to look as Hazel lifted the baby up, patted it, and they heard the baby cry for the first time. Everybody crowded round to see as Hazel placed it on Angie's tummy. Her face was a misshapen mess of dark purple.

'Is she all right?' Angie asked.

Hazel was wiping the baby's head and face, Hugh welcoming the first-born Child of Ceres and attempting to sever the umbilical cord with his teeth. Hazel examined the baby.

'I think she's gonna be fine,' she said, tears spilling. 'I don't think it's permanent damage. I think it's swelling that'll go down. The bruising will go. Well done, Angel. You did so good.' She hugged her. 'Just the placenta now.'

Hazel turned her attention back to between Angie's knees, pushing people away who were crowding round the bed. Angie was passing a lot of blood, probably from the tear. Fern took the baby as Angie hunched forward again with a contraction. The baby was passed around for everyone to hold and bond with, which Hugh said should be done before she was bathed, so that everyone came into contact with the 'birth blood'. A few people abstained until the baby was clean. After Angie delivered the placenta, Hazel examined it to check it had all come out. Hugh was studying it with fascination too.

' . . . sooo full of goodness,' he was saying. 'I've heard the best way to eat it is fried with garlic and shallots.'

It was the last thing Angie remembered before losing consciousness.

★ ★ ★

As dusk fell, she came in and out of sleep. It was sometimes Hazel who woke her, giving her the baby to feed, checking her temperature, her bleeding, changing the cloths between her legs. It had all been as unbelievably surreal as a trip, but, whenever she opened her eyes, there was her battered little miracle lying next to her in the bed. Different people were at her side each time. The children, Willow particularly, were utterly enamoured with the baby, and kept coming to check she was real. She asked for Dave, but he was already locked in his dark room developing the roll of film.

In the middle of the night she woke properly, hungry and needing to move around. A beautiful peace had finally descended. She could hear distant strains of melodious guitar from the hang-out downstairs, where people were finally coming down. The children and a few adults were sleeping in the room with her so she took care not to wake them as she struggled up. She felt the blood sliding from her as she sat. She ate some fruit, then carefully gathered the baby into her arms and walked with her to the window. Physically she was in tatters. Her legs could hardly carry her, aching and wobbly; her abdomen felt as though she had exploded. She could smell herself, pungent and meaty. But none of it mattered.

It was a full moon again, as it had been at her creation ceremony, which filled Angie with a sense of spiritual significance. She admired her daughter, lit up by its silver rays. She began to make her vows.

'My beautiful moon child,' she whispered to her. 'So special and precious. You will be the most loved child in the whole world, I swear, and

I will be the best mother I can. I promise you'll never want for anything you need. I'll do my best to give you everything. I'll show you all that's good on this earth, protect you from everything bad. You'll grow up strong and free and happy with all the love and encouragement I have. I'll keep you close to me, but I won't smother you. I won't try to control you or mould you into something you're not. I'll never let you down, and I'll never make you feel as though you've let me down. I'll give you confidence and a real sense of your own worth. I'll bring you up to believe in yourself, to feel you can be whoever and whatever you want to be. These are my vows to you, little moon girl, and I'll never break them, I swear.'

Angie was crying suddenly, from the exhaustion and the trauma and the overwhelming feelings she had for this new person in her arms. And the wish for the father to be sharing this moment. She heard the footfalls of bare feet behind her, felt an arm slip round her shoulder, and thought her wish had come true. But the person who then leaned down and kissed the baby's forehead was Hazel.

# 1999

# Nat

Nat picked Jade up from Lee's stepmum's. He was right about her being a nasty old bitch. She'd had a go at Nat and it wasn't fair because it was Lee who was meant to be looking after his daughter. He'd agreed to have her a couple of times a week; it wasn't Nat's fault he had gone out. She had to sign on so Lorraine had reluctantly let her leave Jade there while she went. Nat was supposed to go straight back afterwards in case Lee hadn't come home, but she hadn't. Lee knew he was meant to have her. Nat hoped he would come back at some point, and rang Shawna. They met up in the pub and it was nice to just be out for once, so they'd had a few and the day had slipped by. But when she got back to Lee's place she found he hadn't shown up all day. Lorraine hadn't been able to do anything and was mad at her.

'Save it for your fucking waster son,' Nat had snapped, turning the pushchair and bumping it down the steps. Sometimes she regretted kicking Lee out. He hadn't been much use when he lived at hers, but now that he didn't he got away with even more. Really, she'd just wanted to show him, when she found out he'd been screwing some slag. She wasn't going to put up with being disrespected, even if he was her kid's father. Somewhere in her mind she'd thought she'd have him back once he'd learned his lesson, but he'd moved in with the stupid cow instead. It hadn't worked out, and she might have had him back, only by then Kel had moved in, so Lee had gone back to his stepmum's.

She'd fancied Kel for years, ever since she'd first seen him DJing. He was good-looking and cool, and, being TJ's older brother, much more of a man than her mates. He'd been round a few times with TJ and she'd been flattered when he showed an interest after she'd split up with Lee. She'd got off with him. She hoped it would get back to Lee and make him jealous. It had done, but it scared him off as well. She'd found it funny at the time, tried to tell herself it served him right, but in reality it was her that was paying. Kel hadn't really moved in with her as such, he'd just sort of taken up residence in her flat. And now whenever she returned home she felt like a visitor in it, another punter going round to score. She never knew who would be there, or what state they and the flat would be in.

As she walked home she felt the old fear creeping coldly back through her, replacing the nice numb buzz she'd got from the drink. She let herself in. The sitting room was dark but garage music was pumping out of it so she glanced in and saw Kel hanging with four guys she didn't know. She said 'All right?' as coolly as she could, as though their presence didn't make her guts twist. Kel raised his head at her, a kind of half nod. One of the guys turned his head and looked at her, then back. They all looked pretty out of it. Nat didn't know if they were mates of Kel's getting high together or buyers sampling. They were chilled, anyway. She went back through to the kitchen to take Jade out of the pushchair and fold it up by the door.

'TV,' said Jade.

'Not now, babe,' said Nat. Jade's mouth began to turn down for a grizzly protest. 'Here, guess what I've got you?' Jade looked hopeful. 'Chocolate!' She rummaged in her bag and got out the Aero. 'Let's go and play in your room.' She handed the bar to Jade, who grasped it with both hands and went running through. Nat took off her coat and followed her. Tyler wasn't in there. She poked her head round the door of her bedroom, into the bathroom. He wasn't there.

She steeled herself, went back into the front room.

'Seen Tyler?' she asked Kel, as casually as she could.

Kel looked at her through half-lidded eyes. 'Yeah,' he said. 'He went out to play with his mate.'

'Oh. Right.' She gave a small smile and dipped back out of the room. She wanted to ask when that had been, but something in his voice had had an air of menace about it, an air that said, *Yeah — what of it?*

He hadn't put up with Tyler's tantrums for a second.

'He's gotta learn respect,' he'd said, slamming him against the wall when he was creating about something or other, threatening a whack. Tyler hadn't learned straight away, not until he'd got hurt a few times. Then he got the message. He still created when Kel wasn't there — in fact he was worse when Nat had to deal with him on her own than he'd been before — but there was hardly a peep out of him when he was.

She went through to the kitchen and peered out of the window to see if she could spot him. It was raining and none of the kids were out. She checked Jade in the kids' room. She was sitting on the floor holding the whole bar of chocolate to her mouth. She'd be OK for a minute. Nat picked up her coat and keys again and slipped out of the door. She hadn't seen Tyler on her way in, and they usually played around the estate. She knocked at Shane's mum's door, but she hadn't seen him and Shane was home having his tea. She started calling for him, broke into a run towards the main road. She asked some older kids hunching in a doorway smoking, but they hadn't seen him. She ran to the play area, a patch of grass with swings and a slide. At first she thought he wasn't there, but then she caught sight of the red sleeve of his coat along the edge of the slide. What the hell was he doing lying out there in the rain?

She rushed over to him, not calling his name until she got near enough that she could catch him before he wriggled up and ran away. But he stayed lying there until she reached him. 'TYLER!' she shouted again, but he didn't respond. He hated getting wet, but he was just lying there, the rain falling on his sky-turned face. He was awake, but his eyes were weird, as though he couldn't keep them in place, rolling back under his upper lids. She pulled him up and shook him, tried to get him to speak. She yanked him up by the arms to standing, tried to hold his hand to tug him along and see if he could walk. He was clutching something in one of his fists. She prised it open and found one of Kel's baggies, still with a couple of white tablets inside.

'Fuck!' she shouted. 'Did you eat one of these? Tyler! Answer me!' But he wouldn't. She opened his mouth, tried to see any traces of it. 'Oh no, no, no,' she began to cry over and over. She hoisted Tyler and tried to run with him towards home. The vodka in her veins made her stagger and she couldn't think straight. She had no idea what to do. It was only when an older couple came running towards her that she realized she was screaming.

'I've got to get him home,' she cried, battling to get past them at first. The woman managed to grasp her while the man took Tyler.

'What's wrong with him?' the woman was asking her firmly. 'Is he epileptic?'

Nat shook her head as she sobbed.

'Has he taken something?'

'I don't know, I don't know!'

The man had Tyler in one arm as he flipped open his phone and called 999. 'Ambulance,' he said and started talking to the services on the other end of the phone.

The woman was trying to calm Nat down, saying, 'He'll be OK, he'll be OK. They'll get him to hospital really quick.'

Shit. The consequences of it suddenly hit Nat. 'He can't go there!' she yelled at them. 'He'll be all right. I need to take him home.'

But the couple had taken over now and the ambulance was on its way. The man was still talking on the phone, telling them where they were. The woman tried to reason with Nat, going on and on in her calm voice about why he had to go to hospital.

'But I've got another kid at home. I've got to get back,' said Nat.

'Is it on its own?' the woman asked urgently. 'Is there anyone else at home? Can you phone anyone?'

Yes, she had to phone Kel. Her mobile was in her pocket and she called his, trying to control her sobs as she willed him to pick up. She moved away from the couple, who were following instructions over the phone, lying Tyler down on a bench. A few more people had gathered round the commotion.

'Yo,' Kel said finally. 'What's up?'

'Tyler's taken something,' she said in an urgent whisper. 'The ambulance is coming. Get rid of everyone and clear up.'

'What the FUCK?' hissed Kel. 'What are you fucking doing calling an ambulance, you stupid bitch? Shit man.'

'It wasn't me,' Nat tried to protest. 'I'll say he found them outside.'

'Yeah, you do that. Fuck.'

'And look after Jade.' Nat didn't know if he'd heard her before he rang off. She was sure he wouldn't hang round the flat waiting for the police to turn up. She couldn't imagine him taking Jade with him wherever he went.

'I've got to get my baby,' she said to the woman.

'There's no time,' the woman said, but Nat was already running.

★ ★ ★

She got back as the ambulance men were loading Tyler into the back. She pushed past everyone with Jade, covered in chocolate, bumping and screaming on her hip, and climbed in with him.

'Do you know if he's taken something?' one of the paramedics asked. When she didn't answer, he added, 'It might save his life if we know.'

She took the baggie out of her pocket and showed the tablets to him.

'He had these in his hand. I think it might be E,' she said. 'I don't know. He must've picked them up in the park.'

'Did you see him do that?' he asked.

Nat shook her head.

'How long has he been like this?' he asked.

'I — I don't know,' Nat admitted.

'Were you looking after him?'

'No. Well, yes.' Kel would be mad if she said he was meant to be watching Tyler. Best leave him out of it altogether. 'But he, he ran off when I was feeding her. I didn't realize he'd gone.' Nat desperately tried to sober up so that she could get the lies straight in her head. Tyler found the tablets outside. Kel wasn't at her flat dealing drugs. Kel didn't exist. She hadn't been in the pub all day but home with her son.

★ ★ ★

She stuck to her story to the doctors, to the police, to social services. Hours and hours of questions into the night before they went back to the flat. Kel had done a good job of clearing out; they found no sign of him. He'd done what she'd said when she'd run in for Jade — to take his clothes as well as the drugs and to stay away until she called him. They believed she lived there alone. Her story was checking out. She thought they believed her when she said she'd only had one drink earlier when a friend, whose birthday it was, had come round. She gave them Shawna's name and hoped she'd have time to text her with the story. She said the bottles in the kitchen had been there for months, since a party. But then they found some skunk down the side of the sofa cushion. At first she said she didn't know anything about it, it must have belonged to someone who came round, perhaps at that same party. But then they started asking her for names of friends who took drugs. In the end she said it was hers. It wasn't enough for a big sentence, she was sure. They asked who she got it off and she said she didn't know, someone on the street. It was in a baggie exactly like the one she'd shown them with the pills Tyler had taken. She tried to convince them it must have been from the same dealer working the patch. They said forensics could prove it. She said eventually that the pills were hers too.

Tyler was kept in hospital for a couple of days for observation. He was going to be OK. Even so, they took him from her, and Jade, put them with foster carers. They said it was temporary, while she was charged and sentenced. That when it was over, if she worked with the services and cleaned up her act, she would get them back.

The following night was the first one Nat had ever spent alone. She sat in shock under the strip light in the kitchen, unable to do anything but chain-smoke as the silence pressed down and smothered her.

# FIVE

*A painting. A woman at a window,
looking out.*

*She sits on an old wooden chair, leaning for-
ward with her arms on the sill, a loose dress
draping over her form to her feet, which are
bare. Her hair is swept up at the back to reveal
the nape of her neck, stray locks falling around
her shoulders. Her face is in profile, highlighted against the glass.*

*The large window takes up most of the
painting, placed at the very centre of it, looking out onto a dark sky. All that can be seen
of the room surrounds the window at the
edges of the painting: the bare white walls,
the lack of curtains, the unpolished floorboards, a discarded stocking. The perspective
of the lines of the floorboards leads the eye
up to the woman's feet, taking in the figure
tilting forward and following her gaze through
the window, but we do not know what she
can see outside.*

*It is lighter inside than it is out. Because of
this all that can be seen through the window
is the artist's reflection suspended in mid-air
in one of the panes. He half-sits against a
tall stool, painting at an easel. The way he is
painted contrasts with the detail of the woman*

— each contour, each lock of hair, each toe-nail, each fold of her dress, painstakingly captured. His figure, a barely-there impression.

The kind of painting in which the image can only be made out with unfocused eyes. If she looks straight at him he disappears into so many indecipherable daubs of paint. She has to look slightly away from him to make him out. The figure, the easel, his arm holding the brush.

# 2003

# Luna

The second time they met it was as natural as though they had been doing this for months. Luna had emailed to ask what she should wear, and Jon still didn't know, so he had told her to wear anything she liked. She wore the same long boots but with faded drainpipe jeans and a tight long-sleeved T-shirt that she knew was too tight once he started looking over her figure. It was flattering, she knew, perhaps too much so. He still couldn't decide how his painting should be, so he sketched again, this time asking her to stand at the window in bare feet, looking in, so he could catch her silhouette.

The third time she came, the week before Christmas, she wore a black dress made out of soft jersey that clung and yet also slid over her figure, while the hem skittered above her knees. This time he asked her to recline on the sofa, and she lay with her arms behind her head, a position which raised her breasts, as well as the hem of the dress.

It felt different, that third time, perhaps because they had agreed to meet later in the day and the darkness set in on the sitting so much sooner than it had before. Jon too seemed different. He was distracted, unable to concentrate for long periods. After only a couple of hours, he put down his charcoal and stretched and asked her if she'd like to go for a Christmas drink. An anxious reflex made her look at her watch, even though Pea knew she was 'out with friends' and wouldn't be home until late. In fact, having a drink would be a good idea, if she wanted to arrive home in the right spirit for someone who'd been out with friends, with a relaxed demeanour and a boozy tinge to her breath when she kissed him. But still, she hesitated. Sitting for a painting was one thing, even grabbing something to eat during the course of it — part of the same thing. But finishing early and going for a drink was something else. She wondered if Jon had planned a later meeting specifically for this reason. He had certainly been more fidgety today, unable to settle and focus on drawing the way he usually did, as though he had something on his mind.

'I just can't do any more today,' Jon said to her silence.

He came over to her with his sheet of paper, and she sat up and took it. He sat next to her on the sofa and pointed vaguely at the drawing.

'I've done enough of this pissing about now,' he said. 'I know what you look like. Sitting, standing, lying. I feel I know your body — I mean, its lines and that, you know.' He scratched his head, embarrassed. 'I've got to decide how to paint you and just bloody start. Stop messing about.'

Luna looked at his drawing. He had extremities — hands, feet, a knee, but very little of her actual torso beyond an albeit very

294

accurate outline. Still, she loved the strong, swooping nature of his strokes. They seemed to somehow perfectly suit her long limbs and angular frame, the way she held herself.

'It's not exactly finished,' she said. 'Isn't my body supposed to be here somewhere?' She peered at the painting in mock search.

He coughed and stood up, muttering something about 'the problem'.

'Sorry?' she asked.

'Nothing,' he replied. 'Come on. I can't do any more today. Let's go out and we can talk about the proper portrait.' He seemed frustrated with himself, and so Luna acquiesced, reaching down for her boots.

'Do you know anywhere round here?' she asked, looking up at him. As she did so she saw from his face that as she bent down her dress was gaping. She clasped the front of it to her chest, saying, 'Sorry.'

'Don't apologize. Really,' he said, in his dry way, which made her giggle.

He was still staring, and so she had to say, 'Excuse me,' to make him turn away while she pulled the other boot on. She supposed she should be offended, but found instead that she was amused. Flattered. He didn't appear lechy so much as — awestruck. It felt good to have so much admiring attention for a change. And it was especially good coming from Jon, although she wasn't sure why: Was it because she felt he had such a good eye, artistically speaking? Or was it that he seemed so self-composed, so immovable? Whatever it was, it filled her with a sense of potency, a feeling, she realized, which had been missing, and which, as she strode along beside him, made her more aware of her sexual prowess than she had ever been.

'So. What does Christmas mean for you then?' he asked, over their Happy Hour cocktails.

It was the first time either of them had addressed directly what happened in their actual lives.

'Well, I'd usually spend it with my mum and her random bunch of waifs and strays. Which will probably include Tomas this year.' She crossed her eyes comically. 'So for one reason and another, I'll be giving that a miss this year.' Jon looked more concerned than amused.

'Why's that?' he asked.

'It's kind of a long story.'

'I've got time.'

She looked at him and saw that he really meant it, that he really wanted to know. So she told him, about the row with Angie and what had caused it, about her upbringing in the commune, her now-deceased grandparents, the recent hook-up with her dad's side of the family.

'So you're a Yorkshire lass!' he exclaimed, looking exceptionally pleased.

'If it means you'll stop typecasting me as the villain, then yes,' she laughed.

'I haven't been doing that! Have I?'

'Well, admit it — you're now suddenly seeing me in a different light!'

He looked at her appraisingly. 'I suppose I am, actually,' he admitted. 'I don't mean I'm thinking more highly of you. But you don't fit the stereotype I had you down for. All that hippy stuff as well — I just thought you had a posh middle-class background, you know. Safe. That you could lean on Daddy to pay the rent while you twatted around being arty-farty. But in fact it wasn't so easy. You've had to be pretty independent from the word go, by the sounds of it.'

'Yes, I suppose I have,' Luna said, blushing at the praise.

'You've done well,' he said. His directness was unnerving, but at the same time Luna was enjoying revealing herself afresh to this new person who appreciated her, for herself and for her achievements. It was good to feel interesting to somebody again, when at home all this stuff about her was taken for granted. Her life story was tied to Pierre. There was only one new aspect to herself she could share, one new dimension, one new aspiration, and he didn't want to hear it.

'So. In answer to your question,' she said after a pause. 'I'll be spending Christmas with just my boyfriend.' She was glad to have got the mention of her boyfriend out. Both of them seemed to have avoided any talk of their partners, and it had started to feel odd.

'Right,' said Jon. He took a long gulp of his drink.

'What about you?' she asked. He looked uncomfortable, so she added smoothly, 'Will it just be you and your wife, or do you have to do a trawl of a thousand relatives?' He looked taken aback, then relieved that she had brought up the fact that he was married.

'It'll be a bit of both. This year it's my mam and dad on Christmas Day and Hannah's lot on Boxing Day.'

'Have you got a big family?' Luna asked. They couldn't be more different. Jon had a brother and two sisters and a shed-load of cousins, all still living in the same area where they were brought up. They were close. His extended family knew his wife's extended family. She'd been right about the childhood sweethearts.

'It must be nice,' she said.

'Isn't that just normal?' he replied.

'Yes,' she said. 'I suppose it is.'

They were talking so much she missed the nine o'clock train she'd planned to catch, and had to run for the nine-thirty. Jon escorted her all the way to the train door, as always.

'Happy Christmas,' he said, as she turned to say goodbye before climbing into the train. 'Email me. And try to make that one before New Year.'

Jon had been at pains to point out that he wouldn't be off with his family the whole week in between Christmas and New Year. He was pretty much having a regular working week, he said, although there wouldn't be that much work to do, and he was sure he'd be able to get away for a sitting if she could. It seemed so vital to him, as though he couldn't last somehow if they missed a week.

'I can't promise anything,' she said. He looked so forlorn that she added, 'But I will try.'

The whistle blew, so she quickly reached up to

kiss him on the cheek. Next thing she knew he was pulling her into him for a hug. She was aware of his hands somehow being inside her coat, sliding tightly round her waist, his face in her hair. Their bodies pressed together and he seemed to breathe her in as her arms moved round his big shoulders. Her cold nose met his hot neck, and then he was lifting her effortlessly onto the train. They watched each other through the window as it pulled out of the station. She could feel the imprint of his body along hers all the way home.

★ ★ ★

The Christmas period was much better than Luna expected. Her dread of it had gone, and instead she threw herself into the festivities. The commission cheque helped. No money worries for a while, and, with some decent earnings, her confidence came back. Amelia performed the grand unveiling at her home Christmas party, which was, as expected, a fabulous extravagant affair. The portrait was incredibly well received (it actually drew a gasp of admiration as it was revealed), and Luna received several approaches regarding further commissions. Julian threw a great party at his club, to which Luna invited Alex and Danny as well as everyone else she knew. Even Pea, surprisingly, was in festive spirits, and they had fun in a way they hadn't for years. Everyone commented how great she looked, and she felt it. She found she was enjoying dressing up, finding funky clothes she'd forgotten she had hanging in her wardrobe. It felt good, to just enjoy the sensation of being a woman, for a change. Pea was over his angsty phase, now that his sculptures were on schedule for the show, and he caught her mood to let go and party.

They had such a good time at Julian's do, they went out on a kind of date a couple of days later, spending a fortune on a night of clubbing. Pierre looked gorgeous, sweating on the dance floor, a close-fitting shirt sticking to his light, sinewy body and his wavy hair forming damp tendrils around his gleaming, wonderful face. Luna was lately accompanied by an ever-present out-of-body awareness of how she looked, and she watched herself now with Pierre, admiring how they looked together. They fitted well, and she enjoyed the feeling of being in such a sexy couple. They actually smooched all the way home in the cab as though they'd only just met. They had fabulous couldn't-wait-to-get-their-clothes-off sex when they got home.

Pea sank immediately into a deep satiated sleep and she lay, her heart beating with excitement in the guilt-tinged afterglow, knowing it was the perfect time for making a baby.

★　★　★

'D'you fancy going to Paris for Christmas?' said Pierre, suddenly, coming off the phone to his parents just days before.

'What — now?' asked Luna, looking up startled from her emails.

'When d'you think? Yeah, why not?' said Pierre. 'You refuse to go to Angie's and we haven't seen my folks for ages. We've been working really hard. I fancy a few days away. Let's see if we can get a flight or the Eurostar. What do you say?'

Luna closed her email and looked at him, two thoughts arguing in her mind. One jumped excitedly at the prospect, the other slyly suggested that if she encouraged him to go, she could take up Jon's suggestion of meeting for another sitting before New Year.

'Um — I don't know,' she wavered. 'I've got loads to do, but . . . you could go.'

His face fell.

'Aw, come on, Lu. What've you got to do that can't wait a few days? We haven't been able to spend time together for ages. And I've really enjoyed this last week with you.' He came over and put his arm round her, kissed her head. 'Can't you get out of your shifts at Trey's? You've been doing loads lately, surely he can spare you for once? I'll make the call for you, if you like — say I'm taking you on a surprise trip.'

'No, no — I'll do it,' Luna replied hurriedly. 'I'm not worried about that.'

'What then?' Pierre said, turning her round in her chair. 'Give me one good reason why I can't whisk you off to Paris tomorrow.'

His face was so eager Luna could only laugh. The fact it would be her money doing the whisking didn't matter. He was right, it would be fun. Like old times. His family was sweet and spoiled them rotten when they visited, and they

301

had a to-die-for apartment in the Marais. Christmas in Paris. It would be romantic, start the new year and their future in the right way.

'OK, you win. There are no good reasons for turning down a trip to Paris. Let's do it.'

Within an hour Pierre had found and booked flights from London City Airport for just over a hundred quid each. They had to leave early in the morning, and Luna headed up to the bedroom excitedly to pack while Pierre called Maman back to tell them of their sudden arrival.

'She's made up,' he called, bounding up the stairs afterwards. 'Although be prepared, it sounds like the entire extended family will be there. God knows how many nieces and nephews I've got now — they'll all be charging around the place. If we need some privacy, maybe we can get a B&B or something.'

'It'll be fine, I'm sure,' Luna answered. All but one of his younger siblings were married now, and three had kids at the last count. There had been a newborn recently, to his youngest brother, she thought. Maybe that would make him see things differently. His mother's influence would be good too — it used to be annoying, the constant pressure about marriage and children, but now Luna was grateful for the help. Finally things seemed to be moving in the right direction. She wished it wasn't too soon to try a pregnancy test. It would be perfect to confirm it and break the news while they were there, in the bosom of his family, hopefully cushioning his initial shock. But she daren't say anything unless it was absolutely definite. If she was pregnant she was sure Pierre would come round, but if he found out about her deception when she wasn't he would never forgive her. It would be all over for them and she would never get another chance.

⋆　⋆　⋆

Paris was wonderful. They stayed for the entire week, and spent New Year's Eve surrounded by four generations of Pierre's family, looking out from the veranda and watching fireworks explode and shimmer over the beautiful city. The future seemed bright and exciting and Luna was filled to the brim with hope. The family, always warm and welcoming to her, seemed to treat her especially fondly, particularly the grandmothers, and she was sure they had guessed her condition. She supposed it wasn't hard to anyone observant and tuned in to that particular frequency, the way elder matriarchs were. Especially somewhere like France, where the traditions of what should be drunk with which part of the meal were still formally upheld and it was perhaps more apparent if you were declining anything alcoholic at all. They didn't say anything, but Luna saw the two old ladies exchange glimmering glances with each other, and they outdid themselves showering her with extra hugs and kisses and fuss. Luna longed to make the announcement, for their expectant sakes as well as her own. The atmosphere went to her head so much that she almost did, but managed to stop herself. In any case, in this environment, it should be Pierre to do it, while she stood in his embrace, glowing, simply receiving everybody's praise and admiration.

Gradually, a specialness was being endowed upon her that she had known nothing of. She didn't even have to do anything to earn it, the way she had done with her art. It was inherent within her, and the minute it was announced everyone would flock to her to celebrate her achievement. It made her want to laugh aloud. It seemed so easy, this natural ability she had dismissed for so long. Yes, you could be dismissive about it, yes, anyone could do it. It wasn't really an achievement as such. You couldn't make a baby with your own bare hands, with all your talent and skill and effort. And perhaps this was the reason that it was so very priceless. Because, really, nothing else Luna had ever done had come close to making her feel the way she felt now.

Her high spirits continued when they arrived back home. She said goodbye to the precarious old year, setting off for her new chapter as though it were a brave new world. Pierre went back to work with a vengeance, but she no longer felt lost and adrift, not knowing what to do or how to move forward. It was happening for her without her having to try, nature was taking care of it. They were happier together than they had been for ages. She bought a pregnancy test and planned how she would tell Pierre. It would be hard to do, but everything would be all right in the end, she was sure. He would understand that this was what had brought them closer together again, that it was the right thing for them. She filled the excruciating time until the first day of her next period secretly surfing the Net for information about pregnancy and motherhood, or drifting around Mothercare and the baby section of Boots, buying folic acid and Pregnacare vitamins. It was like a new kingdom, which smoothly opened its gates to her now she had a pass.

A need to take care of herself overwhelmed her, as though she was something incredibly precious. She kept thinking Pierre would guess — surely he could tell there was something different about her? But he didn't seem to. He only seemed happy that she was happy. As the days moved along, she felt her senses become more acute. Her beloved coffee began to repel her, her breasts hurt and her stomach swelled. A faint nausea hit when she got out of bed.

*   *   *

Going to sit for Jon again didn't matter as much as it had. She still went, still looked forward to it, but she couldn't remember why on earth it had felt so crucially important before. It made her feel slightly silly, and she hoped Jon hadn't noticed the air of need she'd had about it. As she stepped off the train and looked for his inevitable frame she felt at her most supreme — the most attractive, the most confident, the most powerful. She moved towards him, aware of how the wind blew her loose hair from her face and her flowing dress against her body, how enhanced her femininity was by her big Eskimo boots (no more jarring heels), knowing she looked at her ultimate best. The perfect timing for a portrait. How wonderful to have this moment captured, before the new life was confirmed and declared, but there within her all the same, showing itself through her. She had to have this portrait, she realized. She would offer Jon any amount for it. How she would explain it to Pea she didn't know, but, as with everything else, she had absolute certainty that it would all turn out right. She could see herself in the future, looking back on this painting as the start of it all, passing on the story to the person who was now forming.

She saw Jon take her in, but a pained, almost haunted expression overcast his features. She kissed his cheek and smiled hello.

'All right?' he responded grimly and turned for the exit.

'Happy New Year and all that,' she said after a pause.

'Oh yeah. And you.' He was moody, disapproving almost.

'How are you?' she persisted. 'How was Christmas?'

'Oh — you know. All right. Quiet.' He turned his collar up against the cold. 'Nothing as glamorous as yours, I'm sure.'

Luna glanced sideways at him but he stared resolutely ahead of him towards the car.

'I'm sorry I didn't make the sitting after Christmas,' she said softly. 'You did get my email before you came all the way here, didn't you?'

'Oh yes. Don't worry about that. I wasn't

really expecting we'd be able to make it. I had work to do anyway.' He looked at her finally as he opened the passenger door for her, and managed a small smile.

'Is everything all right?' she asked. She saw him soften then, as though he wanted to keep it up but couldn't.

'I'm sorry. I'm fine.' He walked round and got in the driver's seat. 'I suppose I'm jealous. Spending the season in Paris sounded sickeningly fantastic.'

Luna laughed. 'It was. Sorry.' She reached out and touched his knee in a gesture of apology.

'Yeah, you look as though you are,' he said. Luna giggled. He glanced across at her. 'You look wonderful,' he said. She felt the colour rise to her cheeks.

'Thank you.'

He looked at her again. 'Especially now.' He took his eyes off the road to watch her glowing cheeks, seeming to take the greatest of pleasure in them.

'Stop it, will you?' she said, waving his gaze away and looking out of the window.

'I've got to get my revenge somehow,' he said.

★ ★ ★

That day, Jon began the portrait proper. He'd arranged a wooden chair for her to sit on at the window, leaning forward with her arms up on the sill, her hands supporting her face as she looked out. Something about the pose pleased her, the way she had her back turned to what was in the room and she was facing out, as though she was looking into the future. Jon's viewpoint, from the side and slightly behind, emphasized the forward motion into what was beyond the room. What he could see through the window she couldn't tell. He only said he might want to use the window for something other than background, but he didn't yet know. Also, the position was comfortable and allowed her to watch the world go by out of the window. It gave her stomach lots of room, which — and the thought made her catch her breath — she would need over the weeks as her baby grew.

'Are you happy with the clothes I'm wearing?' she asked as Jon stood back and appraised her once he'd finished arranging her limbs — her boots were off, her feet planted wide.

'They're perfect, as it goes,' he said. 'I wasn't sure about the dress at first. It's a bit — well — hippyish for you. Not what you usually wear. And I thought the lines wouldn't be right. But the way the material hangs is great. Really great. A real contrast to the sharp lines of the window frame. And you look kind of Pre-Raphaelite. A bit of a challenge to paint, mind. Thanks for that.'

She smiled apologetically at him before settling into the position. She wondered how long it would take him to finish the portrait. Would her bump show under the fabric of her dress by the end? Would he paint it in? Would he notice, even? And would she tell him? She suddenly found she wanted to, desperately. She supposed it was something to do with already

308

sharing secrets with him. He felt like a confidant. There was something easy about talking to him, especially in this pose, where she was looking away. There was something freeing about that, when you were trying to express yourself.

For today, though, she decided to keep it to herself. She probably would tell him, maybe even before Pierre. But in the meantime she would just lean forward with her secret pushing at her breasts and stomach, unseen beneath the loose drape of her dress.

★   ★   ★

The blood came, thick and globby and late, on the train on the way to the next sitting. The test she had taken on the day it was meant to come had been negative, but still she had been convinced she was pregnant. She took the other test in the packet the following day — still negative. But she hadn't believed either of them. She'd clung to the thought that they were often wrong, which meant that it still came as a shock and a blow when she bled. It was so heavy, dragging on her womb as she cried silently in the train toilet, doing her best to tidy up with paper towels, finding some tampons in the bottom of her bag. She had no painkillers on her and wished it had at least happened before she set off so she could have cancelled, drugged herself up and gone back to bed. She sat back at her seat, trying to curl her knees up into her to relieve the cramps. No position was comfortable. It made her convinced she was having an early miscarriage, whatever the pregnancy tests had said. Hormonal emotions and dashed hopes came over her in waves, like the pain. There would be no telling Pea anything after all, and, by extension, no comfort from him either. And here she was, hurtling towards Leicester, of all places, and some man she hardly knew.

The clarity of how estranged she'd become from Pierre hit her like another thump to her stomach and she went to the toilet again to weep. It was just as well. She crouched over the toilet bowl as long as her thigh muscles would let her. She felt woozy, not sure if it was the copious loss of blood or the motion of the train. A practical voice in her head told her she mustn't faint in there, like that. It was no way to be found. She cleaned up as best she could and staggered back, pulling herself from seat to seat. She wondered if she should get off at the next station and get the first train home, but she felt as though she'd never make it. An image of Jon, sturdy Jon, standing with his feet firmly planted on the platform wafted into her head as she collapsed into her seat and closed her eyes.

Anyway, the next time the train stopped it was at Leicester. She had no choice but to get off. She did her best to alight from the train in a normal state, to walk towards Jon and smile.

She saw him register that something was wrong. She knew she was walking gingerly, could feel a light film of sweat on her forehead that her wisps of fringe stuck to.

'Are you all right?' he said, taking her arm.

'Yes. No. I think so.' She tried to laugh it off,

wafting a hand, but the enforced breeziness took a huge effort. 'I'm sorry. I've come over a bit faint.'

He led her to a bench and sat her down. 'D'you need some water?' He looked up and down the platform and into the top of her bag. 'Take some deep breaths. I'll run and get some.'

She grabbed his arm as he rose. 'Don't go. I think I'll be fine.' She leaned her head on her hands, elbows on knees, for a few moments, and then sat back. 'Am I green?' she asked as she took careful breaths of air.

'Pretty much, yeah,' he answered. He reached up and swept back a lock of hair that had stuck to the moist skin on her face.

'It's passing,' she said. She was trembling.

'Are you OK to walk? Can you get to the car or should I get help here?'

'No. No. Let's get to the studio. I'll lie down for a bit there. I'll be all right after that cup of tea you're making.'

He offered his arm and she slipped her hand into the crook of it, leaning on him as she weakly pulled herself up and they walked slowly through the station. He asked how she was every few minutes, making sure she wasn't feeling worse again. She tried to dismiss his concern, tried to ask after him instead and apologized for being 'boring'.

'Don't be daft,' he said. 'You're really unwell. I can see that.'

After helping her up the stairs he settled her on the sofa, pulling off her boots and tucking the blanket round her. He brought her a glass of water while he put the kettle on and opened the new biscuits he'd bought.

'I couldn't,' she protested as he raised one to her mouth, but he insisted.

'It'll do you good,' he said, sitting on the edge of the sofa and looming over her while he offered her a bite of biscuit followed by a sip of tea.

'Your tea chaser,' he said. She smiled. He was sweet to remember that she'd called it that before.

'I'll be right as rain in a mo, I promise,' she said. 'I don't want to waste your time.'

'Don't be ridiculous,' he said. 'God — I don't care about the painting, if that's what you're worried about.'

'I'm sure you have better things to do than come all this way just to nurse me,' she said.

'Believe me, I really haven't.'

She shot him a look. 'What would you be doing otherwise?' she asked.

'Spending the day discussing the finer points of brand recognition with a risk management consultancy.' Luna managed a wan laugh. 'And trying to make it sound really exciting so they take us on.'

'OK, you win. This is definitely more fun than that.'

'Hands down,' he agreed. As he squeezed her hand to emphasize the point, tears welled in her eyes and she felt her face crumple. She sat up, wiping her eyes, and said sorry again. Then she abruptly staggered from the room to the loo at the end of the corridor. When she came back she attempted a bright smile, but he didn't look convinced. Although she had splashed cold water on her face, she could feel her skin, puffy and tight round her eyes.

'You don't have any painkillers, do you?' she asked.

'God, are you all right?' he said, coming forward. She saw him register her hand over her stomach.

'It's women's trouble,' she said.

'Oh right. Actually, yes I do.' He rifled through his briefcase and found a packet of Ibuprofen. 'I often get headaches in my meetings, I have no idea why,' he said.

'I can't imagine,' she said. She tried not to wince as she walked across to the bed he'd made for her and collapsed thankfully on it. He gave her the tablets and watched her as she let her head fall back and closed her eyes.

'Are you sure that's all that's wrong?' he said.

She looked at him and opened her mouth to speak, but nothing came. She closed her eyes again and put her hand across her forehead.

'Yes and no,' she said, in the end. He waited. 'I may have just lost a baby.'

At first Jon was so stunned he didn't react. Then when he did it was strong.

'Oh my God! We should get you straight to a hospital.' He lunged at her and grabbed her hands, jolting her eyes open.

'No, no!' she answered, embarrassed. 'Sorry — it's not that bad. I just mean that I thought I was pregnant. I might have been. But if I was it was all very . . . early. I mean, there wouldn't have been a . . . an actual baby. Not yet.'

313

'Oh. Oh . . . OK.' He reddened at his overdramatic reaction. Luna fell back again with her hands over her face and sighed.

'I'm sorry,' said Jon. After a while he said, 'Do you want me to call Pierre?'

She parted her hands and looked at him. She saw what that would mean for him as well as for her.

'And I'll take you back down to London in the car. You shouldn't go on the train.'

'You are so kind,' she said. 'But there's no need for all that, honestly. I'll be all right in a minute.' She rolled onto her side and drew her knees up. 'Actually,' she added, 'Pierre doesn't know.'

'Doesn't know . . . what?' asked Jon, sitting down on the sofa where her legs had been.

'Any of it. He doesn't know I was — might have been — pregnant. He doesn't know I'd stopped taking the Pill. I suppose it's all for the best, really.'

Jon didn't speak, just sat watching her with a concerned frown.

'It was wrong of me,' said Luna. 'He doesn't want kids.'

'What — ever?' he asked, incredulous.

'Maybe not. Neither of us did. But I changed my mind. Or not my mind really. It was more like a change of heart.'

They stayed in silence for a while.

'I don't know what I was thinking. I guess I just hoped it would happen and he would come round to the idea. I knew it wasn't right, somewhere. But I couldn't come to my senses.

314

When I thought it had happened I was . . . so happy.' Her voice cracked as she spoke the word. 'But of course, I shouldn't have been. I had no right to do that against his wishes and be happy. You must think I'm an awful person.'

'No,' he said quickly. 'Not at all.'

His response made her begin to cry again, and she sat up to wipe her eyes and sniff. He put his arm round her, while she tried to compose herself.

'I think you'll be a wonderful mother,' he said, at last. It was the best thing he could say, and the worst. He held her while she leaned back into his shoulder and cried.

⋆　⋆　⋆

Jon had gone to the shops while she slept. When she awoke he was heating up what he thought she'd be able to manage for lunch: a posh ready-made soup in a carton and some rolls, a couple of microwaveable chocolate puddings. He'd bought some extra-strength painkillers that said they were suitable for period pain, as well as the sanitary pads she'd asked for. Curiously, there had been no embarrassment from either of them about it. Luna was touched by how well he looked after her. He wouldn't let her travel until he was convinced she was revived enough to make the journey home. She allowed him to keep his arm round her as he helped her out of the car, even when they had stopped walking and sat together on their bench waiting for the train. As it drew in she stood and thanked him and rested her head against his shoulder.

'You will take care of yourself, won't you?' he urged her, speaking into her hair. 'Please let me know how you are. Text me when you get home. And tomorrow. Or email. I'll be worrying.' It was hard to pull apart. But then whistles were blowing and the guard was moving along the platform slamming the doors shut, and Luna had to hurriedly board the train. She smiled at him as the train pulled away, and watched him, standing resolutely where he was, as though he wouldn't move until the train got to London.

★   ★   ★

Incredibly, it all passed Pierre by. She was so late back that her first thought as she came through the door to find him not there was that he was at the police station raising the alarm that she was missing. But then she found his scrawled note on the table saying that Tony had called round and they'd gone drinking with the gang in Spitalfields. *Come after work if you feel like it*, he'd written, with the name of the bar they'd be at.

She was glad of the time alone. She surprised herself with how immediately and automatically she thought to dutifully text Jon that she was home safe and sound, as though he was family. She added that she had the place to herself so could just make a cup of tea, have a hot bath and go to bed. Two minutes later her phone rang, and as she saw it was Jon she hesitated briefly, and then answered.

'I just pulled over when I saw you could talk,'

he said. 'How are you?'

She heard herself laugh with genuine pleasure at the sound of his voice and the image of him immediately swerving into a lay-by when he thumbed through her text at the wheel.

'I'm fine,' she said. 'Much better. Thanks to you.'

'I didn't do anything,' he said. 'I was just glad to be able to be there for you. You shouldn't go through that on your own.'

'It was nothing, really. But what about you? Aren't you home yet?'

'Nearly. Don't worry.'

'But — how will you explain?'

'I'll think of something. It'll be fine. I'm just glad you're back. Glad I could talk to you.'

'Thanks for calling. Thanks for everything. I'm so sorry about today.'

'You've got nothing to be sorry about. Really. I'm sorry you . . . I understand how you must be feeling. It must be really upsetting.'

'I'm all right, really.'

Luna tried to make light of it, but his seriousness moved her. He called a loss a loss. Even if she hadn't been pregnant after all. There was something so caring in that, something she didn't get from those closest to her, or even herself really. She, Pea and her mother were all for shrugging things off like they were nothing.

'Like I said,' she added, true to form, 'it really is for the best. Considering Pierre's feelings and everything.'

'What about your feelings?' he said, surprising her with the sudden force of his voice. 'What about what you want? Look, I'm probably speaking out of turn here, but . . . you shouldn't feel so bad about what you did. There's nothing wrong with it. Your boyfriend isn't being fair to you. You only want the most natural thing in the world. How can he not see that? How can he not love you for that?'

Luna was taken aback by his strength of feeling.

'I've gone too far. I shouldn't've said anything,' said Jon to her silence. 'It's none of my business, I know. I'm sorry. I just — feel for you. I'll stop now. Don't be mad at me.'

'I'm not,' said Luna. 'Of course I'm not mad at you. How could I be? You've been so sweet. You — you're — my champion!' She had meant it humorously but realized as she said the word that she meant it. He made a slight noise as he sighed out, a moan of sorts, which Luna couldn't quite interpret. 'Now go,' she said. 'Don't get into any more trouble on my account than you're in already.'

'It doesn't matter,' he said. 'As long as you're all right.'

'I am. Thank you. Goodnight, Jon.'

'Take care, won't you?' he said, and she turned her phone off quickly before he could say anything else, sensing it was difficult for both of them to break off with a simple goodbye.

She sat curled up on the sofa with her tea, looking out at the night sky, tonight cloudless and plastered with stars. They shouldn't have been through today together, these two strangers with lives that were great distances apart. But despite the rights and wrongs of it, they had been through something together all the same, something that had brought them closer than was usual between friends of the opposite sex. Thanks to Jon taking care of her, and the bit of luck of Tony turning up, Pierre would not know what she had been scheming all these weeks and what the outcome had been today. She would text him now to say she had period pain and was getting an early night, and he would flop in beside her at some ungodly hour, and they would start again together in the morning just as before. It was strange but, as she had thought before and said to Jon, probably just as well and for the best.

*   *   *

When Luna went into her studio the following morning, the photograph of herself as a baby promptly made her cry. She marvelled at how undeniably gorgeous she was at that age — what was it? One? Two? She felt somehow inherently lacking, that she didn't know. Old enough to be standing on her own two bare feet anyway, naked in a field, with wisps of curly fair hair filled with light. She was coming towards the camera — her father — with the biggest, dimpliest grin. It was the happiest picture she had ever seen, somehow, the brand-new experience of joy radiating from the child as she revelled in the sensations of the grass underfoot, the air on her skin, her new-found ability to run towards someone she loved, someone who would wrap her in his arms

319

and keep her safe. The pure trusting innocence of her pierced Luna with a sharp sorrow for the grown woman she had become, struggling as she was to cope with the sad adult burdens of disappointment, of failure.

# Angie

## 1973

Angie watched from the farmhouse doorway, a reflexive smile mirroring her daughter's. Luna loved the discovery of her new-found feet, and although she often still teetered and stumbled and suddenly bumped to the ground on her bottom, it only ever seemed to make her laugh. Angie resisted her maternal urges to rush to pick her up and mollycoddle her, determined to let her child experience the freedom to be, confident in her own skin. It was hard though. She missed the early days, when she had Luna strapped to her body most of the time in a home-made baby sling, like a kangaroo with her offspring in a pouch. She still felt the loss of the heat and weight on her front, now feeling exposed and vulnerable without her baby there, filling the space that had been left inside her by her operation. Luna herself seemed perfectly delighted to be let loose to discover the world beyond her mother. It was a good thing, Angie told herself; it showed that she was secure, a happy, healthy baby.

Dave had stood up from his crouch and backed up a few paces, encouraging Luna to totter forward towards the camera. Her giggles as she lurched forward again drifted across to Angie on the breeze. Luna reached her hand towards the lens and after taking a few snaps, Dave put the camera down to protect it from grubby little fingerprints. He reached forward and swung the girl into the air, and she shrieked with unadulterated delight. Tears filmed over Angie's vision and she wiped them away quickly, not wanting to miss the precious scene. It was the first time she had seen Dave with Luna, just the two of them, and she wished she had a camera herself to click the image and keep it, make it eternal. Instead she would have to let the moment go into the ether, and she watched intently so it would at least live on in her memory. She felt a hope rise like a butterfly. Perhaps as the child grew he would acknowledge her more, now that he could identify her as his. For surely he couldn't fail to see the echoes of him in her face now — the dark eyes, that grin? Perhaps he couldn't connect before with the arrangement of features, at first grotesquely distorted by the force of the birth on her face. But elements of him were inevitably beginning to come out, just like truth. Perhaps he would one day have no choice but to acknowledge his flesh and blood, grow to love her, even.

At that moment, Poppy and Allun arrived back from hospital, where Poppy had had her scan. Angie felt a clutch of envy at seeing Allun help Poppy jump down, beaming, from the Land Rover, her bump proudly protruding. Poppy's was not an accidental pregnancy. They had decided together to become parents, filled with the fervour after Luna's birth for populating their community. But Allun was very definite about being the father, involved every step of the way, and he and Poppy had decided she would have the baby in hospital. It was causing a big rift in the commune between those, like Hugh, who were adamant that it wasn't the natural way and the others who believed it was every individual's right to have the birth they wanted. Each side used Angie's experience as proof of their point of view. Hugh said how wondrous it had been for everybody; his opposers said how wrong it had gone, how they should learn from it and not run that risk again. How lucky, looking back, Angie and Luna had been.

Not that lucky, Angie had thought, but she had kept it to herself. The memory of how very wrong it had gone could still drench her at times now, over a year later, like a downpour. She had had to go to hospital anyway in the end, the day after the birth, regardless of all her hopes and plans. She was still in severe pain and haemorrhaging blood. Hazel had driven her to Accident and Emergency, where they had whisked her to the operating theatre. When she came round Hazel had had to tell her it had been very serious and that they had not been able to save her womb. She wouldn't be able to have any more children.

'You have your beautiful girl,' Hazel tried to comfort her. 'And she won't have to share you with anyone else.'

Angie was devastated. The trauma seemed to make confusion cloud everything that had previously seemed so clear. In many ways, her daughter had to share her with everyone else. Was she more loved or less, having no particular father? Was it really love at all, not to lay claim to a child you'd made? And was she, Angie, wrong to have risked her baby's life by having a home birth? Would her baby's sense of security be damaged irreparably by the hours, spent without her mother while she was operated on? Would the bond between them have a permanent fault, a crack that made it weak? While these worries swarmed around her head, she also tried to cope with the grief for the big brood of children she'd imagined she would bring into the world, the lives she'd thought were her reason to be. For Angie, the shining simplicity of the commune ideal became forever tarnished.

★   ★   ★

Poppy was bending down, admiring the handful of grass Luna was thrusting towards her. Luna did have other children who would be like brothers and sisters, Angie reminded herself, and there was another on the way. Luna was fine. It was her own need for more children that tugged, like an unhealed wound. Dave was taking pictures of Luna and Poppy together. Allun came up and put his arm round Poppy, then picked Luna up and sat her on his hip. They formed a tight nucleus together, while she and Dave stood on the periphery looking on. It didn't feel right, and Angie took an instinctive step forward towards her child, wanting to reach out and extract her from Allun's embrace. She stopped herself, thinking of Luna, how good it was that she was comfortable with people other than her birth mother. Dave was laughing with the couple. He moved forward and stroked Poppy's rounded belly, gave her a kiss on the cheek. He was as loving with her as he'd been with Angie when she was pregnant. No more, no less.

They hadn't been intimate since. Angie had not wanted physical love for a long time when she came back from hospital. She needed time to recover, and her intimacy with her baby was enough. But sleeping again in the private room, she began to feel excluded. If anything it was worse when she and Luna took up residence once more in the main bedroom. She never seemed to recover her desire. The sexual act seemed almost brutal to her, an invasion of her private injury, and loss. She found more often than not that she would pair with Hazel or Fern, but the men, although quite happy with it at first, later objected to the exclusivity of the arrangement. Nobody seemed in sync any more. Some people wanted when others didn't. Angie felt uneasy with her baby daughter sleeping in the room. Some of the children were too old now to sleep innocently through. What of Crispin? He was of age and certainly more than willing and able, but the others in the group were parental figures to him — never mind the fact that his actual parents were there in the group. However free they all were, there were still taboos. It was decided he should have one of the private rooms, to bring back any girlfriends he could find.

Poppy and Allun had taken over the other private room, opting out of the group love and even calling themselves a couple, which not only went against the commune's ideals, but left no other private rooms should anyone else ever need one.

It was hard to know what was breaking the rules when there weren't any. Trying to impose rules went against the rules too. More often than not morning meetings consisted of grumpy arguments that went unresolved and resumed again the following day, or the day after that. People refused to work alongside others who held strongly opposing views, and factions began to form. Bad feeling settled in with the autumn chill. Hugh tried to restore the sense of harmony but others resisted his attempts to control and order.

'You're not our leader, man,' Roger challenged him, when Hugh tried to remind him of his commitment to 'making this work' by doing something useful around the place instead of spending the day taking mind-bending drugs.

'This isn't a free ride for losers,' Hugh had shouted, finally losing his temper. 'If you're not going to do as I say, get out of my fucking house.'

Roger had simply smirked in triumph, sat defiantly at the breakfast table, and calmly dropped a tab of acid.

'I didn't mean that as it sounded,' Hugh added. But he couldn't take back what he'd said. While most people certainly agreed that Roger was a becoming a waste of space and were sick of carrying him, Hugh's authoritarian slip of the tongue went completely against the ethos of choice they believed in. Dilemmas were moving in among them like unrested souls.

Poppy got so upset with the arguments over what she could and couldn't do with her own pregnancy that she and Allun made a shock announcement that they were leaving.

'You can't leave!' Hugh said, incredulous.

'That's just it, see,' said Allun, gesturing at Hugh himself as though he were the proof of the pudding. 'We can.'

There were such vicious accusations of selfishness and betrayal that they left sooner than planned, before they'd even sorted anywhere else.

'A bloody hostel's gotta be freer than this,' Allun mumbled, gathering up a knapsack and the few baby things they already had. Angie embraced Poppy sadly.

'You must do what's best for you and your baby,' she said. She walked with them to the gate to wave them off, with a few of the others. She would miss them terribly. She wondered if she would ever get to meet the baby she already loved as Luna's sibling.

★　★　★

The gap that was left by the first leavers was keenly felt, and Hugh was determined to fill it as quickly as possible. He encouraged everyone to go out more, to fairs, to concerts, to try to find some tuned-in replacements. It was Dave and

Justin who came back one morning with two more young women, Debbie and Tina. They were giggly, spirited best friends, who loved the idea of taking on names of nature, and christened themselves Bluebell and Daisy. Somehow, though, the names never stuck, and Debbie and Tina they stayed. They certainly brought renewed enthusiasm to the place for a while, especially to the night-time activities in the love room. Tina immediately solved the Crispin conundrum, happy to couple up with him separately much of the time, to his delight and relief, as well as joining in with everyone else. The girls seemed to most enjoy loving as a pair among the men, which certainly went down well with them. They had a good-time feel about them, reminding Angie of call girls or groupies, and she began to feel in the love sessions as though they were all acting in a bad porn film. She and the other women did their best not to seem like prudish disapproving first wives, but all the same she suggested turning the remaining private room into one for the children. For the first time in ages, there was unanimous agreement in a morning meeting.

# 2001

## Nat

When she got there, all the little streets of houses looked the same and it wasn't as easy as she thought it would be to remember which was theirs. She'd already been on two buses and must have got off in the wrong place. She wandered around for ages until she found it, and then when she did nobody answered her bangs on the door. She began to shout for Tyler and Jade, and finally someone came out of a house a few doors along. It was Cathy.

'There you are! I got the wrong house!' she laughed, stumbling towards Cathy.

'Nat. What are you doing here?' said Cathy.

'I've come to see my kids! What do you think I'm doing here?' Nat laughed again. Cathy didn't seem to be finding it as funny as Nat did.

'We didn't arrange it, Nat. I don't think you're meant to be here.'

'Yes we did,' said Nat. 'Tracey sorted it out. Didn't she tell you?' Cathy wasn't making any move to go into the house, so Nat stopped by the front gate.

'That was last week, Nat. You were meant to come at half-term.'

Nat tried to think what day it was, but drew a blank. Standing here like this was making her feel ill, and she leaned on the gate post.

'I can't believe it. Tracey told me it wrong. I've come all this way,' she said. 'Are they in school then?' Cathy was staring at her. Nat suddenly felt exhausted by her hours of getting there and wished she could lie down. She felt herself slumping, as if the tiredness was sucking the insides out of her and they were pooling around her feet.

'No Nat. They're here. It's Saturday,' she said. 'You'd better come in.'

'Tyler! Jade! Mummy's here!' she called as she followed Cathy indoors.

'Shh,' Cathy said, taking her arm and guiding her into the front room. 'Sit down and get yourself together for a minute,' she told her. 'They're in the back garden. I think you could do with a strong coffee before I call them in.'

'I wanna see them now.' Nat lurched, trying to release herself from Cathy's grasp, but Cathy was stronger and pushed her back her into a squidgy armchair that seemed impossible to climb out of. 'I've got them presents,' she said as Cathy went through the sliding doors to the kitchen.

'Jim?' Cathy called, banging on the kitchen window for her husband. She had a whispered conversation with him as he looked over at Nat, then came through. She tried to get up again but couldn't.

'It's OK, love, don't get up,' he said, and sat in the chair opposite her. 'This is a surprise. We weren't expecting you.'

'I've come to see my babies,' said Nat, lifting the plastic bag with her presents in.

'I know, love, course you have.' Jim sat forward with his elbows on his knees. 'Thing is, Nat, you're only supposed to see them when it's been arranged. It's for their sake really. So they know what's what. Do you know what I mean?'

'They won't mind!' said Nat. 'Kids wanna see their mum!'

'Yes, they do, they do. But it's better if they know they're gonna see you. If they're prepared, like. It's better all round for everybody. You too.'

'I'm fucking prepared,' Nat said. 'I'm always prepared.' The word prepared was hard to say and it didn't come out right, so she laughed. Cathy came through with a coffee. The cup was really hot and as she took it she spilled it down her front.

'Silly me. It's fucking hot, Cath.' Cathy took the cup back off her and went to get her a cloth.

'You're not really in a fit state to see them, Nat,' said Jim. 'It'll upset them. You don't want to do that, do you?'

Nat pointed a finger at him and struggled forward. 'I'd never upset my kids,' she said, stabbing the air between them.

'I know you wouldn't, Nat, not deliberately. But . . . you're not yourself at the moment, are you?'

'Course I'm myself! Who else would I fucking be?' said Nat.

'You just seem a bit — out of it,' said Jim. 'And we don't really like swearing in this house.'

'Fuck your house!' shouted Nat. It seemed like the funniest joke and she flung herself back, laughing.

Cathy came back with the coffee. 'I've put

some cold in it. Drink it down.'

'I'll give you a lift home,' said Jim. 'Come back and see them another time when you're feeling better.'

Nat held her coffee in both hands, looking down into it. The thought of going home after all that, without having even seen them was too depressing to face and she began to cry, quiet tears at first, but then she was bawling, with Cathy sitting on the arm of her chair squashing her into her fat side, saying, 'It's all right. It's all right.'

When she got up to get Nat some tissues Nat summoned all her energy and made a dash for it, running through to the back door and shouting for her kids. Tyler and another boy were racing remote-control toy cars and Jade was watching. Nat flung herself on Jade.

'Hello, my beautiful little girl!' she said, smothering her in kisses. She did the same to Tyler, who told her to get off, he'd lose the race.

'I've got you presents,' Nat persisted, sitting on the ground with her arm round him. The other little boy stopped racing his car anyway, to look at Nat. Cathy and Jim came out.

'Isn't that nice?' said Cathy to the kids. 'A surprise visit! Your mum can't stay long though. Go on, Tyler, open your present.'

Tyler looked at the bag, then away.

'There's some things for you as well,' Nat said to the other boy. She reached in to hand the things out, sweets and chocolate that she shared between them, a Barbie for Jade and a cowboy set for Tyler, plastic guns and a holster and sheriff badge. Jade smiled and was trying to tear into the packaging to get to the doll.

'Isn't she beautiful?' Nat said, leaning over to help her. 'Just like you!' Jade clutched the doll, turned round to show Cathy.

'Isn't she lovely?' said Cathy, resting her hand on Jade's head. 'No, dear, you mustn't chew her leg. She's precious.'

Nat turned back to Tyler. 'Aren't you going to play with yours?' she said. He'd put it back in the bag and was playing with the car controls, frowning. Nat picked up the bag. 'I'll help you open it,' she said.

'I don't need help, I'm not a fucking baby,' he said.

'Tyler, that's enough,' said Jim. 'You should say thank you nicely when someone gets you a present.'

Tyler threw the remote, banging it on the ground as hard as he could. 'But it's stupid,' he yelled. 'She's stupid,' and he leaped up and shoved Nat, just managing to slip through Jim's fingers and slamming the door to the house behind him. Jim followed.

'I'm sorry, love,' said Cathy. 'It's not you. I think maybe the present's a bit young for him and he felt embarrassed and didn't know what to say.'

Nat got up off the grass, wiped her jeans. She felt herself crashing. 'I don't need you telling me about my son,' she hissed, bashing Cathy's shoulder as she passed. She ran through the house and up the stairs, following the sound of Tyler yelling.

'It's OK, Mummy's here,' she called.

'I don't want you!' Tyler shouted. At the door to his room she saw Jim trying to get hold of his flailing arms as he grabbed toys and threw them. He snatched up a Game Boy and directed it at her. 'Fuck off,' he screamed.

She swung to the side to avoid it, and it clattered down the stairs behind her. The sound of it breaking enraged Tyler even more and he tried to pick up the computer off the desk. It was too heavy for him and Jim managed to restrain him finally. He relented to Jim's embrace, turning to cry into his chest. Nat stood for a moment, reeling.

'I'm sorry I got you the wrong thing,' she said. 'I'll get you something else next time. I'll get you a new Game Boy.' She didn't know if he heard her over his sobs.

Jim tried to smile at her over Tyler's head. He was a nice man. Tyler seemed to like him and his rage was subsiding. Nat took in the room before she turned to go. He had everything he could want for, not only a computer but a TV as well. It was really nice for a boy's room, with a thick carpet and football-pattern curtains, the duvet cover in the design of some football team's strip, she didn't know which one.

'Jim?' Cathy called from the bottom of the stairs.

'We're all right,' Jim said. 'We'll be down in a minute.'

Nat made a move towards Tyler to kiss him goodbye, but his cries started up again. She turned and went downstairs. Cathy was jigging

334

Jade, who was grizzling, frightened by all the commotion.

'Don't be upset, babe,' said Nat, stroking her hair and kissing her. 'You'll see Mummy again soon.'

She had to get out of there. She heard Cathy asking if she wanted a lift and then calling Jim, but she broke into a stumbling run as soon as she was out through the gate. She didn't stop until she reached a bus stop, when the effort it had taken made her throw up. Her head was pounding and she felt awful; she lit a cigarette, taking lungfuls of the soothing smoke. Desolation came down like a fog blinding her to everything. She knew there were other real things out there that she should be grasping for, but all she could see was the fog. By the time she got home she was shaking with the need for the fog to lift. The only way she could think of was to get high again. It would obliterate it, make everything clear and sunny again.

★　★　★

Nat saw the face through the view hole and recognized it. She undid the locks and opened the door.

'Hello?' she said. She couldn't put a name to the face, or work out how she knew it.

'Hi, Nat. It's Tracey.' The woman looked down at Nat's bare legs beneath the T-shirt. 'I started to think you weren't in. Were you asleep?'

'Uh — yeah,' said Nat.

'Can I come in?' said Tracey.

Nat widened the door and let her past. She still couldn't think where she knew her from, but she knew she was someone she let in. Tracey peered through to where people were crashed.

'Have you had a party?' Tracey asked. She came into the kitchen, looking around.

'What?' said Nat. 'No.' There was an awkward pause. 'Do you want a cup of tea?' she asked, opening the fridge. 'There's no milk though.'

'No, it's all right thanks. Nat, I've just come for a bit of a chat about what happened the other day.' Nat looked at her, waiting. 'When you went round to see the kids?'

Finally Nat understood. Shit. She looked around. The place was disgusting and she was meant to have it nice for when Tracey came round. Kel and everybody usually made themselves scarce as well.

'Sorry about the mess. We — I did have a party. That's why they're all here.' The sudden nerves had made her break into a sweat but she was shivering cold too.

'Nat,' Tracey said. 'Cathy said you were in a state when you went round — '

'It was her!' Nat interrupted. 'She didn't want me to see my kids! She's turned them against me!'

'Nat, calm down and listen to me,' Tracey said. 'You'll never get them back if you carry on like this. You missed your proper time with them, and then you showed up out of the blue not knowing what day it was, out of your head on drink or drugs or whatever it was. Can't you see that that's really disturbing for them?'

Nat looked away. She heard someone stirring next door. Kel came to the door of the kitchen, eyeing Tracey.

'What's going on?' he said. 'You all right, Nat?'

'Yeah, fine. It's about the kids.' She signalled with her hand that he shouldn't get involved. He went through to the bathroom, pissed loudly with the door half open.

'Is that your boyfriend?' Tracey asked.

Nat shook her head but couldn't raise her guilty eyes to meet Tracey's.

Tracey lowered her voice. 'We can help you, Nat,' she said. The kind words made Nat begin to cry hard and silently. 'We can get you into rehab or whatever you need, rehouse you away from . . . here. But until you clean up, I'm sorry to say it, Nat, you run the risk of not being allowed to see your children. We have to put them first. Make sure they're safe.'

Nat wiped roughly at her face as Kel came out of the bathroom in case he came in and saw her. But he went through to the lounge, put a sudden stab of loud music on.

'Are you frightened of him?' Tracey whispered.

Nat didn't want to say, but the truth of it made her cry harder and she gave a quick nod.

'You need to get out of this situation,' Tracey said. 'And fast. If you stay in this — We can protect you from him. You know that, don't you? Can you come and see me?' Nat nodded. 'Come and see me as soon as you can and we'll get things moving.'

Kel appeared at the entrance to the kitchen and Nat jumped.

'What's going on?' he said, seeing Nat's tear-streaked face.

'It's OK. I — I just missed a visit to the kids,' said Nat. She stood and went to the front door to show Tracey out.

'Come and fix up that appointment,' Tracey said on her way out, darting a polite smile at Kel.

'Interfering bitch,' said Kel, as Nat closed the door behind her.

Nat went through to the bathroom, shut the door, and slid down against it, hugging her knees and crying. The thought of what she had to do filled her with terror. She knew she had to do it, but she didn't think she could, not yet. All she wanted right now was the void shooting into her veins and making her disappear.

# SIX

*A painting. A woman at a window,
looking out.*

She sits on an old wooden chair, leaning forward with her arms on the sill, a loose dress draping over her form to her feet, which are bare. Her hair is swept up at the back to reveal the nape of her neck, stray locks falling around her shoulders. Her face is in profile, highlighted against the glass.

The large window takes up most of the painting, placed at the very centre of it, looking out onto a dark sky. All that can be seen of the room surrounds the window at the edges of the painting: the bare white walls, the lack of curtains, the unpolished floorboards, a discarded stocking. The perspective of the lines of the floorboards leads the eye up to the woman's feet, taking in the figure tilting forward and following her gaze through the window, but we do not know what she can see outside.

It is lighter inside than it is out. Because of this all that can be seen through the window is the artist's reflection suspended in mid-air in one of the panes. He half-sits against a tall stool, painting at an easel. The way he is painted contrasts with the detail of the woman

— each contour, each lock of hair, each toe-nail, each fold of her dress, painstakingly captured. His figure, a barely-there impression.

The kind of painting in which the image can only be made out with unfocused eyes. If she looks straight at him he disappears into so many indecipherable daubs of paint. She has to look slightly away from him to make him out. The figure, the easel, his arm holding the brush.

And there, the thing that doesn't make sense. In the reflection, something else floating, like a low-slung moon. When she doesn't look too hard, slightly to the left or right, she thinks it is a child's face she sees hovering somewhere between them. But it cannot be, because it would have to be in the real room if it was really there, the back of its head in the foreground of the painting as it stood somewhere between its mother and father, in the way. She finds herself looking at the painting often, trying to work it out.

# 2004

## Luna

Luna got through the ensuing days by working long hours at Trey's and numbing herself to the pain. She felt dampened down and subdued, like a watercolour. But not so as Pierre noticed. The momentum of his series of pixel sculptures was carrying him along — he had several figures in various stages of creation crowding him out of his studio. He began to complain about the lack of room and talk about finding a bigger space to complete the work.

'In the meantime you could spread into my studio,' Luna suggested.

'Haven't you got anything on the go?' Pea asked, an aghast look on his face, and despite Luna answering, 'No,' he looked into her room as though he just couldn't believe it. 'Why not?' he asked, going over to inspect the experiments she hadn't touched for weeks on some of the competition themes Julian had suggested she work on.

'Nothing's coming to me just now. It's OK,' she assured him.

He turned to look at her, perplexed. 'Why not?' he asked again.

'I don't know!' she managed to laugh. 'It's just a dry spell, I guess. I'm not inspired. I'm not bothered about it. I'm sure enough waitressing will soon get me in the mood to paint instead.'

He stared at her with an unreadable face. 'Is there anything you need?' he asked. 'Anything I can do?'

'No! Course not!' Luna smiled back. 'You need to concentrate on your show. It's good timing really. My job's taking care of the bills so you don't have to worry about anything else. In fact, we could afford the rent on a bigger space if that's what you need right now.'

'Oh no, I couldn't ask you to pay for that. I'll try to get something free through the gallery, or at least something I can pay for later.'

'Honestly, Pea, don't let that hold you up. That's going to seriously limit your choices. And you haven't got time to fuck around looking. Find your ideal place and go for it. We've got the money.'

'I don't know, Lu. That doesn't seem right.'

'Course it is. We are a couple. My money is your money is my money. Isn't it?'

'Yes, but . . . '

He will do it, she thought. For all his protestations now, he would be on the lookout for the space he needed within a couple of hours and probably have found something within a few days. Luna even bet herself that before the week was out he would casually mention a space he'd seen that was great, but that cost x amount and he'd have to pay a deposit of y amount, and he didn't like to ask her, but what did she think? Could they manage that? He'd pay her back, of course, when he sold his next piece. And x and y would probably be higher than she had mentally calculated, because hadn't that happened more than once before? When she had been generous with her earnings and, despite attempting to resist her money at first, Pierre had ended up spending more of it than she'd expected to give? She couldn't remember for sure. She was certain he never meant to deliberately take advantage. Certain he was absolutely genuine when he said he'd pay her back, even though that didn't seem to happen, other than the impulsive impractical gestures when he was flush — a holiday, or a new TV. Much as she loved him he was just so . . . immature.

Luna suddenly felt like the mother of a teenage son.

Maybe it really is just as well not to have children with you, she thought as he gave her a happy squeeze on his way out of her room. Maybe I could do without having to deal with any more of your genes than I do already. It was a mean thought, but it made her feel strangely better. She crossed the room to her Mac, where she found she already had three emails from Jon since the last time she'd written to him at 7.30 that morning before she'd set off for Trey's.

★　★　★

She caught Jon eagerly straining to see her. It made her grin long before he actually picked her out of the people getting off the train, so that as soon as he did her smile was there to greet him. The concern on his face lifted as she approached and he saw how much better she was, and he came towards her, unable to wait for her to reach him. They embraced easily and kissed each other near the mouth, Luna linking arms with him as they left the platform.

'You'll be glad to know I don't need carrying today,' she said, leaning into him. She had her heeled boots on again, which clacked confidently on the pavement, inexplicably heightening her good mood.

'That's good,' he replied. 'Can I carry you anyway?'

'Oh, OK then,' she said with a smile, and made a sudden playful lunge at him, throwing her arms round his neck and swinging her legs up.

Even though she took him by surprise he somehow caught them and staggered to the car with her while she threw back her head and laughed. He managed to fish for his car keys, open the passenger door and drop her into the seat, although it meant he lost his balance at the last and squashed her as he fell forward onto her. Their bodies pressed together before he pushed himself up with his hands on the back of her seat. The position was so sexual, her body trapped beneath him, their faces close enough to kiss. But instead they were laughing. He pushed himself back so that her arms slid away from his neck, bumping his head on the door frame. She reflexively reached out and rubbed his head and said 'Ow' for him. It felt almost more intimate than a kiss would have done.

In the studio they fell easily into their roles,

Luna kicking off her boots and not even waiting until he was busy making tea with his back to her before peeling off her black woollen hold-up stockings. She noticed him notice, then turn away abruptly to the sink. She smiled to herself and scraped her chair to the window, getting into the pose and arranging her dress around her bare legs. After some time behind the easel Jon came to her to make some alterations to her position and dress.

'Er — excuse me,' he said gruffly, 'your dress . . .'

She turned to look where he pointed and saw that it had caught up as she sat down, revealing a small amount of milky flesh on her thigh. She lifted herself to smooth it down. He helped her then with the folds of material, moving her body into exactly the shape she had held before. His hands seemed to linger slightly and she felt the heat of their imprints on her body. They seemed to extract her tension as they left and she sighed and felt herself relax.

He settled at the easel and after some shuffling finally seemed to become caught up in the work. They fell into silence for a long while. Being in the pose she became aware of the flatness of her stomach and all the room between its skin and her loose dress, the empty space that she had been so looking forward to filling. He seemed to read her thought clouds again, because he asked, 'Are you all right?'

'I'm fine. Actually, hold on a mo.' She took the moment to stretch her arms up above her head, arching her back before resettling.

'I meant — you know. After last week and that.'

'Oh. That. Yes. I really am.' She apologized again, thanked him again.

'Stop doing that,' he said. 'It was nothing. I'm just really glad I was with you. Really glad you look so much better today. Thank you, for still coming.'

'Why wouldn't I?' she asked. 'Actually I've been looking forward to it all week. I like it. It's kind of peaceful here. It's nice to have this to come to. It's ... freeing, somehow. Like a holiday from my life. Myself. My inability to paint at the moment. Waitressing. Everything else.'

He paused before asking, 'What do you mean by everything else?'

'Oh. You know. All that business you were witness to last time. Me. Pierre. The baby thing.'

At Jon's silence, she glanced round. He was just sitting, looking at her.

'How about you?' she said, turning back round. 'You reacted as though it was strange to not want children. When are you going to have them? Are you and your wife trying?'

'Oh no,' Jon said quickly.

'What's stopping you? If you want them?'

'Well. My wife. She wants to get her career established first.'

'Oh. Well. That's understandable. I was the same. You're both young. You've got plenty of time.'

'I know,' Jon replied. 'I know all the arguments for waiting.' He looked up to see Luna smiling at him in the reflection in the window. Understanding passed between them like the same sweet breeze.

'They don't help, do they?' she said. 'The arguments for waiting. When it doesn't really feel as though it's about logical points for and against.'

'No,' he agreed. 'Although you really try to use your powers of logic. Reason.'

'It's not something you choose in your head.' She had refocused her gaze on what was outside the window, to free the thoughts she was trying to express. 'But something your heart chooses for you. It's more of a . . . want, or a need, than a choice. More than that. A yearning perhaps.'

'A yearning. Yes. That's it exactly. That's why you can't persuade someone. If they don't feel the yearning themselves.'

'Of course.' It felt like a revelation, the putting into a few simple words in a moment exactly the weeks and months she had spent, struggling alone and trying to deny it. And such an amazing sense of relief, to find someone else who knew.

'You can't force it on someone,' Jon said. 'If they don't have it.'

'You just have to wait until they do.'

Jon didn't reply. He got up abruptly and put the kettle on. Luna leaned back in her chair and curled her legs into herself, rubbing at her feet to warm them up.

'Are you too cold?' he asked, and she turned to see him halting mid-bend, having picked up one of her stockings. He seemed to be looking at the rubbery tops that made them cling to the thighs to keep them up, and was suddenly unsure whether it wasn't a little ungentlemanly to be touching them. Luna laughed at him.

'Thank you,' she said, and emboldened by his shyness, swivelled to extend one of her bare legs towards him. Speechless, he moved forward and pushed the stocking fumblingly over her foot. He was too embarrassed to slide it all the way up her leg, instead reaching for the other and putting it over her other foot. She left them bunched like that to her calves as she stood up. Her dress fell back over her knees as she got up and moved to the kitchen, where she began poking around for biscuits. Surely she shouldn't feel sexy like that, with these things that at the moment looked like baggy old socks hanging around her ankles? Perhaps it was the knowledge of the bare flesh above that they should have been covering, or the fact that she felt dishevelled, like she'd just left a bed. Or was it that she had left them exactly as he'd placed them, as though she was happy with however he wanted to put them on — was happy, in essence, with him?

★   ★   ★

Sterility formed over Luna's home-life like frost. The skies that set the atmosphere through the window-walls were endlessly grey or white or black, her white studio was sparse and barren, and when Pierre began to work as predicted in a massive ground-floor warehouse space in Hackney Wick, her home was abandoned. She switched herself off to endure the monotony of work at Trey's, acted her way through her relationships with workmates and friends, with Pierre. Only in her time at Jon's studio did she feel she was really herself, really there, connected with the moment and the person she was with. He knew her now, better than anyone else. In the studio, with its vibrant hotchpotch of randomly put-together things and colours, the feeling of invisibility lifted and she found herself revealed, noticed. Jon's attention, focused so intently upon her, seemed to give her back what, elsewhere, she appeared to have lost. The rest of her life — her painting, Pierre — seemed frighteningly elusive, the things that were her absolutes now seeming to slip away, leaving nothing but a vague shadow of what had been.

Jon's touch on her, rather than a fleeting peck or squeeze as Pierre hurried past on his way somewhere else, seemed to end with her, as though she was the destination herself. She became aware that she wanted his touch to remain on her, looked forward to it even before she got to him, and found herself remembering how it was to feel good as he hugged her hello, placed the folds of her dress, re-pinned her hair. She sat as he painted, aware only of her body still rippling to his touch on her surfaces like the wind over a lake. She found herself craving more, and knew what she was doing when she took a break before she really needed one, so that he would have to arrange her again on her return. His hands carried more weight than Pierre's, who tended, she realized now, to only flit over her lightly, minimally. Jon's felt as though they left a print like thumb marks in clay. They were heavy as they rested on her shoulders, as healing on her body as a massage, purposeful and strong when they moved her limbs.

She knew her legs were too close together as she sat back into her pose, and dared herself to leave them that way so that he would have to do something about them. He stood back at his easel appraising her in silence. She wondered disappointedly if he wouldn't be able to bring himself to move her.

'Is this OK?' she asked, encouragingly.

'Er . . . ' He scratched his head. 'Almost. Your legs aren't quite in the right position.'

'What's wrong with them?' she asked.

'They were . . . I think you had them . . . um . . . wider apart.' The words — so sexual — hung in the air, causing him a discomfort she could feel. She looked over her shoulder at him.

'Like this?' she asked, keeping her eyes on him as she slowly opened her legs and arched to lean forward.

He cleared his throat. 'That's it,' he mumbled, pushing up the glasses that were suddenly slipping down his nose, and turning to fumble with his brushes.

Luna rested her chin on her hands and looked out, trying to hide her smile. It was pretty tame really, parting her legs under a baggy old floral hippy dress. But even doing that had such an effect on him. She was powerful. Underneath the dress, her pose was almost pornographic: legs apart, back arched, bottom thrust out and breasts — well, were it not for her bra and dress, they would be deliciously suspended and exposed. Sitting in the pose was erotic, she couldn't stop imagining being nude. She tried to picture herself from Jon's angle — what would he see? One long leg, her hips, the roundness of her belly perhaps, her back, strands of her hair falling onto her shoulders, her arm, and possibly, probably, a glimpse of the side of one breast, its fullness tapering to the point of a nipple.

She closed her eyes, drifted into a reverie of roaming firm hands undoing buttons and lifting skirt hems and sliding inside clothing, cupping.

The feel of his actual hand on her back felt like a natural progression, rather than an interruption, although it caused her to take a quick in-breath and open her eyes.

'Sorry,' he said softly, taking his hand away. 'I didn't mean to make you jump. You drifted off. I didn't want you to hit your head on the window.'

'Oh. Right.' She laughed. 'Thank you.' Her face flushed guiltily. She rubbed it with her hands, faking a yawn to hide it. 'That would have been embarrassing.'

She tried to return to a normal daytime propriety. She got up, moved away to make coffee, but somehow could not shake the feeling that he knew where her mind had wandered. He watched her as often as he could, she realized, not just when he was studying her to paint. When she turned to speak to him, his eyes were ready to meet hers. She couldn't remember ever having to search them out, waiting for them to tear themselves away from something else. She usually talked to the back of Pierre's head or his profile while his attention was held by his work. But Jon's eyes were always looking at her, waiting. Painting her portrait was the perfect alibi for a voyeur. The thought excited rather than alarmed her. She wondered if this was the kick that strippers got from male watchers, the one she had previously thought they mistook for real power. But it was a potent thing, she found, to be so alluring, the cause of such steady fixation.

When she passed him his cup their hands brushed. When they went for lunch, his arm fell on her back. When they sat together on the same side of the table, their thighs touched. He responded to her every mood, laughing when she did, quiet when she was, as though she was conducting him. She could talk about anything and he listened and reacted, cared. And she seemed to cause the same release in him. He didn't seem used to talking, really talking, about his life and his relationship. He was a loyal husband, she thought; he loved his wife. A fact which increased her sense of potency as he unburdened himself to her, only her. His secrets passed into her like a transfusion. All he'd ever wanted was a big family. He'd gone into the best-paid career he could think of, so he'd be able to support it. He'd worked his arse off. And now he was a slave to it, waiting until his wife was ready.

'What about you?' he asked, looking at her sideways over his beer glass. 'What are you going to do? Are you going to keep trying — you know — with Pierre?'

She shook her head. 'It wasn't right. That experience told me that. I don't even know if he'd be a good father any more. Certainly not if he's not ready. He's such a kid still. He can't take care of himself, let alone anyone else. Maybe it's not meant to be for us. Anyway, chance would be a fine thing. He's got a proper studio space to finish his pieces. I doubt I'll be seeing much of him for a while. It feels like we're just people who share a flat right now.'

'He's a fool,' he said finally, quietly, looking into his glass. 'He doesn't appreciate you.'

'You're sweet,' said Luna, putting her hand over his and squeezing it.

It felt so different to when she held Pierre's thin boy's hands, practically the same size as hers, which she could easily encompass. Whereas his were all bone and veins, Jon's were muscly, fleshy. And his wrists were thick and wide, unsnappable as branches. It looked as though he could spread his fingers and make a seat, and lift you up single-handed. Her hand, so dainty on his.

'Your hands are so big,' she said.

'Oh. Thanks a lot,' he said.

'No! I didn't mean it badly,' she said, rubbing her hand up and down his forearm in comfort. 'You're strong. It's nice.'

Her hand stilled on his and they both looked down at them lying together on the table like mating frogs. Neither wanted to take their hand away, but when it became too intense Jon lifted hers to his mouth and kissed the back of it quickly and said, 'Come on then.'

His lips left a hot wet print on her skin. As the pair left the pub still holding hands, Luna sneaked glances at him, studying his mouth. His lips were full, unusually so. She wondered how it would be to stick her tongue between them, suck on his lower lip. And then of course his lips would be wet and begin to stray down her neck . . .

It didn't bode well for the afternoon's sitting. Now his lips were in her thoughts along with the hands, and the wrists. She tried to turn her attention away from them, but both she and Jon seemed to have run out of things to say. Their hands began to sweat together, but neither pulled theirs away. His thumb rubbed rhythmically on her skin. They remained hand in hand all the way up the stairs, as he unlocked their door, right to her chair, where he only let go to place it elsewhere on her body, his other one joining in, on her shoulders, her legs, bolder this time. Both hands were on her hips as he stood behind to angle them correctly on the seat, before he put one of them on her upper back and pushed her gently but firmly forward into position. She heard his breathing, felt it around her hair and neck. As she put her arms on the sill she felt herself trembling. She tried to still herself but couldn't, wondering if he could notice from the easel the quiver of her dress giving her away.

★  ★  ★

It was she who kissed him. She had put her arm through his as they walked to the platform but he had kept his hands firmly in his pockets.

356

When the train showed in the distance she faced him to say goodbye. And it was she who reached out and drew their bodies together and leaned in so that their noses touched and lips met. Although the kiss was on the mouth, at first it was just a goodbye kiss — one short, sweet, dry kiss, and she pulled back. She stood and looked at him — at his mouth in particular, then up into his eyes, then back to his mouth. He stared helplessly back. And then, she brought her hands up and placed them on his neck, just below his ears, and kissed him again, and this time it was for longer and there were tongues involved. Only hers at first, for he was still reeling from the shock of it parting his lips and pushing into his mouth, but then his joined in. She pressed her body against his inside his undone coat and her hands slipped round his shoulders, into his cropped hair. His hands at last left the pockets where he had resolutely thrust them. He slid them under her coat and round her waist and pulled her closer to him.

It was hard to break away once she was swamped in Jon's embrace, and they struggled to the train doors as though they were something coming undone that was meant to be fastened together. She bent for a last kiss from the train, their hands reaching for each other, and when Jon finally had to shut the door she leaned against it as though it was him. He kept his hand on the door until the train began to move and then Luna straightened and tried to pull herself together. She walked through the carriages, light and floaty since Jon had let her go. His embrace had encompassed her like a protective shell, the hard exoskeleton of a crab or a tortoise, and she was just so much soft pink flesh inside.

She sat on the train, shock and a smile alternating on her face like a flickering neon reflection. Jon's physicality kept returning to her, causing electrical hums to run down her body the whole journey home. She wanted to collapse into him, let him take her over, crush her even, anything that let her know she was really there. His hands let her know that, and his mouth. The parts of her that she could feel the strongest were the parts that he had touched. She could feel her outline as it had been drawn by him, her back and hips, her sides, her lips. She felt unfinished, and ached for him to complete the rest of her.

★　★　★

By the following day a sense of moral reasoning had returned and Luna felt ashamed of herself. Jon was a married man, and whatever problems he had with his wife, it didn't excuse her leaping on him and taking advantage. And she loved Pierre, for all their lack of current intimacy. It was only a month ago she had been desperately trying to have a baby with him, for God's sake, and here she was seducing someone else. She was out of control. Maybe it was hormones, out of balance and overthrowing her self-discipline. Poor Jon, innocently taking the brunt of her wild emotions. She had to get a hold of herself. She emailed him straight away.

Jon, I'm so sorry. I feel really bad for lunging at you like that. I don't know what came over me. I hope it didn't cause you too much guilt when you got home to your wife — it shouldn't have done, it was completely my doing. I can't explain it at all, but I know it was wrong. You must think I'm awful. I completely understand if you think I shouldn't come and sit for you any more. In fact, perhaps you've got far enough to finish the painting without me there now? I hope so. Please accept my apologies — I hope you don't think too badly of me. Lu

As soon as she had sent the email she tried to get back into her painting, rereading the briefs for the competitions Julian had sent and sifting through her collage experiments. She didn't have to go to Trey's until the afternoon and tried to regain her previous ability to make herself work when she didn't feel like it. She didn't allow herself to check her emails until she was ready for work and had ten minutes before she had to set off to the cafe.

There were five emails from Jon. As she was reading through them her mobile rang.

'It's me,' said Jon, the familiar way lovers declared themselves. 'I've just come out of a meeting. Did you get my emails? I wanted to phone last night but I couldn't. I didn't know if you'd want me to. I didn't want to ruin things. Don't feel bad, Luna, I — It was me too. It wasn't such a terrible thing, was it? It just happened. Don't stop coming — I need you to sit for me some more. It won't be weird, I promise. We can pretend it never happened if you like. But please, please still come. Are you there?'

Luna laughed. His desperation to see her again shouldn't make her feel happy, but it did.

'OK, stop already! I'm here!' she said. She picked up her keys and left the flat, saying she had to get to work and that she'd lose her signal in the lift.

'I'll call you in three,' Jon shouted down the phone. He sounded as though he was on the move too, obviously in the middle of things. Her phone rang the second she got out at the bottom and cleared the looming building's foundations.

'Where've you been?!' he yelled at her, all his usual composure gone. Luna tried, all the way to work, to keep hold of herself, suggesting again that he finish his painting without her, but he wouldn't have it.

'Please, Lu, we both know it shouldn't have happened so of course it won't happen again, it was just a thing of the moment, all by the by, forget about it — I've forgotten it already! What are you talking about?' Luna laughed, stopping outside Trey's, waving in. 'But I *need* you to sit again, even if it's just once. If you're uncomfortable next time, fine, we'll call it a day, but I swear it'll all be OK.'

'I really have to go now,' she said. 'So OK, I'll come. With reservations, but . . . anything to get you off the phone!'

'Brilliant!' Jon whooped. 'Can you do Monday?'

'I thought we said Thursday next week?' said Luna.

360

'I've got an important presentation Thursday — Monday's my best bet. Afternoon anyway. Into the evening. If you can?'

'I'll check the rotas today and see,' Luna replied. 'I'm not promising anything. But I'll email you later.'

'No — text me. Else I might not get your email till tomorrow.'

'But . . . does that matter?' Luna made winding-up-the-call signs through the window to Gina, who was looking out at her with interest. 'Is it OK to text your phone in the evening?'

'Yes, it matters, yes it's OK, yes, yes, yes! Please try to make Monday!'

'OK, OK! Later.' Luna flicked her phone off and hurried inside, apologizing.

'Who was that?' asked Gina, with raised eyebrows.

'Oh, no one,' was her only response, but she held Gina's gaze for a guilty fraction of a second too long.

'It's nothing — just a guy who's painting my portrait.'

'Oh.' Gina looked disappointed. 'The way you were talking it looked more intriguing than that.'

It was true, without mention of the snog, it didn't sound very juicy. Treat the kiss as if it never happened and there was nothing wrong about it. Luna swapped her Monday shift with Tuesday and texted Jon on the way home, to let him know.

★　★　★

She came towards him in an overdone casual saunter. When she reached him, he turned to walk to the exit before she could give him the light kiss on the cheek she'd decided upon.

'Good idea,' she said.

'Sorry?' he asked.

'No kissing whatsoever.' She emphasized her words with a drawing-the-line hand gesture, and he laughed. They were too used to this ritual journey, to each other, walking in step to his car, to act in any way other than the way they were together.

'I had decided on a quick peck on the cheek,' he admitted. 'But I had second thoughts. When you got close.'

'Me too,' she said. They gave each other a glance as they parted and rounded the car to get in, in perfect step, as though they were performing a dance. Their smiles met.

In the car they stared straight ahead. They were held up in a traffic jam, the cause of which they couldn't see. After a long silence, Jon seemed to summon up the courage to say something.

'You know that thing?'

'What thing?' said Luna.

'That thing that never happened . . . '

'Oh. That thing.' She took a breath to speak, but he carried on quickly.

'I'm glad it did,' he said. 'I just wanted you to know that. Before we move on.'

They remained at a standstill in the traffic, like an ironic illustration.

Luna sat silently. She had meant to be chatty

and breezy, to really act as though nothing had happened, to be at ease herself and to put Jon at ease in her presence. But instead she found herself now tongue-tied and shy, overwhelmed with the same feeling that had engulfed her last time and made it so impossible to not kiss him. Sitting in a car chatting breezily did not feel enough. She wanted to be beyond words with him, as close to him as she could get. And now that he had mentioned the thing that never happened and let her know he was glad of it, she could not recover.

'That's nice of you to say,' she managed eventually. The car before them finally moved and Jon placed his hand on the gearstick and she kept her eyes fixedly in front of her, trying to be unaware of it in the corner of her eye shifting forwards and back and forwards again.

In the studio the ritual continued. He'd been here already — so sweet that he still came to pick her up even though it was walkable from the station — and the place was already warmed up, kettle boiled. She went straight into pose, not knowing how to have tea with him, talk, in any surface way that didn't involve the way they really spoke to each other. Any amount of superficial chatter couldn't hide what they really said. It had been easier to forget, when she was away from him, quite what it was like when they were together. She felt her chemistry alter around him, reacting with him in a way that fizzed and changed her into someone else, someone that felt good to be.

He started painting without arranging her and

she felt bereft. The absence of his touch almost hurt.

An hour or so passed until he cleared his throat and said, 'Actually, your hair isn't right. Do you mind putting it up more at the back? There were less strands hanging down.'

She did her best to catch her hair in the grip exactly as it had been. He tried to give her spoken directions from where he was at the easel, until she laughed and gave up.

'This is silly!' she said, turning and holding out her hair clasp to him. 'You come and do it.'

\* \* \*

Jon moved to Luna, took the clasp and, standing behind her, began to scoop up tendrils from the back of her neck. He couldn't work the grasping teeth of it, so she laughed and helped him, pushing the thing into place as he piled the hair at the right spot. He began gently releasing the locks that had to fall exactly right around her neck. She sighed as he brushed her skin, and inclined her head so that his fingers touched the side of her face. She reached up and took his hand and held it against her face, then to her lips in a kiss. She leaned back in the chair, rested her head against his ribs, and he watched his hands as they moved down along her shoulders, the tops of her arms. She raised her arms up to his shoulders and tilted her face and he bent down and began to kiss her as his hands moved further down the sides of her body, over her stomach and round her ribs, where they hesitated. Her hands reached round his neck and into his hair as the intensity of the kiss increased, a rhythm beginning to insist itself. As the kiss grew fierce he slid his hands over her breasts and inside her dress. She twisted as he dropped to his knees between her legs, and then she was sliding down onto his lap and they were wrapped in each other as tight as they could get in a ferocious embrace. He pulled open the buttons at the front of her dress, slid it off her as he lay her on the floor, and she was tearing off his trousers and shirt and then, at last, she felt the weight of him possess her.

★　★　★

Hours later, they lay squashed together on the sofa. He confessed everything, how hopelessly in love with her he was, from the moment they met, how he'd never felt like this before. How the studio didn't in fact belong to any friend of his but that he had spent days searching for it, rented it off a stranger, a woman who was leasing it while she went off to have a baby. He kept saying Luna's name over and over as though she was the most beautiful thing. They were ravished, exhausted, but yet not satiated. The assault of his desire on her raised her body into a state of sore bliss. Even after coming so many times, even when darkness fell and they knew they had to check for the time and leave, even then there was no sense that their passion was spent, that it was over. Instead having to go felt like a brutal interruption to a beginning. They walked to the station clinging together instead of taking the car, so that they didn't have to pull apart while Jon drove. Waiting for the train Jon wrapped his coat around them both so that nobody could see his hands crawl up inside her dress as he pressed her against the waiting-room wall and she pulled him to her. Her eyes shone through the darkness into his.

'Come back soon, Luna,' he pleaded low into her ear. 'Make it this week. Tomorrow. Whenever you can. I'll be here.' On the train she pushed the window down and leaned out so they could touch until they were finally wrenched apart.

⋆　⋆　⋆

The affair became her real life, vivid and ringing, while the time spent apart and inhabiting her old world consisted of avoiding, lying, excusing and planning. Her connections there seemed severed, like cut veins, stopping feeling. She somehow couldn't feel that it was wrong, even though she tried to, to refer to an afternoon of hardcore adultery as a shift, or shopping. She just couldn't feel guilty when the crucial thing of life was happening elsewhere. Her life with Pierre became a series of annoying daily things that had to be done, like jobs or housework, to be got through with the cheering thought that later, or tomorrow or in two days' time she would be released again in Jon's presence. Pierre became an obstacle, too present and in the way yet distant at the same time, to be got round or over or through. This new sex was unlike anything she had experienced before, raw and violent with need. She was devoured by lust that was never satisfied. She hurt on her journeys home, with disguised bruises and bite marks and chaffed skin, something that only added to the feeling of being utterly present, in the moment, full of life and joy. She became reckless, for why did it matter? When the life she had been leading until now was coming to a natural end? She shared whispered, giggly conversations from her mobile to Jon, with Pierre and Jon's wife only rooms away, texted in the middle of the night when their partners were sleeping, and sent blue emails to Jon's office for him to read while his colleagues sat beside him.

Luna was amazed how little Pierre was aware of the bubbling change in her, how vivacious she was in herself, how absent to him. It only made her feel that what she was doing wasn't wrong — how could it be? He didn't care. They weren't a proper couple, this confirmed it. Only sharing a space, a habit, an old situation that they continued to act out because it was what they had been doing for years and were used to it. They just hadn't acknowledged that their time was over. She had tried, after all, she justified to herself. She had told him it was time for her to enter the next stage in her life, that she had wanted to do that with him but he had said no. How could he possibly object to her moving on with her life instead of letting it stall and stagnate? It would be unfair of him. She imagined that when it came to it, it might not even be a trauma. She would be able to tell him calmly and he would take it that way too, unsurprised. He might even give her his blessing. They would stay friends, even. After all, wasn't that what they already were to each other? Friends that shared a flat and a past.

★   ★   ★

Luna cut her hours back at Trey's, giving a fictitious commission as a reason to her boss, and failing to mention her new rota to Pierre. They kept completely different hours from each other, she retiring to bed much earlier than the time he crashed in beside her. On the rare occasions he quit the studio at a reasonable time, hinting at an early night together, she said she had work to do, keeping in mind that to Pierre she was still waitressing full-time and could only work on her art in limited periods. 'I'm just going to do a few hours,' she would say, and disappear up to her studio with her laptop. 'I'm trying to get some inspiration from somewhere.'

Trips to Leicester doubled, sometimes trebled in the week. There was no time to do anything but the basic minimum in her usual life — work, sleep, eat, have functional conversations with as few people as possible.

★   ★   ★

Life at the studio was becoming home. It was the moment of crossing, like one scene in a film fading slowly out while the new scene faded in, the point in which elements of both scenes were equally visible, merging. Luna and Jon began to recognize and greet other artists at the complex, who grinned at them knowingly when they met. They began to befriend them, as though they were just a new couple in town and in love, with no mention of their separate home lives away from the studio. New characters were coming into play, who may or may not have a significance in the next part of the story. Luna felt like a new character herself, Jon's admiration for her as affirming as applause. It allowed her to be generous with people, as though she was the star of the show, open and gregarious and sparkling. He was good for her. They found themselves idly looking in the free papers at galleries, jobs, flat rentals. The future opened up with possibility. They could live here in this town if they wanted, or somewhere else. It wouldn't matter where it was, with Jon, because he would make the important thing happen, take care of the rest.

★   ★   ★

Nothing was ever said, about the fact that condoms were never used — why would either of them have had them on them, the first time? When neither had meant for it to happen. Even so, they understood in each other a disappointment at the first month's blood. Shock even, that their combined lust and yearning hadn't created what they had expected, despite the exhaustive efforts made. Still without admitting to each other the planning, they tried harder the following month, timing the days that they met and making love as many times as Jon could muster, which was an impressive count. Still the second month's blood came, and the third. It was difficult to believe they had missed a window of opportunity. But perhaps their afternoon slot had been a fraction too early, or late. Still they never discussed what they were attempting, even though they spoke freely of everything else, as if putting words to it would break the magic spell. Luna believed that simply the sheer force of their sexual ecstasy would make their dream happen. She clung to Jon's trust in it, dependably impregnating and impregnating again, with every faith in the potency of their coupling.

Even so, Luna secretly bought an ovulation kit, just to be sure. She suggested they spend a whole night away in a hotel — maybe two nights, even. She wanted to lie in a bed in his arms while their ingredients brewed, where they could wake up and try again, and again. 'Somewhere romantic,' she said, 'not Leicester. Somewhere by the sea.'

'Leave it to me,' he told her, and Luna was happy to. It was a relief to have someone else take charge, to have the responsibility lifted. She believed in his machismo, that he could make it happen when she had failed on her own. She began to think that was why it never happened with Pierre, when they had tried only once at roughly the right sort of time in the month, with his ignorance and her guilt. Just look how hard she and Jon were trying, and it still hadn't yet worked. She marvelled at the miraculous chance involved for women who fell pregnant easily, accidentally even, as though you could catch a baby like a cold.

★ ★ ★

As soon as the test indicated a change in her LH levels she texted him: *Can you make it tomorrow?*

He replied immediately: *Get the first train to Leeds you can in the morning. I'll pick you up from the station.*

Luna told Pierre she was going to visit her new relatives again. She had the perfect alibi, as her uncle Robert, sweetly, had emailed her about an open exhibition at their local art centre he thought she might be interested in. She was always welcome to stay, he had said, and he'd help with anything she needed if she had a piece she wanted to enter.

'I think I will stay the night,' she said, lightly. 'If that's OK.'

'Sure,' said Pierre. 'You don't mind if I don't come too, do you?'

'Course not!' Luna exclaimed. 'I didn't expect you to. I do know how it is when you've got a show coming up.'

'I fancy a break away, as it goes,' he said. 'I'm knackered. But we can do something cool when the show's over. Not long now.'

She turned to leave the room, wondering if she would still be here when his show was over.

'D'you want to take the van?' asked Pea after her. 'I won't need it.'

'No, I'm used to the train,' she replied, before she could stop herself. 'You know, I mean tubes and that. It'll be quicker.' She turned back to see if he'd noticed — she didn't even travel on tubes very much — but he hadn't.

He was sprawling on the sofa, tapping on his laptop, and just answered, 'OK. It's there if you want it,' not bothering to look up at her as she stood in the doorway.

★ ★ ★

Jon had parked in a corner of a dark multi-storey close to the station, affording them some privacy before they even set off. He was nervous about being in his home town as they drove away, but he said he wanted to show her his favourite place. She put her hand in his lap, stroked his thigh, and as soon as the traffic separated out, playfully opened his fly. He could hardly drive. They kept looking at each other and laughing aloud. It was a beautiful spring day and she wound down her window and the wind blew her loose hair everywhere and it felt good as it brushed her bare shoulders. She kicked off her shoes and placed her bare feet on the dash and he kept looking at her, adoration lighting up his face. He whooped as he wound his window down and turned the stereo up. She sang along loudly and carelessly, and he joined in. He opened the sun roof, and she flung her arms up and danced in her seat, and as he watched her, it made her feel like a girl in a film. He slid his hand up her leg and she let her seat back and reclined and he put his hand on her through her jeans and soaked up the warmth of her.

Life sang through her veins. It was exciting to be driving somewhere she had never been, seeing the strange city give way quickly to suburbs, to soothing green countryside and picture-perfect villages, and then the soulful, expansive moors. She felt herself unfurling to the place, abandoning herself yet more to Jon. Here his solid frame seemed perfectly set in the rugged terrain, and she found herself completely held by him, the place, the experience, as though she had been lifted out of the gritty mire of her usual life and gently placed in a hammock, to swing suspended above it without a care in the world. Soon he had to turn off the main road and take a detour down a lane and find a hidden, isolated track, because there was no way they could wait a whole hour until they got to the hotel. They found a soft spot under a tree and released each other from their clothing and lay together between the grass and leaf-dappled sky.

They drove on afterwards, in quiet joy, her hand resting over his.

He'd booked a luxury suite in the heart of the seaside town, overlooking the harbour and beyond it the sea. It was expensive, and the effort he'd gone to lent their liaison a specialness that touched her. She said thank you and wrapped her arms round his neck. She felt him breathe in the warm, earthy, sun-kissed air that had caught in her hair. He made love to her again on the crisp white linen of the king-size bed with a serious care and attention that filled her with gratitude, and she drifted into sleep afterwards filled with the peace afforded by the release from the constant awareness of passing time and trains to catch.

★ ★ ★

Later he led her by the hand down to the pier and the beach, where they kicked off their shoes and paddled and kissed, the sort of time that should be caught on bleached-out, ticking Super 8 film. They strolled with their trousers still rolled up like teenagers dating, sat on the pier with sandy feet swinging. He talked about his family and his childhood and what a perfect place it was to grow up. Kids should grow up in places like this, she agreed.

As the sun began to slide away, he pulled her up to her feet and took her back to the hotel where he ordered champagne and they got dizzy with bubbles, made love again. Perhaps for the first time, Luna felt completely taken care of. Every new moment was like shedding her old self, like a chemical peel. She was emerging newer, younger than she was before. If she came to Jon, not only would her life completely change, she would too. She could leave her damaged old skin behind and start again all pink and shiny, let herself be looked after and adored, sheltered from the world by Jon and his salary. She could rub everything away, strip it all back until she was just a woman. Have children. What would be so wrong about that? Why had she made life so hard for herself, when it didn't have

374

to be? She could still paint.

Or she could give it up if she wanted to.

The thought had never ever entered her head before. She didn't have to be an artist. If you had children what else did it matter what you did? The children became your reason, your identity, what you did. You could fail at art, or not even try, and it really didn't mean a thing, because you had something else to put in the empty space it left behind. Something else that mattered more.

They ate dinner in the hotel, an expensive gourmet affair, holding hands by the candlelight. It was romantic. He insisted on paying. They went for a last stroll along the seafront, and stood several yards apart to make their last duty calls home. Pea didn't pick up so Luna left a cheery message from 'outside Robert's house', hoping Pierre wouldn't hear the surf rolling in the background. She hung up, couldn't help but hear the odd phrase from Jon's conversation — the meeting had gone well, he still didn't know what time he'd be home tomorrow. It didn't sound as though his wife was best pleased, and he winced a little as he came off the phone. They switched their mobiles off and strolled along the front again in the moonlight, which had taken over the sky and was casting a silvery glaze, like icing on a cake. He took her to bed and afterwards she slept, small in his embrace, surrounded by him so that she could forget everything like a child hiding from a nightmare.

★ ★ ★

They approached the subject of plans tentatively, as though they were delicate and fleet as a deer, easily disturbed and unwittingly chased away.

'I could live somewhere like this,' said Luna, lying in the sheets after breakfast in bed. 'It's lovely.'

'Me too,' said Jon, casually stretching. 'I'm not chained to where I am. I mean, I could reach work from here, but I could easily switch companies. I could go anywhere. Anywhere would be good. With you.'

'It's just a question of making it happen,' said Luna.

'You're the sort of person who can make anything happen if you want it to,' said Jon. He turned to her. 'And you are making it happen. Right here, now. And you deserve to have what you want, Luna. You deserve to be happy.'

'So do you,' she said, looking into his eyes as she began to touch him again, making sure they made full use of the two hours left before check-out.

*   *   *

It was gone twelve by the time they switched their mobiles on again. It made Luna jump when hers beeped to let her know she had messages she wasn't expecting. Her heart began to thud. There were four, all from Pierre. He never did that, called and called when she was away. She stopped in her tracks, where they had sauntered down to the pier again after loading up the car. Jon had wandered a little way ahead, to check his. She saw that the time of the first message was six o'clock in the morning. Her heart was in her mouth as she put the phone to her ear to listen. What if he'd found Robert's number and tried to call her there? Reality rushed at her, like the ground when you were falling.

*Shit, your phone's off — call me as soon as you get this, Lu.*

She pressed through to the next one. *It's me again. Um . . . Call me straight away, OK?*

And then, *Fuck, Lu, this is urgent. I haven't got Robert's number. I'm gonna see if I can find it. You need to come home straight away.*

She held her breath before the last one, praying he hadn't found it. His voice was immediately different, flooded with rising panic. *Luna, I can't find the number, I don't know where you've put it. I've tried to get into your computer but I can't — have you changed your password? Why have you got your mobile off? Ring me.*

Just as she finished playing them her phone rang.

'Pea?' she said quickly, turning and walking further away from Jon.

'Oh, thank fuck,' he said. 'Why the hell have you had your phone off?'

'What is it?' said Luna.

'Come home quickly, Lu,' he said. 'It's your mum. She's in hospital.'

It took Luna a few seconds for what he'd said to sink in. Whatever she'd imagined, it hadn't been anything to do with Angie.

'What's wrong?' she finally got out. 'Is she all right?'

'I don't know. I think so, but . . . Luna, she's had a stroke.'

'Oh my God.' Luna clamped her free hand to her mouth. Jon came towards her, concerned, but she turned away.

'Is it . . . ? Is she . . . ?'

'I don't really know anything, Lu. Her neighbour heard her fall on the front steps. Just get Robert to get you on a train as soon as possible. I'll come and pick you up from the station and we'll go straight to the hospital.'

'I've got to go,' she said to Jon, turning to run towards his car. Jon took charge, insisting on driving Luna all the way back to Leeds, where trains to London were quicker and more frequent. He drove expertly in his smooth car, constantly breaking the speed limit and over-taking. Even so, Luna felt far too far from home. Whenever they came to a standstill at red lights or queues, Luna couldn't bear it, repeating 'Come on, come on,' through gritted teeth. Jon tried to keep her calm, comforting her by squeezing her knee and saying everything would be all right, taking back streets to avoid the worst of the traffic to get to the station. He carried her bags, rushing to find the right platform while she queued for her ticket, hoping she wouldn't miss the next train by minutes.

The relief she felt, finding there was a train to King's Cross in ten minutes' time, was overwhelming. She wouldn't have known what to do with herself if she had had to wait any longer. The minutes seemed to last for hours. Jon tried to console her, even offered to get on the train with her for part of the journey, but she found it was the last thing she wanted. She wanted to ring Pierre the second the train pulled out of the station.

'You must keep in touch with me, Luna, every chance you get,' Jon said. 'I wish I could be there with you.'

'There's nothing you can do,' Luna said. 'You've done enough already. Thank you for getting me here. Thank you for everything.'

'Promise me you'll phone, or text, or email — whatever you can do,' Jon said as the train pulled in. 'I'll be worrying so much. I want to take care of you.'

Luna climbed the steps into the train, urgency forcing her into quick movements as though they would get her home faster.

'I love you,' Jon said. 'I should be with you.' There was a desperation in his voice that made Luna feel uneasy, and it occurred to her that he might do something stupid, like drive down to London and turn up at her front door.

'The best thing you can do is go home,' she said, clutching his hands through the open window. 'Just be normal and I'll be in touch when I can. OK?' She wasn't sure he was convinced, and she squeezed his hands to emphasize her words. 'Please? For me. Don't do anything . . . rash.'

The train pulled away, leaving Jon standing helplessly on the platform. It was a relief to turn away from his anguished face. She called Pierre before she found a seat. His voice was all she wanted to hear to pass the unbearable few hours it took to get to London.

The familiarity of Pierre's face when she got off the train made her time with Jon seem like a dream.

'I'm so sorry,' she kept saying on the way to the hospital. He dismissed her apologies, thinking they were about leaving her phone off.

'It's OK,' he said. 'How were you to know? You're here now, that's all that matters.' His belief in that made her cry again, his forgiving, encouraging smile. The thought that her being here was all that mattered seemed so innocent and so far from the truth that it almost broke her heart.

★ ★ ★

The sight of her mother lying in the hospital bed was shocking. She seemed to have aged so much since Luna had last seen her — God, how long had it been? Lying there, her face was sunken, the flesh of her neck where it was visible above her hospital gown sagged towards the bed like melting wax. For the first time Luna saw her mother was growing old and vulnerable, and was horrified at herself for not knowing it before. All she could say was sorry to Angie as she had done to Pierre, but the word was hopelessly inadequate. Angie was conscious, recognized Luna as she sat by the bed and attempted a smile. It wasn't as bad as they'd initially feared, the doctor was saying. The heavy fall on stone steps had made it appear worse, as she'd hit her head and blacked out, bruised herself horribly along one side. She was lucky she hadn't broken anything. Tests were encouraging. She'd possibly had a mini-stroke, a small haemorrhage in the brain that she could recover from completely. It was an early warning sign though, and Angie should take preventive steps.

'You might have to stop smoking pot, finally,' Luna joked through her tears. Angie shook her head. 'What the hell were you doing out on the steps in the middle of the night anyway? Trying to fly?'

Luna felt Angie's hand moving under hers. She let it go and saw her attempting to point at something. Following the direction of her finger, Luna's eyes finally alighted on her mum's bag, which Angie acknowledged with an effortful nod forward. She gestured for Luna to look through it for her, making a croaking noise when Luna pulled out her house keys; she pointed to Luna.

'Is there something you need from home, Ange?' asked Pierre. 'I could drive over and get it?' She blinked a no and pointed to Luna again.

'You want me to go round?' Angie gave a lopsided twitch of a smile. 'You need me to bring you something?' A frustrated frown: no. 'You want me to check the flat?' With a last effort Angie grabbed her hand and pointed to her again. 'OK.' Luna glanced quizzically at Pierre. 'We'll go round later.' But Angie gave a groan and let her hand go, turning her face away. 'Now? You want me to go now?' Angie sighed and closed her eyes, the small smile returned. She seemed to drift back into sleep then, as if

381

that was the end of the matter. Luna didn't want to leave her, but Pierre said they might as well do as she wanted.

'We ought to check it's all secure anyway,' he said. 'The neighbour said she'd cleared up the mess in the hall, whatever that was, and put the things in Angie's flat, made sure she had her keys and bag with her in the ambulance.'

Luna sat for a few moments longer holding Angie's hand, tucking the loose gown round her mother's exposed shoulders, smoothing her tangle of hair from her face and the back of her neck so she would be comfortable. She found it hard to leave. She had the strongest sense she'd ever had of the three of them together like that, like a family.

★ ★ ★

The neighbour heard them arrive and came out to ask how Angie was doing. She was obviously hugely fond of her, so relieved that it might not be as bad as it looked.

'She's the heart of this building,' she said. 'So friendly and helpful. It was a horrible shock to see her like that.'

'So what happened?' asked Luna. 'Do you know why she was out there, even?'

'She'd obviously come back from somewhere really late — my bedroom's at the front and I'm a light sleeper, so I heard the car reversing into a spot. Then I heard the front door open, and I listened out to make sure it wasn't someone breaking in, and I heard Angie's door go too, so

I knew it was her. She went back and forth again a couple of times, like she was carrying something in. And I thought she must've been away 'cos actually I realized I hadn't seen her for a few days, and I usually do. And then I heard this almighty crash and she cried out, so I rushed up to the window and peered out, and I could see from the street light she was lying there at the bottom of the steps, not moving. Well, I called the ambulance straight away and went down, knocked for Hassan in number two on the way 'cos I didn't like to try to move her or anything on my own. Anyway, they told us not to move her if she'd banged her head, and she had, so we checked her breathing and that. They came ever so quickly, thankfully, and we picked up all the stuff that had gone flying out of these boxes and just put it in her flat, just inside the lounge door there. And I found your number by the telephone. I knew you were called Luna, as she'd talked about her wonderful daughter many times.' Luna tried a painful smile. 'I hope it was the right thing to call . . . ' This she addressed to Pierre, as it was him she'd spoken to. Luna felt another guilty shard pierce her like broken glass.

'Absolutely it was,' said Pierre. He grasped her hand. 'Thank you so much for everything you did. We really can't thank you enough. You've been wonderful.' She blushed with a pride that made her uncomfortable in the inappropriate circumstances.

'Would you like a cup of tea?' asked Luna, unlocking Angie's flat door.

'Oh no, thank you, I'm sure you have things to

do for your mother.' She wouldn't be persuaded, so Luna promised she'd let her know as soon as Angie was coming home.

'We should get her some flowers or something,' she said to Pierre as they entered the flat.

The lounge was full of grubby old storage boxes and piles of manila folders with a dank smell as though they'd come from a loft or a garage.

'What the hell is all this?' said Luna, beginning to flip open cardboard lids and flick through yellowing papers.

'Lu,' said Pierre, still standing at the lounge door, looking through the dishevelled box that must have been the one that spilled on the front steps. 'It's loads of old photos and diaries and stuff. There're dates on these. Here.' He passed her a handful of black and white shots, began turning the crinkly pages of a biro-filled notebook. Luna took the photos, flipped them to see names and dates on the back: *Roger tripping to Led Zep, '72; Poppy preggers, '73; Harvest, '71.*

'My God,' said Luna. 'It's all from the commune.' She turned and pulled out a pile of papers from a box, children's drawings with names and ages. 'Look at this!' she exclaimed, passing one to Pierre. *Luna, aged* 2, it said in grown-up writing on the bottom of a wild scribble of colour. She delved in some more, found a large art block of black paper, used as a formal photo album called 'The Creation of Life Ceremony'. Luna didn't know whether to sink into the details of each item she found, or scrabble through everything at once.

'Where did Angie get it all from?' asked Pierre.

'I don't know — someone must have been keeping it all these years.' She picked up another ledger-style book, Hugh's 'Daily Life Diary, April-August 1970'. It was meticulously detailed: what was planted when, who did what, the meals they cooked each day. In another box, loose leaves of paper with penned poetry, song lyrics, and druggy-looking drawings; in another, dog-eared self-sufficiency manuals and books on crops and flowers and herbs. Another box was entirely filled with material, vile-smelling bile-green woollen shawls and patchwork maxi-skirts. Luna stopped sifting through it for a moment, pushed her hand through her hair and breathed out. It was a lot to take in. Pierre came over and put his arm round her.

'I think she might've tracked all this stuff down for you, hon.' Luna put her face against his chest and sobbed.

'Don't make me feel any worse than I do already,' she said.

'I didn't mean to do that, Lu,' he said, hugging her. 'It's not your fault, what happened. And she should have told you what you wanted to know a long time ago. She was just trying to make up for it.'

'It's me that needs to make up,' Luna said, muffled against his jumper.

'I think you both already did,' answered Pierre.

But her mother wasn't the only person she meant.

It was a few hours later, sitting cross-legged on the floor and going through every precious scrap, that Luna began to find the evidence she'd been looking for. They'd been sorting as they went, putting things in the right chronological order, and were beginning to piece together the commune's decline. At first the cataloguing was ordered and meticulous, but a few years further along even Hugh's paperwork seemed scatty. Luna wanted to get back to the hospital as soon as possible to talk to Angie and thank her, so there was no time now to be thorough. But even skip-reading journal entries, she could tell that the sunny optimism of the early days had been overcast by fractious clouds. Notes of the meetings detailed arguments over who wasn't pulling their weight, or who could sleep where. She studied what appeared to be a drawing of a proposal for putting up partitions in the upstairs communal area.

It was the photographs that Luna pored over the most. There seemed to be hundreds and hundreds of them, mostly her father's. She could tell which were his, proper photographer's photographs, with thoughtful composition and sharp focusing, capturing perfect moments. Some scenes she even felt she remembered as she saw them, faces of people who had inhabited her memories suddenly coming to life. 'That's Rosie! We played together all the time! I wonder what she's doing now! She must be nearly forty!'

But there were other photographs too, when

more amateur hands got hold of the camera, especially towards the latter days. A blurry self-portrait of a teenage boy in a mirror, a timer shot of a kind of classroom with a woman and the children — 'That's me!' Luna exclaimed. A man began to appear in front of the camera who had been absent or at least invisible early on, like a ghost manifesting, a man she recognized as her father from the picture she already had. He was paler, scruffier, more brooding than the image she had from the festival picture. With a beard he looked far older, even allowing for the few years it must have been since the first shot.

Luna came across some photographs inside one of the files used to document meetings. For a few minutes Pierre didn't notice how quiet and absorbed she'd become. She started rifling through a pile from a previous year, picking up some photos to compare.

'What've you found?' Pierre asked, finally seeing Luna staring at two photos in her hands. The expression on her face as she looked up at him made him ask, 'What's the matter?'

'Who would you say these two people are?' she asked, passing one of the pictures to him with a trembling hand. It was a bad photograph, dark and blurred. Wonky, as though it had been snapped hurriedly. Wooden supports from floor to ceiling made it look like a barn or a stable. There appeared to be bales of hay stacked up along a wall but it was hard to see. What you could tell was that the photographer was a voyeur, taking a secret picture of two bodies close together. Pierre looked at her uncomprehending.

'You're not going to get all shocked now, are you, after everything else we've seen?' he asked, trying to lighten Luna's mood.

'I am, yes,' Luna said, seriously. 'If that female is who I think it is.'

Pierre looked back at the photo, trying to figure her out. Luna handed him the other one she had in her hand, a stunningly beautiful portrait, radiance personified, seen through her father's own unmistakable artful eye.

# 1974

# Angie

At first, Dave's obsession with photographing everything continued into the commune's difficult period. Angie felt in some way validated, now that she wasn't the only one who found it invasive and infuriating when he was suddenly there, camera in your face, at one of your worst moments. He loved catching someone at the height of their ugly anger in an argument, or losing their temper with a squalling child, or slumped on drugs — usually Roger. In fact, a whole film once, following Roger on a bender, some close-ups of his eyes that really showed the wildness behind them, as his mind unravelled. They were Dave's proudest series of the moment, but the others cared less about his artistry and more about the fact that Roger was becoming a casualty. They called yet another meeting to address the problem of him. He was refusing to wash now, let alone do anything useful, and could sometimes be heard at night ranting a low steady stream of paranoid nonsense that was beginning to disturb people and frighten the children. Everything seemed to divide the group more, like cells splitting. Some thought he was a selfish waster who shouldn't be tolerated. Others were more tolerant, said he should be looked after as he wasn't well in the head. There were never any decisive outcomes, and people often opted out of meetings altogether, knowing they would never get to an agreement but trudge round and round the same problems, like a tricksy Escher drawing.

Dave's last series was of the children, as if it were a last-ditch attempt to capture the innocence before it fled. It was the final 'exhibition' as such at Ceres, not confined to just one room but spread all over the house, like religious icons. There was Crispin, in metamorphosis from child to man, backlit by sunlight as he threw up his head and laughed, the focus on the protrusion of his Adam's apple, his wisps of beard caught white by the rays. The little ones, Rosie, Daniel, Luna, sometimes mischievous earthy imps sprawling in the farmyard dirt, sometimes transcendent angels, so pure they seemed to hover in the shining air. The beautiful Willow, at her Coming of Blood Ceremony. Many exquisite close-ups of her, catching the moments of transformation. Sitting cross-legged on the ground like a girl still, but those gangly limbs and knobbly knees smoothed over as though worked in clay by a sculptor. Or her breasts budding through the thin muslin round her chest. Or that smile, with teeth still too big for her delicate face, somewhere in an unknowable fraction of a moment tipping sweetly from childish goofiness to a languorous, suggestive overbite. The flirtatious innocent-knowing in the eyes of her own beauty, like a secret gift. Self-worth flowed through her, intrinsic as blood. Her mother, Fern, and all the women had nurtured it and were proud of her as though she was their greatest achievement. They had tended the blossoming of a girl into womanhood free of shame. People looked on her in wonder, stragely awestruck in her presence. It felt like a privilege to touch her. She had the sort of incandescent beauty that could make you believe in gods.

Despite the praise heaped on him for these photographs, Dave lost his passion for the art, or at least for documenting the commune. Hugh had to make a point of asking him to photograph particular events or special occasions. He seemed bored by it all, like a wedding photographer churning out the same old scenes. Crispin showed an interest, and Dave taught him how to use the camera and the dark room. It became Crispin's thing for a time, before he grew frustrated that his pictures never came out like Dave's. He never got the light right, or the composition, never quite caught the special moments. They always blurred as he missed them, fractions of a second too late.

Angie could feel Dave's restlessness like the choppiness of the sea when a storm was coming. He took off by himself a lot, and only then did he seem to have renewed interest, when he took photographs of different things, the market in town, holidaymakers on a faraway beach, fans and musicians at a Pink Floyd concert.

He'd said he was going to the gig alone, which pissed off a lot of people who would have liked to have seen Pink Floyd themselves. Debbie was particularly upset. She had fallen in love, however hard she tried to seem casual and free. Angie had been jealous at first, when Dave took good advantage of the fact when she was first there, but now she felt only sympathy. Falling in love seemed a curse for young women here, for actually, in this house of love, there was strangely no place for it. Debbie had done her best to persuade Dave to take her to the gig, said she'd take a chance of getting a ticket once she got there. But Dave was adamant that he'd only feel bad if she didn't and it would ruin it for him. He was only trying to find new things to photograph, he said. It was kind of work, really.

Sleepless, Angie heard the Land Rover return in the small hours. She heard whispers and a giggle, and thought perhaps Debbie had won him over in the end. She knelt up on the mattress and peeked out, straining to see. It was too dark. All she saw was a girl jumping down. She flinched back, tried to see who was missing in the bedroom, but it was impossible. She looked back to the figures, caught in the moonlight by a break in the clouds as they crept to the back door. Dave had his arm round the girl. He shushed her laughter, an intimate, conspiratorial shush. Angie heard the back door being gently opened and closed, and holding her breath, she crept through the sleeping room, wincing at every creaking floorboard. She got to the top of the stairs and craned to see through the banisters. She got to see only a glimpse, now and again, of Dave as he moved back and forth in the kitchen, making drinks perhaps. One particular flash of his face stopped her heart. Angie hadn't seen him smile at somebody like that for an age.

She thought she saw a flick of long blonde hair as she slunk back into the shadows.

⋆ ⋆ ⋆

In a moment alone with Debbie, Angie asked if she was OK now about not going to the concert. 'Oh yeah,' Debbie shrugged. 'It's no big deal, right? It's not quite my scene anyway.'

The hurt that she was trying to cover, still etched in her face, let Angie know it wasn't her. She wished it had been. There was only one other girl it could have been, the only other one with long fair hair that hung straight as a waterfall. Willow.

Angie secretly watched him over the days, and nights. It didn't have to be as bad as she feared, but her fear was telling her it was. In the rare moments she caught them together she saw the old intensity in Dave's eyes as they met Willow's, the depth that had drawn Angie in, that he had used too on Debbie for her brief moment in the glare. But instead of the control he'd exerted before, the magnetism that had drawn her and Debbie helplessly in, this time he was the one who was losing himself. He was smitten, obsessed. When he didn't know anyone was watching, his eyes followed Willow's every move. Now that Angie was looking, she often caught him watching her from an obscured place, through a window or from round a door, for as long as he was left undisturbed.

Poor, sweet Willow just bathed innocently in the glory. Angie remembered well the delicious power of attraction over older men she possessed as a teenage girl — the drama teacher at college, for instance. But, God, Angie was eighteen then. Eighteen was old enough.

Willow was still shy of fourteen.

It was wrong. It felt strange to say so, in this land of freedom, where everything was unre-pressed and out in the open. But she felt it, not an opinion but an absolute truth, way down inside. She had to do something to stop it before it went too far. She monitored Willow, tried to have a talk with her even, about boys, sex, asked if there was anyone she was interested in. The blush that crawled round her white neck as she said, 'No one in particular,' let Angie know for sure.

She confided in Hazel, who couldn't believe it — surely it was harmless infatuation, something that would pass? But then she too watched Dave, saw his arm linger on Willow's back for a moment too long, the praising smile at a pretty dress, the tuck of the hair behind her ear. The eyes, drinking her in.

'My God, he's crazy about her,' Hazel said to Angie, in a shocked whisper.

Hazel tried to talk to Dave, thinking that hearing it from the older matriarchal figure of the commune would make him see sense. His response shocked her.

'He laughed at me,' she reported to Angie. 'I said wasn't Willow becoming a beautiful woman, and he said, 'Becoming? She already is!' I said yes that's true, but she is only thirteen. That's still too young. He realized what I was getting at then, that I knew. He looked so full of hate I thought he might hit me. Then this look of scorn came over his face and he said, 'Or maybe it's that you're too old, Hazel.''

Hazel was still shaken. He'd gone on to call her a jealous old cunt, to say that it wasn't for an old crone like her to dictate the law, or oppress Willow and make her as frigid as she was. Girls all around the world had babies at thirteen; it was only our fucked-up culture that went against our natural biology for ridiculous concepts of decency. It was sexual repression. He'd threatened her to mind her own business, in a way that had truly scared her.

She and Angie discussed talking to Willow or her mother or both, but they remembered too well how incendiary it was when older women warned you off, the danger only adding sparks to the already explosive allure of male interest. It was something that had to be dealt with by a higher authority. But there was no authority. All they could think of in its place was the collective moral of the group. But they needed evidence.

Quickly, secretly, Angie got Crispin to show her how to use the camera. She began to trail silently after Dave, like the ghost of their lost love, waiting to capture the moments. It was not easy to do. Most images she caught she knew just made her look like the jealous, spurned one, as she zoomed in on Dave chasing Willow, laughing, in the field, or took a shot through the banisters of Dave teaching Willow how to play the guitar. Angie lay awake at night, only pretending to sleep, the camera hidden under the bedclothes.

She saw Willow silently rising on a night she had noticed Dave had not come to bed. Willow picked up a shawl on her way out, and Angie listened to her use the taps in the bathroom, heard the creak of her feet on the stairs instead of back to the bedroom. She rose with the camera and followed her. She heard the scrape of the back door over the stone floor, and when she reached it herself saw the darting light of a torch heading towards the hay barn. Waiting until the light had disappeared inside, she quietly let herself out. Peering in from the barn door, she made out the torch light behind the hay bales, a beam rising up to the roof from where the torch had been stood on its end as a lantern. She slunk along the stacks of hay until she was near enough to hear the rustles and whispers in the corner. Her eyes adjusting to the dark, she could make out a makeshift bed behind the stacks of hay, where it couldn't be seen from the door. When she rounded the corner she would see them. She raised the camera, made a guess at the focusing distance by the light thrown from the torch. She crouched down and inched around the bale of hay, her hands trembling with the camera, waiting for them to make some noise to disguise the shutter clicking. As she took the photograph she was aware of seeing hands — his up inside Willow's nightdress, hers on the fly of his jeans.

The shutter sounded so loud to her, but

incredibly they didn't hear it. She quickly backed away, then stepped as fast as she could to the entrance of the barn, stuffing the camera in between the bales to be retrieved in the morning. She ran to the back door, opening it loudly.

'Willow,' she called. 'Are you out here?' She moved near the barn again, standing in the courtyard and calling a bit louder each time. Suddenly Willow appeared.

'What is it?' she asked nervously.

'Ah, there you are,' said Angie, trying to act natural. 'Are you all right? I heard you get up and then I thought I heard the back door and I was a bit worried about you.'

'Oh I'm fine,' Willow said. 'I — I couldn't sleep and . . . I thought a bit of fresh air would help.'

Angie put her arm round the shivering girl and guided her back inside.

'You're freezing,' she said. 'You'll catch your death coming out like that in the middle of the night.' Willow had no choice but to allow Angie to steer her back inside. 'Let me make you a hot drink. Something milky might help you sleep.'

'No — I'm really OK,' said Willow. 'Go back upstairs. I'll be up in a minute.'

But Angie insisted, putting a pan of milk on the stove to warm.

'Really, Angel, I don't want one.' She was petulant now, but Angie wouldn't budge.

Eventually Willow sighed and climbed the stairs. Angie made herself a milk and honey anyway, sitting up for as long as she could. She allowed a small glow of pleasure, like the draw on a cigarette in the dark, at the thought of Dave, freezing his balls off out there, not being able to come back inside. She heard a sound, something like a flowerpot being knocked over, and was bold enough to open the back door and say, 'Is anybody out there?' to the silent darkness, before shutting the door and locking it. Her grim smile did not last long. She had only just caught them in time. They needed to act fast.

★   ★   ★

The next morning Angie retrieved the camera and locked herself in the dark room, leaving Hazel to keep Willow under her watch in the classroom. She prayed the photo would come out. It was the only one that was enough proof in its own right. Nobody could say it was just a harmless passing phase. Angie watched the image form in the developing tray. It was hard to make out, but the things that there could be no mistake about were who the people were and the position of those hands. She printed some of the others too as back-up, and she and Hazel went to Hugh straight away. He called an urgent meeting with everybody.

★   ★   ★

It was decided, unanimously except for Crispin and Roger. They were the only ones who weren't appalled, but both were deemed by the others to be incapacitated for reasons of youth or mental health. Fern flew at Dave, scratching great chunks of flesh from his face before she was wrenched off him, sobbing. Dave lost his temper and started pacing around shouting about Willow's right to her own sexual expression, that this community was based on liberation and there were no rules against what they were doing.

'There are now,' Angie said. 'Without rules against what you were doing, there is no community.'

Dave had drifted so far away from the others' morality that he sneered at Angie, looking to the guys in the group for support. It was then that Hugh decked him with an astonishing punch to the side of his head that seemed to fly out of him like a demon. Willow screamed and ran to Dave as he went sprawling across the Aga, and tried to take the blame, saying that it was she who led him on. This sparked a rage in Angie that made her feel she'd just erupted into flames, a rage that would burn forever.

'Never, ever,' she said, shaking Willow's shoulders, 'feel that a grown man taking advantage of you is your fault.'

'But it is! He didn't take advantage! I love him,' she wept. Angie grabbed her then and hugged her fiercely to her.

'You beautiful girl,' she said. 'What he was taking from you was not love. Believe me. You're too young to understand now, but one day you will.'

Dave, stunned, nursed his jaw as he got back to his feet.

'Get out,' said Hugh, his voice low and even. Still Dave couldn't seem to comprehend the fury directed at him.

'What?' he asked, incredulous. 'Mr Hippy Peace and Love — the Great Dictator!'

'He's not a dictator if it's what the whole community wants,' said Hazel. 'Bar one.' Dave looked round at everyone, realization dawning like a bruise.

'Those who want Dave to leave, raise their hand,' said Hugh. Everybody did.

'I didn't do anything!' he argued, helplessly. 'Roger, man . . . ?'

But Roger was sitting at the table transfixed by Willow's sorrow, matching every one of her heartbroken sobs with one of his own.

'Take a bag of clothes,' said Hugh. 'I'll give you some money to get yourself wherever you need to go.'

'I'm not going anywhere, man. I've done nothing wrong.'

'If you're still here in ten minutes you can tell it to the pigs,' said Hugh.

For a few moments Dave tried to stare him out. But the mention of the police seemed to make him see reality, that his part in Willow's sexual liberation was in fact illegal, something he could actually go to prison for. He tried to swagger slowly out, but was actually back downstairs with a bag packed within minutes, looking frightened as he overheard them deciding perhaps they should hold him and call the police anyway. It was only Willow begging them not to that gave him the chance to snatch the cash in Hugh's hand and bolt out through the door.

★   ★   ★

'We still ought to tell the police,' Angie said later, privately, to Hazel and Hugh, still sitting at the table hours after the day-long meeting. 'He shouldn't be free.'

'But what about Willow?' said Hazel. 'She'd be dragged through it. Do we want that start for her? That damage? And we'd be dragged through it too. How do you think free love would go down in court? That we all share a bedroom and each other? That we're open about it with our children? We're more likely to get them all taken away from us than get Dave convicted. They'd all be like Willow and think: who could blame him?'

After the shocking revelations and violent events, everyone was reeling. Willow was inconsolable, desperate to run after Dave to be with him, full of hate and fury towards her mother and the commune for denying her the love of her life. It was painful not to be able to make her understand more than her years would let her. However much they tried to make their words hit home from their many years ahead, they fell short like ineffective arrows. Finally exhaustion sent her weeping to bed, and the adults, sadly, and much against their ideals, secured all doors and windows and hid the keys so that she wouldn't run away in the middle of the night.

Several other ideals were redefined over the

course of the day, and would continue to be over the next days and weeks and months. Hugh admitted he'd run out of money and they would have to think about how they would survive without it. It was finally agreed that Roger needed the intervention of a qualified doctor. And they began to hammer out a consensus over the sleeping arrangements. Somebody suggested dividing the top floor into individual compartments, almost like sleeper carriages on a train. Willow wasn't the only one, Angie thought, who had travelled the perilous journey recently from innocence to experience.

She lay down that night coiled round her tiny daughter like a conch, knowing she would protect her to the death. The sleeping people around her twitched and moaned as their dreams processed the adjustment that had been made to their world. The sun had gone down eventually on a day of renewed vows to make the commune work, optimism for a better way forward. But still she felt a sense of something else coming and realized, although it was still far too far away in the distance to see or even to think about yet, what she now had the wisdom to recognize as the beginning of the end.

# 2004

## Nat

Nat could never shift the feeling of being watched. It had been with her since she could remember, the sense of eyes on her, waiting, like hunters creeping up on prey. The first belonged to the mother's friend, and even when she had fled from them, far enough to be safe, she still felt the danger out there, the gaze. With Lee and the gang she had relaxed a little, felt safety in their numbers, yet the gaze had found her again, singled her out as weak. She almost felt she had sought it out herself when she had first flirted with Kel and let him happen to her, as though she knew it was her destiny to be the hunted, like a rabbit.

When her kids were first taken away she'd been free of him, kept away by the threat of the authorities around her. But their observation of her had been so much more frightening while they judged whether she was fit to have her children back. She didn't believe she was herself, that was the thing. After her sentence, when only social services and not the police were still monitoring, Kel came sniffing around again. Nat had been relieved at his returned presence, helping to at least banish the searing loneliness that gnawed her bones since she had been on her own, spooked by the unknown forces that were bearing down on her. Kel was like her natural predator, something she instinctively understood. And with him came the only escape from the predatory eyes of others, in the drugs he supplied — the anaesthetic that put the beasts to sleep and let her rest.

For three years she had numbed herself, until it no longer sheltered her from the harm but made her crazy and ravaged with pain. Tracey had thrown her the lifeline and somehow her survival instinct had come through and she had turned and fought. Not straight away, not on her own, but finally she thought of her kids and went to the police about Kel. They'd raided when he had a huge stash and he'd been given five years. Nat was put straight into rehab to protect her and help her start again.

★ ★ ★

It had taken a long time but she had done it.

'You should be really proud of yourself,' Tracey had said, giving her a hug. 'You've turned your life around.' No one had ever said anything like it to Nat before.

It was no fairy tale. She had done rehab three times and fallen. Now she had been clean for eighteen months. A day didn't go past without her thinking about getting high, to make disappear the eyes that never shut, even with Kel inside. But she didn't. The temptation for the escape was so strong sometimes, but she thought about Tyler and Jade, and she didn't. She needed to protect them. They'd never think of her as their proper mum again, she knew. She had a lot more to prove before they ever came and lived with her. But she never missed a visit with them, and now they were allowed to come and stay for whole weekends.

They had had a few foster families by now and hadn't stuck anywhere. The last family hadn't worked out because Tyler bullied the younger boys. It always seemed to be the problem, him fitting in with the other kids. Nobody minded Jade, anyone could love her. She was too quiet, they said, had learning difficulties at school, but she was no trouble. They were in a care home at the moment, waiting to go somewhere without any other children. Nat felt guilty because she couldn't help be glad about it, even though it wasn't the best place for them. She thought it gave her more chance of getting them back if they weren't settled in a nice house with nice parents. She tried hard not to think it as it made her feel like a bad mother, to not want what was best for her kids. But lately she had even started to think that maybe what was best for her kids was for them to be with her. She could do this now. She could be a good mum.

Tracey had driven them all over in the car and had a cup of tea with Nat while they settled in. Tyler was sulky and not speaking and just went through and put the TV on, but Tracey said he probably wouldn't be able to keep it up all weekend. Now he was older he was no longer hyperactive, but slumped around the place in a fug of pheromones and lethargy like a stoner, sleeping loads. Jade slipped down and ran through after him.

Nat was used to Tracey now, and even loved her for the help she'd given, but all the same she was nervous in front of her, feeling judged. She kept looking around to make sure everything was right in the flat, getting up to tidy things away or clean the surfaces again.

'Don't worry, Nat,' Tracey said. 'The place looks lovely. I've got every confidence in you. Just call if there's anything you're worried about.'

They went through Nat's plans for the weekend. Lee was coming over and they were taking them out to the shopping centre. They'd have pizza and go to Blockbusters to get DVDs. A Disney one maybe for Jade, and she'd let Tyler choose what he liked for after Jade had gone to bed, even a horror one as long as it wasn't over eighteen. It'd be fun, sitting in between her two blokes on the sofa, trying not to scream.

Still, though, her heart began to thud when Tracey said she'd be off. She was scared to be alone with these people her little kids had become, solely responsible for them, but knew she couldn't admit it. She had to look like she was in charge. To keep Tracey there a bit longer she asked again about the rehousing. Now the kids were bigger Tyler had to have his own room so Jade slept in with Nat. She'd have to have her own room soon too, even if they only ever visited and never stayed for good. Nat was on the waiting list for an exchange. The thought of a three-bedroom place, a proper house even, with carpets and an upstairs, gave Nat the biggest hope. It made a future look possible. She could imagine herself a proper mum then, hoovering and hanging out washing in a back yard or garden, talking over the fence to another mother. The kids walking through a front gate after school, like at Cathy and Jim's.

And somewhere very far away from here. They were looking at properties right out the other side of the city, or even in a little town, somewhere Kel would never find them once he got out.

'I'll write another letter, if it helps,' said Tracey. 'You should do it soon. Get right away from here.'

She hadn't meant it to, but her comment hung in the air when she'd left, like a threat. When she was sure Tracey had gone, Nat sneaked her cigarettes out of their hiding place behind the microwave. She knew she shouldn't smoke around the kids, but she needed to quell the panic attack that was rising. Even when she did make her new start, even if she did escape the actual danger, would she ever feel as though she'd truly got away from the feeling of someone out there wanting to cause her harm?

★　★　★

Lee still hadn't shown by the afternoon and wasn't picking up his phone. It was fucking typical, but Nat refused to let it spoil their weekend. They went to the mall anyway, the three of them. Nat promised Jade she would see

Daddy soon and cheered her up with entice-
ments of new clothes and getting her nails done.
Tyler was changing his mind, saying he'd stay
behind, but she finally got him off his backside
with the suggestion of getting him a mobile
phone if there was a good offer on.

When they finally sat down to eat in the food
hall on the top floor — the kids chose
McDonald's instead of pizza — Nat was thinking
this was the best day of her life. Only once had
her heart stopped, when she felt the presence of
someone, looked round and thought she saw a
glimpse of the man. It was stupid. He wasn't
from round here and she hadn't seen him for
years and he wouldn't look like that any more
anyway, if he was even still alive. He certainly
wouldn't recognize her. Looking at Jade, holding
her chips like a princess so she could proudly
admire her long spangly nails, Nat realized with
sickening horror that the little girl was closer to
the person he had known than the adult woman
she was now. She saw what had happened to her
from the outside for the first time. The surge of
love she felt for Jade at that moment felt almost
like a love for herself. This is what love is, she
thought. I know it, because I can feel it, flowing
through me as strong as a fix. She looked at Tyler
and felt it again, physically felt it. He was leaning
back in his seat trying to be cool. He'd already
wolfed his burger and was flicking through
the manual for his new Nokia to check out the
features. He was ready to go home now so he
could charge it up and use it. He had tried to
stay in a mood all afternoon but his surliness was

having a battle with excitement, and excitement kept winning. It was sweet to watch. He was getting bum fluff on his upper lip. That was sweet too, but she didn't dare say so.

⋆  ⋆  ⋆

Back home, Nat put *Pirates of the Caribbean* on for Jade. Tyler pretended he wasn't interested, but he sprawled on the sofa with Jade anyway. They'd bought Coke and popcorn and chocolate, and Nat pulled the curtains so it was dark like the cinema. She was having a fag at the window in the kitchen while the adverts were on when the doorbell went. It was bound to be Lee, finally remembering and, she supposed, better late than never. She opened the door without looking to see who it was.

He barged the door with his shoulder so that it hit her on the forehead and knocked her back against the wall. He seized her by her shoulders and flung her sideways onto the kitchen floor.

'So the stupid bitch is still here,' he said, looming over her as she struggled to get up and whacking her across the cheek with the back of his hand, and his heavy rings. 'Hasn't even got the sense to fuck off.' Nat tried to turn and struggle away on her knees but he caught the top of her jeans and punched her ear. 'What d'you think, that you're above me now? That I can't touch you now you're friends with the pigs? Think you can just swan around here like you're the queen of cunts?' He turned her back round and kicked her in the side.

Tyler came rushing in and leaped on his back, biting his arm. Jade was screaming in the doorway. He roared and tried to fling Tyler off him, but Tyler was much bigger than he remembered and he clung on with his long limbs. He grabbed the boy by his sweatshirt and pulled him round, slamming him into the table. Tyler cried out as the sharp edge of it dug into his ribs.

'Leave him alone!' Nat shrieked, rushing at Kel and headbutting him in the stomach. It winded him and as he was doubled over she grabbed her bag and threw it to Jade, making a frantic sign for the phone and pointing to the farthest room, the bathroom. Kel saw Jade running.

'Oi! Fucking get back here!' he roared, chasing her.

But she was quick and had already slammed and bolted the bathroom door before he'd got there. He hammered on it but it didn't give.

'What's she doing, calling your friends?' He charged back at Nat, got her by the throat against the door jamb. 'Well, it doesn't matter 'cos you'll be fucking dead by the time they get here.' Nat kicked at him, but she only had bare feet; tried to knee him in the balls. She tried to shout but he was gripping so tightly no sound came out.

'Let her go!' In her blurring vision she saw Tyler coming at him, something flashing.

Kel yelped and jumped back, dropping her. Tyler stood with a kitchen knife, blood dripping off it. Kel looked down at the gash on his arm in disbelief, then back at Tyler. You're gonna wish you hadn't done that, you little fucker!

'Fuck off or I'll kill you,' said Tyler as Kel moved slowly towards him. Nat saw the hate in her son's eyes and knew that he meant it. She'd let her son get in a lot of trouble and become a lot of things, but she wasn't going to let him be a murderer and go to prison, not because of her. With an almighty lunge, she threw herself at Kel's back, unbalancing them both and hurtling them towards the glass kitchen door. There was a wild shattering as they fell through it and landed against the railing of the balcony. Disorientated for a moment, she struggled fast to keep her advantage over Kel and crouched low to heave against his body with her back, trying to push until his weight tipped him up and over the railings. She saw Jade come running back through, screaming. Tyler was coming out on the balcony to help her but she shouted, 'No! Stay back! Stay back!'

She saw Tyler grab Jade, hold her head to his chest — the last image before she screwed up her eyes to use every last ounce of strength in her body to force the badness out of their life once and for all.

# SEVEN

# 2004

Jon kept phoning and texting. It jabbed Luna every time her mobile went, like a guilty conscience, and she wanted to leave it off but couldn't, with everyone wanting to know how Angie was doing. Luckily she was able to tell Pierre that the calls were all from concerned friends. She texted Jon in moments by herself to let him know she couldn't speak, she was with family, that he should just not think about her at all while her mum was in hospital, just get on with his life. It had the opposite of the intended effect, as he called with increasing urgency, insisting she speak to him, threatening to come down to see her. He was sounding disturbingly irrational, completely unlike the idea Luna had of him as being solid as a rock. Something about him coming loose seemed particularly danger-ous, as though she was standing under a cliff before an avalanche.

She managed a quick conversation with him when she went to the drinks machine at the hospital.

'You have to stop calling me,' she said, low into the phone. 'I'm with my mother and Pea all the time. I'll talk to you when it's calmed down here, when my mum's all right.'

'I can't go on like this,' he said. 'I'm a mess. My wife keeps asking what's wrong with me and I just want to tell her. I'm going to have to tell her. I've got to see you.'

'No, you can't!' Luna insisted. 'It's impossible. I can't deal with this right now. I'm in a crisis, Jon — can't you understand that?'

'But what about us? You can't start something like we've started and then shut me out of your life, expect me to go back as if nothing's happened. I feel like I'm losing you. Promise me I'm not losing you.' He was sounding deranged and Luna wondered where he was — crying outside his office? Not even at work at all?

'Jon, please, just keep it together for a bit longer. I really need you to be strong right now. And for God's sake, don't tell your wife, especially not when you're in this state. You need to calm down and we need to plan how we're going to do this. I just can't do it yet, OK? Promise me, not yet.'

The thought of planning together seemed to give him solace and she managed to wring a promise out of him before she rang off. She didn't know if she trusted him though, whether she would any day now pick up the phone to a distraught wife, or open the door and find him standing there. She felt as though she was in the plot of a thriller, a character who hadn't realized the stranger she'd met was unhinged, as her mind raced back to try to recall whether she'd ever given him her full address. She tried to stop herself being so melodramatic. She thought back to the man she'd first met, the self-composed, reliable man she'd studied and painted. It was Jon, lovely Jon, who only days ago she was deciding to spend her future with. A future whose seeds she had already sown in a hotel room. There was no going back. But she felt herself wobble, like a tightrope walker losing confidence. The moment of doubt that made you fall.

★   ★   ★

'How's our Child of Ceres?' said Luna, squeezing Angie's hand as she woke, and leaning over to kiss her.

'No Peter Pan, that's for sure,' said Angie, hoarsely, slurring a little. Luna poured her a glass of water from the jug on her bedside table. 'You found it all then?'

'Mum,' Luna replied, 'thank you for digging out all that stuff for me. It's incredible. Every detail documented. Who'd kept it all these years?'

'Hazel,' said Angie. 'Hugh first, it was his thing. He died, years ago. Sons sold his cottage — found it all in the attic. Hazel still lived round there and they found her number in Hugh's phone book. She's had it all these years.'

'Were you still in touch?' asked Luna.

Angie shook her head. 'Had to track her down.' She looked pleased with herself. Luna laughed.

'Thank you,' she said. 'And sorry. I didn't need to know badly enough for you to risk your life to get it.'

'I should have just told you.'

'Well, I know now why you didn't,' said Luna. Angie looked at her.

'Do you?' she asked. Luna pulled the incriminating photograph from her bag and showed it to Angie. She flinched, as though it still caused her pain all these years later.

'I read Hugh's report too,' said Luna.

'I'm sorry,' said Angie.

'You've got nothing to be sorry about,' said Luna. 'I'm sorry I was so mean to you over it. Sorry I built him up into this great — idol.'

'I did that too, once,' Angie smiled.

Luna paused before she spoke again.

'Do you think he — ' She stopped. 'Was he sick? Were there . . . others?'

Angie shook her head. 'I'm sure not. It was the situation. Drugs and no rules and everything wild.'

'But . . . Thailand.' Luna winced as she said it. It was vile to think of him living there for the underage girls.

Angie shook her head, vehemently this time. 'You saw his work afterwards. He had a conscience.'

Luna wasn't convinced.

'And anyway,' Angie added, 'there's a letter. For you.'

'From him?' said Luna.

'Yes. I've only just seen it. It went to the farm after the commune had failed and I'd left. But it's there. I kept it separate. I hadn't decided whether to show you. It admitted what he'd done — he was full of remorse. I still wasn't sure you'd want to know about it.'

Luna didn't say one way or the other. She didn't know herself which version of her father she preferred to have, the perfect one or the one that was true.

'Even though I got all the commune stuff, I still wanted to sort through it and censor what you saw,' Angie went on. 'But now I'm glad my fall stopped me doing that. I think it's time I stopped trying to protect my little girl from the truth of things.'

Luna began to cry.

'I should have let you just be yourself,' said Angie, squeezing her hand. 'That's what I meant to do. But then I tried to make you tough, to cope with the world. Not a soft dreamer like me. Someone who could make it and have something for herself, without men and children. I was hurt and bitter. I tried to mould you. And I never meant to do that.' Her voice broke with the effort of trying not to cry herself. 'I meant you to just be. Yourself. To know what you wanted and go for it. Be happy.'

The word made Luna break down completely. She had to grope blindly in her bag for a tissue to blow her nose.

'Aren't you happy, Lulu?' said her mum.

'Yes. No. I was,' Luna tried. 'But . . . I found out I wanted children. And now . . . I think I might be pregnant.'

Angie looked startled, as though she'd spoken Yiddish, then joyous. She pulled Luna to her and said, 'That's wonderful! Congratulations! There's no reason to cry about that!'

'But Pierre doesn't want kids, Mum. Or not yet. I was worried we'd — I'd — run out of time. He doesn't know yet. And we've got no money and no house and . . . '

'Good God, Lu. You really did grow up in a different era, didn't you? Money and houses don't matter!'

'But they do. They shouldn't but they do. If you're going to be responsible. And you need a man who's ready to be responsible.'

'But he will be, Lu. He's a really good man. You'll all be fine, I know it. He loves you very much. He'll be a great dad.'

Luna took a deep breath, ready to tell Angie everything. 'That's just it, Mum — '

'Hello, Pea,' said Angie. Luna jolted up, saw Pierre coming towards the bed.

'Are you all right?' he said, his concerned tender smile filling her with pain. She loved that face, so familiar, so *hers*. It was the face, she realized, she wanted her genes to mix with, if they were going to at all. And now it no longer belonged to her, she'd given up all her rights to it.

'Is this, like, a mother and daughter moment?' he asked, giving Luna's shoulders a squeeze.

'Well, yes,' said Angie. 'But we'll let you in on it.' She winked at Luna.

He bent over and gave her a kiss. 'How you doing, Ange?' He sat on the bed with his arm round Luna, teasing Angie in that way he did, calling her an old hippy but making her feel cool at the same time. Luna realized how subtle and brilliant it was, the way he handled her with such fond ease. Not everybody could cope with a mother-in-law like her. But they were really close, Luna could see that now. What they had was love, born out of knowing each other, going back a long way, and loving Luna, who was there in the middle between them, ruining what they had like a bad apple. The sweetness of the feeling of them surrounding her was so unbearable Luna had to get up and make an excuse to be off.

'I've only just got here!' said Pierre. 'We don't have to get back for anything, do we?'

'I think you probably do,' said Angie emphatically, giving a knowing grin. Pierre looked questioningly at Luna but she looked down, frowning as she did up the buttons of her jacket.

'Go and have a romantic evening together,' Angie went on. 'Just the two of you. You've been looking after me far too much.'

'Steady on, old girl,' said Pierre. 'You're getting soppy in your old age. You'll be calling us a lovely couple next.'

'You are a lovely couple,' said Angie.

'God, stop it, the pair of you,' said Luna, as though she was joking.

'And I've revised my opinion on marriage too, by the way,' she added. 'If you're interested. It's not such a bad thing, you know.'

'Fuck, you really did bang your head,' said Pierre, bending to kiss her goodbye. 'Luckily we haven't. Unless it turns out you're loaded, of course.' Angie chuckled.

Luna hugged her and kissed her, unable to

speak with the effort of holding back the emotion.

'Don't worry, darling,' said Angie in her inimitably bad effort at a whisper. 'Things'll work out. Just talk to him.'

★   ★   ★

'Talk to me about what?' asked Pierre.

'She's never quite mastered the art of discretion, has she?' said Luna.

'What's worrying you?'

'Can we talk about it when we get in?' said Luna. She kept her eyes on the corridor lino but felt him searching her face.

'Sure,' he said, trying to keep his tone light but falling quiet as he walked beside her in the knowledge that something big was coming.

★   ★   ★

She found it easier to stand, facing out of the vast window as the day began to fail, her arms wrapped round herself, her eyes avoiding Pierre's in the reflection. He'd busied about at first, asking if she was hungry, offering tea. She'd shaken her head no, so he'd flicked the kettle off again, opened a bottle of wine and poured two glasses, leaving hers on the table. He'd sat down finally, taken a couple of gulps, and now he waited.

'I've been untrue to you,' said Luna. It was an odd, old-fashioned phrase and she wondered where the hell it had come from. Her voice sounded unemotional, as false as her heart. She saw the movement as he slowly put down his glass.

'What do you mean?' he asked, in the same peculiarly flat way, as though they were delivering lines in a read-through.

'It started months ago. After my dad died. When I said I wanted a baby.' The word baby was hard to say, and she struggled with herself for a moment. 'I tried to be reasonable, like you asked of me. Wait for a while. I knew you were right about our situation and everything. But somehow I couldn't. When I went away on that weekend, I met . . . '

She saw him lean forward and put his elbows on his knees. He bowed his head as if he was bracing himself and looked down at his hands, twisting together. She faltered, not knowing how she would ever get it out.

' . . . I met Alex. I talked to her about it. Something she said convinced me that it was up to me when I had a child. No, that's wrong. I'm not trying to put the blame on her. It's just . . . she's got a daughter and it didn't stop her doing the other things she wanted in her life. She struggled but it didn't matter. It was worth it. She said at my age it wasn't fair of you to put it off much longer. And it just made me think, why should it be you that gets your way, and not me? I became convinced it wasn't fair. That it was my right. So I stopped taking the Pill.'

After a pause he looked up at her.

'I should have told you, of course. But I wanted to get pregnant. I didn't want you to use anything to stop it. So I deceived you. I tried to steal a baby off you.' She gave a small mirthless laugh. 'I thought I was pregnant in Paris. But I wasn't. Or I lost it.'

'Luna,' Pierre said, wanting to cut to the chase. 'Is that what it is? Are you pregnant now?'

Here it was then.

'I don't know. I might be.'

Pierre exhaled slowly. She waited for him to digest what she'd already told him before she went on. She wondered if she would have been better to have blurted out about the affair first. But it was so hard, and she had wanted to explain why. It wasn't that she didn't love him, after all. That she loved someone else better. She realized it wasn't that at all.

And now she knew that yes, she had said it all the wrong way round. Pierre was adjusting to it, as her mother had said he would, standing up and coming towards her to hold her and say it was all right. His face was full of love as he turned her to him and tried to make her look at him.

'Don't forgive me,' she said, turning her face away.

'There's nothing to forgive,' he said, bringing her head to his chest — the dip in the breastbone that felt like home. This was the worst thing imaginable. He was meant to be already furious with her and cold, so that it didn't hurt either of them so much when she delivered the final wound.

'There is, Pea,' she tried to insist. 'I've done something we can't come back from.' She found she was having to raise her voice, over another less well-behaved domestic from one of the neighbouring flats.

'You haven't,' said Pierre. 'Don't say any more.'

'I've got to. I've got to get it out,' she cried, and tried to push him away.

At that moment there was the sound of a huge explosion, glass crashing somewhere above them, and they both flinched together instinctively.

'What the FUCK . . . ?' shouted Pierre, his hand over Luna's head.

They heard screams, an irate man bellowing, and they rushed to the window to see glass falling like hail. Pierre flung open the sliding door to the balcony. The sound intensified and he leaned out to see what was going on above them.

'Oh GOD!' he shouted. 'STOP! STOP!' Luna saw what was happening above them in the terror on his face as he looked up. The sounds of fighting became a single blood-chilling scream, and Luna saw a body drop past their window. Pierre shot his arms out wildly, as though he could catch it on its way down, shouting, 'NO!'

They looked over the railing in horror to see a girl hit the concrete below and smash.

Luna was struck dumb, paralysed.

'Oh my God, oh my God,' Pierre said, looking up again at the balcony above, where children's screams still curdled the air. He raced back into the flat to the front door, yelling at Luna to call the police. 'It's two floors up,' he yelled. 'There was a guy, I saw a guy.' Luna snatched her mobile and ran after him, dialling 999. She saw the door to the stairs still swinging, and followed. She was just in time to see a man holding his bloodied stomach crashing past her on his way down.

'PEA!' she screamed, and began to race up the steps.

'I'm all right,' he said, in a tight, winded voice.

She got to him just as he was struggling up from where he'd been slammed out of the way. He staggered upwards.

'Did you get a look at him?' he shouted over his shoulder. She had.

'Yes,' she shouted, following him up. The image of the man's scared and hate-filled face was scratched into her mind. 'Yes I did.'

At the thirteenth floor, Pierre caught the door before it clicked back into place. Terrified residents had opened their doors and come into the corridor. Pierre followed the sounds of the screaming, through the open door to a flat. By the time Luna got there he had pulled the kids back in off the balcony and was easing the knife out of the boy's fist. He was dazed, the girl hysterical. When Pierre had put the knife in the sink he held the girl to him tightly, saying, 'It's OK, it's OK, it's OK,' over and over like a mantra. Even though it wasn't OK, it helped the girl, and her desperate shrieks subsided to breathless, juddering sobs. The boy stepped back against the units and slowly sank to the ground, staring ahead with eyes that had seen too much.

Luna approached him quietly, lowered herself to sit next to him and put her arm round his shoulders. She felt them stiffen but he let her leave it there. They heard the sound of sirens in the distance.

★ ★ ★

426

Pierre insisted they go with the kids, stay with them as long as they needed. He made out to the police and social services that he and Luna knew them well, even though in reality they'd only seen them around the estate sometimes. They were usually up to no good, especially the boy, who they'd suspected of being the one who'd graffitied the lift, who Pierre had chased for breaking the wing mirror off his van.

They made their statements. Pierre had seen the man first, his upper torso leaning out over the balcony. Then somehow he'd twisted and when he wrenched back up he had the woman in his grasp. They had struggled for several horrible moments, and then he'd seen her hanging momentarily in space, trying to twist and grapple to clutch the railing. And then the lurch as her whole body was flung. Pierre broke down then.

Luna gave her description. Tyler couldn't speak, not a word or a nod, as though he had atrophied with the shock and horror, but the girl managed to say the man's name and the social worker confirmed who it was. She was distraught. He'd been let out from prison early and a fuck-up meant they'd somehow not known of his release. The family was meant to be rehoused by now.

'How could this have happened?' she said, over and over.

When, hours later, the police said Luna and Pierre could go, Pierre said no.

'We'll stay with them until you find some-where,' he said. 'We want to know where they're going.' The girl had clung to him like a baby

427

animal. The social worker was trying to find an emergency foster home. They finally got hold of the girl's father, who'd been out drinking. He wanted to have them but social services had already deemed his home unsuitable; there wasn't room and his stepmother was known to the services. Luna and Pierre stayed with the children all night and into the following day, when they were put temporarily with a family they'd stayed with before. They found it hard to let them go. Luna couldn't go back to the flat, not while the screams still rang in her ears and the body still fell in front of her eyes, the stain still fresh on the ground. So they stayed at Angie's at first. They went to see the children every day in a round trip that included a visit to Angie in hospital. Their lives before then were completely obliterated by the event, as though it had been a bomb.

★　★　★

'How are you doing yourself, Lu?' Pierre asked.

They were finally back at their own place on the evening of the day they had taken Angie home from hospital, curled together on the sofa against the ghosts. They'd wanted to stay with her overnight but she'd sent them home, saying it was time.

'I'm OK,' Luna answered.

'Do you — know for certain yet if you're . . . ' Pierre asked.

Luna shook her head.

'Can you take a test yet?'

'Probably.' Luna stopped there.

'Don't you want to know?' said Pierre.

Luna looked down.

'Because I do,' Pierre went on. 'If that's what's worrying you. Honestly. I'll be really happy if you are.'

'It's not that,' said Luna, her voice tight. 'There's something else. Something I never got to say because of what happened. I need to tell you.'

'No you don't,' said Pierre quickly. Luna glanced up at him. He took her hands in his and blew his fringe away. 'I mean it, Lu. I really don't want you to tell me anything else. About the baby.' He was emphasizing his words as if trying to make her understand. 'What I mean is . . . I really don't care how — how it got there.'

Luna's heart lurched. He knew. Of course he knew. When she thought back over the weeks she saw it was hardly possible for it to be his.

'What I'm trying to say is that I love you more than anything in the world and I will love that baby as much. I want to be with you. Both of you. You're the love of my life, Luna. There's only ever been you. Whether you want to be with me is another thing, I know that. But I really hope you do. I can't imagine my life without you. But I want what you want. I want you to be happy. I just hope against hope that you feel you can still be happy with me.' He was trembling. His brow was stitched tight with emotion.

Luna started to speak but he shushed her.

'Please don't say anything else about it. Really.

429

Ever. If — if you decide to leave me . . . ' His voice cracked and he swallowed. 'You must do what you must do. I don't want to guilt-trip or pressure you, or . . . I just want you to know how I feel. So that you know what you'll get with me if you stay. You'll get everything I can give. Always. You both will. That's it.' He released her hands and held his up in a gesture to signal the end of the matter.

He breathed out and stood up, reached for his weed box and changed his mind.

'Cuppa tea?' he asked from the kitchen. Luna smiled at him through her tears and nodded.

She wanted to run over to him and squeeze the hurt out of him, make him feel all right again, tell him how much she loved him and that she wanted to stay. But she held on to her knees as though it would help her stay where she was. She knew he didn't want that. He wanted her to really think about what she was going to do, properly, not in an unthought rush of gratitude. He wanted her to consider the baby, consider the father. Consider herself. Not now. But when everything had settled and she really knew.

★   ★   ★

Jon's messages had changed. After the Angie incident, when she hadn't been in touch for days and then finally emailed him about the horrific murder and their involvement with the victim's children, his desperation for her hardened over with a sullen crust. It occurred to her that he thought she was a compulsive liar coming up

430

with wildly absurd excuses for not seeing him. Did he really imagine she would make all this up just to avoid him?

*You can just tell me, you know,* he said in a tired voice in the last message, *if you had no intention of getting together with me. Now I know why you were so adamant I didn't tell my wife. Thanks for that advice, by the way. I'd be looking pretty stupid if I had done.* His voice began to rise in temper. *If you were just using me to get what you wanted at least have the balls to say so. But whatever it is you're up to, that's my baby as well, you know. I have rights . . .*

He didn't finish his sentence. There was a pause and then the phone went dead. It was true; it would be his child as much as hers and Luna would have to do the right thing.

And then there were no more messages or texts or emails. Luna missed him. Without him she felt herself deflate back to normal. She saw herself as she really was again, no longer omnipotent and able to transform into who and whatever she wanted to be like some kind of superhero, but the same person she'd been before, with all her human failings.

But the strange thing was that it felt OK. It wasn't that she had the richest life anyone could ever have, but she was blessed. She saw it now. Instead of seeing the holes and the gaps and all the things that were missing, everything she did have was suddenly apparent, like islands revealed in a lifting mist. The knowledge of her own blindness felt almost as sad as everything else.

Finally, she was alone in the flat for the first

time. It was strange to be without Pierre, who'd been there so constantly for her, for her mother, for those children. He had changed. Or perhaps the serious situation had brought out the deep character that was always there but never had cause to reveal itself, until now. They said that, didn't they? That it was a crisis that brought out who you really were. He seemed to be shouldering everybody's burdens now on his skinny frame. At the mother's funeral he had cried for everyone yet still somehow bore the weight of all their sorrow too. He seemed to know exactly how to be with the children. He worried how they were when he wasn't there, talked about them all the time. 'I'm haunted enough by what happened,' he said. 'Imagine what it's like for them.' They had affected him so deeply Luna couldn't quite remember the person he was before they'd come into their life.

Eventually she had suggested gently that he should to get back to work. His exhibition was approaching and he was way behind. He said it was hard to care about it. She had managed to talk him round by suggesting maybe the kids would like to see what he did. Their foster mum was having trouble even coaxing them out of their rooms. Maybe Pea taking them out, maybe a ride in the back of his van, maybe just being somewhere completely strange, anything, would help. If it only gave their suffering a second's respite it would be something.

He asked her to go along too but she said not this time, there was something she had to do, and he seemed to understand. He had offered to be there with her but also knew why she had to be alone.

They were the longest minutes. She stood at the window waiting, knowing they were the most important minutes of her life, fractions of time that would decide her whole future one way or a very different other. She was torn over what she wanted the outcome to be. So torn she had to shut off her thoughts and wait for fate to give its verdict on what she must do. She looked at the clock and took a breath. Heart thudding, she looked quickly at the result. Seeing it made her realize what she had truly wanted in her heart of hearts, the way tossing a coin did when you couldn't decide. She smiled.

*A painting. A woman at a window, looking out.*

She sits on an old wooden chair, leaning forward with her arms on the sill, a loose dress draping over her form to her feet, which are bare. Her hair is swept up at the back to reveal the nape of her neck, stray locks falling around her shoulders. Her face is in profile, highlighted against the glass.

The large window takes up most of the painting, placed at the very centre of it, looking out onto a dark sky. All that can be seen of the room surrounds the window at the edges of the painting: the bare white walls, the lack of curtains, the unpolished floorboards, a discarded stocking. The perspective of the lines of the floorboards leads the eye up to the woman's feet, taking in the figure tilting forward and following her gaze through the window, but we do not know what she can see outside.

It is lighter inside than it is out. Because of this all that can be seen through the window is the artist's reflection suspended in mid-air in one of the panes. He half-sits against a tall stool, painting at an easel. The way he is painted contrasts with the detail of the woman — each contour, each lock of hair, each toenail, each fold of her dress, painstakingly captured. His figure, a barely-there impression.

The kind of painting in which the image can only be made out with unfocused eyes. If she looks straight at him he disappears into so many indecipherable daubs of paint. She has to look slightly away from him to make him out. The figure, the easel, his arm holding the brush.

And there, the thing that doesn't make sense. In the reflection, something else floating, like a low-slung moon. When she doesn't look too hard, slightly to the left or right, she thinks it is a child's face she sees hovering somewhere between them. But it cannot be, because it would have to be in the real room if it was really there, the back of its head in the foreground of the painting as it stood somewhere between its mother and father, in the way. She finds herself looking at the painting often, trying to work it out.

The painting pleases her. It reminds her of the time before her first child was born, the time she sat at that very window, with a child who was there, and yet not there.

She hung the painting in the very same studio on the opposite wall to the window, despite the artist throwing it out. He'd said it was no good and she had not been able to persuade him otherwise. At least let me reuse the canvas, she'd said, so finally he did, along with the paints and brushes and sketch pads he said he no longer had a use for. But she'd lied. She was never going to paint over it. It was a better painting than he thought, his Hackney Venus. She had told him he shouldn't be giving up when he came for the last time, but he wouldn't expand on why, just left as abruptly and decisively as he'd arrived. Some of the other artists had met the woman in the painting. They'd thought the couple were in love. Then she stopped coming. He had carried on for a while, kept himself to himself, until he phoned when the six months were up and arranged to give her back the key. It was a while before she got back to painting after her baby was born, but she didn't want to lease the studio out again. So she found the money for the rent somehow, and took the time to move back in slowly, gradually filling the room again like a picture, until she was all here.

# 2009

# Uffizi Gallery, Florence

I was so thankful for his presence as we turned and saw you. He was speaking into my ear, unaware of the effect of your sudden appearance on me, so that I could feign intent listening and also lean on him a little more for support. I was proud of him too, glad to have him with me as I turned into the imposing face of you and your family. I knew you had one now, of course, as try as I might I am not above Googling you every once in a while — your company profile, your Facebook page. I wonder if you ever succumb to that temptation? I am easy enough to find now, I suppose, and I wonder at times what you know about me, what you think of my work — whether, if things had turned out differently, I would have gone on to produce it at all. Do you know about the commune exhibition I did with Angie? Maybe you even saw it. Or the prize I won for *Perception*, the piece with the words torn from my father's letter? The highest achievement of my career, the point which finally satisfied two hungers at once: my ambition and my need for my father's love. The time I came to terms with, even cherished, his legacy, the vigilance it taught me in searching for the truth of things. Were you impressed, proud of me?

You're the first person I think of even now when I find myself needing validation. I bathed in your admiration as though you were the sun.

And now I have seen how a daughter turns to her father for this, I feel I understand.

'You all right, Lu?' We had left behind the Botticelli room and my step faltered finally from that great splash of memories, and I took a breath to compose myself.

'D'you wanna sit down for a bit?' He gestured to the cafeteria at the end of the corridor with an incline of his head, the way cool young people do. But I imagined you finding your way there soon after passing through the famous rooms and so I said, 'We should probably go,' and we sauntered back towards the stairs and walked down, stepping in unison.

Had we been alone, you and I, I may have changed my mind about walking past and turned back, to actually say the things I've often told you in my mind. First, I always say sorry again, for how things turned out between you and me. But now I think perhaps that is no longer necessary. Seeing you with your addendums felt like living proof that we were not meant to be. You have grown into a family and it suits you so well. Your children are just like you. Your wife too. I wonder if you have always looked like such a pair or if you have grown into each other over the years. Your round face, your colouring, replicated around you like flowers blooming on the same plant. It cracked the seam in my heart momentarily, for the seeds that wouldn't grow in me.

But I am happy for you. Your children meant everything to you before they were even born. It was something so attractive in you. I'm glad I did not deprive you of the one thing you had to have. That's another thing I would say. That I will never forget the way you made me feel. I fell in love with the way you saw me. The same me, yet different. The woman I wanted to be but, as it turned out, couldn't. Around Pea I am just the person I am. He has always loved me for being that person and always will, and I discovered the same is true of how I feel about him. We will never know that about each other, Jon — whether, if we had ever had children or not, we would still love each other for the people we are.

★ ★ ★

Tyler and I stroll to the Ponte Vecchio and lean on the bridge, where we wait for Angie and Jade. Angie has taken her shopping, has promised her a pair of fancy Italian boots. I don't know if either of them quite realizes what she's let herself in for. And then we'll go to the gallery where Pierre is installing pieces for his show. He never loses his hope that this will be the one that does it, and I love him for that. For in spite of his dreams of accolades and pots of money, it's not what it's about for him, not at all. Then later we'll drive to the airport to pick up some more of the gang. How bizarre that you're here in this place too, now, when everyone's come for Pierre's opening — Gina and Adam and Billie,

Hazel, Fern and Willow. It's amazing to think you may even run into Alex or even Tomas, while you're here. You'll think you're having the most peculiar dream.

I watch the light reflecting from the river, daubing the contours of Ty's handsome face. He asks what I'm smiling at and I say nothing, but sometimes how I feel for him just comes bursting out. He may not be my flesh and blood, but he's my son just the same. He and Jade are my pride and joy, as much as if I had given birth to them myself. Worth every second of the labour we went through to adopt them. Sometimes I forget, see a gesture of Pierre's as Tyler sweeps a hand through his hair, hear Angie's cheeky tone as Jade says a bad word and giggles.

That's the main thing I'd like to tell you. That I found what was meant for me. That I too know the love we were missing that we thought we'd find together.

It was good to see you complete, Jon. You looked so right, the childhood sweethearts who built a life together, you and the woman who never loved anyone else, who gave you what you waited for all your life. That is a good, proper love story, a better one than ours.

And as for me — well, you know what they say. You can take the girl out of the commune, but . . . Do you know that we live here now? In a tumbledown villa outside Florence that we intended to renovate but is too much of an artwork in itself to touch. Just me and my collage of a family, stuck firmly together solely with a bond of love. And this one won't fail, for I have fallen in the deepest love with my life and this place and all those it embraces, a till death do us part kind of love, and will always be here.

I am happy. I hope you are too.

## MY VINTAGE SUMMER

### Jane Elmor

It all began in the summer of '76. The year the sun scorched the grass the colour of sand and no one could sprinkle their lawns or take a bath, and the year Lizzie could no longer run around without her top on . . . Schoolgirl friends Lizzie and Kim grow from small-town adolescents to women on the hedonistic stage of London in the early eighties. There they join Kim's older sister, Vonnie, an untameable force of nature who is everything they'd like to be . . . or is she?

# SONGS OF TRIUMPHANT LOVE

## Jessica Duchen

While the celebrated opera singer Terri Ivory is in hospital, facing what could be the end of her career, her daughter Julie discovers a long-buried secret. This forces her to question her past and her place in her mother's affection. Their empty house no longer seems a home. Mother and daughter try to keep their closeness to each other and to the men they love: damaged Teo, whose passion for Terri borders on the self-destructive, and Julie's first love, Alistair, who fails to predict the consequences of his decision to join the army. When calamity strikes, all four must make vital choices to find their way forward. Can love and music heal when medicine cannot? And are there some secrets that should never be shared?

# THE WELL AND THE MINE

## Gin Phillips

It's 1931 in Carbon Hill, a small Alabama coal-mining town. Nine-year-old Tess Moore watches from the darkness of her back porch as a strange woman lifts the cover off the family well and tosses a baby in without a word. It is the height of the Depression; while Tess's father, Albert, performs backbreaking and dangerous work at the mine, her mother, Leta, makes do without meat on her table. But the family are luckier than most; the food they grow on their plot of land has saved them from the crippling poverty and near-starvation that besets their neighbours. As Tess tries to unravel the mystery of the woman at the well, the family and community struggle to survive the darkest of times.

# A WINDING ROAD

## Jonathan Tulloch

Spring 2008. The art world is awash with money. The celebrated art mogul and 'adviser' Piers Guest has a client list which includes the wealthiest of individual collectors and an international merchant bank. A newly discovered masterpiece leads him away from his gallivanting through London's galleries and cafes, and takes him onto altogether different terrain . . . 1933. Under the shadow of the Nazi party, Helga and Ernst Mann bring a disabled child into the world. While Ernst drifts near the baleful influence of the Third Reich, Helga is determined to keep her child safe. 1890. In Auvers-sur-Oise, Vincent Van Gogh lives out his last days. Tormented by illness and regret, he takes up his brush, and paints the picture that will draw many disparate lives together.